The Set Up

Paul Erdman

The Set Up

WHEELER
PUBLISHING, INC.
ROCKLAND, MA

★ AN AMERICAN COMPANY ★

Published in Large Print by arrangement with St. Martin's Press
in the United States and Canada

Wheeler Large Print Book Series.

Set in 16 pt Plantin.

NOTE TO READERS: This is a work of fiction. All the people, businesses, establishments, and events portrayed in this novel are either fictitious or are used fictitiously.

Library of Congress Cataloging-in-Publication Data

Erdman, Paul Emil, 1932–
    The set-up / Paul Erdman.
        p. (large print) cm.(Wheeler large print book series)
    ISBN 1-56895-502-2 (softcover)
    1. Large type books. 2. International finance—Fiction. 3. Banks and banking—Switzerland—Fiction. 4. Conspiracies—Fiction. 5. Switzerland—Fiction. I. Title. II. Series
[PS3555.R4S4   1997b]
813′.54—dc21

                                                              97-34579
                                                                   CIP

To Helly

The Set Up

part
One

1

It was early evening on Saturday when
the domestic Air Inter flight from Paris
touched down on the tarmac of
Bäle/Mulhouse, the provincial Alsatian
airport located directly on the border
with Switzerland. From the looks of the
other twenty or so passengers, Charles
Black had concluded that, as usual, he
was the only American on board.

"As usual" because he'd been on this
exact same flight very often during the past
four years—probably almost fifty times in
all. The routine was always the same.
First, TWA from Dulles to Paris. Then a
two-hour layover at Charles de Gaulle.
Finally this connector flight to Basel.
Always on the first Saturday of the month.

As he deplaned, Black also knew what
normally awaited him on the ground. He
would walk a hundred meters to the terminal. Inside, he would go on to the bar-
rier that divided the terminal in half and
represented the frontier between France
and Switzerland. There he would clear
Swiss immigration and customs, go to
the baggage carousel and pick up the single suitcase that contained all that he
would need for a two-night stay, and walk

to the limo waiting outside. It would take him to the Euler Hotel in downtown Basel.

Ten minutes later his limo would take him to the Schützenhaus, a medieval hunting lodge converted into the best restaurant in Basel. There, one by one, the ten most powerful men in the world of finance would begin to arrive. They were the heads of the central banks of the ten most powerful nations on earth. All would come alone to the restaurant: no wives, no administrative assistants, no bodyguards. The discussions around the dinner table in the private room on the second floor would be informal, unofficial, and strictly for their ears only.

Discussions of the official business at hand would be reserved for their meeting the next morning in the boardroom of the Bank for International Settlements, located directly across the Bahnhofplatz from the Euler Hotel. There they would spend most of the day mapping out the future path of the world's key interest rates—those prevailing in the doliar, the pound sterling, the deutsche mark, the Swiss franc, and the yen—and also the exchange rates that would link these currencies together.

Collectively, these ten men made up the inner sanctum of global finance. He who was privy to their discussions possessed the formula that could predict what would happen in all the major financial markets during the next days, weeks, and months.

For the past four years, Charles Black, as Chairman of the Federal Reserve Board of the United States of America, had been the key player in developing that formula, as had his predecessors, who included such renowned personalities as Paul Volker and Alan Greenspan. Their power stemmed from the fact that *dollar* interest rates, *dollar* bond prices, *dollar* exchange rates, affected everything else in the financial world, from the price of oil in west Texas and Kuwait to gold in London and Zurich to stocks in New York and Tokyo.

But now Charles Black would no longer play the pivotal role here in Basel, because four months ago he had decided to resign from the Fed. Consequently, this time, Charles Black would not be attending the dinner.

After the November elections, the new President of the United States had not specifically asked him to stay on; he had also not asked him to resign. But then "leaks" began to emanate from the White House, suggesting that either the Fed chairman should lower interest rates in the face of the increasing threat of renewed recession, or get out of the way. As the pressure continued to mount, rather than cave in—and be responsible for the rising rates of inflation that would inevitably follow— Charles Black had decided to resign.

The post was still vacant. Since the Fed's vice-chairman, who had temporarily assumed Black's position, lacked sufficient expertise in international matters to represent properly the interests of the United States in Basel, the chair usually occupied by an American at the monthly meetings remained empty. To bridge the gap, Black had agreed to stay on as a special temporary envoy to the Bank for International Settlements until the new Fed chairman was appointed and confirmed. Because protocol was protocol, and because Charles Black was a very proud man, during the past three months he had consistently declined each invitation extended to him, despite the change in his status, to attend the traditional Saturday-night dinners.

Strangely, however, it had not been necessary for him to politely decline a similar invitation this time. None had been extended.

Rather odd, Black thought as he approached Swiss customs. I wonder why?

He found out almost immediately.

2

"Are you alone, Mr. Black?" the Swiss border policeman asked.

"What do you mean?"

"Is your wife with you?"

"No. I'm by myself." During the past two years, Sally had often come along, but this time she had been too busy working out arrangements for the move from their old home in Georgetown to the new apartment in San Francisco. In fact, she was in California now.

"Why do you ask?" Black then added.

The Swiss did not answer the question. Instead he posed another one.

"Do you have baggage?"

"Yes. One piece."

"Would you please show me the baggage check?"

It was attached to his ticket. He pulled the ticket out of his pocket and shoved it across the counter. "I'm afraid you'll be disappointed," he said.

Now a second man in uniform approached him. The uniform was different. So was the attitude. The gun that hung at his side might have had something to do with that. He reached up to the counter and was given both Black's passport and the airline ticket.

"You will come with me," he said in very guttural English.

"Where?" Black asked.

"You will come with me." The policeman took Black by the arm, then firmly led him down a corridor and into a small conference room.

Two men in civilian dress were waiting inside. Both immediately rose as Black entered.

The younger of the two spoke first. "I am Lieutenant Paul Schmidt. I am with the police department of the city and canton of Basel-Stadt."

"What do you want of me?" Black asked.

"We will get to that in due time," came the answer.

"Do you have any idea who I am?" Black asked. It was more an angry shout than a question.

"We are fully aware of who you are, Mr. Black." It was now the second man in civilian clothes who spoke.

"And who are you?" Black demanded.

"Dr. Rolf Wassermann," he replied. "I am the *Staatsanwalt*—the state attorney—of the city and canton of Basel-Stadt. In your criminal justice system, Mr. Black, I would be called the chief prosecuting attorney."

Criminal justice system? Prosecuting attorney? A stunning chill went down Charles Black's spine. What in the world was going on here?

"Look," he said, "there must be a mistake here. Despite what you just said, you obviously do *not* know whom you are dealing with. I am a very high official in the government of the United States of America. You have no right to detain me, if that is what you are attempting to do. Therefore, I am leaving."

He turned to the uniformed policeman and held out his hand. "My passport, please. And my ticket."

"Sit down, Mr. Black," the prosecuting attorney now said. "We want to handle this in as civilized a way as possible."

"Handle what, for God's sake?"

"Sit down, and then we can discuss this as gentlemen. We do not like this any more than you do."

"And then I will be free to go?"

"Of course. But you must first answer a few very simple questions. Please sit down."

Black pulled out a chair directly across from the two men and sat. So did his two interlocutors. The uniformed policeman who had been standing behind Black went around the table to his superior, handed over Black's passport and ticket, and left the room.

Lieutenant Schmidt then pulled two pieces of blank paper from a dossier and slid them across the conference table to Black. "Do you have a pen?" he asked.

"Of course," Black replied.

"Would you mind signing your name, using your usual signature?"

"Why?"

"Sir, the sooner we get this over, the sooner we all can go home and have dinner," the police lieutenant replied.

Black went to the breast pocket of his suit jacket for his pen. "Where?" he asked.

"Anywhere. Twice. One signature on each paper."

Using the same old-fashioned Parker fountain pen that his wife had given him many Christmases ago, he signed his name twice.

"Anything else?"

"Your address—home address. Your

9

home phone and fax number. Your Social Security number. On each paper. Under your signature."

Black hesitated a full half minute, but then he acquiesced. When he was done, the prosecutor reached across the table and retrieved the two papers. Then he opened a dossier—a thick dossier—that lay in front of him. For the next minute, as the room remained silent except for the muffled noise of jet engines outside, Dr. Rolf Wassermann seemed to be meticulously comparing what Black had just put to paper with another document inside the dossier. Finally he seemed satisfied.

"Do you have a client relationship with a lawyer in Zurich by the name of Zwiebach? Hans Zwiebach? To use his title, *Doctor* Hans Zwiebach?"

"I did, yes. Years ago."

"How many years ago?"

"At least ten."

"Do you have an account with the General Bank of Switzerland in Zurich?"

"*Had.* Past tense."

"Pardon me?"

"I used to have an account there," Black said. He paused. "Come to think of it, the account probably still exists. But it has been lying completely dormant for more than ten years."

"I see. Does Dr. Zwiebach have signature power over that account?"

"Yes. It was a fiduciary account—a so-called B account."

"Which means that although the account was in Dr. Zwiebach's name, you were—in fact, still are—the beneficiary owner of that account."

"Technically, yes."

"Does that mean yes?"

"Yes. It was my account."

"Do you recall the account number?"

"No."

Dr. Wassermann pulled a card from the dossier in front of him. "This is a photocopy of the original signature card for the account. It bears the number J 747-2239. You must also have a copy of it."

"I probably do. But it would be among my personal records, back in the United States."

"You must also have a copy of your fiduciary agreement with Dr. Zwiebach among your records."

"I'm sure I do. But as I already told you, my account there has been dormant for at least ten years. So the documents you refer to are no doubt buried at the bottom of a deep pile in my safe."

"How did you normally communicate with Dr. Zwiebach?"

"By phone."

"That is how you gave him instructions regarding your account?"

"Among other things, yes."

"I see. From where did you phone?"

"From wherever I happened to be at the time." Actually, it had been both he and his wife, Sally, who had used that account.

Both had signed the fiduciary agreement with Zwiebach, and both had phoned him on occasion. But that had stopped years ago. Still, it was better she be left totally out of this.

Black's mind was now trying to keep ahead of the questions. They were on to something very specific. Probably it dated from the time when he was still with the investment bank, before his appointment to the Fed. Had the Securities and Exchange Commission uncovered something his former partners had been up to way back then? And was it now trying to implicate him? But why now? And why here?

"For example?"

"For example what?"

"Phone calls."

"You can hardly expect me to recall phone calls that occurred over ten years ago."

"You're quite right." The prosecuting attorney reopened the dossier in front of him, turned a few pages, and then asked the next question.

"How about a more recent one? From London. The Savoy Hotel. It occurred in January of last year. To be precise, the call was placed at 10:45 A.M., Greenwich Mean Time, on Monday, January thirteenth. From room 507. Your room."

"I told you that my account in Zurich has been lying completely dormant for at least ten years."

"I know what you told us. What about

12

another call, this time from the Bäle/-Mulhouse airport, again on a Monday—"

Black stood up.

"That's enough. Where's the nearest telephone?"

"Why always Monday?"

"There were no such calls."

"Come now, Mr. Black. There are more. And each phone call was duly logged by your lawyer's secretary."

"What does that prove?"

"It is evidence—suggesting that perhaps you are not telling us the truth, Mr. Black."

"This is ridiculous. I want to get to a telephone. Right now. Otherwise I can guarantee you that there will be severe repercussions."

"We wouldn't want that, would we?" was Dr. Wassermann's response.

"Don't get smartass with me," Black said.

"I'll ignore that," Wassermann responded. "Just once." He then directed an icy stare directly into Black's eyes. "Remember, Black, this is *my* country and *my* canton. Here *I* make the rules. Understood?"

Black maintained the eye contact for the next thirty seconds. It was the Swiss who broke it off.

"I will have a phone brought in," Wasserman finally said, in a very tight voice. He motioned to his colleague.

The police lieutenant immediately left the room and, minutes later, returned with a cellular phone. He handed it to Black.

"You have ten minutes," Wassermann said. "Make as many calls as you want."

"Does this work for overseas calls?" Black asked.

"Of course. You're in Switzerland. If you need help, dial zero."

With that Wassermann rose from the table and, with the policeman, left the room.

As soon as the door closed behind them, Black began to dial his own new number in San Francisco. It rang. And rang. Twelve times. No answer.

"Dammit!" It was almost 10:00 A.M. there on Saturday morning, and Sally was probably out shopping for things for their new apartment.

He dialed again. This time it was the main number of the Federal Reserve in Washington. It rang twice. Then he got the recording telling him that the offices were closed until 8:00 A.M. Monday. He hung up for the second time.

"A lawyer," he said. But what lawyer? If he called Dan Lash, his longtime friend and established lawyer in Washington, it would be the same story. A recording. And if he got him at home, what could an American lawyer do anyway? It would take him days to get up to speed. As that goddamn Swiss prosecuting attorney had just told him, this was *their* country, and they were playing by *their* rules.

Hold on. He had a lawyer who knew the rules here. Zwiebach.

Bad idea. Really bad. Whatever was going on here clearly involved Zwiebach. They'd already gotten to him. That was how they knew about the fiduciary agreement. More important, that was why they knew about the telephone log. All total bullshit. But it had to be Zwiebach, not the Basel police, who had made up all that crap. Why?

Black looked at his watch. He had already blown four of the ten minutes they had given him. And after the ten minutes were up, then what?

The watch did it. It was seven. His colleagues would be just arriving at the Schützenhaus restaurant for their traditional Saturday-night dinner. Forget the lawyers. What he needed now was muscle, political muscle, enough political muscle to get him out of here. Then he could work on getting a lawyer.

Who had that kind of muscle? He knew the answer immediately. Who could have more influence here than Samuel Schweizer, the president of the Swiss National Bank? Everybody knew that Switzerland was run by a small number of men. All had gone to the same universities, where they had all been in the same fraternities. All were high-ranking officers in the army. All had married the daughters of rich, old, patrician families as their means of gaining both social status and financial reinsurance. By now they were the leading industrialists, lawyers, merchants, politicians. And by now they also had one more thing in common: close links with at least one of Switzerland's three leading banks. Such a relationship was a sine qua non for members of the Swiss establishment. For it was the bankers, the gnomes of Zurich, who controlled the Swiss power elite. Through their control of the purse strings, it was the bankers who controlled the government, the army, the legal system.

And the chief Swiss banker of all was Samuel Schweizer.

Charles Black dialed zero.

"Schützenhaus," he said when the operator came on.

"Twenty-six, ninety-seven, thirty-five," she answered, in German. Black wrote the numbers down. His knowledge of German stemmed from his undergraduate days at Georgetown's School of Foreign Service.

He dialed again, and it was the maître d' who answered.

"This is Charles Black, the American banker. Do you remember me?"

"Of course, Mr. Black. You will be late for the dinner upstairs?"

"No, no. I'm calling for another reason. It does relate to that dinner. Would you mind checking to see if Dr. Samuel Schweizer has arrived? If he has, I would very much like to speak with him."

"I will check immediately. If you will give me your number, I will have Dr. Schweizer call you back."

"No. This is extremely urgent. I would prefer to hang on while you check. Otherwise, I will call back."

"Certainly, sir."

Two minutes later, another voice came on the phone with a single word: "Schweizer."

"Is that you, Samuel?" Black asked.

"*Ja.*"

"This is Charles Black."

"*Ja.* I was told that it was you."

"Samuel, let me explain. I'm at the airport, and for some reason I'm being detained by the Swiss police. I need help. Would you mind coming out here? Or at the very least, could you speak to the man in charge? I believe his name is Wassermann. Dr. Wassermann. I'll get him on the phone right away."

"I'm sorry," the Swiss banker said.

"What do you mean?"

"It's out of my hands."

Schweizer hung up.

One minute later the police lieutenant returned to the conference room. He was accompanied by the uniformed policeman.

"You will come with us," Lieutenant Schmidt said.

"Where?"

"You will see."

"I refuse to go anywhere until I've spoken to my embassy."

"You have had ample time to do that. You will now come with us. Either you cooperate or we will use handcuffs. We would prefer not to make a fuss."

Realizing he had no choice, he did as ordered. Five minutes later he was alone in the back of the police van as it pulled away from the airport entrance.

Out of my hands? What in the name of God did Schweizer mean by that?

3

Twenty minutes later, just as Charles Black was being fingerprinted at Basel's central jail, which was known locally as the Lohnhof, nine of the world's ten leading central bankers sat down to dinner in the private room upstairs at the Schützenhaus. They started with foie gras, fresh from the Alsace, just a few miles away. The wine came from the same region of France—a Riesling made from grapes grown near Ammer-schwihr. The main course was venison from the Black Forest, also just miles away. It was served with spätzle and Breiselbeeren. The wine was a Pommard.

As dessert was being served—Vacherin Glacé, a speciality of the house—Dr. Samuel Schweizer summoned the chief waiter and whispered in his ear. Minutes later all the waiters left the room, and the door to the private dining room was firmly closed. As if on signal, Schweizer tapped the only wineglass in front of him that was still empty, although it would later be filled with Dom Perignon. Then he rose to his feet.

He did not rise very far, since Dr. Samuel Schweizer was only five feet six. But he more than made up for his lack of physical stature through the pompousness of his bearing and the fastidiousness of his dress. He sported a small mustache and spoke in a clipped manner that was more British than Swiss. His command of the English language was, of course, complete, as he was about to demonstrate yet again.

"Gentlemen," he began, "it is unprecedented during the six years that I have hosted these dinners in my capacity as your chairman that I feel obligated to interrupt in this manner in order to discuss business. But we are, I am afraid, faced with an unprecedented situation."

This produced no noticeable reaction around the table.

"We have had a Judas in our midst," Schweizer declared.

Now he had caught their attention.

"He is not among us this evening. Nor was he invited. Nor will he ever be invited again. Because it has been ascertained that our colleague misused his high office—both in his home country and here at the BIS—for personal gain. The profits he has personally accumulated during the past four years as a result of his insider trading are unprecedented. We believe they are in the range of a half-billion dollars."

The room was now deadly silent.

Dr. Samuel Schweizer continued. "It was Sir Robert Neville of the Bank of England who first suspected that something was going on. He brought it to my attention. I then asked him to make a thorough investigation and to report back to me when all the salient facts were in. He did so earlier this week. He will do so again—this time to all of you and in detail—at our ten o'clock meeting tomorrow morning.

"It began when Sir Robert and his staff determined that a series of highly suspicious transactions in Eurodollar futures and in the foreign exchange market in London were being made by the General Bank of Switzerland, and that they originated from its head office in Zurich. Ultimately, the chairman of that bank, Dr. Lothar Zopf, was contacted and gave Sir Robert immediate access to all of their records that appeared pertinent to these trades. As you all know, Switzerland has very strict bank secrecy laws. So this was highly unusual—in fact, unprecedented to my knowledge—and only possible because of my close personal relationship with Dr. Zopf."

The head of the Dutch central bank could not restrain himself. "Pompous ass," he commented to his neighbor.

Herr Doktor Schweizer continued. "It allowed Sir Robert to get to the heart of this matter swiftly. All of the suspect trading activities could be traced back to one account—the account of a single private client. It goes without saying that Dr. Zopf and his associates at the General Bank were completely unaware that this trading activity was a result of insider information. In fact, the bank was completely unaware of the true identity of the client involved. Dr. Zopf and his bank were victims, as are we all, of a totally corrupt man."

"And who is that man?" It was the head of the Banque de France who posed the question.

Schweizer replied. "Until an hour ago I would have been very hesitant to name him, lest injury be done to an innocent party. That changed when I received a call from the state attorney of the City of Basel, informing me that the man in question was arrested this evening. He is now imprisoned at the Lohnhof, Basel's main jail. He will be charged with fraud and the misuse of public office for private enrichment."

"Who is it?" another voice demanded.

"The ex-Chairman of the Federal Reserve Board of the United States of America," Schweizer replied. "Yes, our mutual friend Charles Black."

Now it was the head of the Bank of Canada who immediately intervened.

"I find this impossible to believe. I know Charlie Black very well, probably better than any of you. I can say without the slightest reservation that he is one of the

21

most decent men I have ever had the privilege to deal with. It will take a hell of a
lot more than your accusations to convince
me otherwise."

Samuel Schweizer, his face flushed with
anger, responded immediately, speaking
directly to the Canadian: "When you hear
the evidence tomorrow morning, I suspect
you will change your mind." The dinner
broke up shortly thereafter. It was now a
very somber group of central bankers
who returned to their waiting limousines.
There was but one subject on their minds.

4

Charles Black had dined much less sump-
tuously, in quarters that fell far short of
the elegance of the dining room where
his former colleagues had spent the evening.

His cell at the Lohnhof was narrow,
dank, and dimly lit. The mattress on the
single bed was stained and smelled of
urine. His dinner tray, which had been
shoved through an opening in the steel door,
lay untouched on the small rough wood-
en table over which Black was slumped.
The meal consisted of two slabs of heavy
Swiss bread, a slice of Gruyère cheese, and
a metal mug half full of lukewarm milk coffee.

The prior hour had been one of never-
ending humiliation. This was new for

Charlie Black. Life so far had simply left him totally unprepared to respond to what had come so suddenly, so unexpectedly. He was used to people looking up to him, both physically—he was well over six feet tall—and, more important, where his achievements were concerned. He had been at the top of his class at Georgetown. Although he had not made the basketball team, he had ranked number one on the swimming team. He had even tried his hand at boxing while doing his graduate work at Stanford, where he had received his Ph.D. after only three years of study under two Nobel laureates in economics.

Professionally, his career had also been one of uninterrupted success. After Stanford he'd spent a year as a White House fellow. Then he'd joined the international division of the First National Bank of Manhattan, a New York bank and the fifth largest in the United States, working first in New York, then London, then Hong Kong, then back in New York. By the time he was forty-one, he was already being talked about as a possible CEO of the bank. But he had had enough of commercial banking, and had decided that it was time to switch to investment banking. So he'd moved to Whitney Brothers & Pierpont, one of the leading investment banks in the country, where he ran their international investment activities, first in London, then at their head office in New York, where they eventually made him vice-chairman. When, at fifty, he was asked to replace the Chairman of the Federal Reserve Board, who was stepping down for health reasons, he agreed to do so. Since it was generally recognized in Washington that Charlie Black was probably the man best qualified for the job, the nomination received almost instant confirmation.

This consensus, however, did not include the politician newly elected to the presidency of the United States. So, rather than fight what would have been a losing battle with the White House, four months ago Black had decided to retire at the pinnacle of his career, move to California, visit Europe on a regular basis—as with this trip to Basel—and finally begin to smell the flowers.

Now the smell was that of urine.

The swiftness of it all had left Black disoriented and bewildered.

The trip from the airport in the police van had taken only twenty minutes. At their destination the rear doors of the van had been opened, and he'd been hauled out by two uniformed policemen. He had found himself standing on cobblestones at the far side of a square surrounded on three sides by high walls. Facing him was a massive three-story building, a medieval structure built from native red sandstone. It was, he later found out, a fifteenth-century monastery that had been converted into the city jail in the late eighteenth century.

From its looks, very little had been done with it since.

The interior of the Lohnhof was even more intimidating than its exterior. The floors consisted of uneven, pocked tiles; the thick walls were covered with gray, chipped plaster. Three heavyset guards, armed with pistols and nightsticks, had watched as Black was led through the entrance hall into a small room off to the right, whose furniture consisted of a single table. Some paraphernalia lay on top of it. A man in a white coat was waiting there.

"Bitte," he had said as he grasped Black's right hand and pulled him in front of the table. He had then opened the lid of a flat metal case on top of the table and, one by one, pushed Black's fingertips onto the ink pad within. Next, each was firmly rolled onto the paper that lay ready, within its individual square. His left hand came next. He was given a damp cloth to wipe his fingers and told to stand up against the back wall. The man in the white coat had then lifted a Polaroid camera from the table and taken six quick shots of Black's face. That done, he had moved forward to a position directly facing Black.

"Hände hoch, bitte," he said, motioning to indicate what he wanted.

Black had raised his hands. The body search had begun. His wallet, his keys, his belt had been removed. Minutes later he had been led down a corridor past a long

25

row of gray steel doors until he had reached the cell that was to be his for the night. It bore the number 17.

They had left Black his watch. He now looked at it. Only eight-thirty. Only eight-thirty on Saturday night.

"Dammit," Black said when the significance of that sank in. It might not be just for a night. Realistically, even after he got hold of Sally there was probably no way she could arrange to get him out before Monday. But you never knew unless you tried.

He went to the steel door, raised his fist, and pounded on it. Nothing. He pounded again. This time it produced a response. First a whistle. Then a howl. Then somebody else started to pound. It sounded as if it came from the cell next door. For the first time the obvious dawned on him—that it was not just he who was locked up here. And whoever the others were, they sure were not here because of phone calls they had purportedly made to their Swiss lawyer from the Savoy Hotel in London.

This time Black really smacked the door with his fists. And this time it produced the desired effect. The small eye-level slot in the steel door slid open and a guard's eyes peered in at him.

"What's wrong?" the guard asked in English.

"I must speak to your superintendent."

"Please?"

"Your boss," Black said. "Bring him. Please."

"No boss," the guard replied. He raised his arm to the small window and pointed at his watch.

"When?" Black asked.

"*Montag,*" came the answer. Monday.

What was there to do? In any case, it wasn't this guy's fault.

"Okay," Black finally said.

"You stop noise?" the guard asked.

"Yes. I stop noise."

"Good. I bring blankets."

The steel door opened, and the guard entered, bearing two of what appeared to be clean woolen blankets. He threw them onto the bed. Then he pointed at the food on the table.

"No eat?"

"No."

"You're American?"

"Yes."

"You're the only American here."

Black shrugged.

"Get sleep now. It's better," the guard said, as he looked at Black in obvious sympathy. Then he gathered up Black's untouched dinner and left, slamming the steel door behind him.

Outside it had quieted down. A half hour later the light in his cell went out. Fully clothed, Black lay down on the blanket he had spread across the filthy mattress, and covered himself with the other. No pillow had been provided.

It didn't matter. The last thing Charlie Black was about to do now was go to sleep. It was time to think. Somebody had set him up. Big time. So big that even Dr. Samuel Schweizer had been scared off. "It's out of my hands," he had said on the phone before hanging up so abruptly.

So who were they? And why were they doing it? Where the *why* was concerned, the answer seemed obvious. To make money. But why use his account at the General Bank of Switzerland for cover? Because, from what he sensed, whatever had been going on must have involved highly sophisticated international transactions that only someone at the top could have managed. Which would explain why Samuel Schweizer had said what he did. But if they had needed the "footprint" of someone at the top for cover, why his? Charlie knew maybe one reason. He had a reputation as a so-called trusting type. He hadn't fostered it, but somehow he had always known that that was how he was regarded. He was also aware of the downside of being looked at that way. Nice guys don't go out of their way to question things. They tend to trust people. They don't check their accounts. They go with the flow, are ready to accept explanations, and are thus natural suckers where the more devious types in our society are concerned. It was a sort of "Don't worry. Charlie Black's in charge."

The guys at First National's branch in London had been maybe the first to find out otherwise. That was almost twenty years ago. The place was run by one of those insufferably lazy Englishmen who had gone to Cambridge and thought that from then on the world owed him a living. Via the old-boy network, he had recruited three other Oxbridge graduates with similar attitude problems. Collectively they ran First National's U.K. operations— when they got around to it. The situation had gone from bad to worse, prompting New York to send Charlie over. After Charlie arrived to take charge, he had just let things ride for a while as he watched, waited, and sniffed around.

The short, fat Englishman and his three buddies simply ignored his arrival on the scene. They continued to show up at ten, leave for lunch at noon precisely, and, after too many glasses of wine, lurch back to the office, only to leave again at four to catch the train to Surrey or Bucks.

As Charlie's sniffing around soon revealed, they charged off these daily lunches on their expense accounts, purportedly for entertaining clients. That meant four times two hundred pounds times five days a week when they were in town. Their out-of-town habits weren't too great either. They booked first class, flew economy, and pocketed the difference, which was bad enough. But as he looked further, it became apparent that the bank was buying first-class tickets for trips that never took place. They called it "fiddling" in England. Charlie regarded it as stealing.

So one fine day Charlie had simply fired the lot. They'd tried to gang up on him in his office after they'd gotten their notices and their last paychecks. First they'd threatened to sue, and when that had no effect, their "leader" had gone face-to-face with Charlie, suggesting he might just beat him up. Whereupon Charlie had grabbed the short, fat, red-faced Englishman by the scruff of the neck, marched him to the elevator, pushed him in, and then reached into the elevator and pressed the button for the ground floor. When he'd returned to his office, it was empty. Subsequently, with them gone, everybody else in London had gotten down to serious business. Word had never leaked out concerning what happened that Friday afternoon, since nobody sued and none of those who had been present thought it wise to challenge Charlie Black ever again.

The "nice guy" reputation seemed to have followed him to Whitney Brothers when he switched jobs. That also changed. Almost from the day he took over Whitney's international operations at the head office in New York, there was something about their foreign exchange trading in Hong Kong that bothered him. Their results were just too good to be true—too *consistently* good. Hong Kong never had a down month. On his first swing through—he had deliberately scheduled himself to spend a full week there—he made it a point to meet the chief foreign exchange dealer right away. His name was Sammy Lee, and it was immediately apparent that Lee considered Charlie Black to be just another dumb American; they came and went, and were best ignored. Charlie, however, knew Hong Kong pretty well because, years earlier, he'd run First National's office there. He immediately started asking around among old friends about Sammy. All the answers he got spelled trouble. Lee lived in a house that was too big. Drove a Jaguar that was too expensive. And was known to gamble heavily in Macao, accompanied by a different girl each time.

So, just before the office closed for the weekend—and after Sammy had gone home in his brand-new red Jaguar, sure that he'd seen the last of Charlie Black—Charlie called in the head clerk from the foreign exchange department. He didn't even try the "good cop" approach. After getting ten minutes of stonewalling, he just grabbed the guy by the tie, hoisted him in the air, and pushed him against the wall of the conference room.

"You tell me the truth, you little son of a bitch, or I'm going to take you apart piece by piece," he told him, and, for good measure, whacked his head against the wall. Then he dropped him to the floor.

The two of them spent the next twenty-four hours alone in the bank at the computer. Charlie never let the fellow out of his sight. He warned him not even to think about picking up a telephone. Charlie even accompanied him to the john.

Slowly but surely it came out.

Sammy Lee had been dummying up phantom trades for at least eighteen months. In the process he had generated almost a quarter of a billion dollars in phony profits. The chief clerk knew it, of course, but Sammy Lee had taken care of him and his family—for life.

One by one the clerk identified the phantom trades. Then Charlie had them printed out. To what extent Lee had used these "trades" to cover up losses, and how much he had simply stolen, was not clear. Nor did it make a difference as far as Charlie was concerned. At 11:00 P.M. on Sunday—10:00 A.M. in Connecticut—Charlie had phoned the country home of his boss. He described what had been going on and recommended that first thing Monday morning New York dispatch an audit team to Hong Kong. In the meantime he'd arrange for the local police to lock up Lee and his partner.

The latter recommendation did not go over too well on the other end of the line. It was suggested that until all the facts were in, there was no sense in causing undue anxiety among the clients who had entrusted their investment bank with billions of dollars. Maybe Charlie could "finesse" the situation in the meantime.

"No way," Charlie had said.

Lee and his buddy were both in jail an hour later. New York "confessed" right away Monday morning that they had detected a problem in Hong Kong and were already in the process of assessing its dimensions. Black's boss and the audit team subsequently took full credit for their "discovery" and the swift punishment of the Hong Kong perpetrators. No mention was ever made of Charles Black. So as far as the rest of the world was concerned, his "nice guy" reputation once again remained intact.

When the President nominated him to head the Fed, during the confirmation hearings before the Senate's finance committee, there were also moments when the other Charlie Black surfaced momentarily. With his Washington attorney, Dan Lash, at his side, it had been, for the most part, clear sailing. Until the senator from Nevada decided to take him on.

"I understand, Dr. Black, that you are considered an expert in the field of derivatives," he began.

"I'm familiar with the techniques employed in that field, yes."

"I further understand that as an investment banker you were responsible for various operations in that field."

"At times, yes."

"Do you recall one of those operations that took place in the spring of 1994?"

"Not really."

"Then let me refresh your memory. Alan Greenspan was chairman at the time. Very unexpectedly he began to raise short-term interest rates. It especially caught bond traders by surprise, particularly those who had been dabbling in interest rate futures in Europe."

"Now I know what you are talking about. It caught some by surprise, yes. But not me."

"Exactly. I certainly appreciate how forthcoming you are on this, Dr. Black."

"Why shouldn't I be?"

Dan Lash leaned toward his client and whispered three words in his ear: "Be careful, Charlie."

"I'll get to that. Was it not so that even the greatest and most successful speculator of that time, George Soros, got caught by surprise?"

"According to reports in the press at that time, yes."

"How much did he lose, according to the press?"

"I believe they said six hundred million."

"Did you believe those reports?"

"Yes. More or less."

"What's that supposed to mean?"

"I thought the loss might have been more than that, not less."

"You probably were in a better position to make that judgment than most, were you not, Dr. Black?"

"I don't know exactly what you are driving at, Senator," Charlie said. This time it was a warning nudge that his lawyer directed at him.

"Because," the senator continued, "although it was not reported by the press at the time or since, I have been given to understand that it was you, Dr. Black, who was on the other side of those trades. And as I further understand it, trading in such financial derivatives is regarded as a zero-sum game. This means that for every winner there's a loser. Or, in this case, when George Soros's hedge fund lost six hundred million in the month of February 1994, it was Dr. Charles Black's investment bank that won six hundred million. More or less. Some say it was more, not less. That it was closer to a billion dollars. They are also saying that you personally directed the operation from beginning to end."

"I was involved in that operation, yes. And we did come out well. Very well."

"You sound proud of it," the senator said.

"Really? Well, I certainly am not going to apologize for it."

"Maybe you should."

"Why?"

"Because what you were doing was nothing less than out-and-out gambling. I'm not sure we want a man who gambles at the head of the Federal Reserve."

"The financial community has a better term for it, Senator. They call it risk management."

"I call it gambling. And I condemn it."

"That surprises me."

"Why?"

"You are, after all, the senator from Nevada. Your state encourages gambling like no other state in the Union. It encourages those in our society who can least afford it to stuff their savings into slot machines and then go home broke. What I and other investment bankers do is totally different. We help large investors—no, the largest investors in the world—to manage risk. They are all big boys, they know the deal: win some, lose some. Well, in 1994 some lost and some won. But nobody that I know of even had to consider selling his yacht."

The chairman of the committee stepped in right there. The senator from Nevada never spoke up again, at least until it came time to vote on whether or not to refer Charles Black's nomination as Chairman of the Board of the Federal Reserve to the full Senate. The vote was eleven to one in favor. The sole dissenter was the senator from Nevada.

After he had been elected their chairman, the board of governors of the Federal Reserve discovered the truth about Charlie Black pretty fast too. At first, it was generally assumed that, like his predecessors, he was a numbers guy, a scholar with superb academic credentials who had returned to the fold, a man of consensus. It soon became apparent that someone in that fold thought he needed a few lessons. Just three months after he had assumed office, the leaks began. Elements of what were supposed to be discussions held behind closed doors began appearing in *The New York Times*. If the desired effect was to put the new chairman in a bad light, it worked. The third time this occurred, Charles Black convened a special meeting of the board of governors, at which he told them that if it happened just one more time, he'd track down whoever was doing it and, one way or the other, get him off the board.

Word of this spread throughout the building on Constitution Avenue. Nevertheless, six weeks later it happened again.

Shortly after that, as he was leaving the elevator on the ground floor, headed for home, he was approached by the secretary of the Vice-Chairman of the Federal Reserve Board. She asked if she could speak to him privately. He took her to a coffee shop down the street. It soon became obvious that she hated her boss, who, it seemed, was a "fanny patter"—almost any fanny within reach. The problem was that it was *her* fanny that was in reach most of the time. So, when she'd heard about the "leaks," she'd recalled that her boss spoke regularly to the financial editor of *The New York Times*. The last time he had done so, she had listened in. She had worked at the Fed long enough to know the lingo used there. So, when her boss told the *Times* man that, despite the reservations of key members of the board, the chairman was nevertheless probably going to ram through another half-point increase in the federal funds rate, she realized both the import and the impropriety of what had been said. Then she read it in the next day's *Times*, which was put on her desk each morning, to be delivered to her boss immediately upon his arrival.

When her boss arrived the next morning, along with the paper she brought in a sealed, handwritten note from his boss, telling him he was expected in the chairman's office immediately. The confrontation lasted less than ten minutes. The vice-chairman did not even attempt to deny what he had been doing. He simply defied Charles Black to do anything about it. The vice-chairman had been there for many years. The rest of the board and he—most of whom had been appointed by Bill Clinton—were of a like mind on most issues. If the choice was between growth and fighting inflation, they would opt for fostering growth every time, regardless of the consequences for inflation. They had immediately sensed that Charles Black was not one of them. Black was not just a hawk on inflation, but a superhawk. His goal was a zero rate of inflation. The public had a right to know this. Thus the vice-chairman's "conversations" with the man from the *Times*.

"And you intend to continue this practice?" Charlie had asked him.

"Until you begin to listen to the opinions of the entire board instead of simply acting on your own, yes," was his answer.

Black called a special meeting of the board of governors for later that day. First he told them what had transpired between the vice-chairman and himself. Then he asked the vice-chairman to leave the boardroom. He told the remaining governors that he would demand the vice-chairman's immediate resignation. He'd talked to the White House and had their full backing. The issue at stake was the traditional role of the chairman and his ability to reach and implement decisions with or without the agreement of individual members of the board. The vice-chairman obviously wanted to change the rules. Did anyone else agree with him?

Not a hand was raised. The vice-chairman resigned. And the word spread throughout Washington: Don't mess with Charlie Black.

Unfortunately, the word had not reached Switzerland. Yet.

Once an hour, the bell in a nearby clock tower chimed. The last time Black had heard it was when it chimed four. He decided that he had taken things as far as he could. Before he could even begin to find a way out, he'd have to know a lot more. Zwiebach, and whoever his partners were, had done such a job on him, for whatever reasons, that even the authorities appeared convinced that they had an airtight case on their hands.

So play dumb for as long as it takes. Talk to them. Draw them out. Wait them out. Be patient.

And then, when I find out who's doing this to me, I'll personally nail him to the fucking cross! Nail by nail by nail.

With that final comforting thought in mind, Charles Black fell asleep.

5

Six hours later and ten blocks away, the central bankers of the world were taking their places around the oval table in the boardroom of the Bank for International Settlements. The building itself was a twenty-story circular tower, an architectural disaster that had been inflicted on a city that otherwise took pride in its cultural heritage. The money that the BIS brought with it had more than made up for its lack of architectural standards in the eyes of the city fathers. This was understandable because Basel was, after all, part of Switzerland, where money has *always* ruled supreme.

The man in charge of Switzerland's money matters, the president of the Swiss National Bank, Dr. Samuel Schweizer, opened the meeting at precisely ten o'clock that Sunday morning. He immediately turned over the proceedings to Sir Robert Neville.

As Governor of the Bank of England, Sir Robert Neville enjoyed, for historical reasons, a special status among the men who gathered each month in Basel. All recognized that the Bank of England was the mother of all central banks. Further, it was one of Sir Robert's predecessors, Montague C. Norman, who was the "father" of the Bank for International Settlements at its founding in 1931. The BIS was not a bank in the usual sense of the word, since it did not deal with the general public, taking deposits and making loans. Rather, it was established to facilitate intergovernmental financial transactions. Its founders included every major Western European nation as well as the United States and Japan. Initially, its primary mission was to facilitate Germany's reparation payments to the victors in World War I. But gradually its activities were extended to arranging loans to member governments to help them bridge financial crises during the turbulent decade of the 1930s.

It was Montague Norman who spearheaded this expansion, because he felt that, in the face of the Great Depression that had engulfed the world after the Crash of 1929, there was an urgent need for the creation of a "central bank of central banks," and that the Bank for International

Settlements was uniquely qualified to fill that need. There the handful of men who ran the world's finances could meet regularly, informally, and in total secrecy, and jointly engineer a global economic recovery. The BIS was, then, the forerunner of those other two multinational financial institutions, the International Monetary Fund and the World Bank, which were created at the end of World War II to help finance the reconstruction of the global economy and the reestablishment of a functional international monetary system. The BIS, however, almost did not survive World War II. It was another Englishman, John Maynard Keynes, the greatest economist of the twentieth century, who had used his enormous influence to save it from Franklin Roosevelt's Treasury Secretary, Henry Morgenthau, who was trying to close it down, claiming that the Bank for International Settlements had acted as an agent of the Nazis during World War II. So, when the representative of the Bank of England spoke, everybody gathered in Basel listened with particular interest.

"As you know," Sir Robert began, "I represent the Bank of England at these meetings. At the request of all of you, a number of years ago I was also given a particular charge: to maintain a constant surveillance of the activities of the major players in the international banking community and to report regularly to our chairman. The purpose of this surveillance was to prevent a recurrence of two recent scandals. The first was the BCCI scandal of the 1980s, when criminal elements gained control of that Luxembourg bank. The second, much closer to home, was the bankruptcy in 1995 of Barings Bank. That two-hundred-thirty-year-old bank, as you all know, was one of our most prestigious financial institutions, and counted the Queen among its clients. The cause was a billion-dollar loss brought about by 'unauthorized' trading in financial derivatives in Singapore. The lesson in both cases is that the key to prevention is early detection. We also learned from the Barings fiasco that we had to pay special attention to those markets where financial derivatives were traded. To that end, I have a small staff— six in all—who are constantly looking for suspicious behavior."

He paused, then continued. "Five months ago they came upon something. What originally aroused their suspicions was this: From the beginning of last year, every three months or so there would be an exceptional flurry of speculation—involving three-month Eurodollars traded on the London International Financial Futures Exchange and the dollar in interbank futures trading in London. I immediately reported this to our chairman, Dr. Schweizer, and he agreed that I should pursue the matter. Further investigation showed that the surge of activity involving these financial derivatives always occurred on the Monday after the first weekend of the month. Subsequently—sometimes after a few days, and other times after a few weeks but no longer than that—the dollar always—I repeat, always—moved up relative to the pound sterling. Precisely the opposite happened to three-month Eurodollars. They always went down.

"Let me now remind you of the situation back then. The economic recovery in the United States had turned into a boom, and the danger of inflation was increasing. So, at the beginning of the year, the Federal Reserve Board had no choice but to slow down the economy by raising interest rates. Higher interest rates would slow down everything from home sales to new housing starts to car sales. Initially the Fed raised the federal funds rate by a half-percent. Then, every three months or so thereafter, it would announce a further half-percent increase. A half-percent increase in the prime rate would immediately follow. A similar increase in the discount rate would follow that. And so forth. You all know the drill. You also know that as short-term interest rates ratchet up in New York, so, *subsequently*, does the value of the dollar as international investors move their funds into the dollar, seeking those higher rates. On the other hand, rising interest rates mean lower bond prices.

"So those investors who went long dollars, betting they would rise in value, and short-dollar bonds and particularly Eurodollar futures, betting they would fall in price, made out like bandits."

He paused again, and the head of the Belgian central bank took advantage of it to whisper to his Dutch colleague, "He thinks he's still lecturing to undergraduates at Cambridge."

Sir Robert went on: "Now, as you all know better than anyone, the key to success in both interest rate futures and currency futures is timing. Even if you get the *direction* right, it won't do you much good if you don't get the *timing* right, since the related carrying costs will eat you up. What began happening in London last year was nothing short of *uncanny*—or, as my staff put it, 'too good to be true.' The more data they collected as they moved further and further back in time, the more suspicious they became—and the more frustrated. It was like a puzzle to which there had to be a solution, probably a very simple solution. How could someone, singular or plural, be guessing so right, so often?

"I told them to look for correlations with other cyclical phenomena. Phases of the moon. Tides. Earthquake activity in California. I'm joking, of course, but the cyclical nature of these bursts of always successful speculation was one of the only real clues that we had. What appeared most odd in the pattern was 'always following the first weekend of the month.' Which raised this question: What always happened the first weekend of each month that enabled our unknown speculator or speculators to always make the right bets at the right time?"

He paused as if waiting for someone to come up with the solution.

"You, of course, all know the answer," he finally said. "This meeting. We always gather in Basel on the first weekend of each month, and meet at ten o'clock on Sunday morning as we are doing right now. We always discuss the same subject—interest rates—because we, as a group, *control* the world's interest rates. Therein lies our unique power. It is we, and only we, who can force a country or a continent into recession by massive increases in interest rates. The classic example occurred in the early 1980s when our former colleague Paul Volker, in order to stop runaway inflation that had been triggered by the massive increase in oil prices, pushed the American prime rate to over twenty percent. The cost of money was so high that it no longer made sense to take out a mortgage in order to buy a new house, or even to finance the purchase of a new car. So housing starts plummeted and car sales collapsed, and the United States plunged into the deepest recession since World War II. It is also we who can pull a country out of recession, by engineering declines in interest rates to the point where borrowing by consumers and companies alike becomes very attractive, spurring the purchase and building of everything from houses to cars, and thus lifting the entire economy. Though it is the business cycle that we affect in the longer run, it is every financial market on earth that we affect in the short run. Month after month. *And in a thoroughly predictable manner.*

"So there was the correlation. At this point in our investigation we knew the 'what.' Now came the question of the 'who.' "

Although everybody in the room already knew the answer, they continued to hang on Sir Robert's every word. For he was the master sleuth who had traced the crime to this very room, and was now about to explain how he had reduced the number of suspects from ten to one.

Sir Robert's next words indicated that he knew exactly what they were thinking.

"Narrowing down the *who* was not an easy task. All signs pointed to someone at the BIS. Theoretically it could have been one of the staff or at least one of the senior members of the BIS management. But those possibilities were soon rejected. As you know, it is we ten—today just nine, owing to the absence of an American—who meet *in camera*. No minutes are taken, no observers are present. No staff, other than the secretary of the BIS, who has been with us for over twenty years, partake in these Sunday meetings, unless invited to present a paper on a particular subject, after which they are asked to leave. So, after pursuing this line of logic, we were back to ten.

"Then another thought occurred to us. Because our initial data indicated that all the bursts of speculation involved the dollar, it could well have been someone very senior at the Federal Reserve in Washington—a person privy to the thinking and plans of the Fed's chairman—who knew in advance what would be discussed here, allowing him or her to act accordingly the following week in London's foreign exchange and Eurodollar markets.

"But as we continued our investigation—going further and further back in time—this theory was soon shot down also. The year before last, dollar interest rates had stayed flat the entire year. The international financial markets were driven by changes in interest rates here in Europe. An American insider in Washington could hardly anticipate what Dr. Schweizer intended to do with interest rates in Switzerland, or what the head of the Bundesbank would reveal on Sunday morning about his planned actions the following week, which would affect interest rates in Germany. Well, guess what? Precisely during that period, an eighteen-month hiatus in dollar interest rates, our unknown speculator switched tactics. Instead of speculating in Eurodollar futures he began to concentrate on Euromark and Euro Swiss franc futures, with the usual infallibility. We later found out that he had also switched tactics where foreign exchange was concerned. Now it was the mark, and especially the Swiss franc, that he became interested in.

"So it had to be one of us."

"How long ago did you reach this conclusion?" It was Dr. Mannesmann of the Bundesbank who posed the question.

"Two weeks ago," Sir Robert answered.

"Who was your prime suspect then?"

"Despite what I just said, owing to the central role of the dollar in most of the transactions we had discovered thus far—both before and after that eighteen-month hiatus—all evidence pointed in the direction of the American in our midst. But when it was subsequently discovered that these transactions had all originated in Switzerland, executed through the London subsidiary of the General Bank of Switzerland in Zurich, doubts were raised even about this conclusion."

"How did you find out about the General Bank of Switzerland's central role in all of this?"

"By talking to traders on the floor of the London International Financial Futures Exchange—the LIFFE—where Eurodollar futures are traded, and by identifying the big losers in these suspicious FX transactions—Citibank, Bankers Trust, Lloyd's, Mitsubishi, Deutsche Bank. They were more than happy to name the counterparty in those foreign exchange trades—i.e., the bank that had taken them to the cleaners time and again. It was always the General Bank of Switzerland that was named. We were told that the biggest loser of all was another Swiss bank—the United Bank of Switzerland—but when I approached them, they clammed up, claiming they were unable to cooperate because of the constraints imposed by the Swiss bank secrecy laws—which we know is no longer true, since those laws have been amended, but—"

Now Dr. Samuel Schweizer broke in for the first time. "That matter is not closed by any means. If their losses were as high as is rumored, the shareholders of that Swiss bank were seriously injured, meaning that a massive fraud was perpetrated against them. The United Bank might have rebuffed Sir Robert, but it will have no choice except to cooperate when the fraud squad of the Basel police force moves in on this."

Sir Robert resumed command. "Be that as it may, because of Dr. Schweizer's intervention, the General Bank of Switzerland agreed to cooperate completely with me. That led directly to the account where all the trades started. This was still not the end of the road, for it was one of those so-called B accounts—controlled by a lawyer for a client unknown. The law firm headed by Dr. Hans Zwiebach ranks among the most prestigious in Zurich. He teaches law at the University of Zurich. He is a colonel in the Swiss Army Reserve. He is an elder of the Swiss Reformed Church. His family's connection to the church goes back to the early sixteenth century, when they were very supportive of Zwingli's reform movement. The Zwiebachs have been regarded as pillars of Zurich society ever since. So it is natural that he is also on the board of directors of the General Bank of Switzerland. *Summa summarum*, Zwiebach is a man of impeccable credentials and held in the highest respect throughout Switzerland. I have dwelt on this because our case against Charles Black rests to a substantial degree on the information provided to us by Dr. Zwiebach."

Samuel Schweizer immediately intervened. "What you have just said, Sir Robert, is true, but it could also lead to a misunderstanding. It is the *records* of Dr. Zwiebach's law office, and those of the General Bank of Switzerland, that have provided us with the totally damning and irrefutable evidence of the culpability of Charles Black. In Switzerland, our laws demand severe punishment for crimes of such magnitude. I, for one, will insist that such punishment be meted out. It is our reputations, gentlemen, our collective reputation, on the line here. We either make sure that Charles Black is punished to the limit of the law, or the world will punish us."

Heads all around the table nodded affirmatively. The exception, again, was the

Canadian. But he was outnumbered eight to one.

Charles Black's goose was already as good as cooked.

Charles Black was of, course, oblivious of all that was being said about him just ten blocks away. In fact, he was oblivious of anything that was happening outside of the two thousand cubic feet he was inhabiting. He knew that his cell measured two thousand cubic feet, since, for lack of anything to read or to do, he had figured it out in his mind at least fifty times. Since then, he had also figured out that he was being deliberately kept in total isolation. At six o'clock that Sunday morning, the guard from the night before had shoved his breakfast— two slabs of thick bread, jam, and lukewarm milk coffee—through the slot in the door.

"I want to get to a telephone," Black had said quickly, before the slot was again closed.

"No talk," had been the response.

"You don't understand. Telephone. Bring me to telephone."

"Orders. No more talk to you," the guard had said. The metal plate slid back in place.

"The bastards!" Black exclaimed.

He was ready to pick up the tray holding his breakfast and slam it against the wall. But then he realized that he was hungry.

He also realized that if he threw the tray, it would be he who would have to clean up the resulting mess. No maid service here.

Two hours later the jail seemed to come alive. First there was the opening and closing of steel doors. Then the corridor outside his cell was full of men. Five minutes after that, he could faintly hear the sound of voices in song. It could only be a church service for the inmates, being held somewhere in the building. Without him.

Sally would probably be headed for church about now, too, he thought. Then he realized that Switzerland was nine hours ahead of California. This meant she was just getting ready for bed in their new apartment, probably after watching a movie on television.

The picture of his wife in that setting flashed across his mind. It drove home the unreality of his situation. No, the reality. This was not just a bad dream.

During the next twenty-four hours, the slot in the steel door opened three more times. Three more meals were shoved through. Not one word was spoken.

6

That all changed at exactly ten o'clock on Monday morning. Without warning, the door to Charles Black's cell opened. A guard—not the one from the weekend—entered bearing Charles Black's suitcase. He placed it on the bed.

"You are wanted by the state attorney. But first you are to take a shower. Then you come back here, you shave, and you dress properly. Okay?"

"Yes."

The guard pointed to the open door. "You go first."

It was with a feeling of relief that Black emerged from his cell into the corridor. The softening-up process was over. The battle would soon be joined.

The shower room was at the end of the corridor. Black stood under the hot water for at least five minutes, hoping that it would soak out the prison odor. Back in his cell, he removed his kit from his suitcase, and then began shaving in the basin that hung from the wall beside the open toilet. He didn't look all that great. Puffy eyes. Pallid skin. He looked *guilty*, for God's sake.

But five minutes later, when he rechecked himself in the mirror, the image he saw was much improved. The change of underwear had already helped. Then a clean white shirt, a new tie—they had taken the one he had worn on the plane—and the blue pinstriped suit that Sally had insisted he buy just a week earlier. She'd also picked out the tie. Then he noticed that his belt had been returned to his suitcase. So had the other tie. But don't fall for it, he told himself. First, total isolation. Now they're all heart.

Same approach when the guard came to fetch him. No leg irons. No handcuffs. They walked side by side down the corridor, this time in the direction of the entrance where he had arrived. Surprisingly, they did not stop there, but, as Black followed the slight lead of his guard, they left the building and he was back on the cobblestones in the courtyard where he had been unloaded from the police van after being brought in from the airport.

It was spring. The sky was blue. The sun was warm. And the air was sweet. You never know how good this world is, Black could not help but reflect, until you have been deprived of it. But don't get maudlin about it. Don't let them sucker you into letting your guard down. You're dealing here with some very devious bastards, and don't ever forget it.

There was to be no police van this time. Wherever they were headed, it would apparently be on foot. They walked through the main gate leading from the courtyard of the Lohnhof onto a narrow medieval street that curved along the top of a low hill overlooking the center of Basel. The blue and white street sign said HEUBERG. Many of the narrow, three-story buildings on each side bore plaques indicating the dates when they were built, and the names of some of the more famous people who had lived there.

On the right, one read, BUILT IN 1347. ERASMUS OF ROTTERDAM DWELT HERE 1509–1521.

Next door: BUILT IN 1498. HANS HOLBEIN THE YOUNGER LIVED AND PAINTED HERE BETWEEN 1519 AND 1526.

How civilized could a city be!

In fact, although centuries older, the street reminded him very much of where he and Sally had lived on the 3400 block of N Street in Georgetown during the years he had spent at the Fed. This was, after all, not Turkey or Paraguay. This was Switzerland. Land of William Tell. Birthplace of a democracy. Domicile of the International Red Cross. Home of Heidi, for God's sake.

Dream on, he reminded himself silently. *These Swiss are probably the most amoral people on earth. And they're out to get you.*

"We're here," his guard said, after he had stopped in front of another ancient, three-story house, this one bearing the number 21 and a plaque:

STAATSANWALTSCHAFT BASELSTADT

The reception area on the ground floor inside the house could have been that of a very high-priced law firm in Washington or New York. Except, perhaps, that the eighteenth-century furniture was real. The guard approached the receptionist's desk and placed a paper in front of her. She signed it and gave it back. The guard left without saying a word. Obviously he had just officially handed over the prisoner and been relieved of any further responsibility.

For a fleeting moment, Charles Black, alone with the receptionist, was seized by a not-so-crazy idea. This might be the last chance for a while. Get out of here and then run like hell. What was there to lose? But seconds later, that chance—if it had been one—passed. A door opened and a man entered the room. It was the police lieutenant from Saturday night at the airport.

"Mr. Black, we meet again," he said, moving forward to shake his hand. Charles Black accepted it very reluctantly. "I am not in a mood for pleasantries," he said. "I want immediate access to a telephone."

"You will get your telephone. But first the state attorney wants to have a word with you."

The door through which the policeman had come opened again, and two men emerged this time. When Charles Black glanced at them, he could hardly believe his eyes: Dr. Samuel Schweizer and Sir Robert Neville. They appeared to be equally startled when they recognized him. Schweizer regained his composure immediately and, without saying a word, strode past Black, out the door, and into the street. Sir Robert was about to follow him, then hesitated. Finally he approached Black.

"Charles," he said, "I hope you're all right."

"Hardly," Black replied. "But seeing you is the best thing that has happened so far. These bastards have held me incommunicado for the past forty-eight hours. This nonsense has got to end. I want out, and I want a lawyer. Arrange it."

The tone was that of the man who was used to being referred to as the second-most-powerful man in the America—second only to the President of the United States. He was also accustomed to having his orders carried out immediately. Though Governor of the Bank of England, Sir Robert Neville was definitely outranked.

But it didn't work. Sir Robert's hands rose in a gesture of helplessness. "Charles," he said, "I would if I could. Believe me. But it is out of my hands."

It was the second time Black had heard that sentence in the last two days—first from Samuel Schweizer when he had telephoned him from the airport, and now from Sir Robert Neville.

"At least you can tell me what's going on here," Black said.

As he spoke, another man entered the reception area. It was the state attorney himself, Dr. Rolf Wassermann. And it was he who answered Black's question.

"You are about to find that out. In my office." He then motioned to the police lieutenant, who took Black firmly by his left arm and escorted him from the reception area into the adjacent office.

Sir Robert watched helplessly. "Perhaps

I could have a private word with Mr. Black," he said to the state attorney.

"I'm sorry," came the reply. "Our procedures do not allow for that."

"If not now, then when?"

"I will let you know when it is convenient."

"But—"

"I appreciate your coming by, Sir Robert," Wassermann said. "You will hear from us." He turned and went into his office, firmly closing the door behind him.

Sir Robert knew a dismissal when he heard one. He had no choice but to leave.

Inside the state attorney's office, Charles Black was seated in a chair facing the elegant desk. The police lieutenant picked up a large briefcase standing beside the desk and left the room.

Immediately after that, the receptionist appeared with a tray bearing what appeared to be a full coffee service. She waited for instructions.

"In Switzerland, we always pause for morning coffee," Wassermann said. "Would you care to join us?"

Black ignored the question. "Enough of this nonsense," he said. "Either charge me with something or release me right now."

"Certainly," Wassermann replied. "But first, coffee." The receptionist handed him a porcelain cup and saucer, and then poured. She added two cubes of sugar. No cream. The state attorney sipped. She watched him. Assured that he was satisfied, she withdrew.

Black had never been treated with such complete contempt in his entire life. It was with enormous difficulty that he restrained himself from lunging across the desk and grabbing the smug son of a bitch by the throat.

Wassermann finally put down his coffee cup. "Read this," he said, as he reached across the desk and handed Black a single piece of paper. It was a legal document, the text of which was in German. Black attempted to read it, but he soon realized that his knowledge of German was not up to the task.

"Having a problem with it, Mr. Black?" Wassermann asked. "But of course. You Americans are not known for your language skills. If you wish, I will tell you what that document says. But first I want you to look at the signatures below the body of the text."

Black looked. The signatures were those of Samuel Schweizer and Robert Neville. He looked back up to the state attorney, who said, "What you have in your hands is a complaint. A formal complaint that has been lodged against you by Dr. Samuel Schweizer, acting on behalf of the Swiss National Bank, and Sir Robert Neville, acting for the Bank for International Settlements."

"What is the substance of their complaint?" Black asked.

"Suspicion of misuse of public office for private gain under Article 312 of the Swiss Federal Criminal Code. Suspicion of misuse of state secrets for private gain under Article 267 of the Swiss Federal Criminal Code. Suspicion of fraud under Article 148 of that same code."

"This is absolutely absurd."

"Perhaps. Let me continue. If found guilty under Article 312, you would face a sentence of five years at hard labor. Article 267 stipulates a similar period of incarceration. Article 148 requires an imprisonment under conditions of hard labor for at least ten years if the fraud involved is less than one million francs. If however, the criminal acts are regarded as professional fraud—that is, if the fraudulent activities took place over an extended period of time—and if the amount exceeds one million Swiss francs, the sentence could go as high as fifteen years. Your case appears to be in that category. Finally, you should be aware that, in cases such as yours, Swiss courts almost always require that these sentences be served consecutively. Thus, we are talking about at least twenty years at hard labor, and as much as thirty."

If he expected Charlie Black to fall over in a faint upon hearing all this, he had guessed wrong. "You are dead serious about this, aren't you?"

"Yes, we are, Mr. Black."

"Then you are a greater fool than I

thought you were. I suspect that even in this country you need more than accusations to arrest a man and then keep him locked up. Even a foreigner. So the time has come either to put up or shut up. Are *your* linguistic talents up to understanding that?"

"We *arrested* you on the basis of an oral complaint, Mr. Black. Had we not, you might have heard about the suspicions of your former colleagues at the Bank for International Settlements and fled the country. We are now *holding* you on the basis of the written complaint that you hold in your hand. In addition to formally lodging that complaint, Dr. Schweizer, Sir Robert, and his aide from the Bank of England also provided us with documentation that we are now in the process of examining in detail."

"Let me try to understand this. You have just begun the process of examining the documents that purportedly support the accusations that have been made against me?"

"That is correct. Lieutenant Schmidt is continuing the process now."

"Yet you have no qualms about holding me on the basis of complaints without charging me with anything? I find that incredible."

Wassermann shrugged. "The complaints—both the oral and now the written—hardly come from just anybody. Dr. Schweizer and Sir Robert Neville are men of impeccable integrity, both holding high office in their respective countries as well as at the BIS here in Basel."

"And I?"

"As I understand it, Mr. Black, you no longer hold *any* office. You are retired. And apparently you have been making sure that your retirement will be worry-free, at least as far as money is concerned."

"I resent that."

"You do, do you? Well, we Swiss resent your using our institutions to perpetrate your crimes. We will not allow you or anybody else to get away with it anymore. In fact, we intend to make an example of you as a warning to others who might be tempted to emulate you."

"I've heard enough," Black stated. "Either you allow me to exercise my rights or I will refuse to speak any further with you or anybody else here. We'll let our two governments fight it out."

"What rights are those, Mr. Black?"

"To begin with, the right to speak to my wife so that she can help me secure legal representation and inform our embassy in Bern about what's going on here."

"You may speak to your wife right away. But let me warn you about your so-called rights. This is Switzerland, not the United States. *Our* government defines 'rights' here, not yours. Keep that in mind."

Wassermann stood up. "There is a conference room right next door. You may use the phone there to call your wife."

He came around from behind his desk and opened a door leading directly into the adjacent room. "Please," he said, motioning for Black to enter. He watched as Black took his seat in front of the phone. Then he turned and closed the door. And locked it.

7

She picked up on the second ring.

"Is that you, Sally?"

"Charlie!" she exclaimed. "Where are you? I tried the Euler Hotel a dozen times, and they kept saying that you never arrived. Are you all right?"

"Yes and no."

"Did something happen? Are you in a hospital?" She sounded increasingly frantic.

"Take it easy, Sally. I'm perfectly healthy. I'm not in a hospital. I'm in a jail."

"Jail! Charles, did you say *jail?*"

"Yes. Jail. In Basel. They call it the Lohnhof."

"But why?"

"Believe it or not, Sally, I really don't know. That is, I know that a criminal complaint has been filed against me, but I have no idea on what basis it was filed."

"I don't understand what you're talking about. You said 'criminal complaint'? Criminal? *You?*"

"Me. I just finished talking to the state attorney here. I'm telephoning from his conference room, and I'm sure the line is bugged. He is what we would call the chief prosecuting attorney. A few minutes ago he handed me a piece of paper with the complaint. They're talking about misuse of public office for private gain, misuse of state secrets for private gain, and fraud, massive professional fraud."

"My God! That's insane. How did they come up with that?"

"It obviously has something to do with that bank account we had with the General Bank in Switzerland. Remember it?"

"Of course. But it's been dormant for years."

"Maybe not."

"What's that mean?"

"You also remember our lawyer in Zurich?"

"Of course. Zwiebach. But I haven't talked to him in about ten years."

"They claim that I did."

"When?"

"Early January of last year, for instance."

"Sure. You told me about it. You wanted him to get hotel rooms at the Palace Hotel in St. Moritz for Laura and her friends. Remember?"

He remembered. He had called from the Savoy Hotel in early January. He'd gone to London after the meeting at the BIS.

"Is he with you now?" his wife asked.

"Who?"

"Zwiebach."

"No. He's on their side, not mine."

"How can that be?"

"I have no idea."

"Then who is representing you?"

"No one. That's where I need your help. Immediately."

"But it's two o'clock in the morning here, Charles."

"I know."

"Who should I get?"

"Dan Lash. You know him. He was at dinner at our place at least a half-dozen times. The firm's name is Lash, Evans and Scott. It's on M Street."

"It's still only five in the morning on the East Coast. When does he normally go to the office?"

"Early. Eight."

"Can I do it on the phone, or I should I get on the next plane and fly back to Washington?"

"Do it on the phone. Otherwise we lose another day."

"Is it bad, Charles?"

"No, not really. Reminds me of the dorm at prep school."

"Should I come over?"

"Not yet. Let's first line up the lawyers. I'm going to have to depend totally on you, Sally. These sons of bitches are going to hold me incommunicado as long as they can get away with it. And as I'm rapidly finding out, in this country that could be until Christmas."

"Don't worry. I'll get you out of there. But first I'll need some exact information. Exactly where you are. The name of that state attorney. Phone numbers over there. Hold on while I move to my desk."

8

When Sally Black finally hung up, she just sat there in her nightgown in front of her desk in the bedroom.

"Dammit," she said, "just when everything seemed to be working out perfectly."

It had, of course, been something of a shock to her when Charles came home and told her that he was going to resign as Chairman of the Federal Reserve. She had known about his difficulties with the new President, and especially with his smartass staff in the White House. But somehow she had thought, even hoped, that it could all be worked out. She had liked her life in Washington, and so, she knew, had he. She also knew that when he made up his mind to do something, there was no turning back.

After his resignation had been accepted with all-too-apparent relief, it was clear to both of them that it would be impossible for them to stay on in Washington. And it was also clear, and totally logical, that when they moved, it would be to California. Because that was where she had grown up. She had gone east to college, and it was at Georgetown University that she had met Charles Black. But it was at her parents' ranch in the Alexander Valley that they had been married. And it was back to California and that ranch that they had returned whenever possible, even though Charlie's banking career had taken him first to New York, then to various places around the world, and finally to Washington, D.C. After her parents had died and she had inherited the ranch, both knew that it was there where they would eventually retire.

But "eventually" came a lot earlier than both had expected, and she knew that Charles was not ready for the rural life. Thus the apartment in San Francisco. Not that she was ready, either.

She looked in the mirror. And what she saw was a damn well-preserved woman of fifty. She inevitably drew admiring glances when she walked into a room, and the men who eyed her seemed to be younger every year. Sure, she loved it. But she had never depended on her good looks to get ahead. She'd been smart enough to go to Georgetown, smart enough to marry Charles Black, and then she had been smart enough to handle their private finances—with great success.

Charles had made a lot of money from the word go, first at First National, then at Whitney Brothers. But like so many men in business, he had never set aside time to take care of the money he earned. So, after their daughter Laura reached school age, she did. First it had been real estate in the suburbs of London in the 1970s, when the housing market there took off like a rocket. They had lived out in Gerrard's Cross—a forty-five-minute train ride from London's Marylebone Station—in that area of Buckinghamshire known as the Stockbrokers' Belt. All of a sudden it seemed as though stockbrokers in London were multiplying like rabbits, each wanting the status that went with owning a house in "Bucks"—plus the quick return on their investment that now was a sure thing. As a result of her American breeding, she had no fear of mortgaging a property to the hilt. So, one after another, she did. Then she started to dabble in the European stock markets, and did all right there, too. By the time First National transferred Charles to Hong Kong five years later, she had gotten their net worth up to almost $2 million.

In Hong Kong she picked up where she had left off in Europe. First in property, and then in one of the most volatile stock markets in the world. By the time they were transferred back to New York, their net worth was up to $4 million.

Then Charles had moved over to Whitney Brothers, where sometimes his bonus alone ran to over $2 million dollars a year. And that was in the second half of the

1980s, when the greatest bull market in Wall Street history began its run. She plunged right into it, often on margin, and often trading in Zurich—through Zwiebach—so as to be able to take advantage of the liberal margin lending facilities there. But she also kept her hand in Hong Kong, Singapore, and Malaysia, since she knew that territory better than even most American professional investment managers did. By that time, when Charles joined the Fed, between his bonuses and her market plays, their net worth had increased to over $29 million.

She turned on the portable computer she kept on her desk. It was all in there. She knew the answer, but she wanted to see it again. On Friday, as she always did, she had keyed in the last update of their securities portfolio. The Mac screen gave her the exact number ten seconds later. Their net worth was $29,537,456.97. She checked it, category by category. Twenty million could be made liquid within twenty-four hours.

Not that she'd need anything like that. But Charles needed lawyers right away—the best that money could buy. And she was a big enough girl to know that *only* money could get them. She scrolled further on the computer. Their cash balance at Bank of America was $152,789.16. She'd wire $100,000 of that to Dan Lash the moment the bank opened. That would get him moving fast. But first she had to talk to him. She looked at her watch. It was now going on two-thirty in the morning—five-thirty in Washington. So she had to wait three hours before she could get the lawyers moving and get Charlie out of that jail.

Fraud...Misuse of office for private gain... Her blood boiled when she even thought of such words being mentioned in connection with her husband. Charles had always bent over backwards to avoid any possible conflict of interests between his professional activities and their private ones. So he had always been very careful about discussing anything he was doing at the bank with her, lest it might later be misconstrued. It was as if a blind trust had been created—financed by him and run by her—with a Chinese Wall in between. Often it became ridiculous. At dinner he would sometimes stop in midsentence lest he say something that might clue her in regarding a merger deal that Whitney Brothers was working on.

But now, somehow, the trading account in Switzerland that they had never closed had caught up with Charles. Which simply did not make sense.

What was going on over there?

9

What was going on at the moment was the first official police interrogation of Charles Black. The man in charge was Lieutenant

71

Paul Schmidt, the head of the Fraud Squad of the City and Canton of Basel.

It was Schmidt who had taken him from the state attorney's conference room up two flights of creaky stairs to his office on the third floor. The inside of the building resembled Black's grandmother's house outside of Chicago. And the police lieutenant's office could have been one of the upstairs bedrooms. It was an oddly lulling atmosphere—probably deliberately so, Black thought. Part of the "good cop, bad cop" game. So don't fall for it, he told himself yet again.

"Take a seat while I clean up the mess on my desk," Schmidt said. "Or, if you feel like it, you might want to take a look out the window. You get a great view of old Basel from here. I hope you don't mind if I smoke."

He began to pack a pipe, and then, satisfied, lit it with a long wooden match. Then he got up from behind his desk and joined Black at the window. They shared a view of medieval downtown Basel, which lay below.

"That red sandstone building with the murals is our City Hall. Inside, some of the paintings were done by Holbein."

"When we walked here from that jail, I could not help but notice the house where he lived," Black said, despite the warning that he had just issued to himself.

"*Ja*," Schmidt said. "We are lucky that we are able to work in this neighborhood.

Every house up here is full of history. The other police buildings in Basel are like police buildings all over the world. We share this house with the state attorney because we deal with nonviolent criminals. You call them 'white-collar,' I believe." He took a puff on his pipe, and went on: "That square in front of City Hall is where they hold a farmers' market in the morning. That's why all the umbrellas. To keep the fruit and vegetables protected from the elements. At noon, the farmers—actually it's mostly farmers' wives—all pack up and go home, most of them back across the border to the Alsace."

It was all very relaxed, even chummy.

"But now, Mr. Black, if you don't mind, I'm afraid that I must ask you a few more questions. Let's both sit down."

Black took the chair facing the policeman across the desk.

"My job," Schmidt said, "is to get to the core of this matter as soon as possible. If we reach the conclusion that the allegations raised in the complaint filed by the Swiss National Bank and the Bank for International Settlements are unsubstantiated, you will not be charged and you will be able to go home."

"And if not?"

"If the facts support those complaints, the state attorney will formally charge you. And you will be detained further."

"I think that I should speak to a lawyer before I answer any more questions."

"That is your privilege. However, as I understand it, you do not yet have an attorney. And even when you do, I can assure you that he will give you the same advice that I am about to give you. The sooner we talk, the sooner you will be released. Or, put another way, if you choose not to talk, you will be held indefinitely. In your case, I can assure you that no bail will be granted, because there is an obvious danger of your leaving the country."

"How long can a person be held purely on the basis of unsubstantiated accusations?"

"As I said, indefinitely. If you decide not to cooperate, the process will no doubt be long and, from our point of view, very arduous. The status of your case will be reviewed every thirty days by the state attorney. Only if he sees fit will bail be granted. Unless you and I make some progress, I can assure you that his review will not be favorable."

"All right," Black said. "Let's get on with it."

"Good. Believe me, Mr. Black, you have made the right decision. Now let me explain how we will proceed. I will bring in a stenographer who will record our conversation. At the conclusion of each session, she will type it up. Periodically, you will receive copies of those transcripts and be given ample time to review them to make sure they accurately reflect my questions and your answers. If you agree that they are correct, we both will sign them. Any problem with that?"

Black thought it over, then said, "Fine with me. But one thing bothers me. You said 'each session.' How many sessions do you have in mind?"

"One this morning. Then we break for lunch. Another this afternoon."

"And how many such sessions in all?"

"That is really up to the state attorney. I merely follow his orders."

"But don't I get a preliminary court hearing before a judge?"

"We do not have preliminary court hearings in Switzerland."

"But then the state attorney acts as both prosecutor and judge."

The policeman shrugged. "That is our system, Mr. Black." He picked up his telephone, dialed an internal number, and spoke a few words. Almost immediately an attractive young woman entered the room, stenographer's pad in hand. She avoided looking at Black.

"Please take your usual seat, Maria," Schmidt said. "We are going to begin." He looked back across the desk at Charles Black. "I will start with early January of last year. I want to go through it day by day."

"How can you expect me to remember what happened that long ago?"

"I will try to help you recall. As I understand it, you arrived in Basel on a Saturday, just as you always do, at the beginning of each month. As usual, you stayed at the Euler Hotel. And, as usual, you attended a private dinner with your colleagues at the Schützenhaus."

"In order to confirm any of that, I would have to check my agenda for last year."

"We have the record of your stay at the Euler Hotel. You paid with an American Express Platinum Card when you checked out on Monday. You also signed the hotel bill. Is this your signature?" He shoved a copy of the hotel bill across the desk to Black.

After just a cursory glance, Black confirmed that indeed it was his signature.

"You then attended the weekend meetings of the Bank for International Settlements. Because of the holiday season, that meeting apparently was held on the second rather than the first weekend of the month, as it usually was. The secretary of the BIS has provided us with a brief protocol, noting the times of the meetings and who was in attendance. Apparently he does so every month."

"I was not aware of that, since I really have nothing to do with the internal procedures of that bank. I do know, however, that at the meetings proper, only cursory notes are taken by the secretary of the BIS, and no protocol concerning what was discussed is ever issued. In fact, from its founding to the present day, no protocols of such meetings or any other internal records of the BIS have ever been made available for public scrutiny."

"Is that common practice among central bankers?"

"Not necessarily. At the Federal Reserve, the secretary does compile a written summary of what is discussed at the meetings of the Federal Open Market Committee. But these protocols are only made public many weeks later. However, if a specific course of action is agreed upon at these meetings, such as setting a new target for short-term interest rates, this is normally announced immediately, following a practice begun by one of my predecessors, Alan Greenspan."

"You continued that practice?"

"Yes. With just one exception, as I recall."

"This is very interesting," the policeman said. "Explain more about those Federal Open Market Committee meetings."

"What do you want to know?"

"How often they take place. Who is involved. What is discussed. That sort of thing."

"Normally they take place every six weeks or so at our headquarters in Washington. However, should a special situation develop during the interim, which happens quite often, we hold meetings via conference calls on the telephone. So there is really no firm, predetermined schedule. The meetings are attended by the seven governors of the Federal Reserve Board, all located in Washington, plus the presidents of five of the twelve regional Federal Reserve Banks. They rotate annually. So at the meetings we have twelve in all."

"Going back to the beginning of last year, we are told that such a meeting was held in Washington on Wednesday, January eighth."

"Let me think a minute," Black said. Then, "Yes. I now recall that meeting. It was an important one."

"Why was it important?"

"Because we had to decide whether or not to increase the federal funds rate."

"What does that mean?"

"The federal funds rate is the interest rate at which banks borrow from each other on an overnight basis. It's the shortest-term interest rate there is, and the most sensitive. Where the Federal Reserve is concerned, it is also the easiest rate to manipulate."

"How do you do that?"

"If we want to get the rate to go up, we sell U.S. government bonds at a competitive price to bond dealers in New York, who pay for them by withdrawing cash from their New York banks. If those banks now want to make new loans, they are going to have to raise new cash. The easiest and certainly the quickest way to do that is to borrow overnight from other banks around the country. In order to entice other banks to lend to them, they will have to bid up the price of the money. When that happens, up goes the federal funds interest rate."

"It's that simple?" the Swiss policeman asked.

"That simple. One of my predecessors said that when the chairman of the Federal Reserve arrives at the office each day, he really has but one decision to make: buy, sell, or do nothing. If he issues the order to buy bonds, interest rates go down. If he says 'sell,' interest rates go up. If he does nothing, short-term interest rates remained unchanged. Job done, he can go golfing for the rest of the day and let the bureaucrats run the place."

The detective chuckled and then drew some smoke from his pipe.

"You make it sound so easy," he said. "What decision was taken on January eighth?"

"To very gradually raise the rate."

"Why raise it? And why gradually?"

"Because after the last recession, the economy had picked up steam—but too quickly. We wanted to issue a mild warning that we would not allow growth to get out of hand. If it did, bottlenecks would develop, which would lead to supply shortages, which would lead to price increases. That's all. By raising the specter of higher interest rates, we wanted to begin to discourage borrowing that could have fueled a too-rapid expansion of the economy and the development of such bottlenecks. In other words, we wanted to make a very limited preemptive strike against the possible return of inflation twelve or eighteen months down the road. We did not want to scare the financial markets and send both bonds and stocks into a downward spiral. So, first, as an exception to recent practice—the only exception during my tenure, as I already told you—we would *not* announce our decision. And, second, we would exercise our open-market operations very carefully by not draining too much liquidity from the market at one time."

As he replayed those days of well over a year ago, it seemed as if Charles Black had completely forgotten where he was.

"Did it work out as planned?"

"At first nobody noticed what we were doing. But then, a week later, *The Wall Street Journal* ran a story suggesting what was going on. Nobody believed that the Fed was just issuing a mild warning. They thought that inflation was just around the corner—which would mean that the Fed's action was just the first step in a ratcheting up of short-term interest rates. If long-term rates followed that lead, it would mean death for bonds. So all the fund managers started to dump their bonds at the same time, sending long-term interest rates straight up. That spooked the stock market, which thrives on low interest rates. So stocks also went into a dive. It was a mess."

He paused before continuing.

"They were right, of course. During the remainder of the year we *did* have to ratchet up interest rates because the economy was in much greater danger of overheating than we had originally thought. As guardian of the currency, I did what I had to do, regardless of what was politically correct at the moment. But what happened in January was at least one of the reasons why, when eleven months later the President made it obvious that he wanted me to leave, very few people on Wall Street came to my defense. The market drop that they felt I had triggered ultimately cut the value of the portfolios they were managing by a half-trillion dollars. They don't like being blindsided like that. It made them look bad. Not many in Washington thought much of my performance, either, especially after those higher interest rates eventually slowed growth and resulted in much higher unemployment. In the long run, however, I was right. I stopped inflation, and in due course the economy revived and we moved back to full employment."

"But between that meeting on January eighth and the sell-off on Wall Street, you came to Basel."

"Yes. We've already covered that. There was no reason whatsoever to cancel that trip."

"But weren't you afraid that this shift in Federal Reserve policy would sooner or later be noticed or leaked? Would it not have been more prudent to stay in Washington, where you could exercise damage control by temporarily injecting some liquidity into the market?"

This drew an odd glance from Black.

"That's why the BIS meetings are held on weekends—so that the number of working days we central bankers are away from our desks in Washington or Tokyo is kept to a minimum. But, tell me, how come you are so familiar with these things? Most policemen I've ever met wouldn't know a bond from a stock, much less how the Federal Reserve operates."

"My father is with the Swiss Bank Corporation—one of their general managers. He wanted me to follow in his footsteps. After the Mathematical Gymnasium, I studied economics at the university for a while. Got my diploma. Then I worked for his bank, where I did interest-rate swaps. Until I'd had enough."

"And why now a policeman?"

"At first it was to get out of the rut that my father has been in his entire life. Do something exciting for a change. Then, after a few years, I was given this job with the Fraud Squad because of my background—and, let's face it, because of my father's influence. What I do here is extremely interesting. It still requires that I keep up with financial matters, but it allows me to get involved in cases like this. How else would I ever get to meet a Charles Black?"

Black could not help admiring the candor of the young man. Schmidt looked about as clean-cut as you could get. He was neatly dressed. His hair was cut close, almost a crewcut. He was maybe thirty-two or thirty-three. And he had none of that smart-alec attitude of his boss, the state attorney.

"I'd like to move on just a bit before we break for lunch," Schmidt said.

"Let's do it. As you said, the sooner we get through this, the sooner both you and I can move on to other things."

"So, after the meetings in Basel, you went to London the morning of January thirteenth."

"Yes."

"Let's now return to what we discussed at the airport Saturday night. I want to go back to your phone call to Dr. Hans Zwiebach in Zürich, which you made from your room at the Savoy Hotel in London on January thirteenth."

"Good. Because in the meantime I remembered that I made such a call."

"Now we're getting somewhere. For what reason did you call Zwiebach?"

"To ask him if he could help us book a room at the Palace Hotel in St. Moritz for our daughter, Laura. She wanted to ski there in late January with two of her friends."

"I see. However, I'm afraid that we've been told otherwise, Mr. Black."

"By whom?"

"By Dr. Zwiebach."

"What did he tell you?"

"Something very damaging, I'm afraid."

"Like what?"

"That you gave him instructions to execute various financial transactions, using your account at the General Bank of Switzerland in Zurich."

"That's preposterous! Absolutely untrue!"

"Dr. Zwiebach has provided us with his log of that conversation, Mr. Black."

"There was no such conversation."

"But you just admitted that there was."

"You know damn well what I said."

"So you claim that you telephoned Dr. Zwiebach on Monday, January thirteenth, but that you only talked about a hotel room for your daughter."

"That's right."

"But the record shows that the conversation lasted six minutes."

"So we might have engaged in the usual exchange of pleasantries, with him asking me about my family and me asking him about his. I can't remember. I told you, Zwiebach's records mean nothing."

"I'm not talking about Dr. Zwiebach's records. I'm talking about the record received from the Savoy Hotel."

For a moment, Charles Black was at a loss for words.

"What in the world is going on here?" he finally asked.

"Zwiebach also remembers that he called you back—at the Savoy— to verify that all the trades had been executed as ordered. He remembers it well, he told us, because this was very unusual, his calling back. You had given him strict orders *not* to call you unless explicitly told otherwise. In no instance was he to *ever* call you in the United States."

"I've never heard such total rubbish in my entire life. Yes, he did call me back. To tell me that he was having difficulties getting a room in St. Moritz for my daughter. Every hotel seemed to be fully booked. So I told him to forget it. Laura ended up skiing at Aspen in our Rocky Mountains."

"So there is no record of any hotel booking in St. Moritz."

"No."

"That might have helped you," Schmidt said, and it was apparent that he really meant it.

"Why do I need help? It's Zwiebach's word against mine."

"Not really." Schmidt now reached for a large dossier, and methodically began to extract a series of documents. He shoved the first one across the desk.

"You probably recognize this. It is the fiduciary agreement with Dr. Zwiebach governing your account at the General Bank of Switzerland."

Black took it and looked at it. "It is just as I told you at the airport. I had an account there. And yes, this is my signature on the fiduciary agreement with Dr. Zwiebach governing that account. At the time we made that arrangement, it was common practice, I was told. In fact, we did it on the specific advice of Dr. Zwiebach."

"I remind you that a transcript is being taken of this conversation, and that you will be asked to sign it."

"Yes." Black glanced over at the stenographer, who was duly taking notes. From the bored look on her face, she was not paying much attention to the import of the words she was taking down.

"Do you also recognize the second signature on that fiduciary agreement?" Schmidt asked.

"Yes. It's that of my wife, Sally," Black replied. Then he added, "In fact, that was the principal reason we went the fiduciary agreement route—for estate reasons in the event of my death. It was like the living trust arrangements we make in the United States. All legal and aboveboard."

Schmidt interrupted him. "We understand. It is common practice in Switzerland. And perfectly legal, just as you said. Let's move on to the bank signature card governing account number J 747-2239. Here. Whose signature is attached?"

"It's that of Dr. Hans Zwiebach," Black said. "But it was our account."

"And you realize that your fiduciary agreement gave him authority over that account."

"Yes, of course. I'm a banker, you know."

"Please excuse me, Mr. Black, but as I just pointed out, these matters must be put into our record."

Now Schmidt shoved a small pile of documents across the desk at Black. "I want you to examine these very carefully, Mr. Black. And tell me what they mean."

Black laid the signature card back down on the desk and picked up one of the new documents. "This is a confirmation from the General Bank of Switzerland of a trade they made."

"For what account?"

Black searched the document, and replied, "It just gives an account number. No name."

"Would you please compare that account number with the number of your account?"

Black did. They were the same. "I never ordered any such trade," he said. "As I have already told you more than once, as far as I knew, my account at the General Bank of Switzerland has been dormant for over ten years."

"What is the description of the trade?"

"I told you. This trade has nothing to do with me."

"Then I will tell you. Along with all the other trading slips in front of you, it confirms that on January thirteenth of last year, in a series of transactions for account number J 747-2239, the General Bank of Switzerland bought puts on 16,666 December Eurodollar contracts at a strike price of 95. As the contract was trading at 96.43 at the time, short-term interest rates would have had to rise precipitously in a short period in order for these puts to have any value. Because of this, the options were dirt cheap. On each contract, which controls one million dollars, the General Bank of Switzerland paid an average of three ticks, or seventy-five dollars a contract. I know these things because when I did interest-rate swaps for the Swiss Bank Corporation, I dealt in that Eurodollar market almost every day. You were, of course, going short Eurodollars, betting that short-term dollar interest rates would go up, meaning that Eurodollar contracts would go down. Precisely what happened, of course. They fell to 94.75, making those three-cent put options now worth over twenty-five cents, at which time the General Bank of Switzerland covered your position by selling out those options and crediting your account with the proceeds."

Schmidt held up a bank document. "It says here that on the original $1.25 million you had 'invested,' you earned $9.25 million." Then he pushed another pile of General Bank of Switzerland trading confirmations at Black.

"These are U.S. Treasury bond futures trades. Same dates. Same account. With the December contract at 119 17/32, you bought eight thousand out-of-the-money 115 puts at 16/64, or $250 per contract. Bond prices plummeted to 109 19/32, allowing you to sell those puts for over $5,410 per contract. On your investment of two million dollars you made around $41.3 million. This was not luck, Mr. Black. This was a sure thing. And the only man on earth who knew that it was a sure thing was you."

"That's sheer nonsense. I told you what happened. The last thing in the world that I expected was that interest rates would spike up that way."

"I talked this over with my father, Mr. Black," the police lieutenant said. "And he remembered vividly that your predecessor, Alan Greenspan, did almost *exactly* the same thing in February of 1994, with *exactly* the same results. The only difference is that Greenspan did not have a secret trading account at the General Bank of Switzerland where he could personally profit from a process he had singlehandedly set in motion."

"So there it is," Black said. "Finally."

"You admit it, then?"

"Don't fuck with me, young man. Of course I don't admit it. But I finally know what's going on here."

"And that is?"

"Somebody is setting me up."

"Who?"

"Who? Certainly one of them is Zwiebach."

"But how could Zwiebach know what only you could know?"

How indeed? Schmidt got up from behind his desk.

"Let's break for lunch, Mr. Black," he said. "It will give you time to search your memory further."

Black had no choice but to get up from his chair.

"We're going back downstairs," Schmidt

said. "A guard will escort you back to the Lohnhof. You will be returned here at two."

Ten minutes later, Charles Black was back in his cell. Shortly thereafter, a lunch tray was shoved through the slot in the steel door. It held meat loaf, carrots, mashed potatoes, and gravy.

Black took the food over to his small wooden table, determined to leave it untouched. But hunger got the best of him. He took up a fork and tried the mashed potatoes. They were good. Then he tried the meat loaf. It was very good. Within minutes he had wolfed down the entire meal. Then he lay down on the bed, trying to figure out a convincing response to what he had just heard. He came up with nothing.

At exactly two o'clock the guard came to fetch him.

10

At almost exactly the same time, Sally Black got hold of Dan Lash in Washington. "I'm calling about Charles," she began. "He asked me to call you. We need your help."

"What's the problem?" the lawyer asked.

"Charles is in jail in Switzerland."

"Charged with what?"

"He's not been charged. He's being held under suspicion of fraud and a few other things."

"How come there's nothing in the papers?"

"It just happened. They arrested him on Saturday."

"Who's 'they'?"

"The police in Basel."

"What was Charles doing in Basel?"

"He went there to attend the monthly meeting of the central bankers at the Bank for International Settlements, like he always does."

"But he's no longer with the Fed."

"They asked him to help out over there for a few months until his successor is appointed and confirmed."

"Why haven't the people at the Fed gotten him out?"

"I don't know."

"But they must be aware of what happened."

"I don't know if they are or not, Dan."

"When did you talk to Charles?"

"Three hours ago."

"Tell me exactly what he told you."

"He told me very little. The conversation lasted less than five minutes. Charles was sure the line was tapped. But he did say that it had to do with an account at the General Bank of Switzerland in Zurich."

"Charles has an account there?"

"Charles and I *had* an account there. We opened it years ago when we lived in London. I used it to do some trading. I also used their margin facilities at times. It was a so-called B account, meaning that we used a fiduciary—a local lawyer—to keep an eye on it for us. He had signature rights. And that's the second problem."

"Namely?"

"Charles says the lawyer's involved in this. On their side."

That produced a pause on the other end of the line.

"The press is bound to get hold of this very soon. How do you intend to handle them?" the attorney asked.

"I don't give a damn about the press," Sally said. "I just want you to get Charles out of that jail."

"I brought it up, Sally, because we want to keep the media on our side."

"Then you'd better handle them."

"Good. If any of them call, say nothing and refer them to me."

"And what are you going to tell them?"

"Nothing either. Until I learn more. Which means I'm going to have to talk directly to Charles right away. That will require my contacting the Swiss authorities first. They will, of course, want to know if I am authorized to represent Charles."

"You are, as of right now. I will wire you a hundred thousand dollars within the hour," Sally said.

"That's hardly necessary," Lash said.

Sally knew better. "How much will it take to get a Swiss lawyer?" she then asked.

"Enough. Swiss lawyers charge the highest fees on earth. Even more than we do, believe it or not. And I know for sure that whoever we get will want money up front."

"How much?"

"Another hundred thousand."

"Will I pay him directly, or will it go through you?"

"I'm not sure."

"Then, just to be safe, I'll wire two hundred thousand." She would have to transfer some funds from her money market account to her checking account.

"What's your bank and account number?" Sally asked.

He told her.

"When are you going to start?" she asked.

"Right now," Lash answered.

"You'll need the name of the state attorney over there. It's Dr. Rolf Wassermann. His phone number is 011–41–61–44–73–23. His address is Heuberg 21, CH–4058, Basel, Switzerland."

"Fax?"

"I don't know. It's already the middle of the afternoon over there, Dan," Sally said.

"I'll call right now."

"And then you'll call me right back." She gave him her number in San Francisco and hung up.

11

The afternoon session on the third floor of Heuberg 21 began at exactly 2:12 P.M. It was duly noted by the police stenographer in Lieutenant Paul Schmidt's office.

"Was lunch satisfactory?" Schmidt asked Black.

"Yes."

"Good. We are now going to move on. Or, more accurately, move back—way back—to the end of your first year in office. To the weekend of December third of that year. Do you recall attending the BIS meetings held then?"

"Actually I do, yes."

"Do you recall what was discussed at the meetings?"

"I would have to think about it. But I would hardly be free to discuss their content with you. I think I've already explained the strict policy of the BIS regarding confidentiality."

"You did mention it, yes. However, in this instance they have made an exception."

"Who is 'they'?"

"The chairman and secretary of the BIS."

"You mean Dr. Samuel Schweizer?"

"Yes. And a Monsieur Henri Boeglin."

"That surprises me."

"All I know is that we have a transcript of what was said at those meetings," Schmidt said. He held up a bound set of legal-length sheets of paper.

"I have no idea what they have given you, but it can hardly be a transcript. No precise notes are taken at these meetings."

"But the secretary is always in attendance, isn't he?"

"Yes. But he only takes notes when instructed to do so by the chairman of the meetings."

"Yes, we also have those handwritten notes. What I am referring to here"— again he held up the bound sheets—"is a verbatim typed transcript of the meetings held the weekend of December third. It was left up to us to sort out what was germane to our case."

"But how did they produce this so-called transcript?"

"Apparently, shortly after Dr. Schweizer was elected Chairman of the Bank for International Settlement, he installed a tape-recording system in the boardroom there. It is activated by the secretary when signaled to do so by the chairman."

"How does the secretary activate it?"

"We asked the same question. He presses a button installed beneath the table immediately in front of where he always sits. As I understand it, his place at the conference table is always immediately to the left of the chairman."

"I'll be damned," Black said. "I'll bet I know where he got the idea to do that."

"Where?"

"From my predecessor. Alan Greenspan installed exactly the same system in the boardroom at the Fed in Washington. Same button in the same place, pressed, on signal, by the same type of secretary."

"When you were chairman of the Fed, did you use the system?"

"Of course. It was the only way to keep a truly accurate record of what was said, and especially who said it."

"So you have no objections to our using the recorded transcript of certain portions of the BIS meetings attended by you that weekend?"

"No. Why should I?" Black replied.

He soon found out why.

"Let's begin with the session on December third," Schmidt said. "It had to do with the sharp increase in unemployment that was being experienced in Europe at that time. Do you recall that?"

"I certainly recall the circumstances, yes, even though it was a long time ago," Black replied. "The worries had become especially acute in Germany, and, if I recall correctly, also here in Switzerland."

"That's right," Schmidt said. "Our unemployment rate here has traditionally been the lowest in the world, even lower than Japan's. We were used to getting worried when it got above one percent. That changed in the 1990s. In the 1993–94 recession, unemployment reached five percent. And at the bottom of the most recent recession— about the time that the meeting took place—it went over seven percent. Everybody in Switzerland knew that something had to be done about it."

"Now I recall exactly what transpired at that meeting," Black said. "Both the head of the German Bundesbank and the head of the Swiss National Bank proposed that there be a coordinated effort by the central banks of all major industrialized nations to help alleviate the situation."

"Did everyone there agree to help?"

"Yes—even the president of the Bank of Japan. We unanimously agreed on a first step that would be taken immediately."

"And that was?"

"To readjust the value of the deutsche mark and the Swiss franc vis-à-vis both the dollar and the yen."

"How did you do that?"

"Two ways. By the Germans and the Swiss lowering their short-term interest rates, while the Japanese and we Americans raised ours. That was no problem for me, since I intended to raise rates at least one more time in any case. That would create an incentive for international investors to move out of the mark and the Swiss franc and into the dollar and the yen. In the process, the mark and the Swiss franc would move down, the dollar and the yen up."

"And the other way?"

"To accelerate this process by directly intervening in the foreign exchange markets. We agreed that the Bundesbank and the Swiss National Bank would take the lead by selling marks and Swiss francs for dollars and yen. If that did not suffice to produce the desired effect, then both the Federal Reserve and the Bank of Japan would also intervene by doing the same in New York and Tokyo. The BIS would facilitate these operations by arranging currency swaps among the four central banks."

"Explain how the BIS did this."

"They arranged for short-term 'loans' between the Swiss National Bank and the Federal Reserve, under which the Swiss would 'lend' us Swiss francs in exchange for our 'lending' them dollars. We 'swapped' currencies. We—meaning the Fed—then sold those Swiss francs in the foreign exchange market in New York, thus pushing the exchange value of the franc down still further."

"And how was this supposed to help unemployment here?"

"By making it easier for Germany and Switzerland to export. The lower the mark and the franc sank, the cheaper their products would become in world markets. That eventually would lead to higher demand for their exports. Higher exports would ultimately lead to more jobs in both countries."

"Did it work out as planned?"

"Not immediately. But that was to be expected. There is normally a nine-to-twelve-month lag between exchange-rate adjustments and their effect on exports. Therefore the action we took that December first began to affect employment here in the summer of the following year."

"But your efforts to push down the Swiss franc and mark did succeed?"

"Yes. Immediately."

"By how much?"

"You'd have to check the record. If I recall correctly, we were aiming for a five-percent adjustment. It must have worked out to something very close to that."

Schmidt paused for a moment, then said, "You have been extremely forthcoming, Mr. Black. I thought I would have to read you excerpts from the transcript of that meeting. But now it will not be necessary. You have accurately summed up what was discussed and what was agreed to. Nevertheless, I would still like to include the contents of that transcript in the record. But you have already agreed to that, haven't you?"

"Yes. But what has all this got to do with my being here?"

"A lot," the policeman answered. "In fact, an awful lot."

He picked up what were obviously more confirmations of trades made by the General Bank of Switzerland. He pushed them across the desk, where they ended up in front of Black.

"Look at them," he ordered.

Black took them and began examining them as Schmidt continued: "On December fourth, the General Bank of Switzerland, in two transactions, went long two hundred million dollars against Swiss francs. The next day, in two more transactions, it went long three hundred million dollars against deutsche marks. Four days later it covered all of these positions in a series of trades. All in all, the profits generated by

99

this series of transactions in the inter-bank forward market totaled $45,842,000. All of these transactions were made for, and the profits credited to, account number J 747-2239.

"Then there was the speculation in three-month Eurodollar futures in London, again a sure thing. You went short because you knew that American interest rates were going up. The profit there was $11,479,000. Let's go through those trades, one by one."

"Why?" Black asked, in a voice that was now sharp. "All of this, Herr Schmidt, has absolutely nothing whatsoever to do with me, and it's time you got that into your head. Did I give written orders for any such transactions? No. Did I ever call the General Bank of Switzerland to give oral instructions? Of course not. Then who did? You know the answer. Dr. Hans Zwiebach, who had fiduciary authority over Account Number J 747-2239. It is *he* who should be sitting here, not I."

"But you left out one thing, Mr. Black."

"And that is?"

"The phone call you made to Dr. Zwiebach on December fourth."

"Now we're back to phone calls that never took place."

"Oh no. This one definitely took place. Just as did that phone call from the Savoy Hotel in London three years later. We have the log from the secretariat in Dr. Zwiebach's office. Phone calls are registered consecutively. There is no way that these calls, or any other calls, could have been entered into that log retroactively, Mr. Black."

"This is going too far," Black said.

"That is exactly what the authorities in this country feel also. It was one thing for you to take advantage of a decision taken by American authorities in the United States for personal financial gain, even if you misused Swiss banking facilities in the process. It is quite another thing for an American to take advantage of a decision taken by the Swiss National Bank—a decision you learned about at the BIS meeting on that December third—to make tens of millions of dollars for his personal account. No, that understates the problem. You actually helped *formulate* that decision. The transcript shows that it was in fact you who suggested that a five-percent correction would be about right."

Black stood up. "That's enough," he said.

"You appear to forget something, Mr. Black," the policeman said. "Here it is *we* who give the orders."

"You might give the orders," Black responded, "but from now on you will have to talk to my lawyers, not to me."

Black remained standing and then ostentatiously looked at his watch. It was approaching 10:00 A.M. in Washington. Where was Dan Lash?

12

Dan Lash was on the phone with Sally.

"All right, let me bring you up to date," he began. "I've talked to the people over at the Federal Reserve. I've also talked to the State Department. And I just finished talking to the state attorney in Basel."

"And?"

"I'll be blunt. It does not look good."

"What is that supposed to mean? How can you say that after just three phone calls?"

"Because nobody in this town seems to want to touch this thing with a barge pole. The State Department says that it has only received very cursory information about the case, but that the embassy in Bern has indicated that it seems to be a strictly internal Swiss matter, since it involves alleged criminal activity committed on Swiss soil, using Swiss institutions, and gravely affecting Swiss financial interests."

"Big help there. But what did you expect? The State Department couldn't care less about Americans who get in trouble abroad. They consider them nuisances who only waste their time. Believe me, I've lived abroad long enough to know that."

"Maybe. But when I talked to the spokesman at the Fed, it was even less encouraging."

"Who did you talk to?"

"A Fred Benson. He's apparently the chief of staff in the chairman's office."

"He's a bureaucrat. Been at the Federal Reserve for twenty-five years. He's seen chairmen come and go many times. He considers them as much a nuisance as the cookie-pushers do Americans abroad who ask them for help."

"You're right there. He was no help at all. He said that Charles Black was no longer with the Federal Reserve. And when I asked him whether he had heard about what was happening over there, he said he was not in a position to comment. He also assured me that it would be a waste of time to talk with anybody else at the Fed, since they would give me exactly the same answer."

"But why?"

"I can only guess. And my guess is that the last thing anybody in this town wants is for a story to get going that might totally undermine the country's faith in the men and institutions that control its finances. I'm not just talking Wall Street, either. Most Americans have become very savvy about money matters. They especially know about interest rates, because those rates affect their lives in a very direct way, be it through credit cards or adjustable-rate mortgages. They don't know how the Fed works exactly, but they do know that it somehow controls those interest rates. The last thing anybody in Washington wants is for them to suspect that a crook has been running the place during the past four years."

"Crook? Charles? How can you even say such a thing?" Sally's voice demanded an answer.

"Because that is the message that is coming out of Basel—to the Fed, to the State Department, and, just a few minutes ago, to me. I just finished talking to the state attorney over there."

"What did you expect him to say? After all, he's the guy who has my husband locked up."

"It's not *what* he said. It's *how* he said it, Sally. He's so cocksure that it's—well, it's worrisome. I've been an attorney for a long time, and I have a nose for such things."

"How can he be sure about something that is simply flat-out impossible?"

"Because he claims he has full documentation of trades made through your account in Zurich that generated huge profits. He has records of Charles's telephone calls made to the attorney in Zurich who acted as your fiduciary. During these calls, Charles gave the instructions, the attorney passed them along to the bank, and the bank executed them as instructed. They've got the paper trail, Sally."

"And how come Charles was able to make such huge profits?"

"Because, they claim, he, and only he, had had advance knowledge of what was going to happen to interest rates in the United States, rate changes that inevitably affect other interest rates elsewhere around the world. Knowing that, it was simple. They also say he obtained other inside information from the meetings at the BIS."

"So where is all the money that we purportedly made? Remember, it's a joint account. I sure haven't seen any of it," Sally said.

"I asked the same question. According to the state attorney, the profits were transferred to a bank on an obscure island in the West Indies whose name I didn't quite get. In any case, as far as the Swiss are concerned, the money is out of their reach. That really pisses them off, because for once someone has beaten them at their own game."

"What's that mean?"

"Usually it is crooks who make their money in Colombia or the Philippines or Pakistan who transfer it to Switzerland—knowing that the paper trail will end there. Once the money arrives, all they have to do is go to Zurich or Geneva and pick it up in the form of cash or bearer bonds. Or have someone else do that for them. Then they can stash it or reinvest it wherever they want. And we're not talking isolated instances. There's probably hundreds of billions of dollars like this, floating around the world."

"So Charles has this big stash somewhere that I don't have the slightest clue about, right? Come on, Dan. By the way, how big is that stash supposed to be?"

"The state attorney didn't tell me. But it must be pretty damn big." Then: "Hold on, Sally, my secretary just came in with a note. *The New York Times* is on the phone."

"They can wait," Sally said. She heard the lawyer tell his secretary to get the name and number, and he'd call them back.

"You there?" she then asked, impatiently.

"Yes."

"All this is getting us absolutely nowhere. We need a Swiss lawyer. Right away. So we're going over there—right away—and get one. I can either go via Dulles airport and we can take the same flight to Europe from there, or I can meet you in Basel."

"Hold on, Sally, I can't just drop everything and take the rest of the week off."

"You're not exactly going to take the week off, Dan," she said. "I'm going to be paying you for every hour of your precious time. In advance."

Damn lawyers, she thought.

"I can't do it, Sally. As it is, I've already had to cancel two very important client meetings that had been scheduled for first thing this morning. I've rescheduled them for tomorrow, and I can't cancel twice in a row. And there are other commitments that—"

Sally broke in.

"Then forget it. I'll go alone. That means I'm going to need the names of the best law firms and the best individual lawyers over there. You put the list together and fax it to me. My fax number is 415-950-4142. I want that list within two hours. Then I'm leaving for Switzerland."

Three hours later she was on United Airlines, headed for London, where she just barely made a connection with a Swissair flight that got her into Basel at ten-thirty the next morning.

13

When Sally Black went through immigration at the Bäle/Mulhouse airport, she could not help but notice the glance she got from the Swiss border policeman when he saw the name on her passport.

"Got a problem?" she asked in a very sharp tone.

"No, ma'am."

"Good."

He handed back her passport. But as she walked toward the baggage carousel, she glanced back. The policeman was on the phone. After she'd grabbed her bag, she headed straight for the taxi stand outside the terminal, ready to slug anybody who even came close.

"Euler Hotel," she said. Between planes

at Heathrow, she'd called ahead for a reservation. When she'd occasionally gone to Basel with Charlie, they had always stayed there, and she liked it.

Twenty minutes later, Sally got the same glance from the reservations clerk when she gave her name. But this time it didn't bother her. She would have to get used to it in this town, she reasoned.

She had a small suite overlooking the not-very-scenic Bahnhofplatz. Facing the square on the right was the railroad station. Facing the hotel, on the other side of a small park, stood an ugly, round, twenty-story building—the Bank for International Settlements. That place was high on the enemies list she had compiled in the airplane on the trip over. She'd get to all of them in due time. But first she needed a lawyer. Then she'd demand to see Charlie.

Dan Lash had faxed her a list of six law firms, and had added a note at the bottom explaining that, from what he had been told, this was it.

As Sally found out later, these six law firms ran the town's legal affairs. This stemmed from the fact that the establishment in Basel was small, close-knit, all-powerful, and shaped like a triangle. There were the banks, led by the General Bank of Switzerland, on one side. Industry, led by the pharmaceutical companies—Basel being the home of two international giants of this industry, Hoffman La Roche, and

Novartis—on the second side. The six establishment law firms formed the third side of the triangle that was all but impenetrable for anybody without the right credentials.

What were those credentials? To begin with, you had to be Swiss, preferably a "Basler," and, more preferable still, a Basler stemming from a family that could trace its local origins back at least three hundred years. The ultimate insider was a descendant of the Huguenots who had fled Catholic France in the sixteenth century for a safe haven in Protestant Basel. Their very names demanded respect. Thus, if you were a Sarasin, a Boeglin, or a Läckerlin, you were probably destined for a high position in the establishment. But that alone would not do it.

You must have attended the University of Basel, which dated back to 1456. If you were to end up at or near the top of one of the pharmaceutical companies, you had to have a doctorate from the university faculty known as Philosophy II, where the natural sciences were taught. If you came from the right family and your ambition was to become a successful banker, you were well advised to get a *Doktor rer. pol.* degree from that university. And, of course, if you were ever to be asked to join one of the six establishment law firms, you absolutely had to have a doctor of law degree from the University of Basel, preferably with a predicate of *summa cum laude*.

Then there was the military. Every Swiss male was in the army. One started at eighteen with full-time service at recruit school, and continued part-time through the age of fifty. To become eligible for the Basel Establishment, you had to have officer's rank in that army. Lieutenant was a bare minimum. Captain was better. Colonel was perfect.

Sum it all up, and a Herr Doktor Doktor Balthazar Läckerlin III who served as a part-time colonel in Swiss Military Intelligence was as good as you could get. The double doctorate stemmed from the fact that after Läckerlin had received his law degree, he had stayed on at the university and, at the age of thirty-one, had also received a second doctorate from the prestigious faculty known as Philosophy I, where such luminous scholars as Paracelsus, Friedrich Nietzsche, Jacob Burckhardt, and Karl Jaspers had taught during the past half-millennium.

Though Sally didn't know all this yet, she was impressed by the "Dr. Dr." prefix and called Läckerlin's office first to ask for an appointment. Again the name did its work. After giving it to the secretary, she was asked to wait. In less than half a minute the secretary was back on the phone, inquiring if two o'clock would be satisfactory. It was. It also gave Sally time to unpack and have a sandwich in her room.

Dr. Dr. Balthazar Läckerlin completely lived up to both his name and his titles. From the moment Sally saw him as she entered his office, it was apparent that he considered himself a breed apart. Tall, very thin, with a goatee and slightly graying hair, he awaited Sally's approach with a ramrod posture. When she stood in front of him, he carefully examined her through his pince-nez before finally extending his hand to hers. His handshake was brief and limp.

"Please be seated," he said, pointing to the chair in front of his desk.

After he had assumed his place behind it, he began, "I am, of course, familiar with your husband's problem, but before we discuss that, I am curious about why you have sought me out."

He chose his words deliberately. His pronunciation was precise. But Sally did notice just the slightest hint of a lisp.

"Our attorney, Dan Lash, recommended you," Sally replied.

"I've heard of Mr. Lash, but have never dealt with him. Am I correct in recalling that he is often involved in government matters in your country?"

"Yes. He is very well connected in Washington."

"And he is representing your husband in this matter?"

"*Advising* might be the better word. We need no representation in the United States. We obviously need it in Switzerland. That's why I am here."

"How much do you know about this case?"

"Practically nothing. I have only spoken once to my husband since they arrested him, and then very briefly."

"So I probably know a lot more than you do, Mrs. Black," Läckerlin said. "When I was informed that you were coming, I took the liberty of telephoning the state attorney, Dr. Rolf Wassermann. Are you familiar with his name?"

"Yes. Dan Lash spoke to him yesterday."

"Before we get any further, I want to tell you that I have already arranged for you to meet him. Dr. Wassermann will receive both of us in his office at four o'clock. He assured me that your husband will be there also."

"Thank you. Thank you very much. So you are prepared to represent him?"

"Yes. If we can reach an understanding."

"What does that mean?"

"That I will represent your husband only if he agrees to tell me the absolute truth, and only if he authorizes me to have full access to all of his financial dealings and records during the past ten years. I will especially require unrestricted access to the records of all—all—transactions that were done through his account with the General Bank of Switzerland in Zurich."

"We don't have those records. They were all kept in Zurich with our attorney there, Dr. Hans Zwiebach. Are you familiar with him?"

"Of course."

"I am afraid that he is part of the problem."

"That remains to be seen, doesn't it? I can only tell you at this juncture, Mrs. Black, that Dr. Zwiebach has an impeccable reputation, one unsullied by any improprieties or even rumors of such."

Sally sensed she had touched a nerve. "I did not want to imply anything about Dr. Zwiebach's character. All I said was that he is a problem. As my husband put it, 'Zwiebach's on their side, not ours.' "

"Then we shall have to ask your husband to tell us why he said that, won't we?" the attorney asked. "In any case, I will require his authorization to get the pertinent records from Dr. Zwiebach."

"You will get it," Sally said.

"Good. Then there are a few formalities that must be taken care of."

The formalities consisted of Sally's commitment to have a front-end fee of 250,000 Swiss francs wired within forty-eight hours. Since the dollar and the Swiss franc were almost exactly at parity, and since it would be easier for her to arrange the transfer in dollars, she asked him if $250,000 would be all right. Condescendingly, he agreed.

At four o'clock Dr. Dr. Läckerlin's Mercedes 600 pulled up in front of Heuberg 21. As he and Sally got out, Läckerlin mumbled some words to his driver in

German and came around to escort her inside. The receptionist immediately ushered them into the office of the waiting state attorney.

"*Herr Kollege*," Dr. Wassermann said, moving forward to extend a fraternal hand to his fellow member of the Basel legal community, Dr. Dr. Läckerlin. Then the state attorney turned to Sally.

"I regret that we must meet under such unfortunate circumstances, Mrs. Black. But at least I find you in very good hands."

This produced a collegial smile from Sally's lawyer.

"I am sure you want to see your husband immediately," Wassermann said. "He is expecting you in my conference room."

From the look on Charles Black's face as he rose to greet his wife, it was as if nothing out of the ordinary was occurring. The embrace was brief, the kiss perfunctory. Then he looked past her at the stranger who had come in with her.

Sally, who seemed equally unperturbed by the circumstances, immediately made the introduction. "This is Dr. Dr. Läckerlin, Charlie. On the advice of Dan Lash, I have retained him as our local attorney."

The two men shook hands and then sized each other up. As Sally watched them, she could not help noticing how utterly different they were: the Swiss—ascetic, thin as a rail, morbidly serious, exuding an air of supreme self-importance; the American—tall, rangy, quick to smile, a man, one sensed, who was good-natured almost to a fault.

"So, how soon can you get me out of here?" was her husband's first question.

"That is up to Dr. Wassermann," Läckerlin replied.

"I think he needs a bit of a nudge," Black countered. "A nudge from you, since I don't seem to be getting through to him."

"I will try. But first I must learn more about the allegations and the purported facts that back them up. Dr. Wassermann told me on the phone that he was prepared to provide me with that information. If you agree, I will ask for it now. In the meantime I am sure that you have a lot to discuss with your wife."

With that, he left the conference room to return to the state attorney's office, closing the door behind him.

"So, what do you think?" Sally asked, the moment the door had closed.

"Melvin Belli he ain't."

"I know what you mean. But this isn't San Francisco, either."

"How did you find him?"

"I picked him from a short list that Dan Lash gave me. The theory is that it's not *what* he knows but *who* he knows that is going to do the trick. And apparently Dr. Läckerlin knows everybody. You missed the buddy-buddy act between him and that prosecuting attorney a few minutes ago."

"I'm not sure whether I like to hear that or not. Maybe it won't matter."

"What do you mean?"

"I strongly suspect that it will be Dan Lash who gets me out of here—not Dr. Läckerlin."

"Why do you say that, Charlie?"

"Because of the same rationale that led you to Läckerlin. Both are the local establishment's lawyer of choice. The difference is that the establishment in Washington has a thousand times more clout than the one in Basel. And after Lash mobilizes his friends at the Fed and the State Department—even the White House, though that may be expecting too much—our embassy here will have no choice but to come down heavy on the Swiss. Very heavy. Americans don't like their citizens being held incommunicado without habeas corpus."

Sally said nothing.

Her husband continued. "When will Lash be reporting in next?"

"We didn't set any particular time. But he knows that I'm here in Basel. I'll call him first thing in the morning, Charlie."

"Maybe you should call our embassy in Bern first. On the off chance that Lash has already got something going."

"I'll call them as soon as I get back to the hotel. I'm at the Euler, by the way. I've never stayed there alone." She suddenly reached out for Charlie's hand. "How is it here, Charlie?"

"Not bad."

"What kind of...cell are you in?"

"Single, with running water."

"So at least you're alone. Can you eat the food?"

"So far, yes. It's actually been pretty good. Meat loaf and mashed potatoes."

"Who's doing this to you?" she suddenly asked.

Before he could answer, the door to the conference room opened and in walked their Swiss lawyer with an armload of documents. He was followed by the state attorney.

"I'm afraid," the state attorney said, "that our office closes in a few minutes. That means, Mrs. Black, that we must end your visit. But I have promised Dr. Läckerlin that because of the special circumstances, instead of weekly visits—our normal policy—you will be allowed daily visits. And these visits will take place in this building, rather than in our usual facilities at the Lohnhof."

"I greatly appreciate that, Dr. Wassermann," Sally replied. "But I hope that my husband's stay here will be so short that we will not have to take up too much of your time arranging visits."

Dr. Wassermann chose to ignore the sarcasm. "Also, if you would like to bring anything that your husband might need, please do so. Food, reading material, smokes. Anything within reason. Same time tomorrow afternoon, here, if that is convenient, Mrs. Black."

"It is."

The state attorney looked at his watch, then addressed her husband.

"I believe that Dr. Läckerlin would like to have a few more words with you, Mr. Black. Alone."

He left the conference room, closing the door behind him.

"So how does it look?" Charlie asked.

"I will know more after I have read all this," Läckerlin said, holding up the pile of documents that he had gotten from the state attorney.

"What's supposed to be in them?"

"Evidence," Läckerlin replied. Then he laid the documents on the conference table, reached into his jacket pocket, and withdrew a piece of paper. "I almost forgot. This is a release giving me full access to the financial records of both you and your wife, especially those related to your account at the General Bank of Switzerland. I would appreciate it if both of you would sign it." He produced a Mont Blanc fountain pen and handed it to Charlie Black.

Charlie signed. As did Sally.

Dr. Läckerlin retrieved the pen and then the documents from the table. He looked at his watch. "I'm afraid..."

Sally and Charlie rose to their feet. Sally took both of her husband's hands in hers and, ignoring the lawyer, said, "Don't worry. *I'm* going to get you out of here, Charlie. No matter what."

"I know. Call the embassy now, Sally.

118

Then get hold of Dan Lash first thing tomorrow. And call Laura. Tell her not to worry."

The door to the conference room opened again. This time it was a uniformed guard, the nice one from the weekend. He nodded at Charlie. Charlie nodded back.

"Time to go," he said.

Sally watched as her husband left the room, followed by the guard.

Then she turned to the lawyer. "Let's get out of here."

Dr. Läckerlin's Mercedes pulled up in front of the Euler Hotel less than ten minutes later. "Let's meet tomorrow afternoon at the same time," Läckerlin said. "By then I will have gone through the so-called evidence against your husband. Then I—both of us—can seek to get your husband released. But let me warn you, the state attorney will insist that an extremely high guarantee—you call it bail—be put up. Millions, I'm sure. Can you raise that sort of money?"

"Yes."

Läckerlin's face registered surprise, but he said nothing further.

"I'll be in your office tomorrow at two," she said as she climbed out of the Mercedes.

"I'll be expecting you."

Sally went directly to her room in the hotel, and got the operator to give her the number of the American embassy in Bern. When she dialed it, she got a recording telling her that office hours were ten to four.

"Hopeless," she muttered as she hung up. She had lived long enough in Washington to know that it would be futile to try to track down the ambassador at this hour anyway. So it would have to wait until tomorrow—after she had talked to Dan Lash. Where Charlie was concerned, it hardly mattered, since he was stuck for yet another night in that place in any case.

Now what? Charlie had said she should call their daughter. But that could wait also. First a drink. Then she'd call Laura.

The bar at the Euler looked very English with its dark wood paneling, brass railing, and oil portraits of horses on the wall. Sally had never been here by herself; she had always gone with Charlie, usually to have a drink with one or more of the other central bankers after their meeting across the street at the BIS. So she didn't quite know how to handle it. All the tables were taken, and even the bar was crowded.

Having no choice, she took a stool at the far end.

The bartender came over immediately. "It's Mrs. Black, isn't it? Welcome back to the Euler, ma'am. I trust that Mr. Black will be joining you?"

"No," she said. "My husband's been detained. So I'll have a drink by myself. Just one."

"If I recall, Mrs. Black, you always have vodka on ice, with a lot—a lot—of fresh lemon squeezed over it."

"That's right." The last thing Sally wanted to do was to get into a conversation with a bartender. So, when he served the drink, she pointedly ignored him.

After she took the first sip, she regretted having come down to the bar, because suddenly the trip, the jet lag, the shock of seeing Charlie under arrest—all were now catching up with her. She needed to be alone, not in the midst of a bunch of middle-aged foreign businessmen, a couple of whom were already starting to ogle her. She asked for the bill, signed it, and got out of there, ignoring the glances she attracted as she headed for the lobby and the elevator. Back in her room, she thought about ordering something to eat. But instead she decided to lie down for a little while. So she drew the curtains, took off her shoes, and stretched out. Minutes later she was in a deep sleep.

14

Fifteen hours later she woke up. It was now 9:00 A.M on Wednesday. Sally felt better. She also felt hungry. So she picked up the phone and ordered a real American breakfast—eggs, bacon, orange juice, coffee, the works.

Fifteen minutes later it arrived, and the waiter set it out on top of the coffee table in the sitting area of her small suite.

"I've also brought you the *Herald Tribune*, compliments of the hotel," he said. "If you wish, I can have it left outside your door every morning for the rest of your stay."

"Please do," Sally answered.

She was so hungry that she let the paper lie on the table untouched for at least five minutes. When she finally picked it up and looked at the front page, it leaped right out at her:

Former Head of Federal Reserve Arrested in Switzerland

But it was the first paragraph under that headline that hit her like a body blow to the stomach:

Charles Black, the former Chairman of the Federal Reserve Board, was arrested in Basel, Switzerland, on Saturday. According to the state attorney of the canton of Basel-Stadt, where he is being held, Black faces charges of massive securities fraud. Asked to comment, the State Department, the White House, and the Federal Reserve all stated that they have no intention of intervening, since they regard the matter as a domestic Swiss affair.

"I can't believe this," Sally said. And for the first time since this whole unbelievable mess began, she started to cry.

Dan Lash had warned her that nobody in Washington wanted to come near this, but to see it in black on white on the front page of the Paris-based *Herald Tribune* was too much. How could they just walk away from Charlie like this? No, it was worse than just walking away. It was tantamount to the American government publicly declaring Charlie guilty as charged. And Charlie had wanted her to call the American ambassador first thing in order to see when he would get him out.

She went back to the article.

Apparently the charges against Dr. Black arise from allegations that he took advantage of insider information gained at the monthly meetings of the world's leading central bankers at the Bank for International Settlements in Basel. It is alleged that he used that information to deal in the financial futures markets in Europe for his own account. This was confirmed in a telephone interview with Dr. Samuel Schweizer, Chairman of the BIS. Dr. Schweizer, who is also head of the Swiss National Bank—the Swiss equivalent of the Federal Reserve—further confirmed that it is alleged that Black used a numbered account at an as-yet-unnamed Swiss commercial bank for his illegal operations.

"This would amount to misusing a major financial institution in our country in order to personally profit from a flagrant and unprecedented abuse of office," Dr. Schweizer said.

"It saddens all of us who knew and respected Dr. Charles Black."

Sally had had enough. She crumpled the paper and threw it at the wastepaper basket.

She knew Samuel Schweizer. She'd had dinner with him at least a half-dozen times, both in Basel and in Washington. He was a bit too arrogant for her taste, and a bit too dapper. But there could be no doubt that he was brilliant.

So how could he say such things? *Why* would he say such things?

There could only be one answer. Because he and everybody else completely believed what they were being told by Hans Zwiebach, that Zwiebach had acted solely on Charlie's instructions. But hadn't Zwiebach smelled a rat? Their answer would be, So what if he had? It was not his job to police his own client, was it? Even Sally knew full well that Zwiebach's behavior was no different from that of thousands of other Swiss lawyers who fronted B accounts at Swiss banks. They simply did what they were told—for a fee. She knew because she had used Zwiebach in exactly that way. And he had always done what she told him—no questions asked.

But that had stopped years ago. Yet the trading through that account in Zurich had not stopped. It had obviously escalated to fantastic levels—in terms of both volume and profits.

But if she had stopped using Zwiebach and that account years ago, and if Charlie had not been telling Zwiebach what to do, then who had?

Theoretically, Zwiebach could have been doing it all on his own. But she didn't believe that for a minute. He was a lawyer, not a financial type. She knew. She had dealt with him often enough when she'd lived in London. She knew his limitations where understanding financial transactions were concerned. There was no way that Zwiebach could have made all that money by trading in some of the world's most sophisticated financial markets.

There had to be somebody behind him. Somebody who had known Zwiebach for a long time. Somebody who had found out that Charlie was one of his clients. Somebody who knew how B accounts at Swiss banks worked. Somebody who was so vulnerable to exposure, should his financial machinations become known, that he was willing to let an innocent man go to prison for thirty years—and had the power to make it happen.

Who could be that greedy, that powerful, and that evil—all at the same time?

15

Dr. Samuel Schweizer had arrived at his office at the National Bank of Switzerland at just about the same time Sally Black's breakfast had arrived. The *Herald Tribune* was on his desk, as were five other newspapers that were placed there before his arrival every morning. He picked it up immediately, and his eyes went directly to the same front-page article that had had such a stunning effect on Sally Black.

"Perfect," he said. "Absolutely one hundred percent perfect."

He reached for one of the three phones on his desk—the one designed to be most secure from prying ears. He dialed the direct number of Dr. Hans Zwiebach. The lawyer answered immediately.

"Hans, it's Samuel Schweizer," the banker began.

"What a surprise," the Zurich lawyer said. "A pleasant one, I hope."

"Very pleasant. Have you read this morning's *Herald Tribune?*"

"No," Zwiebach replied.

"Like all the newspapers, it has a front-page article on our American friend. But with more details. I'll read the first part."

"I'm listening."

Samuel Schweizer put on his reading glasses—he only used them in the office—and read the first paragraph of the article.

"You see," he said, "the Americans have turned their back on him. That takes politics out of it. Charlie Black is going to be left twisting in the wind, all by himself. Then that prosecuting attorney in Basel is going to put him away for what will amount to the rest of his life."

"It's a pity it had to come to this," the attorney said.

"I did my best to prevent it, Hans. But once that damned Englishman began the investigation, there was no way I could stop it. And when the investigation led him to the General Bank of Switzerland and then to your fiduciary account there, what choice did we have?"

Silence on the other end of the line.

"I'll tell you the choice," Schweizer said. "Either Charles Black had to go to jail in Basel or you and I would be on our way to jail in Zurich. Have no illusions about this, Hans. You are in this as deep as I. And although it is regrettable that we had to use our backup plan, the need for that insurance was the only reason that you started using Black's account in the first place."

"I'm afraid that, unfortunately, we might have a problem there. I didn't use Black's account the first time. The first trades that you and I made together four years ago were in gold futures. Remember?"

"Vaguely," Schweizer said.

"They were *not* made through Black's account. They were initially made through the Sardinian's account. I subsequently had that 'error' corrected, and rebooked the trades though Black's account. But—"

"So what? Errors like that occur every day at a big bank. Accounts are always getting mixed up."

"I know that. However, this was not the normal type of mix-up. Which brings me to the point. I got a phone call a few minutes ago from Urs Stucker."

"Who's he?" Schweizer asked.

"He was the vice president over at the General Bank who, for years, handled all my accounts there. He retired at the beginning of this year."

"Why did he call you?"

"Because, just before he called me, he got a call from the Basel police. They want to talk to him."

"So?"

"Stucker knows that what happened to those gold trades four years ago was not an error. If, for any reason, the *other* fiduciary account is brought into play, the Basel police will show up in my office and demand that I divulge the client's identity. *That* would bring the Sardinian to the attention of the police, and if they then started to probe still deeper, they might not like what they found. Nor would we, Sammy."

"What makes you think that Urs Stucker will bring this up?"

"I'm sure he won't volunteer that information now. He told me as much on the phone. But when this comes to trial and he is asked to testify before the court under oath, that might be quite another matter. Urs Stucker is a good Swiss who would do his duty. I think that's why he called. To give me time."

"This is not good," Schweizer said.

"No. So we have no choice. We are going to have to tell the Sardinian," Zwiebach said.

"Tell him what?" Schweizer asked.

"Everything."

Now there was a long silence on Schweizer's end.

"When?" he finally asked.

"Right away."

part

Two

16

It had begun in Sardinia four years before, and it had started quite innocently.

Or *fairly* innocently, because on that weekend Dr. Samuel Schweizer had gotten himself a girlfriend. The girlfriend had rapidly evolved into a mistress. And the mistress had soon become an expensive mistress.

Her name was Simone. From the moment he laid eyes on her in the bar of the Cala di Volpe, he knew that he wanted her—no matter what. She came in with another woman and they took a table right next to the bar, where Schweizer was sitting. Unable to restrain himself, he kept turning his eyes in her direction. They both ignored him. But as he strained to hear what they were saying, the opening immediately presented itself. They were speaking in Schwyzerdütsch, that Germanic dialect peculiar to the no more than four million people living in the northern part of Switzerland.

"Entschuldige si," he began, leaning toward them. "Would you be offended if I offered you both a glass of champagne? It is such a pleasant surprise to find out that I'm not the only Swiss here."

They hesitated. And while they did,

they checked him out. It was the other woman who finally responded.

"You sound like you're from Zurich."

"I am. I was in Rome on business and, on a whim, decided to come over here to Sardinia for the weekend."

"All by yourself?"

"Yes."

"What business are you in?"

"Banking."

"Well, we can't let a fellow *Zürcher* be all by himself, can we?"

"Then may I join you?"

"Of course."

He had moved to their table, and after the champagne had arrived, he formally introduced himself.

"My name is Samuel Schweizer. I'm with the National Bank in Zurich."

"My name is Giselle, and my friend's name is Simone."

That was the first time he heard her name.

It was Simone who asked the next question. "And what do you do at the National Bank, Herr Schweizer?"

"I run it."

That produced a lightning exchange of glances between the two ladies. Twenty minutes later they moved on to the dining room.

Schweizer asked for a table, apologizing for not having made a reservation. Without hesitation the maître d' led them onto the outside terrace, which jutted over the shallow waters of the small bay around which the Cala di Volpe resort was built. Strings of lanterns provided the soft lighting overhead. Candles lit the tables. A guitar player added background music for the Mediterranean night. It was the Emerald Coast at its early summer's best.

When they arrived at a table directly overlooking the water, the maître d' removed the RESERVED sign with a flourish before seating the ladies. If they—and he addressed the two women, not the Swiss banker—needed anything, they should simply ask for him. Minutes later another bottle of champagne arrived, compliments of the house.

"You've obviously been here before," Schweizer said.

It was Giselle who answered. "Yes. Because of my ex-husband. He was also a banker. With the General Bank of Switzerland."

"That's the same bank I was with before moving to the National Bank," Schweizer said. "Perhaps I knew him. What was his name?"

"Rudi Stemmler."

"It doesn't ring any bells."

"Probably because he was just a *prokurist,*" Giselle replied. "He managed investment portfolios for clients. Until he lost a lot of their money and got fired."

Giselle appeared to be in her mid-thirties, as did Simone. Both were well built and well dressed—expensively dressed. The jewelry they wore was impressive. The diamond mounted on the ring on Giselle's left hand ran to at least five carats. Simone's taste, however, obviously ran to emeralds—lots of them. The green stones that adorned her rings, her four bracelets, her necklace, and the emerald earrings were perfect complements to her long, dark, red hair and fair complexion.

Both women were absolute knockouts. Samuel Schweizer knew that he was the envy of every other man on the terrace of the Cala di Volpe, especially those in the company of their wives. He knew that feeling all too well. They were probably speculating, as he was, about who—or what—they were. And apparently it showed.

"You're wondering what the ex-wife of a lowly *prokurist* from Zurich is doing here, aren't you?" Giselle asked, with typical Swiss bluntness.

"Not really," Schweizer replied. "I assumed you must be with someone."

"You were right," Giselle replied. "We are guests of someone. Both of us."

That caught Samuel Schweizer by surprise, and it showed.

"No, no," Simone said, breaking in for the first time. "It's not what you think. Our host is an acquaintance of Giselle's. He has a house on the island. It is one of those huge villas on top of the hill over there." She pointed across the waters of the bay. "But he insisted on putting us up in the hotel."

"Is he also Swiss?" Schweizer asked.

"No. He's from here. He's a native Sardinian," Giselle said. "I met him through my ex. That's about all I got out of that marriage, except for some furniture."

"The Sardinian was one of his clients at the General Bank?" Schweizer asked.

"Yes. He used to come to Zurich two or three times a year. After they talked business at the bank, my husband would take him out to dinner. I would go along. Twice we visited him here. Then my husband started losing his money—like he was losing money for all of his clients. Then he got fired."

"Giselle," Simone now said, "don't you think we've talked enough about your ex-husband?"

"You're right," Giselle said. "In fact, I'm starting to get hungry. So let's get some menus. If you agree, Herr Schweizer."

"Samuel," he said. "Sammy would be even better." After all, he was on vacation.

"Sammy it is," Giselle responded.

Sammy signaled to the waiter, and the menus were brought.

"I'm going to need your help," Simone said. "I've never eaten here before."

"So this is your first time at the Cala di Volpe?" he asked.

"Yes," she said. "The first time in Sardinia. I've been almost everywhere else in the world but here."

"Did *your* husband take you to all those other places?" he asked.

137

"No husband. I was with Swissair. A flight attendant."

"Was?"

"Yes. Until a couple of months ago."

"And now?"

"I'm trying to figure out what to do with the rest of my life," Simone answered.

As it turned out, she needed very little help in figuring out what she should eat. She went for the beluga caviar and the pheasant stuffed with goose liver. She decided to stick to the champagne—Roederer's Crystal.

Coffee had just arrived when *he* arrived. The Sardinian.

There could be no mistake that it was he, for he didn't really arrive. Rather, he made an entrance onto the terrace of the Cala di Volpe. He was dressed in a white summer suit, embellished by a boutonniere—a red carnation. His shoes were also white, as were his socks. By contrast, his thick head of hair was coal black. So was the wicked-looking cigar—a Brissago—he carried between the fingers of his left hand. The right hand sported more rings than the hands of both of the women at Samuel Schweizer's table. The Sardinian was tall, thin, wiry. As he headed toward their table, he evoked the image of a bull-fighter swaggering into the arena.

Giselle was on her feet the moment she saw him approaching. Upon reaching their table, he immediately lifted her off her feet in a theatrical embrace. After setting her back down, he turned next to Simone. He bowed, reached for her hand, and kissed it. Rising back to his full height, he finally recognized the presence of Samuel Schweizer by fixing him with an icy stare.

Giselle instantly rescued the situation. "Pietro," she said, "this gentleman is also from Switzerland. He is a banker. We asked him to join us for dinner since he was all alone."

The Sardinian appeared mollified. He extended his hand to Schweizer, saying, "Pietro di Cagliari. Welcome to the Costa Smeralda." He said it as though he owned the Emerald Coast, maybe even the entire island.

From what then happened, it appeared that he actually might. The maître d', accompanied by three other waiters, was instantly on the spot. The table was hastily rearranged to accommodate the new arrival. A place was set. A fourth chair was instantly at hand. And no sooner had the Sardinian taken his place than a glass of dark red wine was presented to him. He raised it in a toast to the homeland of the three other people at what was obviously now *his* table.

"*La bella Svizzera,*" he said, and then proceeded to empty the glass.

After he sat down, he chose to ignore the ladies and concentrate totally on the male foreigner who had encroached on his territory.

"Which bank are you with?" he asked.

"The National Bank."

"But that is like the Bank of Italy, isn't it?" Pietro asked. "It's the government's bank."

"Yes. Exactly."

"Then you do not lend money to people like me."

"No," Schweizer replied. "We lend to commercial banks, to other central banks, to the Swiss government. But never to individuals or private corporations."

For a moment it appeared as if Pietro di Cagliari was going to dismiss Schweizer out of hand and shift his attention back to the ladies. After all, there was nothing to be gained here. But something held him back.

"What do you do at the Swiss central bank?"

"I run it," replied Schweizer, for the second time that evening.

"Really." The Sardinian wheels began to turn rapidly in Pietro's handsome head. "How did you get that job?"

"I was formerly the chief economist at Switzerland's largest commercial bank, the General Bank of Switzerland."

"Aha! So you went from making money to serving your country," Pietro said.

"You could put it that way, yes," Schweizer replied, although as an economist with the General Bank he hadn't made that much money— certainly not enough to afford this sort of thing on a regular basis. His eyes shifted briefly back to Simone, who was in deep conversation with Giselle.

"I used to have an account with the General Bank of Switzerland," Pietro said. "I set it up to avoid Italian taxes." He laughed. "The way it turned out, in the end I would have been better off keeping the money in Italy and paying the taxes."

"I'm sorry to hear that," Schweizer said.

"What brings you here?" Pietro asked.

"I was down in Rome, meeting with the people at the Bank of Italy. I decided to spend a long weekend here before going back to Switzerland."

"And as the ladies pointed out, you're all alone."

"Yes."

Pietro suddenly shifted his attention back to those ladies, interrupting their conversation.

"Giselle, do you remember the discotheque at the Patrizza Hotel in Liscia di Vacca?"

"Yes. It's great."

"Should we go?"

"Oh yes." This time it was Simone who answered. "I haven't danced in ages."

Pietro turned back to the Swiss banker. "Please join us. It's only twenty minutes from here. And my car is waiting outside."

"But first I must sign the check."

Pietro waved his hand. "Consider it already taken care of."

"But—"

"No 'buts.' You are on Sardinia, my dear friend, and here I pay."

The car that was waiting outside was a Rolls-Royce. The uniformed driver who stood beside it snapped to attention the moment he saw Pietro di Cagliari emerge from the front entrance of the hotel. Pietro made the seating arrangements: the three Swiss sat in back, while he took his place beside the driver.

Less than twenty minutes later they arrived at the discotheque. It was packed, mostly with young people. But again the very sight of Pietro di Cagliari entering the place did its magic. Waiters immediately moved forward to clear the best table in the house. Its occupants began to protest—until confronted by the bouncer. No sooner was the Cagliari party of four seated than the headwaiter appeared with another bottle of Roederer's Crystal, along with three glasses. The manager himself brought a fourth glass filled with a heavy, dark red wine, and personally presented it to Pietro. He hovered nervously while the Sardinian tried it. His anxious look turned into a relieved smile when he heard the words *Va bene.*

Then Pietro was back on his feet and headed for the dance floor with Giselle in tow. He proceeded to take over, as he seemed to do everywhere. He moved around the floor with an athletic grace and artistic skill that put to shame the pack of twenty-year-olds that surrounded them. To her credit, Giselle more than held her own. As soon as the band paused, Pietro moved forward to give them instructions on what they should play next—slow music. Of course they did what they were told, as, it seemed, did everybody else in Sardinia when in Pietro's presence.

Samuel Schweizer and Simone, who had remained at the table and watched as Pietro did his thing, now took to the dance floor themselves. Although Simone was a bit taller than Schweizer, they immediately moved well together.

"You must dance a lot," she said.

"I used to," he replied, "but lately there has not been much opportunity."

"Maybe that will now change," she said as her arm tightened ever so discreetly, pulling him into a close embrace for the first time.

Dr. Samuel Schweizer did not know how to respond—either to her implied "invitation" or to the closeness of her body. It was not just that the situation had arisen so unexpectedly. It was that Simone—and he didn't even know her last name—represented a pleasure in life that he had never enjoyed, one that had really never presented itself.

For Samuel Schweizer was bourgeois to the core. Worse, he was *Swiss* bourgeois to the core. And that is as stodgy, as dull, as tedious, as unimaginative, as adverse to risk-taking as one can be.

It was as if his glide path in life had been in full conformity with that dictated by his no-frills Swiss Reformed Church, where the Calvinistic doctrine of predestination was a central tenet of belief. His father had been a teacher of history at the Humanistische Gymnasium in Zurich. His mother had been a *hausfrau*. These straitlaced origins had led to his studying economics at the University of Zurich, and to his chosen profession— that of a bank economist. He had reached his apogee with his appointment as head of Switzerland's central bank.

At fifty-four, Dr. Samuel Schweizer should have been a fulfilled man.

But he wasn't. There was no single obvious reason for this. It could be best summed up, perhaps, by his gradual realization that there had been a total lack of fun in his life. To be sure, he did enjoy certain pleasures, like a good glass of wine, a downhill run on the ski slopes, even those monthly dinners with his professional colleagues at the Schützenhaus in Basel.

But he did all this without having companionship. Real companionship.

Of course, for twenty-two years he had had his wife, Emma. But Emma was a carbon copy of his mother—a *hausfrau* who did not drink wine, who did not ski, and who, thank God, was not allowed to attend those dinners at the Schützenhaus. Her dour manner would have put a damper on even those occasions. As for their "private life"—the less said, the better. They had never had a child because, he was convinced, there had been so few opportunities to conceive one. He had given up even trying a good five years ago.

But the lack of fun went beyond that. He simply had never made enough money to have a lifestyle that even remotely compared with that enjoyed by so many of the other men with whom he associated—such as his counterpart at the Bank of England, Sir Robert Neville. Sir Robert not only had that elegant flat on Cadogan Square in London. His estate in Surrey, with its eighteenth-century mansion, its seventeenth-century furniture, its stables, its tennis courts, the meadows, the forest, ran to five hundred acres. Schweizer had once been invited there with Emma. She had been so utterly and so obviously out of place that he had cringed inwardly the entire weekend. By contrast, Sir Robert's wife was not only a classic English beauty, but she was young, smart, elegant, and witty. She was fun.

Emma and he, on the other hand, had lived in the same five-room flat in Küsnacht that he had bought fifteen years ago. It overlooked the Zurichsee, but that was about all one could say about it. Three years ago he and Emma had "splurged" and bought a second place— that chalet in Crans-Montana. But in order to swing it, he had taken out a mortgage for half the purchase price. While Sir Robert drove a Bentley, he drove a Mercedes 190, the cheapest model Mercedes-Benz had ever brought out. Whereas Sir Robert spent his vacations shooting grouse or salmon fishing on the grounds of a relative's castle in Scotland, or deep-sea fishing off a friend's yacht in the Caribbean, he and Emma went to Crans-Montana, where they hiked in the summer and where he skied—alone—in the winter.

Not that they were poor by any means. At the General Bank his salary, by the time he left, had risen to well over 150,000 Swiss francs a year. He now made double that at the National Bank. Of course, as a Swiss civil servant, he was also assured of an excellent pension, and Emma was a firm believer in pensions. With great regularity she told him how lucky they were. But at fifty-four he wasn't ready to feel lucky because he had a good pension plan.

"You're very quiet," Simone said, breaking into his thoughts.

"I'm enjoying the music. And being with you," he replied.

"So am I," she said.

They left the discotheque shortly after midnight. When they pulled up in front of the Cala di Volpe, it was immediately apparent that Simone and he were being dropped off. It was equally clear that Giselle was proceeding on with Pietro di Cagliari—no doubt to spend the night with him at his villa on the hill overlooking the bay.

It seemed totally natural that Samuel

Schweizer would escort Simone to the door of her room in the hotel, and equally so that she would invite him in.

It was almost ten the next morning when he left—but only to change his clothes. By eleven he was back, to find her still in bed. Three hours later the two of them finally made it down for lunch. A magnificent buffet awaited them, as did Pietro di Cagliari and Giselle, who were seated at the same table the four of them had occupied the prior evening.

Pietro was all smiles as he rose to greet them.

"I hope you slept as well as we did last night," he said, carefully eyeing both of them for telltale signs. "Or should I say last night *and* this morning."

"Now, Pietro," Giselle said, "be good. They want to eat, not talk about last night."

Simone broke in. "I don't mind talking about it. It was the most enjoyable night I've had since—well, since I can remember. Wasn't it, Sammy?"

"Let me put it this way," he replied. "I don't even want to think about going back to Zurich."

"Then don't," Pietro said. "Stay here and be my financial adviser."

"If only I could," Schweizer replied, smiling.

"No," Pietro continued. "I'm serious. I need help."

The Swiss banker said nothing. So the

Sardinian immediately backed off, turning his attention to Simone. "Do you like sailing?" he asked her.

"It depends," she answered.

"What does that mean?"

"Where and on what," she replied. "For instance, I don't like to be on a small boat in a big ocean. I tried it once off the Algarve and got deathly seasick."

"How about a big boat?" he asked.

"You mean a cruise ship?"

"Not that big," he replied.

"How big?"

"I'll show you—if you're game," he replied.

"When?"

"Now. Or at least after you've had lunch. I must warn you, however, we won't return until late Sunday evening."

Simone turned to Samuel Schweizer. "Are you game?" she asked.

"Sure."

"Then I'll arrange it," Pietro replied.

He disappeared into the hotel, while Simone and Samuel Schweizer went to the buffet. There they were confronted by a choice that ranged from cold lobster, scampi, and ceviche to four types of steaming pasta.

"Let's start with seafood," Simone said. He agreed, and followed her lead in every selection she made. They had barely finished that first course when Pietro di Cagliari returned to their table.

"It's all arranged. We're leaving," he said.

"But, Pietro," Giselle protested, "they are in the middle of lunch."

"Don't worry. I'll make up for it at dinner," he said. "Come. We're going to the hotel dock. Just follow me."

They did. A small motor launch awaited them, and within minutes they were headed across the shallow waters of the bay, toward the open sea. Their destination soon became apparent. It was anchored just outside the bay.

"I call her the *Diana*," Pietro said as he pointed toward the huge yacht, "after the ancient Italian goddess of the moon, because I feel a special affinity for her. We are both persons of the night."

As the launch approached, a hydraulically controlled boarding ladder glided horizontally out of the hull. When fully extended, it tilted toward the surface of the water until locked in place. Then two seamen clambered down and stood ready to help the party of four out of the launch. On deck, the captain, dressed in impeccable whites, stood waiting to welcome them. Of course, it was Pietro di Cagliari whom he greeted first—with a military salute.

"*Signore,*" he said, "everything is prepared according to your instructions."

"Then you will take my two special guests"—he pointed to Simone and Schweizer—"to Suite Number One. As I told you on the phone, we will be using one of the other suites."

"Certainly, sir," the captain replied.

Turning to the two honored guests, he said, "Please follow me."

They followed him across the teak deck to the stairs that led them to the quarters below.

The suite lived up to its designation as Number One—from the Gucci leather cushions on the chairs and sofa in the living room to the cashmere covers on the huge round bed. It was difficult to determine which was the *pièce de résistance*: the fireplace—the real fireplace—in the living room or the Jacuzzi in the bedroom.

"My God," Simone said as she walked around the suite for the second time. "I have never seen anything like this in my entire life."

"Nor I," said Samuel Schweizer.

There was a knock on the door, and when Schweizer opened it, a steward stood waiting outside.

"Signore di Cagliari asked me to help you become acquainted with some of the controls and amenities of this suite. May I?"

"Please."

The controls included thermostats separately regulating the temperature in the living room and bedroom, a panel resembling that in the cockpit of a 747 for running the hi-fi system, and switches beside the bed that allowed for remote control of the curtains over the portholes. The bathroom had a bath, a shower, a small TV, and all the soaps and lotions and gadgets usually found in the bathroom of a Four Seasons hotel suite—except that there were even more towels, all bearing the gold initials *PdC*. The steward told them they did not have to worry about water use, since the yacht had its own desalinization plant.

The other amenities included a wide-screen TV in the bedroom and, in the living room, a movie projection system coupled with a screen that descended from above the fireplace when electronically activated. There was, of course, a fully stocked bar in the living room, and inside the closets were two sets of scuba-diving equipment and outfits. On the desk was a Macintosh computer, complete with modem, CD-ROM drive, scanner, and laser printer.

"We are also fully equipped for windsurfing and trapshooting," the steward pointed out. "If you need anything to eat or drink, any time of the day or night, just call on the house phone."

As he spoke, a muffled sound could suddenly be heard in the background.

"That's the twin diesels starting to rev up," the steward said. "So we'll be under way in a few minutes."

"Where are we headed for?" Schweizer asked.

"I really can't say. But the *Diana* can do seventeen knots, so, even on a weekend sail from the Cala di Volpe, we have a pretty good range. Is there anything more I can do for you now? If not, I should probably return to my other duties. And, by the way, Signore di Cagliari asked me to tell you that the captain will fetch you at five-thirty for a tour of the *Diana*, and that he expects you for cocktails on the promenade deck at six."

As soon as he had left, Simone made a third tour of the suite. When she returned to the living room, Samuel Schweizer was sitting on the Gucci leather sofa, taking it all in.

"Giselle said that Pietro was rich," Simone said, "but not this rich. How much would a yacht like this cost?"

"I can only guess," Sammy replied. "But I would think at least twenty million dollars."

"Wow," she said. "If Pietro can afford a toy like this, then how much would you guess he's worth?"

"Quite a bit, even by our standards," the banker answered.

"When Giselle asked me to come to Sardinia with her, she never mentioned the *Diana*. I wonder why?"

"Maybe he told her not to mention it," Schweizer said.

"I think you're right. She did say he was kind of secretive. But don't all Sardinians have a reputation for being that way?"

"I think you might be mixing up Sardinians with Sicilians," Schweizer said.

"I never thought of *that*," she said. "You don't suppose...?"

"No. Of course not."

"Then how do you think he makes all this money?"

"I really don't know. I just met him."

"So did I. Should we ask him?"

"Hardly," Schweizer said. "If he wants us to know, he'll tell us."

He let them know a few hours later.

By that time the *Diana* was moving swiftly across the waters of the Ligurian Sea—now under full sail. After having been given a tour of the yacht by the captain, they joined Pietro di Cagliari and Giselle, who awaited them under the canopy on the promenade deck. The steward was serving cocktails. Both went for Campari and soda.

"So, what do you think?" Pietro asked, once everybody was settled in on the lounge chairs.

"I think I would like to live this way all the time," Simone answered.

"So would I," Giselle said.

"And you, Sammy?" Pietro said.

"I'm afraid this sort of lifestyle is beyond the means of a civil servant."

"Not in Italy," Pietro said, and laughed loudly.

"But that is one of the differences between our two countries," Schweizer said, smiling along with his host.

"Ah, but is it?" Pietro countered. "I

tend to believe that all of Europe—including Switzerland—must today approach these matters much more sensibly than in the past, more rationally. It is better to have persons in high places who are financially independent than those who are not—and thus dependent upon bribes from all directions. That corrupts the entire society. We Italians have learned this the hard way. Thousands of our people who have held high office, all the way up to the man who was our prime minister four times— *four times*—have been charged with corruption. Many are in jail, although the prime minister—Craxi—chose to go to Tunisia, where he is writing his memoirs. We have a name for all this: *Tangentopoli*—'Bribesville.' "

"And that could have been avoided, had they been independently wealthy?"

It was Simone who asked this.

"Absolutely," the Sardinian replied. "Look at America. You could not bribe men like Kennedy or Johnson or Reagan or Bush. They already had enough money."

"But how did they make it?"

"It does not matter how they made it," the Sardinian said. "What matters is that they *had* it."

"I think I agree with you," Simone said.

"So do I," Giselle said.

Samuel Schweizer said nothing. But he kept listening as Pietro di Cagliari continued. "I'm a perfect example of what I've been talking about. Nobody can bribe me. Nobody can tell me what to do or what not to do. Nobody. Because I have more money than almost everybody else. Some may whisper, 'Yes, but how did Pietro di Cagliari make all that money?' I say to them, 'It is none of your business. Money is money.' "

Nobody contradicted him, so Pietro went on. "One must not be niggardly with one's wealth. One must spend it—like this." He waved a hand at their surroundings. "But at some point, one must also do good for others. Don't you agree, Sammy?"

"Of course," the banker said.

"That is what I want to do next. But there I need help. I want to do it quietly, anonymously. Otherwise all I will do is attract the attention of the fiscal authorities. The tax laws in Italy are crazy. If you paid all the taxes the law says you should, you would pay more to the government than you earn. Is that not so, Sammy? You Swiss understand these things."

"There I completely agree with you, Pietro. In such matters we Swiss are, to use your words, both sensible and rational."

"Ah," Pietro said, reaching over to grasp Schweizer's arm, "what an unexpected pleasure it is to finally meet a man who actually understands what I am talking about. What an honor—what a great honor—it is to have you aboard my beloved *Diana*. We will return to this subject later. But now, ladies, we are going to turn our attentions to you, over dinner."

Dinner consisted of just bread, salad, and a bouillabaisse—a bouillabaisse done to such perfection that it stunned the palate. They were given a choice of two wines of Tuscany—a Vernaccia di San Gimignano and a Brunello di Mantalcino. Pietro di Cagliari, of course, drank only the red, and a lot of it. And the more he drank, the more amorous he became. Not that Giselle minded. She ended up sitting on the Sardinian's lap, from where she announced at eleven o'clock that it was time for all of them to go to bed. Simone immediately seconded the motion. Sammy Schweizer, who by this time was deeper in his cups than he had been since his university days, mumbled his agreement.

Soon thereafter, Simone and he were in the private Jacuzzi in their stateroom.

By midnight, when they finally ended up in bed, the food, the wine, and the incredible things that Simone had come up with in the Jacuzzi had taken their toll. Schweizer immediately fell into the best sleep of his entire adult life.

17

When Dr. Samuel Schweizer woke up ten hours later, it was to find himself in total darkness. His bed, for some reason, was slowly swaying back and forth. He reached out for the lamp that was beside his bed in Küsnacht. Instead his hand met the bare skin of what could only be that of a nude woman—who now sighed in a way that suggested the hand was welcome.

Therefore, Emma she was not. But if not Emma, then...?

The woman beside him moved. Suddenly, with a slight whirring sound, the curtains that covered the portholes of Suite Number One on the good ship *Diana* began to slide open. At the same time, the swaying motion stopped. The background sound of engines ceased.

Sammy Schweizer was now fully aware of who was beside him. The only remaining question was, where were they? The same question must have been bothering Simone. As Sammy watched, she slid from the bed and went to one of the portholes.

"Come and look," she exclaimed. "It's fantastic."

Samuel Schweizer was not used to parading around in the nude. In fact, both he and Emma always dressed and undressed separately. But Simone seemed to be as comfortable without clothes as she was fully dressed. Schweizer had no choice but to follow her lead.

The view from the porthole was indeed fantastic. A couple of hundred meters away, the waters of the Mediterranean gave way to the shoreline. Beyond that, the green coastal mountains rose sharply toward an azure sky. And between the shore and the mountains was a small port where the colors of the houses ranged from subtle pinks to gaudy yellows. This had to be the Ligurian Riviera, and the small town could only be Portofino.

He moved forward for a better view, and in the process could not help but press against the cool body of his bedmate of the prior night. She wiggled in appreciation. She also giggled.

"Don't stop there," she said, reaching back for him.

But then the phone rang.

"I'll get it," Simone said, to Schweizer's relief. She went over to pick it up.

"It's Giselle," she said. "They were wondering if we were dead." She listened further.

"We're going ashore in exactly one hour," she relayed to Schweizer. "They want to know if that's all right."

He assured her that it was.

They boarded the lighter at shortly after noon. Ten minutes later they climbed into a stretch Mercedes limousine that had been waiting at the dock, in which they immediately headed south along the coastal highway—the *strada panoramica*—which, after ascending from Portofino, wound its way along the edges of the coastal mountain range before dipping sharply as they approached their destination, Santa Margherita. Soon they were entering the grounds of the Imperial Palace Hotel. When the Mercedes pulled up in front of the main entrance and Pietro di Cagliari stepped out—first, of course—it was the hotel manager himself who stood ready to greet him. The Sardinian's influence in Italy obviously extended well beyond his island homeland.

"They are all waiting for you in the private dining room," the hotelier said as he bowed to Pietro.

"Good. Show us the way, please," the Sardinian replied.

The private dining room was almost totally enclosed in glass, and the reason was instantly apparent. It jutted out into a garden that was in early-summer bloom. Beyond the garden lay the golf course. Below it all lay the blue sea dotted with white sails.

Six people stood waiting for them, all men. Even though it was Saturday, all were dressed in business suits, with white shirts and subdued ties. Their cufflinks were less subdued. None of them spoke until the Sardinian broke the ice. He did so by addressing the biggest man of all.

"*Come va,* Vincente," he said, "and how is Maria?"

"She is home with the new baby, Pietro, but she sends her greetings." He did not mention that she was home with the baby because she had not been invited.

The Sardinian then made the rounds, greeting and hugging each of the other five men in succession. As he did so, the three Swiss stood by, watching what they regarded as the strange but charming rituals of their southern neighbors. Finally their presence was acknowledged when Pietro brought two of his compatriots over to them.

Ignoring the two women, he introduced them to Samuel Schweizer.

"This is my good friend Dottore Francesco Livorno of the Banco Espirito Sancto," he said. "And this is my new Swiss friend, Herr Doktor Samuel Schweizer of the Swiss National Bank. Perhaps you already know each other."

"Regrettably not," the Italian banker said, "but we do have a mutual acquaintance, Dottore Antonio Riva of the Bank of Italy. He always speaks very highly of you, Dr. Schweizer. It is truly an honor to meet you."

"What a coincidence," Schweizer responded as the two men shook hands. "I just spent two days with him and his colleagues in Rome."

"And this," Pietro said, bringing forward the second man, "is Dottore Silvio Pedroncelli, my most trusted legal adviser. His law firm is in Milano. He is also a member of the National Assembly."

The Italian parliamentarian and the Swiss central banker now also shook hands.

"Our law firm has many Swiss connections," the Italian lawyer said, "but we are most proud of our association with the General Bank of Switzerland. We also share a mutual friend there, the chairman, Dr. Lothar Zopf."

"I was formerly with the General Bank," Schweizer said.

"I know. I also know they were very sad when you left. But of course they also understood that you could hardly refuse the high honor which the Swiss government bestowed on you."

"I want the three of you to sit with me at lunch," Pietro said. "But before we dine, I want you to meet the two charming ladies who have been kind enough to join us. They are also Swiss, and old friends of both of our families. They just happened to be staying at the Cala di Volpe and could not resist our invitation to make a day trip on the *Diana*."

Having thus demonstrated his discretion, the Sardinian proceeded to introduce Giselle and Simone to all the men in the room. That done, he personally made the seating arrangements. After placing the two women between the four men at one end of the table, he assumed his place at the other end—at the head, of course. His lawyer and his Italian banker sat to his left. On his right sat the guest of honor, Dr. Samuel Schweizer.

They had barely sat down when the ubiquitous hotel manager once again appeared. He had an announcement.

"At the request of our esteemed Signore Pietro di Cagliari, I have arranged for our chef to prepare a meal made exclusively of Sardinian dishes. Enjoy!"

After the waiters had served the first

course, Pietro began his commentary.

"Allow me to tell you what you are about to eat, ladies and gentlemen. All the ingredients come from San Giuliano, which is near Alghero in the northern part of my island. The most delicate of these are the wild cardoon. Then there are the *antunna* mushrooms, a rare member of the oyster mushroom family, indigenous only to Sardinia. You add sun-dried tomatoes stuffed with anchovies, herbs, and spices and, *ecco,* you have the finest antipasto in all of Italy."

He paused, then said, "But the secret is the *frutatto* olive oil. It comes only from Sartos and San Raimondo, which are in the middle and southern regions of my island. But you must also try the bread— the *pane carasau*—which we Sardinians call *carta di musica.*"

He picked up a piece. "You see, it is as parchment-thin as music paper, and when you crush it in your hand, it crackles. Listen."

He crushed it and, indeed, it crackled. He was like a little kid showing off a new toy.

And so it went, through the fish and meat courses. Between courses, the four men at the head of the table discussed everything from the never-ending saga of Italian politics to the rumors of Fidel Castro being on his deathbed in Havana. The scene at the other end of the table was more boisterous, no doubt aided and abetted by the presence of two beautiful women as well as the fact that the wine was flowing freely.

The incident occurred as coffee was being served.

The two women had taken advantage of the pause to go to the ladies' room. A distraught Giselle was the first to arrive back at the table, but it was only Pietro who appeared to notice that something must have happened. Without interrupting the conversation at his end of the table, he issued a silent command to the largest man in the room— Vincente. After a brief whispered conversation with the Swiss woman, who had reassumed her place to his left, Vincente unobtrusively left the room. Less than five minutes later he returned. Simone was with him. Another silent message was passed between the two Sardinians at opposite ends of the table. Pietro appeared satisfied.

Samuel Schweizer remained completely oblivious of anything untoward having happened, since, when not forced to listen to Pietro's gastronomic lectures, he had been deeply engaged in conversation with his fellow banker from Milano. The main topic was the fate of the lira, now that the neo-Fascists were making ever deeper inroads into the Italian body politic. Pietro picked up on that.

"I too am worried about the lira," he said to his Italian banker, "and it brings me back to a subject I discussed earlier with our Swiss friend. I want to get involved in a charity. Now that I am in my fifties, I feel I must begin to give back some of what I have been so fortunate to earn. I'm thinking especially of helping children—the children who have been victims of the terrible tragedies in Bosnia and Rwanda and especially in our old colony, Somalia."

His lawyer's eyebrows rose ever so slightly when he heard his client's concerns, but he kept silent as Pietro continued. "I would like to do this from a base in my own country, but it would hardly be in the interests of those children to do so under current circumstances. The more the lira falls, the less they will benefit. Do you not agree, Samuel?"

"I'm afraid that I must agree, yes," Schweizer said.

"Unfortunately, I must also concur," said the banker from Rome.

Even though he could see business slipping away, the lawyer from Milano added his voice to what was now a consensus.

The Sardinian went on. "The most obvious alternative is Switzerland. But I have had an unfortunate experience there in money matters." He glanced down the table at the ex-wife of the man who had been responsible for that experience, noting that Giselle seemed to have completely calmed down by now.

"So I will need advice. First I will need a law firm in Zurich that can set up an investment company there—ideally one that is free of taxation. But it will have to be a law firm that I can trust to maintain complete discretion. I want to remain totally anonymous. Charity must be given for charity's sake, not for the purpose of public recognition. Then I will need advice on how best to invest the capital. I am thinking here of unofficial advice. Advice from friends who are of a like mind but who also desire anonymity. I can imagine that occasional meetings would be necessary. But only at venues like the Cala di Volpe or on board the *Diana*—places that guarantee the seclusion we all seek where our private affairs are concerned."

The use of the word *affairs* might have been pushing things a bit, but the Sardinian was sure that after two nights with Simone, the Swiss central banker's mind was working in tandem with his. "What do you think, Samuel?" he asked.

"I've thought this matter over since you first brought it up on your yacht, Pietro," Schweizer said. "And I think I have an ideal lawyer for you in Zurich. His name is Dr. Hans Zwiebach. He is not only an excellent lawyer, but he is fully conversant with financial matters. In fact, it is well known that he is the lawyer of choice in Zurich for professional money managers from all over the world, because he understands their thinking. He is also the very soul of discretion; I can testify to that, since we have been friends since boyhood. When I was still with the General Bank of Switzerland, I recommended him—very selectively, I might add—to others. All have been most pleased with his services."

"Excellent. How long will it take to set up the type of thing I have in mind?" Pietro asked.

"Until it is registered, I would say about six weeks," Schweizer replied.

"Perfect. Will you inform your Dr. Zwiebach that I will be contacting him?"

"Certainly. As soon as I get back to Zurich."

"I'm sure he will want to know how much we are talking about. Initial capital, I mean."

"I think that is a matter that will be between you and him," Schweizer said.

"No, Samuel. It will be a matter between *us*," the Sardinian said. "I am thinking of transferring fifty million," he said, adding, "dollars."

He turned back to his Italian banker. "So I want you to take the equivalent amount of lira from my account and buy the dollars. I want it done right away."

"But why so fast?" the Italian money man asked. "As Dr. Schweizer just pointed out, it will take weeks to get properly established there."

"I want the money in Switzerland right away. Who knows what our crazy government will do if the lira gets into big trouble."

"But we normally require substantial notice where such a large withdrawal is concerned," the Italian banker said.

"I am not a normal client," the Sardinian said.

"But—"

"No more. You will get transfer instructions next week, after Samuel and I work out the details."

Schweizer intervened. "Lest we misunderstand one another, it would be impossible for me to get involved with the management of this admirable undertaking. That would be incompatible with my position at the Swiss National Bank. I trust you all understand this."

"That goes without saying," Pietro hastened to state as his two Italian advisers vigorously nodded in agreement. "But when it comes to the selection of the children who are to be the beneficiaries, perhaps where *that* part of the undertaking is concerned—and that part *only*, I must stress—you might consider contributing your thoughts."

Schweizer reflected a moment before replying. "I see no reason why not."

"And you will call me next week regarding your lawyer friend?" Pietro asked.

"Of course."

"Enough, then, of this serious talk, Samuel. You did not, after all, come to Santa Margherita for that. Unfortunately, I still have a few business matters to attend to. So I have a suggestion: you and the ladies take a tour through the garden. I will remain here for a brief meeting with my colleagues. Very brief. No more than thirty minutes. Then we will head back to Sardinia."

As he spoke, Pietro rose, taking his new friend Samuel by the arm. Together they approached the two Swiss women at the other end of the table.

"Ladies," Pietro said, "follow me."

He steered the three Swiss into the lobby, where they were met by the ever-present hotel manager, who had obviously been given prior instructions, since he immediately volunteered to personally escort the party around the grounds of the Imperial Palace. If they preferred to ride rather than walk, golf carts were waiting for them outside the main entrance. Satisfied that his guests were taken care of, Pietro di Cagliari returned to the private dining room, firmly closing the door behind him.

It was decided that they would take the golf carts rather than walk. The hotelier drove the lead cart, with Samuel Schweizer at his side. Giselle took the steering wheel of the second after assuring the men that she was a golfer and thus quite able to handle it.

As soon as the lead cart was far enough in front of them, Giselle spoke to Simone. "What happened? I thought you were right behind me."

"I was. Then that drunk tried to grab me again. So I turned around and headed back toward the ladies' room."

"I'm sorry, Simone. I had no intention of leaving you in the lurch."

"You didn't. But you missed what happened next."

"What's that?"

"That big man—Vincente—came charging out into the lobby and went right for the German."

"I told him that the guy was wearing lederhosen," Giselle said.

"He grabbed him and literally dragged him out of the lobby."

"What did the other people think?"

"It happened so fast, nobody else seemed to notice."

"Then?"

"A few minutes later, Vincente came back and told me that he had taken care of it, whatever that meant. And he suggested that, if I didn't mind, it might be best not to mention it to the others. That Signore di Cagliari would become terribly upset. So I promised not to. Then we both came to the dining room."

The sound of a siren suddenly broke the tranquillity of the *parco giardino* of the Imperial Palace. From their golf cart they could watch as an ambulance approached the side entrance of the hotel. The hotel manager ahead of them obviously saw it, too, and turned his cart around.

As he passed them, going back in the direction of the hotel, he said, "Please wait here. I have to find out what's going on."

The two Swiss women did as they were told. From afar, they could observe a man on a stretcher being loaded into the ambulance, which then took off at high speed, sirens going full blast.

The manager and his passenger returned immediately.

"What happened?" Giselle asked.

"A German tourist," the manager replied. "Drunk. Must have fallen and injured himself."

"Badly?"

"Unfortunately, yes."

"How awful."

"Yes. I apologize for the interruption. Please follow me. Much more pleasant experiences lie ahead."

As the golf carts began to move again, the two Swiss women exchanged glances.

"Vincente took care of it, all right," Giselle said. "And I think we would be well advised to follow his advice and forget the whole incident."

"What incident?" Simone asked.

They both giggled.

"But you must admit, my dear," Giselle said, "that Sardinians know how to take care of their women."

"If Sammy Schweizer knew about all this, he'd have a fit!" Simone said.

"So don't tell him."

"Don't worry, I won't."

After the *tour de jardin* was over, the hotel manager insisted on offering them tea on the outside terrace of the hotel while they waited for their host to reappear.

"Tell me," Samuel Schweizer asked after they had settled in, "how long have you known Signore di Cagliari?"

"Oh, for thirty years," the hotelier replied. "He and his father have always brought business friends here."

"And his business is...?"

"I can't say exactly. All I know is that the men he entertains here are very important people. Bankers from Milan, politicians from Rome, even cardinals from the Vatican. Also sometimes foreigners. Like the President of Paraguay on one occasion. The foreign minister of Lebanon on another. And last week, Cubans. Signore di Cagliari is immensely well connected."

"It certainly seems so," Schweizer commented.

The hotelier decided to be more specific. "I do know that Signore di Cagliari, following in the footsteps of his father, is involved in property development in Italy, including resorts. Like the Cala di Volpe resort, over in Sardinia, although he actually doesn't own that one. Originally some of the money came from the young Aga Khan IV, who stayed here on various occasions when the hotels were being built. Then it was a Pakistani bank that moved in and financed the villas around the hotels to turn them into resorts. They relied heavily on the Cagliaris. You know how it is with zoning and building permits everywhere in the world. You always need local help. But in Sardinia, you probably need more local help than in most other places. After his father passed away, Pietro di Cagliari expanded his role from that of adviser to partner in these property developments. Then he moved on to other projects."

He paused, then went on. "I do not want to mislead you. I did not learn about any of this from Signore di Cagliari personally. I have been in the hotel resort business for a long time, so I hear these things. But you know how it is with gossip. It is impossible to tell how much is really true. However, this I do know about the Cagliaris: The father was very powerful, and the son is now even more so."

As far as the man who ran the Imperial Palace was concerned, the matter was now closed. He realized that if he continued, inevitably some of the other gossip would begin to come out. For instance, that the Pakistani bank was none other than the Bank for Credit and Commerce International, or BCCI, known otherwise— before its collapse—as the Bank for Criminals and Crooks International. Or that the visitors from the Vatican had been officials of the Instituto per le Opere di Religione—the Vatican's financial operations center—including one who had involved that august institution in some decidedly unaugust financial deals. Or that the delegation from Rome was often accompanied by another infamous gentleman, the Vatican's principal financial "adviser," Michele Sindona, otherwise known as "St. Peter's Banker" before he was kidnapped. That when the Sardinian moved on to those other projects, it had been more than suspected that his financial backers now included both the Vatican and the Pakistanis—an ecumenical undertaking perhaps unique in the annals of capitalism.

But he would have had no choice but to discontinue the conversation with Samuel Schweizer in any case, since the subject under discussion now approached their table. He was alone.

"Here you are. How good that I have found you. And I see that you have just finished your tea."

They had not, but that did not bother the Sardinian. He looked pointedly at his watch, and said, "I suggest that before it gets too late we return to Portofino. The car is waiting."

Waiting by the car was Vincente. He opened the doors for the ladies and helped them in. The Sardinian had a last brief conversation with him. Then Pietro climbed into the front of the limo and they drove off.

The Sardinian was on the car phone immediately. Although he spoke in rapid Italian, it was obvious to the passengers in the rear that he was talking to the captain of the *Diana*, arranging for their departure. The only incongruous part was what seemed to be repeated references to Cuba at the end of the conversation. The two Swiss women in the back, being Swiss, pointedly tried to ignore the conversation up front. Samuel Schweizer had to make no such effort, since he dozed off immediately. He was not accustomed to weekends involving such—by his standards—frenzied activities.

The lighter was waiting at the dock in Portofino, and the *Diana*'s engines were already running when they boarded the yacht. The Sardinian told his guests that he would be busy in the captain's quarters for the next few hours. Samuel took the opportunity to go to his suite, where he continued his nap.

The two ladies, left on their own, decided to have a cocktail on the promenade deck by themselves.

"So what happens next between Sammy and you?" Giselle asked as she took a tentative sip from the gin and tonic that had just been served.

"That will depend on what he has in mind, I guess," Simone responded.

"I think we know what *he* has in mind, my dear."

They both grinned.

"But seriously," Giselle continued, "do you think he can afford what *you* have in mind?"

"Well, he and Pietro seem to have hit it off together. And from what I've seen so far, friends of Pietro all seem to go first class. Right? But as long as we're discussing the future, what about you and Pietro?"

"He has asked me to stay with him for a while," Giselle said.

"And are you going to?"

Giselle shrugged. "I think I just might. I've got nothing else going."

"But how long will you last in Sardinia?"

"That won't be a problem. Pietro is always on the move. He's headed for Cuba at the end of the week. He wants me to go with him. I already said yes."

Simone fell silent.

"Something wrong?" her friend asked.

"Not really. But I'm not sure that Herr Doktor Schweizer can offer anything near this sort of thing—yachts, the Cala di Volpe, trips to Cuba. You know what I mean? From what he told me, he's got a flat in Küsnacht, a small chalet in Crans-Montana, and that's about it."

"But he's a big man in Swiss financial circles. The biggest, as I understand it," Giselle said.

"Maybe."

"Look, Simone, he's nuts about you. And if he wants to keep you, he's going to have to ante up. Right?"

"Keep me? Do you realize what you just said? We sound like two little Swiss gold-diggers on the make, Giselle."

"So what? We're not eighteen, you know."

When the yacht arrived in the waters just off the Cala di Volpe, it was barely dawn.

Despite the hour, Pietro had arranged that they disembark, explaining that he had a lot to do first thing that morning.

On the way to the hotel on the motor launch, he offered Samuel Schweizer the use of his private jet to take him back to Zurich, and Schweizer accepted the offer. As an afterthought, it seemed, Pietro made the same offer to Simone. To Samuel Schweizer's visible disappointment, she declined. She wanted to spend a few more days on vacation.

The Sardinian made a brief phone call with his *telefonino*.

"The plane will be ready to leave at eight," he then told Schweizer, "which gives you just enough time to change clothes and get your belongings from the room. The hotel limo will take you to the airport."

The three of them waited in the hotel lobby while Schweizer prepared for what now amounted to a hurried exit. When he went to pay, he was told that the bill had already been taken care of.

When Schweizer emerged from the hotel, he grasped the hand of the Sardinian and shook it firmly. "Many thanks, Pietro, for everything—the hotel, the dinners, the yacht. And especially the company." He actually bowed his head at the end. Samuel Schweizer, now back in his blue pinstriped suit, had apparently already reverted to his Swiss banker mode.

"It was our pleasure," the Sardinian

replied. "Unfortunately, it is also time to say *arrivederci*. But not for long. If you can arrange it with your lawyer friend, I can come up to Zurich this week in order to get our project under way. Here is my card, with all my numbers. Please let me know."

"You will hear from me," Schweizer replied.

"Wonderful," Pietro said. Then he turned to the ladies. "Giselle, we must be on our way. Simone, why don't you ride to the airport with Sammy? I'm sure he wants to enjoy the pleasure of your company as long as possible."

"No, I'm too tired," Simone said.

So Samuel Schweizer had no choice but to embrace her awkwardly. Then the three of them walked him to the waiting limo and waved as it pulled away. As soon as it was out of sight, Giselle spoke to Simone in a low voice. "Why did you do that?"

"I don't really know."

"Do you think he'll stay in touch?"

"That is strictly up to him."

Pietro broke in. "Giselle, why don't you stay here with Simone? I have to get some work done. We'll meet at seven-thirty in the bar. And, Simone, don't worry. You'll hear from him much sooner than you think."

As usual, the Sardinian was right.

The two Swiss women spent most of the

day on the small beach adjacent to the hotel. At seven-thirty they met Pietro at the bar for a pre-dinner *aperitif*. They were no sooner seated than the bartender came over with a phone.

"It's for you, *signore*," he said to Pietro.

It was, of course, Dr. Samuel Schweizer. He had tentatively arranged for Pietro to meet with his lawyer friend at four o'clock on Wednesday in Zurich, if that was agreeable. It was.

"He wants to say hello to you," Pietro then said to Simone. Turning to Giselle, he added, "Maybe she could use a bit of privacy. Why don't we go to our table out on the terrace?"

Ten minutes later, Simone reappeared. Since Pietro was talking to some of his friends at an adjacent table, Giselle was alone.

"So?" she said to her friend as soon as Simone sat down.

"He wants me to spend next weekend with him at his chalet in Crans."

"Will you?"

"I said yes. But I can always change my mind. He gave me the number of his direct line at his bank."

"He must have been doing some serious thinking on the plane ride back to Zurich. You sure played that one right."

"Now, Giselle. Let's not start that stuff again. I like him."

"So how are you going to get to Crans from here?"

"Didn't you say that Pietro and you were going to Cuba this weekend?"

"If nothing has changed in the meantime, yes."

"Then you can drop me off at the Geneva airport. From there I can take the train to Sierre and the funicular up to Crans. After that, the transportation will be up to Sammy."

When Pietro returned to their table, Giselle immediately asked about Cuba.

"It's all set," the Sardinian replied. "We leave Friday morning."

"Simone asked if we might take her along."

"To Cuba?"

"No, of course not. Just to Geneva. She plans on meeting Samuel at his chalet in the Swiss Alps this weekend—if the transportation can be worked out. I know it's a bit out of the way, but—"

The Sardinian interrupted her. "No problem at all." He turned to Simone. "I'll be seeing him on business the day after tomorrow. Should I mention this?"

"I think you had better not." It was Giselle who answered. "We know Swiss men all too well, don't we, Simone? They prefer to keep business and pleasure in very separate compartments."

"Fine with me," the Sardinian said. "But this calls for a little celebration. How about beluga caviar and some very cold champagne?"

Neither of the ladies declined the offer.

Even though they were also Swiss, *they* had no qualms about mixing business with pleasure.

18

Dr. Hans Zwiebach knew a valuable client when he saw one. And he saw one the moment Pietro di Cagliari walked into his office on the Bahnhofstrasse in Zurich. The Sardinian seemed to fill the space around him with an air of supreme confidence. Zwiebach knew from experience that that sort of confidence stemmed from the fact that his new client was a man of means—lots and lots of means.

"How good of you to receive me on such short notice," the Sardinian said in impeccable English.

"How good of you, *signore*," Zwiebach replied, "to come to Zurich."

It was now the Sardinian's turn to size up his new Swiss attorney. He also liked what he saw. Taller than the Sardinian by at least five centimeters, the Swiss was also probably ten kilos heavier. *Solid, steady, stable* were the traits that immediately came to mind. *Very observant* was another. The clue to that came from his eyes, which seemed to be always in motion, surveying his new client from top to bottom, darting back to his hands and no doubt registering how well manicured they were. But also noting the rings. Maybe it would have been advisable to leave them back in Sardinia.

"May I offer you an aperitif?" the lawyer asked. "Perhaps a Campari and soda?"

"My favorite afternoon drink," the Sardinian responded.

The lawyer went to the bar, which was placed discreetly behind the doors of an elegant eighteenth-century French armoire. The Sardinian noticed that all the furniture in the room, with the exception of the desk, was of this same period. It reeked of good taste and of money, *old* money, and that was the type of money the Sardinian admired. You could *trust* people of old money. It was the nouveau riche who always ended up as troublemakers.

"Our mutual friend mentioned that you are also a great friend of well-aged Brunello," Zwiebach said as he prepared the drinks, adding only two small ice cubes.

The Sardinian immediately noted the oblique way in which Samuel Schweizer had been referred to. So he added discretion to the growing list of favorable attributes he saw in the other man.

"Indeed I am."

"Then we must have one over dinner," Zwiebach said as he handed his guest his drink.

"Another time, I am sorry to say. This visit must be a short one," Pietro answered.

"Then let's proceed. Might I suggest we

sit down over there?" Zwiebach motioned toward the sitting group in front of a fireplace at the far end of the office.

He continued once they were seated. "As I understand it, your intention is to establish an investment company with the ultimate objective of funding a trust to aid charitable causes, especially those involving children."

The Sardinian's next words immediately confirmed what the Swiss lawyer had thought the moment he saw him. This man was destined to become a big client—perhaps one of the biggest of all—and Zwiebach's clients had ranged from Ferdinand Marcos to the young Duvalier to Marc Rich.

Those words were, "That is correct. I want to start with fifty million dollars. Cash."

He paused to let that sink in. "It will be the *proceeds* from the capital of the investment company that will be used for those charitable purposes."

"And how would you expect these proceeds to be generated?"

"I'm afraid I don't understand the question."

"How would you like that fifty million dollars of initial capital to be invested?"

"Aggressively."

That caused a moment of pause.

"Frankly," the lawyer said, "I did not expect that answer. Invariably, clients stress capital preservation as their number-one objective."

"And invariably their lawyers make money, their accountants make money, their banks make money—and the client makes *niente*," the Sardinian responded.

"I see your point," the Swiss lawyer said.

"I knew you would. You come very highly recommended. That is why I am here. That is also why I want you to arrange for the management of these funds. For a fee, of course. I am too busy with other matters to be directly involved. All I will be concerned with are the results."

"It will take me some time to establish the proper legal framework for what you have in mind."

"No hurry. Because at the outset we won't need any 'legal framework.' As far as I'm concerned, just a one-page agreement stipulating that you will act as my fiduciary agent would suffice."

"But that would hardly minimize the possible tax consequences."

The Sardinian's hands rose in a gesture that dismissed his concerns about taxes.

"We can deal with that as we go along," he said. "Perhaps you have a standard form along the lines I have suggested?"

"I do. I will have my secretary bring us one."

Zwiebach left the room very briefly. Upon returning, he said, "She'll be with us in a few minutes. Perhaps in the meantime you could expand on your investment philosophy."

"No property investment. I have enough of that. No blue-chip stocks. No mutual funds. No bond funds. I've been through all of them. They are for old ladies. I want aggressive investment—speculation, if you prefer to use that word—in fast-moving markets."

"Such as?"

"Currencies. Gold. Options. Futures. Using maximum leverage."

"That is very risky," Zwiebach said.

"I am used to taking risks," the Sardinian replied. "Taking *calculated* risks. I am also used to rewarding those who help me minimize the risks and maximize the profits. Very generous rewards, I should add."

"You have obviously thought this through quite thoroughly."

"I have. What else do you need to know?"

"Nothing, really. Except for one detail."

"That is?"

"The management fee you mentioned. The standard arrangement is—"

The Sardinian interrupted him. "Standard arrangements do not interest me."

"Then what do you have in mind?"

"Something very simple. If you make an annual return of ten percent or more—which, I realize, is high by Swiss standards—you keep twenty-five percent of the profits."

"And if it is less than ten percent?" Zwiebach asked.

"You get nothing."

Again Zwiebach's brain worked it out instantaneously. So what? If that happened, the Sardinian's money would go back to wherever it came from—the less known about *that*, the better—and he'd never hear from him again.

"You have a deal," he said.

He left the room. Minutes later he returned, bearing the now-amended standard, bare-bones fiduciary agreement. It ran to three pages. Most of the text was devoted to the client agreeing that no matter what happened to his money, under no circumstances whatsoever would he have any recourse against his fiduciary agent. And if, despite such a solemn commitment, the ungrateful client ever decided to take legal action against such agent, it would be the courts of the Canton of Zurich that would have sole jurisdiction over the dispute. What it did *not* say was that never in the history of the Canton of Zurich had a disgruntled client ever won such a case.

An addendum outlined the fee arrangement. Pietro watched as the attorney, after consulting a separate dossier, now filled in the blank left open in that addendum for the number of the new B account at the General Bank of Switzerland to be assigned to Pietro di Cagliari. Where the bank was concerned, the account would be in the name of and administered by Dr. Hans Zwiebach.

The Sardinian took less than three minutes to scan the three pages with their addendum. Then he got out his gold Mont Blanc pen and signed in triplicate. Dr. Hans Zwiebach did the same, and handed one copy back to the Sardinian. Pietro folded it and stuffed it into the side pocket of his jacket.

"I like this way of doing business," he said. "We Sardinians are, after all, just simple island people. We normally do things only among ourselves, and then only among the very select few we can really trust. The guiding principle is always that all parties must benefit. But the world has changed. So now we must turn to other people. But the guiding principle remains the same. I am sure we will be very successful together, and that all three of us will benefit greatly."

Not one word was said about the starving children in Somalia.

The Sardinian rose from his chair and extended his hand to the Swiss lawyer. Dr. Hans Zwiebach grasped it with obvious enthusiasm. For it was the hand that was about to deliver fifty million dollars to his omnibus account at the General Bank of Switzerland. Neither chose to elaborate on the role of the third party to which the Sardinian had alluded.

An hour later, Pietro had already boarded his plane at Kloten. Once airborne and headed back toward Sardinia, he faxed instructions to his Italian bank to take fifty million dollars from his newly replenished dollar account and wire it to account number 77-65-39-44 at the General Bank of Switzerland in Zurich. Knowing Italian banks, it would probably be Monday before the funds arrived.

This would be his second go at making money in Switzerland. The first time around he had been new at the game and had allowed his money to be run by one of the multitude of mediocre Swiss money managers—with disastrous results. He had lost his money and his money manager had subsequently lost his life.

But there was also the plus side. He had ended up with the wife of the dead man—who, upon reflection, never alluded to her former husband's untimely death. What that liaison had done, however, was to unexpectedly set in motion a series of very fortuitous events. Giselle had led to Simone, Simone had led to Sammy. And Sammy had led to the clever but solid Swiss lawyer. But the lawyer was really just a detail. It was Herr Doktor Samuel Schweizer who was the key. From the very first moment he had laid eyes on him at the Cala di Volpe, Pietro *knew* that the Swiss central banker personified the sort of thing that came along so seldom in a lifetime—a *sure* thing.

But first he had to hook Sammy. If he failed, then he would yank that fifty million dollars back so fast it would singe the wires used for its transfer to somewhere else. The hook had already been baited—

with Simone. Sammy had already nibbled. More than nibbled. Now he was going to be given a chance to really go for it. Once he was hooked, it would only be a matter of reeling him in—gradually, carefully, even lovingly.

Pietro savored all of these thoughts. Islanders understood fishing as no other men did. But Sardinians, like his father, had developed that skill, that art, even further. They had become fishers of men—though hardly along the lines supposedly fostered by his good friends at the Vatican. His father had coined a more apt phrase years ago, over a celebratory bottle of wine. The occasion had been the mysterious death by poison in a Milan prison of the financier Michele Sindona. Proud of his family's role in this, his father had chosen to describe the Cagliaris' mission in life as "fishers of *evil men.*"

Pietro di Cagliari summoned the steward. During the rest of the flight he savored another celebratory bottle of wine—a 1991 Brunello di Montalcino. It was premature, perhaps. But not by much. All he needed were just a couple more breaks.

19

The breaks he had hoped for materialized sooner than expected. The first was the product of a deliberate scheme. The second, however—which Pietro only learned about much later—stemmed from the unexpected machinations of a person who had come down with a bad case of hubris.

The plan's execution began with the first leg of Pietro's flight to Havana that Friday. His Gulfstream IV landed at the Geneva airport shortly before 10:00 A.M. The only passenger to get off there was Simone Bouverie. The other six remained on board the Gulfstream while the ground crew topped off the plane's fuel tanks in preparation for the long flight to the Caribbean.

Simone, as a former Swissair flight attendant, was thoroughly familiar with Switzerland's ground transportation system. She went directly to the cab stand outside the terminal at Cointrin Airport, pulling her single bag behind her. Next stop, twenty minutes later, was the Gare de Cornavin. There she boarded the 10:34 train that headed east along the north shore of the Lake of Geneva to Lausanne, where it hooked up with the Simplon Express that had left Paris four hours earlier. At 12:08 she got off at Sion. After a layover of seventeen minutes she got on a local mountain train, and forty minutes later and 1,600 meters higher, she finally reached her destination, Crans-sur-Sierre. It was the Alpine resort, high above the Rhone Valley, that, summer and winter, vied with Gstaad, Klosters, and St. Moritz as a favored destination of Europe's vacationing elite.

Across the valley lay the Matterhorn and Zermatt, where the other people went, including, of course, lots of loud Americans.

The terrace of the dining room of the Palace Hotel was anything but loud because it was anything but full. The weekend crowd from Geneva and Paris had not yet arrived. The part-time residents, with their luxurious chalets that dotted the high plateau between Crans and its sister resort of Montana, a kilometer to the east, were either lunching on their own terraces or picnicking along one of the many hiking paths.

As soon as she had been seated, Simone checked her watch. It would still be two hours. So why not make the best of it? She ordered a Bloody Mary. Once it arrived, like the good Swiss that she was, she decided to further tone up her Sardinian tan. So she took off her jacket and turned her chair to face the early-afternoon sun. A few sips of thinly disguised vodka, and she was ready to do a bit of thinking before Herr Doktor Samuel Schweizer arrived.

The signals she had gotten from Pietro—reinforced by Giselle— had made it quite apparent that they intended to be "supportive" of her budding relationship with the Swiss banker. Which meant putting at her—meaning *their*—disposal the best suite at the Cala di Volpe, "whenever she needed it." With a couple of days' notice, transportation to and from Zurich in Pietro's jet would also be provided. Not bad.

She took a few more sips.

Then there had been the broad hint of a possible job. Pietro, it seemed, needed someone with professional experience to supervise the travel arrangements of the Cagliari organization—the scheduling of the Gulfstream and the *Diana*, ground transportation, hotel bookings. Who was better qualified than an ex–senior Swissair stewardess who knew the world from Zurich to Bangkok to New York to Tokyo?

A few more sips and it was all gone. So she ordered another one.

But she was no dummy. It had been a *contingent* offer—contingent on what happened next between her and Sammy. Her future job might ostensibly involve booking airplanes and hotel rooms, but her *real* job would be fucking Sammy Schweizer on the yacht, in one of those hotel rooms, or even on board Pietro's Gulfstream.

She surprised herself by even *thinking* the F-word. Maybe it was the Bloody Marys on an empty stomach. But still, it was true, wasn't it? And so what if it was? She *did* like him. Maybe he needed a bit more instruction in bed. But according to Giselle, her husband had been no great shakes in that department either. As Giselle had told her many times, no Swiss woman in her right mind got involved with a Swiss banker for *that*. It was for the money. For the security that their money would provide.

Except in Giselle's case, it hadn't worked out too well.

Which brought up a worrisome thought. She was not sure how Sammy Schweizer would work out, either. For despite his undoubtedly high and powerful position in the world of Swiss finance, he did not strike her as a rich man.

On the other hand, there was not the slightest doubt that Pietro di Cagliari was rich. Better yet, he liked to spend his money. That he had demonstrated during yesterday's trip to Milano.

Just like that, on a whim, he had said, "Girls, let's go shopping." By late morning, thanks to the Gulfstream IV, they were in the Galleria in Milano. At Bulgari's alone he had spent at least $10,000 on jewelry for Giselle.

But there was also a problem with Pietro. She definitely did not want to give even the faintest impression that she was trying to horn in on Giselle. If Pietro offered her that job, fine. But no hanky-panky on the side. Not that Pietro had ever made a move on her. If he did, she was not sure how she would react—or *could* react—because, despite all his charm, despite the hotel and the yacht and everybody kowtowing to him, there was something wrong. Not that she could really put her finger on specifics. Except, maybe, the incident at the hotel in Santa Margherita involving that thug, Vincente, who always seemed to be hanging around Pietro. She knew that in Italy these days, everybody needed a bodyguard. But, still, that did not mean they went around beating up German tourists so badly they had to be taken away in an ambulance.

Then there were those other men on the plane that morning. They all seemed to be cut from the same cloth as Vincente. And there was no doubt that some of them had been carrying guns. As a stewardess, she had been trained to be constantly on the lookout for that. After all, Swissair flew into such places as Teheran and Tel Aviv. And why were they all going to Cuba, anyway?

The waiter reappeared, bearing the luncheon menu. Simone decided that after ten days of Italian food it was time to watch her figure. So she ordered a *Bündnerfleisch Teller*. Somehow that Swiss specialty— beef that was cured outside in the pure air of the high Swiss Alps— brought back to mind Herr Doktor Samuel Schweizer. He *was*, after all, about as Swiss as they came. And pure—at least until he had met her.

There was no sense in beating around the bush with him. Either he was serious or not. And if he was serious, she would have to make it amply clear that she was not going to be satisfied with an occasional tête-à-tête in his crummy little chalet in Montana. She hadn't seen it yet, but she already knew what to expect.

It all came down—again—to money. So if Sammy didn't have enough to provide her with the sorts of things a girl needed, then she would leave no doubt that this weekend with him would be the last. If he wanted their relationship to continue, it would be up to *him* to figure out how to supplement his income.

She knew how. And she knew that he knew how. Pietro. But first he would have to want her badly enough. She had the rest of the weekend to work on *that*.

And then, who knows? A cushy job in Sardinia. A nice new luxury flat in Zurich. A badly needed new wardrobe. A Mercedes sportscar. Red. Maybe another shopping trip to Milano. But this time it would be *she* who would be on the receiving end. She had already picked out the exact piece she wanted at Bulgari's: an exquisitely designed emerald necklace that was a perfect match to the earrings she always wore.

She loved emeralds.

Sammy arrived an hour later. He had arranged for a horse and carriage to take them from the hotel to his chalet, a kilometer away on the road to Montana. As she expected, it was modest in every way.

But that night there was nothing modest about the performance she put on in the bedroom. Or the night after. On Monday morning they took the train back to Zurich. They held hands most of the way.

Sammy was hooked.

20

The second break that Pietro di Cagliari had been hoping for came just a few days later. It started with an early-afternoon phone call in Zurich that occurred about the same time as the two lovebirds were arriving there after the train ride from Sion. It was the head office of the General Bank of Switzerland calling Herr Doktor Hans Zwiebach to inform him that fifty million dollars had just been credited to his omnibus account as a result of a wire transfer from Italy. Were there any instructions concerning the disposal of these funds?

"Yes. Put twenty million into Account Number Q 178-5997."

"And what do you want to do then?"

"I don't know yet."

But after he hung up, Zwiebach could not help recalling the conversation he had had with Pietro di Cagliari the previous Wednesday. The Sardinian wanted action.

In the meantime he had found out where that action was. On Saturday night he had been invited to a dinner party at the home of the general manager of the Rothschild bank in Zurich, in honor of a certain Philippe de Bonneville. French by birth, Cambridge and Harvard Business School by education, with an IQ of 165, it was said, Bonneville operated the world's hottest hedge fund. The crème de la crème of Europe had money with him. At the top of the list were various members of the Rothschild family itself, the Sultan of Brunai, two of the Getty heirs, and Prince Charles. Seven other hedge funds, including the one controlled by George Soros, had placed money in Bonneville's hedge fund, the highest of compliments a money manager could receive. So had the United Bank of Switzerland and the Deutsche Bank. Representatives from both banks had been at the dinner table, and had heaped nothing but praise on the young man with the financial hot hand who operated from an office in the City of London that was said to be second to none where opulence was concerned.

The problem was that in order to get into Bonneville's hedge fund— which had produced a return of sixty-seven percent already that year— you had to make an initial investment of $100 million. This was because in order to remain unregulated and thus exempt from disclosure about what he was doing, the hedge fund manager had to limit his investors to ninety-nine partners. And even at $100 million each, that added up to only $10 billion.

Unfortunately, the Sardinian had sent Zwiebach only $50 million. So far.

But the evening had not been wasted, because, at around midnight, when everybody was well into cognac and cigars, the general manager of the United Bank of Switzerland had asked *the* question.

"If there was one single investment that you would recommend, what would it be?"

To a man, everyone gathered around the dinner table had fallen silent as they waited for the answer. It did not come fast. The young Frenchman first stroked his long, black, curly hair, then fidgeted with his diamond-encrusted cufflinks, gazed at the crystal chandelier above, and finally sighed audibly before responding.

"I'm sure you have all been watching the recent precipitous drop in the price of gold. Well, the time has come to buy it back on the cheap. Not bullion itself, of course. You want to buy gold futures. That way you'll get a lot more bang for the buck. Each futures contract allows you to purchase one hundred ounces of gold in the future, *but at today's bargain price of four hundred dollars an ounce.* The cash margin required for each contract is just twelve hundred dollars."

That pronouncement alone did not satisfy the Deutsche Bank.

"Why will the price of gold go up?" the German asked.

Bonneville answered, "Because the fear of inflation is about to be rekindled."

"By whom?"

"By the monetary authorities in the United States."

"How do you know?"

This question came from one of the Getty heirs who had journeyed to Zurich from his country villa in Italy especially for this dinner. He felt obligated to speak up since, after all, $200 million of his grandfather's hard-earned money was at stake.

Bonneville was ready with the answer. "Because the Federal Reserve Board in the United States is going to make an abrupt about-face in its policy. Instead of pushing interest rates up yet another notch to keep inflation in check as everybody expects, it will lower both the federal funds rate and the discount rate. Why? Because its members are afraid that if they don't, the current recovery of the American economy could falter. That it might even start to move down into recession. The central banks in both Europe and Japan will follow— for similar reasons. As interest rates drop across the board, the investment community will conclude that the monetary authorities have abandoned any further efforts to fight inflation, and the price of that classic hedge against inflation, gold, will finally soar again."

The oracle had spoken. The party broke up shortly thereafter. And here it was Monday morning. The Swiss lawyer turned on his computer to see what was happening in Europe's gold markets. The bullion price had hardly moved during the morning hours of trading in Europe, but suddenly that afternoon it had jumped eleven dollars an ounce after trading had opened in New York. He checked with Reuters. Nobody, the wire service text said, seemed to know why.

Maybe not, but the explanation was clear to Zwiebach. He knew the mindset of the men who had been fellow guests around that dinner table on Saturday night. They would all be thinking the same thing: Come Monday, that young Frenchman would be buying gold. No doubt he had already started do so *before* that dinner party. But now he'd be buying even more. That would add up to a lot of bullion. After all, with the almost $10 billion that Bonneville had under management, by operating in the futures markets in New York he could muster hundreds of billions in real firepower. They, the investors in his hedge fund, would, of course, be the ultimate beneficiaries as he moved the price higher. But why not double up with a little side bet?

Zwiebach knew full well that when the Gettys of the world thought in terms of side bets, they were still thinking in tens of millions of dollars. And everybody who had been at the table Saturday night could muster that amount with a single phone call.

So could he.

Zwiebach picked up his phone again. This time it was he who called the General Bank of Switzerland. He asked for one of the vice-presidents in the trading department, Urs Stucker, who always helped him out when he was investing money for his clients.

"What's happening with gold?" Zwiebach immediately asked.

"It's been going straight up since the opening in New York. Nobody knows why," came the answer.

"I want to buy some for a client."

"Are you sure? Let me check the price again." There was a short pause. "It's up fifteen dollars an ounce now."

"That's all right. And, Urs, I'm not interested in buying bullion. I want gold futures."

Once again, Zwiebach recalled the Sardinian's instructions. He had specifically said that he was more than willing to run the risks inherent in derivatives such as gold futures, provided those risks were calculated ones.

Well, who better to rely on for such calculation than Philippe de Bonneville, the man with the golden touch? Furthermore, it was he who had specifically said gold *futures*.

"Herr Doktor, if you want to get involved in futures," the banker said, "you've got the wrong man. I'm sixty-two years old, and derivatives are far beyond me. Hold on. I'll transfer you."

The young hotshot who came on the line next had no such inhibitions. And although he was a Swiss banker talking to a Swiss lawyer, every other word he used was in English.

"*Was für* futures *interessiert Sie?*" he asked, adding, "*Sie wissen* derivatives *sind* very risky."

"I know that they are very risky," Zwiebach said, deciding to stay with English all the way—just to put the little bastard in his place.

"Good," the Swiss yuppie replied. Now also staying with English, he continued. "So don't come back later and blame me if something goes wrong."

He gave Zwiebach time to let that sink in, and then asked, "How much are you actually planning on investing?"

"Twenty million dollars," Zwiebach replied.

"You are obviously confused," the trader said. "What you really want to buy is twenty million dollars' worth of *bullion*. That will be in the range of fifty thousand ounces. That's a lot of gold, if you ask me."

"I'm not asking you. And I'm not confused. So stop talking for a minute and listen, young man. I'm interested in gold futures. The twenty million dollars I referred to will serve as cash margin for those futures. And if you can't handle it, I'll call up somebody at the Swiss Bank Corporation who can."

The mention of the competition just across the *Paradeplatz* did it. "Yes, sir. But you must realize that I must first check your credit status with us."

"So check. With Urs Stucker. Then call me back." Zwiebach gave him his number.

He called back two minutes later. No further mention was made of Zwiebach's credit standing. As a result of the magic of the leverage inherent in the derivatives market, during the rest of that day, acting on behalf of Pietro di Cagliari, Zwiebach contracted for the future delivery of 1.6 million ounces of gold. That helped push the bullion price up yet another five dollars an ounce. But so what? Zwiebach reasoned. If the price increased by a further fifteen dollars during the next thirty days—it had already gained more than that in one day—the amount of money that Herr Doktor Hans Zwiebach had invested on the Sardinian's behalf would more than double in value, because every one-dollar increase in the price of gold translated into $1.6 million profit for him. After that, the sky might be the limit. The last time gold had taken off, in the early 1980s, it had ended up at eight hundred dollars an ounce! He did not even dare calculate what *that* would add up to in terms of profits—of which twenty-five percent would be his.

The next day the gold price settled down. It stayed there the day after that. On Wednesday it fell two dollars an ounce. On Thursday it fell five dollars. On Friday morning it fell another five dollars. As a result, at eleven o'clock that morning, Zwiebach got a margin call. The General Bank of Switzerland phoned to say that it needed slightly under $5 million in additional cash collateral if it was to maintain Zwiebach's gold futures position. Otherwise it would have to begin liquidating some of his contracts at a loss.

Zwiebach immediately authorized the transfer of the $5 million from his omnibus account to Cagliari's account. He also found himself in a cold sweat after hanging up the phone.

What had Philippe de Bonneville said? That gold was bound to move to a much higher price level because the Federal Reserve was going to change its interest rate policy. But what he had neglected to say was *when* the Americans were going to announce that change.

He could try to get hold of Bonneville in London and ask him. But the French hedge fund manager probably wouldn't even take his call. So who else might know? The American who ran Citibank's Zurich operation was likely to be best informed on the subject. So Zwiebach called him.

"Benny," he began, "I know this will sound a little odd, but do you know how the Federal Reserve sets American interest rates?"

"Sure. They hold a meeting," was the reply. "Anything else I can help you with?"

Benny was known for believing that he had a great sense of humor—one, however, that remained elusive to most Swiss, including Zwiebach.

"Let's stick to that meeting for a minute, Benny. What kind of committee is it, and when do they meet?"

"The Federal Open Market Committee, which is made up of the governors of the Federal Reserve Board and some of the presidents of the regional Federal Reserve banks, like the one in Philadelphia or San Francisco. They meet about every six weeks."

"When's their next meeting?"

"On Tuesday and Wednesday of next week."

"That's what I thought. I heard that they were going to change their policy and lower interest rates instead of raising them further as everybody expects."

"Oh, really? Look, Hans, whoever told you that is leading you down the garden path. There is only one guy in the world who can really know that in advance, and that's the Chairman of the Federal Reserve Board, Charles Black."

"Thanks, Benny," Zwiebach said, and hung up.

The mention of Black's name had brought Zwiebach up short. He couldn't tell Benny, but Charles Black was one of his clients—or at least had been one for a long time, until he moved from London to New York several years ago. Come to think of it, both Black and his wife were, at least technically, still his clients. She used to be a very active client—even calling him regularly from Hong Kong, where

the First National Bank of Manhattan—
her husband had then worked for that
bank—had transferred them. But that
had been years ago. He remembered that
after he had read about Black's appointment as Chairman of the Federal Reserve,
he had dropped him a note of congratu-
lation. He had received a very cordial
reply from Black, saying that he would like
to keep in touch, even suggesting that
Zwiebach look him up the next time he was
in Washington. He had not followed up,
regrettably. It had never occurred to him
at the time that Black would be in a position where any decision he took could
directly affect the fortunes of a client of
his.

He hated to admit it even to himself, but
his newest client—the Sardinian—was
important to him. Times had been a bit lean
of late. Marcos had come and gone. Baby
Doc Duvalier was broke. Tubman, the
President of Liberia, had been a *really*
good client. But he was long dead, and
Liberia was in ruins, so there was no new
business to be gotten from his successor.
Dictators were out of fashion, it seemed.
To be sure, there was a whole new bunch
of potential clients who were now showing up in Zurich loaded with money. The
Russian Mafia. You could see them outside
the Baur au Lac Hotel, getting in and out
of their rented Rolls-Royces with gorgeous young blond girlfriends at their
sides. They moved in packs. But none of

that business had as yet drifted his way. And even if it did, he was not sure he wanted it. Those guys could be dangerous.

The more he thought about all this, the more nervous Zwiebach was getting. Had he been led down the garden path, as Benny suggested? Zwiebach turned on his desk computer and went on-line to the financial database provided by Reuters. He immediately called up the chart tracking the gold price in London.

It was still headed down. If it continued on that path, it was inevitable that there would be another margin call on Monday.

"That fucking Frenchman!" the Swiss attorney yelled at the computer screen.

Maybe he needed a second opinion. Whom else could he call?

Barely a second later he slapped himself on the forehead. How could he have been so stupid? How could he have ignored the obvious? Who in his circle of friends was, after all, in charge of one of the biggest hoards of gold on earth? Who was it who also undoubtedly met with Charles Black on a regular basis? Who, therefore, would be in a better position to tell him whether or not the United States Federal Reserve Board was about to lower interest rates against all expectations and cause the price of gold to go up—and, more important, to *stay* up?

Dr. Samuel Schweizer, that's who. If only he had called Schweizer *before* he had followed that fucking Frenchman's advice and contracted for all that gold. Well, better late than never.

Zwiebach reached for his phone and started to punch in the number of the Swiss National Bank. But then he stopped abruptly and put the phone back down. Not so fast, he told himself. Sammy Schweizer was a very careful, cagey guy. He was also quite taken with himself. Getting that job running Switzerland's central bank had brought out the worst in him. It was only a matter of time before he began referring to himself as "we."

On the other hand, it was Schweizer who had brought the Sardinian to him. This set the Swiss attorney to thinking once more. Why? Why had stodgy, careful, pompous Dr. Samuel Schweizer done that?

To be sure, over the years, when Schweizer had still been with the General Bank of Switzerland, he had referred more than one client to Zwiebach. But they had always been people like Charles Black and his wife. This was different. Radically different. Even the most charitable assessment of the Sardinian would describe him as being of uncertain background, dubious character, and bad taste. Where Zwiebach was concerned, these flaws had been more than compensated for by the fact that Pietro di Cagliari obviously had a lot of money. But Samuel Schweizer knew a lot of people with a lot of money. So there had to be something else. But what?

Maybe it didn't matter. It just mattered that there was *another* something that linked—yes, that was the right word—*linked* his old friend, the Swiss central banker, to his new client, the Sardinian of questionable credentials.

Zwiebach liked this line of reasoning. For it led to the conclusion that if that link existed, then Sammy would have a vested interest in keeping the Sardinian happy. Right? Well, if the Sardinian were to find out that the initial $20 million that Zwiebach had invested for him in gold futures had gone up in smoke, he would definitely be rather *un*happy. Pietro di Cagliari would be even more upset if he knew that the gold price had kept falling and that the same thing was happening to the additional $5 million of his money that Zwiebach had put up following the bank's margin call.

Zwiebach picked up the phone again. This time he finished dialing the number of the Swiss National Bank. He managed to get right through to the chairman's secretary, but then he was put on hold. She obviously was not going to put him through to her boss until she was sure that Schweizer knew who Zwiebach was and, if he did, actually wanted to talk to him.

"*Salü*, Hans," Schweizer said when he finally came on the line, using the same standard greeting that all students, including the two of them, had used when they had attended *Gymnasium* together in the early 1960s. But then the tone changed.

"What is of such importance that you are calling me at the office?"

Pompous ass.

"*Salü*, Sammy," Zwiebach said. "And I must apologize for disturbing you at the office. I'm not calling you on any official business. I just wondered whether you might be free after work today to meet me for coffee. To discuss a private matter."

This produced a long pause on the other end. "Certainly," Schweizer finally said. "Do you have a suggestion?"

"How about five o'clock at the Café Limmat?"

"I'll see you there."

21

The Café Limmat was situated in the old part of Zurich, just a few minutes' walk from both the National Bank and Zwiebach's law office on the Bahnhofstrasse. Zwiebach left his office at a quarter to five that Friday afternoon, umbrella in hand, since it was a typical early-summer day in Zurich, meaning that it was raining off and on. There were a lot of people on the Bahnhofstrasse, many presumably headed for the Bahnhof itself, where they would board trains bound for weekend destinations south of the Alps, where the sun was sure to be shining.

Samuel Schweizer was already seated at

a table well to the rear of the coffeehouse when Zwiebach arrived. The place was almost empty because of both the hour and the weather.

"*Sauwetter*," Zwiebach exclaimed as he took his place across table from the central banker, "although you could hardly tell from that tan you are sporting. Been on a short vacation with Emma?"

"As you know, earlier this month I was on business in Italy, in Rome and Sardinia, but I managed to get some sun in between," Schweizer replied. "Then, yes, last weekend I was with Emma at our chalet in Montana."

"And the weather was good there?"

"Very good. Sunny and warm," Schweizer replied, although he knew this only from hearsay, since he had spent almost that entire weekend in bed with Simone Bouverie.

"Well, you did mention Sardinia, and it is because of our mutual friend there that I asked you to join me here."

At this point the waitress arrived, and both men ordered a cappuccino. They waited until it was served before continuing.

"I assume you are referring to Pietro di Cagliari," Schweizer then said.

"Yes."

"Did he change his mind?"

"No, no. Quite the contrary. The initial sum he wants invested arrived already on Monday. Fifty million dollars."

"So what's the problem? Has it something to do with the person of Cagliari?"

"No. It's something that I did. Quite fool-ishly did, I should add," Zwiebach said.

"Like what?"

"First let me back up a bit. Last Saturday night I was at a dinner party where the guest of honor was a certain Philippe de Bonneville."

"That scoundrel," Schweizer said. "He's nothing but an out-and-out speculator who is going to get his comeuppance one of these days, believe me."

"I'm sure you're right, Sammy. At least *now* I am sure you're right."

"Why now?"

"Because I subsequently followed his investment advice."

"Which was?"

"To buy gold. Because interest rates in America are going to go down instead of up as everybody expects, meaning that inflation fears will be rekindled and the gold price will soar as a result."

"So he's the one who's been behind all this activity in the gold market this week."

"I'm afraid so. I must admit that I also contributed to the action."

"How much gold did you buy?"

"Well, I didn't exactly buy gold. I bought gold futures."

"For your own account?"

"No. In fact, that brings us precisely to the heart of the matter. I bought gold futures for the account of Pietro di Cagliari."

"With his permission, of course."

"Not exactly. He signed a fiduciary agreement under which I could invest his funds at my discretion."

Samuel Schweizer said nothing. But his head began to shake back and forth as he fixed his eyes on Zwiebach.

"How much gold did you contract for?"

"I don't know the exact amount. It involves futures contracts on the Comex in New York. Are you familiar with such things?"

"Of course I am. How many contracts?"

"Sixteen thousand?"

"Sixteen thousand?"

"Yes."

"At what average price?"

Zwiebach told him.

"Hans," Schweizer said, "you are a greater fool in financial matters than I thought you were."

"I'm not going to argue with that."

"Did you get a margin call?"

"Yes. This morning. For five million dollars. That is, of course, on top of the twenty million dollars I put down in the first place."

"Have you at least *now* told Cagliari about all this?"

"No. I first wanted to seek out your advice on the matter."

"Why *my* advice?"

"Because it was, after all, *you* who referred him to me, Sammy."

"Which makes *me* responsible for this

fiasco? Is that what you are saying?" Schweizer was now furious. His tan had even disappeared.

"Of course not," the Swiss lawyer answered.

"Then what *are* you saying?"

"I'm actually *asking*—for your professional advice. Should I just ride this out, knowing that what Philippe de Bonneville said is going to be right in the end? Or should I cut my losses on Monday and tell Pietro di Cagliari?"

"Why do you think I can give you advice on that?"

"Well, because I assume you must know Charles Black, and you'd have as good a feeling for what he is going to do about interest rates as anybody—certainly a better feeling than that of Philippe de Bonneville."

"Why, all of a sudden, are you bringing up the name of Charles Black?" Schweizer asked, obviously puzzled.

Zwiebach told him about his conversation with the man running Citibank's Zurich office. That it had been Benny who had brought the name up.

"Furthermore," Zwiebach added, "as you might recall, many years ago, when you were still with the General Bank, you referred Black and his wife to me. They subsequently became clients."

"So why don't you ask *him* for advice?" Schweizer asked, his sarcasm apparent.

Zwiebach chose to ignore the mockery. "Because if I did, I'm sure he could hardly give me an answer."

"Don't you realize that the same applies to me?" the head of Switzerland's central bank said.

"Of course I do, Sammy. The last thing I would ask of you would be anything that might compromise your official position. Maybe we should just finish our coffee and forget that this conversation ever took place."

"I could not agree more. So let's change the subject."

"Agreed. Tell me more about your chalet. My wife loves to hike. Maybe she and I could visit you and Emma there, one of these weekends."

"I'm sure Emma would love that."

"Then I'll suggest to my wife that she give Emma a ring tomorrow and—"

Schweizer broke in. "No, we won't be here this weekend. We're going over to Basel."

"Business or pleasure?"

"Both. Emma loves the museums there. And I have business. Actually, I'll be having dinner with Charles Black on Saturday," Schweizer said, adding, "not that that will change anything."

"Of course not."

Minutes later the two men left the Café Limmat and went their separate ways. Zwiebach headed home to have dinner with his wife. Sammy hurried to the apartment of Simone Bouverie, where he hoped to resume where they had left off in his mountain chalet the prior weekend.

22

The next night, the ten central bankers who ran the world's monetary system met for dinner as the Schützenhaus restaurant in Basel, as they always did on the Saturday night prior to their monthly meeting at the Bank for International Settlements. As usual, the president of the central bank of the host country, Dr. Samuel Schweizer, took his place next to the most powerful man at the table, the Chairman of the Federal Reserve Board, Charles Black.

Dinner had barely begun when Charles Black, addressing the entire table, asked, "Does anybody have any idea what was behind this week's flurry in the gold market?"

Everybody there knew that this was going to be the principal subject of discussion that evening. For it was they who, either directly or indirectly, controlled the vast majority of the world's gold stocks— stored at Fort Knox and in the subterranean vaults under the Federal Reserve Bank in New York, or in similar underground facilities beneath the marble halls of the National Bank of Switzerland and the Bank of England.

"It did not start in London," replied the

Governor of the Bank of England, Sir Robert Neville. "At the gold fixing on Monday morning, the price barely moved. It was only when the futures markets opened later in the day in New York that all of a sudden the price began to shoot up."

"So it was the Americans," stated the president of the Banque de France, who, like most of the elite who governed the affairs of his country, held Americans in undisguised contempt.

"I don't think so," said Dr. Samuel Schweizer.

"Then who?" the French banker demanded.

"One of your countrymen, *monsieur*," replied the Swiss.

"Really," Sir Robert Neville said. "Do tell us more."

"I am sure you are all familiar with the name Philippe de Bonneville. He runs the Phoenix hedge fund out of London. Exactly a week ago, at a dinner party in Zurich, he advised a small circle of his principal backers that he was investing heavily in gold futures, and that they should do likewise. Apparently they did."

"How could you possibly know this so precisely?" the French banker asked.

"Because a trusted friend of mine was at that dinner party," Schweizer replied.

"And this friend of yours, did he also tell you *why* Monsieur de Bonneville was investing in gold?" It was the Belgian who asked.

"Because of what we will be doing. More immediately, what our American colleague is about to do."

"And that is?"

"Move from a posture of monetary restraint to one of monetary accommodation," Schweizer said, demonstrating his thorough command of the obtuse terminology of Wall Street.

"Is that true?" the Frenchman demanded of Charles Black.

"Of course not. In fact, quite the opposite," Black replied.

After that, the table-wide discussion ended, but the buzz around the table did not. For this had been a moment of high drama for the central bankers gathered there, one that had to be relished, meaning discussed to death.

Samuel Schweizer, the man responsible for what was now proving to be the evening's entertainment, did not participate further. He suddenly appeared to withdraw within himself. He was not really missed, since Schweizer was hardly known as the life of the party.

But that evening it was more than his usual reticence that was reflected in his behavior. Charles Black's answer to the Frenchman's question had set his mind in rapid motion, because that response had been clear and unequivocal. That coming Wednesday the Federal Reserve Board was going to announce that it was raising interest rates, not lowering them, as Philippe de Bonneville had pronounced so convincingly—or at least so he had convinced his old friend Hans Zwiebach. Schweizer spun the numbers through his head.

Before all this had happened, gold had been at exactly four hundred dollars an ounce. The heavy buying at the beginning of the week had sent it soaring to $420. Zwiebach had bought in at an average price of $418. At the close on Friday the price had backed off to four hundred dollars. So Zwiebach had already lost the original collateral he had put up for the gold investment he had made for his client, which had prompted that $5 million margin call for additional collateral.

When the Fed made its announcement on Wednesday, the gold price would not only dip below the four-hundred-dollar level, but probably sink much lower as Bonneville and his followers scrambled for cover and unwound their positions. Which would wipe out the new cash margin that Zwiebach had put up for his client—even more if Zwiebach responded to the next margin call, an event that now appeared as inevitable as night following day.

That was an unfortunate simile. For it would inevitably bring out the dark side of his client when Pietro di Cagliari learned that thirty million of his dollars had gone up in smoke in one week!

That was only half of the bad news. The other related to Simone. Unfortunately, it also involved money.

He had hurried over to her apartment immediately after that meeting with Zwiebach at the Café Limmat. The evening had started off even better than he expected. She had a chilled bottle of Dom Perignon and two glasses waiting—in her bedroom.

But afterwards the conversation had turned to their future. Simone had made it clear that she wanted to maintain their relationship. To her credit, she had made it equally clear that she did not expect him to get a divorce. But then came the apartment. It was too small. It was noisy. It was not private enough—which should now be of concern to *both* of them, she had pointed out. But even when Sammy got her a larger apartment in a proper neighborhood, she could hardly be expected to sit in it all year, waiting for his phone call. Not that she wanted to stay in Zurich all year round, in any case. Just look at the weather outside! Cold, wet, miserable. And *this* was supposed to be *summer*? No, no. She wanted to spend a lot more time in places like—Sardinia.

Sardinia. That was obviously where the conversation had been heading from the very beginning.

Apparently she had gotten a phone call that afternoon from her friend Giselle. The call came from a hotel in Havana, where she and Pietro had been staying for a week now. She was bored to tears, since Pietro was gone most of the days but insisted that, for her own good, she stay in the hotel. Apparently Fidel Castro was on his deathbed, and things were becoming very tense in Cuba. The streets were no longer safe. But they were expecting the arrival of the yacht *Diana* on Monday and would then be flying back to Sardinia two days later.

Then Simone had come to the point. Pietro had specifically instructed Giselle to invite them down to the Cala di Volpe the following weekend. She had, of course, accepted the invitation. It was *very* important to her that they go, because Pietro had offered her a job—a job that could not be more ideal where both of them were concerned. Why both? Because along with the job came a suite at the Cala di Volpe anytime they wanted it. Plus the use of the Gulfstream IV. And the *Diana*.

And all that wouldn't cost Sammy anything.

What choice had he? Two more phone calls between Giselle and Simone, and it had all been arranged. The Gulfstream would pick them up at the Zurich airport at five next Friday and have them on the ground in Sardinia by seven. That evening the four of them could then once again have dinner on the outside terrace of the Cala di Volpe.

What would happen to all this when the Sardinian found out about those gold futures?

Sammy Schweizer knew the answer.

Everything would fall apart. Right there and then.

23

Monday morning at seven o'clock, Samuel Schweizer called Hans Zwiebach at his home in Zurich.

"Hold on," Zwiebach said. "I'm still in the bedroom. I'll go to my study."

Fifteen seconds later: "I'm ready."

Schweizer got right to the point. "Over the weekend I gave some thought to our conversation at the Café Limmat. And I've concluded that I probably have some *moral* responsibility concerning our mutual friend from Sardinia. Have you got a pen and paper?"

"Yes."

"What I want you do to is to immediately instruct the bank to sell all sixteen thousand of those gold futures contracts. Then I want you to go exactly the opposite way. Tell the bank that you are now going *short*, and that you want to go short sixteen thousand contracts. And tell them you want them to act aggressively. I suspect that they'll get good prices—around $397 an ounce—because they will be operating in a very active market. Philippe de Bonneville and probably a lot of his followers will be coming in on the other side, adding to their long positions as they try to get the gold price back on an upward trend."

"But that means that when I sell all those contracts, all the money I have put up so far for my client is going to be essentially wiped out, Sammy."

"I know that. But you still have uncommitted cash left."

"In my omnibus account, yes. Twenty-five million dollars."

"Use twenty of it as new cash margin."

"But if I now put him on the other side with sixteen thousand new contracts, and if the price starts to go back up as you suggest it will, then I'm going to start losing money all over again. I will have switched from wrong side to wrong side. That would be crazy."

"Do exactly as I told you, Hans," Schweizer said. "Otherwise I am going to wash my hands of this entire matter."

"All right, Sammy. Anything else?"

"I'll give you a call tomorrow morning. Same time."

"I'll be here. And thanks, Sammy. I'll do exactly as you said."

Forty-five minutes later, Hans Zwiebach was in his office and on the phone with the General Bank of Switzerland. That day he went short sixteen thousand gold contracts on the Comex exchange in New York. The average price was $397 an ounce, just as Samuel Schweizer had predicted. But just before the close, the price moved back up to four hundred dollars an ounce—which meant that Pietro now had a new paper loss of almost $5 million.

That night, Zwiebach slept badly. The next morning, again at seven exactly, his phone rang. This time the attorney was in his home study, waiting for the call. He picked up on the first ring.

"This is Sammy Schweizer," the caller said.

"Thank God you called. Have you been watching—"

Schweizer interrupted. "Of course. Now tell me, how much of Pietro's cash do you still have left outside the account?"

"About five million dollars."

"Okay. Tell the General Bank you want to apply all of it to increasing your short position on the Comex."

"I can't do that. We're already down another five million."

"I know what I'm doing, Hans. I'll call you again on Thursday morning."

With that, Schweizer hung up.

An hour later the General Bank had its new instructions. The rest of that day, Dr. Hans Zwiebach did not check the gold price even once. When he got home that evening, he had two scotches before dinner, a bottle of Dôle with dinner, and two cognacs after dinner. Even so, when he finally went to bed he had trouble falling asleep.

When he woke up, he decided to stay home that day. He phoned his secretary to tell her that. While he had her on the line, he asked if, by any chance, the General Bank of Switzerland had called. When she said no, Zwiebach already felt a little better. At least it was not another margin call. Because if it had been, he could not have met it. All of the Sardinian's original $50 million had either been lost or was tied up as collateral in New York.

That thought bothered him the rest of the morning. He decided what he needed was a change of scenery. So he got into his car and headed south along the Lake of Zurich. When he got to Rapperswil, he decided to have a late lunch. He chose a small restaurant right on the water. After lunch he dawdled over a glass of white wine, watching the tourists strolling the promenade. He then decided to join them, and took a long walk along the lake. It was seven o'clock that evening before he was back in his car. He immediately called his wife on the car phone to tell her that he was running late, and not to bother preparing dinner for him.

He'd barely entered the house an hour later, when the phone rang. It was the hotshot derivatives-trading yuppie at the General Bank of Switzerland.

"Herr Doktor Zwiebach?"

"Yes. What can I do for you?" he asked, his voice as cool as he could manage.

"I apologize for calling you at home like this—I got the number from Urs Stucker, by the way," the young banker said.

"But all hell broke out on the Comex in New York. The Federal Reserve Board bumped up interest rates this afternoon. The Comex just closed in New York. At the close, gold was down twenty-five dollars an ounce."

He had twenty thousand contracts outstanding. Each dollar drop in the gold price therefore represented a profit of $2 million. Zwiebach's mental calculator went to work:

If one U.S. dollar = $2 million profit
Then twenty-five U.S. dollars = $50 million profit

But that was only part of the picture.

"How much cash margin is still intact?" Zwiebach now asked.

"Twenty-five million dollars," came the answer.

Zwiebach's mental calculator went back into action:

$25 million ;pl $50 million = $75 million

Pietro di Cagliari not only had all his money back. He was now ahead by $25 million. He, Zwiebach, had just gotten an investment return of fifty percent in a matter of a couple of weeks!!

"But just so you don't get too excited yet, Herr Doktor," the yuppie now said. "Although you now have a big profit *on paper*, even if we decide to start liquidating your position tomorrow, who knows what prices we will get. Gold could move right back up to where it came from. Then again, maybe not. What do you want me to do?"

"I'll let you know."

With that, Zwiebach hung up.

Should he now call Samuel Schweizer?

No. That might upset him. It might also be asking for trouble. This was a very touchy matter. Which raised an issue: What if a connection were ever to be established between what had just happened to Zwiebach's client's account and Samuel Schweizer? Big trouble for both of them. Real big. So no more phone calls from his office to Schweizer's office at the Swiss National Bank, where secretaries were always involved. He would wait for Sammy to call him at home in the morning, as he promised to do.

Zwiebach's lawyer mind kept working.

It wasn't just phone calls. What about the paper trail at the bank? Or even in his office?

So, what to do?

Answer: Put the trades in some other client's account at the General Bank of Switzerland. It would have to be a B account governed by a fiduciary agreement, just like the one he had set up for Pietro di Cagliari. And the beneficial owner of the account would have to be, like Cagliari, a foreigner who showed up only occasionally to find out how he was doing.

But even that could lead to complications. What if the client showed up unexpectedly and wanted an instant computer printout of the activity in his B account since his last visit? No, that wouldn't do.

But he was getting closer. Then he had the answer.

It had to be a *dormant* B account—still open, but with a zero or token balance.

But whose? He had dozens of such accounts that were still on the books of the General Bank of Switzerland, but in which there had been no activity for years. One never knew why. In some cases, no doubt, it was simply because the reason for opening the account in the first place was no longer valid. Maybe the client had moved. Or run out of funds, temporarily. Or died.

But in this case a dead client wouldn't work, because if, for whatever reason, the transactions in this account became a subject of investigation, it had to be perfectly logical that it had *not* been he, Zwiebach, who had masterminded the trades, but rather the client who was hiding behind the facade of the B account that was *technically* in Zwiebach's name.

But still, *any* client who was not dead— really dead—might show up. Unless there were compelling reasons for him not to.

Now he was getting closer still.

A Colombian came to mind. In fact, *three* Colombians came to mind. None of them would show up now that the Swiss government had reversed its former liberal policy regarding drugs, meaning that the Swiss border police arrested anyone who even faintly resembled a drug dealer. And his three Colombians definitely were drug dealers. But one might still slip through, and if *he* then got suspicious, Zwiebach might have to face some very unpleasant consequences.

So it had to be a nonviolent type of client who had good reasons for not showing up.

Then he had it. It had been staring him in the face all along. Who filled the bill in all respects?

Charles Black.

His account had been dormant for years—ever since he moved away from London. But it was still alive and well. Because it had been set up as a B account, it, like Pietro di Cagliari's, was also in Zwiebach's name.

Zwiebach agonized another half hour, pacing up and down the entire time. Then he finally made up his mind. He picked up the Zurich phone book and went to the listings of Stuckers. There was only one *Urs* Stucker, so he noted the number and then dialed it.

"Urs, it's Hans Zwiebach," he began. "I hate to call you at home like this, but—"

"No problem, Herr Doktor. What can I do for you?"

"Well, I just discovered that there's been a mixup in two of my client accounts at the bank, and I'd appreciate your help in straightening them out right away tomorrow morning."

"I apologize for any—"

Zwiebach cut in. "It wasn't your fault. It was that yuppie in your trading department who handled some of those derivatives for me."

"I remember. Gold futures."

"Exactly. Well, he got it right the first go-round, when he went long sixteen thousand contracts on the Comex for account number Q 178-5997. He also got it right when he sold those contracts. Follow me so far, Urs?"

"I'm writing it down. What was the client's account number again?"

"Q 178-5997."

"Got it."

"Now the *subsequent* trades in gold futures *should* have been made for *another* client's account. It begins with *J* as in 'Jacques,' and the numbers are 747-2239. I repeat: J 747-2239. Got that?"

"J 747-2239. Got it. So what do you want me to do?"

"Cancel all those subsequent trades in the first account, and enter them in the second."

"Got it."

"After that, all additional transactions should have gone through sub-account number J 747-2239."

"Where did the cash margin come from?"

"All of it came from my omnibus *Kontokurrentkonto* number 77-65-39-44.

That's the general account I use for incoming cash before I disburse it to the appropriate individual accounts. You've got all that on file in the bank."

"I'll get to that file first thing tomorrow. How did this get so screwed up?"

"It all started when funds from my omnibus account were allocated to the wrong client account. Half should have gone to one account. The other half to the second account—the J account. That yuppie trader of yours talks so much he never gets a chance to listen."

"The bank is now full of those types. I've got three more years to go before retirement, and believe me, Herr Doktor, I can hardly wait."

"I believe you, Urs."

"I assume you will follow up in writing with all this," Urs Stucker now said.

"I'd prefer not to. It would mess up my records something awful. I would prefer, Urs, if you could just do this internally. Simply cancel those transactions"— Zwiebach used the German term *Stornieren*—"and have them posted to the account to which they should have been posted in the first place."

There was the slightest of pauses on the other end. Then: "Let me think about it, Herr Doktor. I'll handle it personally and discreetly. But after this, if you intend to keep investing in derivatives, maybe I should handle them for you. I'm not an expert in the field, but if you tell me exactly what you want done, I can certainly do it for you."

"Perfect. I'll probably be calling you again, early tomorrow morning at the bank. And, Urs, I know you like cigars— Partagas, if I remember correctly."

"You have an excellent memory, Herr Doktor."

"I've always enjoyed working with you, Urs," Zwiebach said before hanging up.

The next call went to the Caribbean Bank for Trade and Finance— CBTF— where it was midafternoon. The owner and general manager of this obscure financial institution was a German Swiss who had risen to the level of managing director at the United Bank of Switzerland in Zurich before he got into a bit of trouble. Zwiebach had represented him, and— after arranging for "reparations," meaning restoring a portion of the funds that he had mistakenly misappropriated—had gotten him off before the authorities were brought in. His grateful client had subsequently moved to the Turks and Caicos Islands in the West Indies, where he had founded the Caribbean Bank for Trade and Finance, using those misappropriated funds that were left over as capital.

"Werner," Zwiebach said, once his ex-client was on the line, "I'd like to open up two new accounts. The first will be a joint account in the names of John Smith— that's not his real name, of course—and myself. The second will be in the name of

Samuel Schweizer. Both will be simple checking accounts. The utmost discretion is required. Utmost. Understand?"

"Perfectly."

"I have some of your signature cards here. I will arrange for them to be sent. But activate the accounts immediately."

"Consider it done. Would you like to have the new account numbers now?"

"Why not?"

"Hold on." Then: "S 1111 and S 2222. Easy to remember, right?"

"Thanks, Werner. How's the weather there?"

"Better than in Zurich."

"Maybe I'll come to visit you one of these days."

"Then you'll be my guest. I just built a new beach house on Grand Turk. You'll love it."

After Zwiebach hung up, he went to the coffee table in front of the fireplace where he kept a humidor. He withdrew a Partagas 8-9-8 and lit it carefully. As he did so, he decided to not only send Urs Stucker a couple of boxes of the same, but to throw in a humidor. He'd have to go back to the phone book and look up Stucker's home address, since it would hardly look good if a package like that was delivered to the bank.

24

At exactly seven the next morning, the phone in Hans Zwiebach's study rang. It was Samuel Schweizer again.

"Feel better this morning, Hans?" were his first words.

"I've never felt better in my life," the lawyer replied. "But what now?"

"Tell the bank to cover your entire short position as quickly and aggressively as possible."

"But wouldn't that mean that we will be helping to push the gold price back up again?"

"Listen. Gold was down twenty-five dollars an ounce at the close in New York. Right? Why?"

"Speculators panicked when the Federal Reserve moved interest rates up instead of down."

"Right. But for the moment the operational word is 'panic.' I'm not just talking about the Comex in New York, where we've got our position. Remember, the spot bullion markets in Europe were closed *before* that panic started in New York. Now they are going to *open* five hours before New York does. And what's going to happen? The speculators who were on the wrong side, and couldn't get out before the close yesterday in New York, are now going to try to get out first thing this morning in London. That will cause the spot bullion price to drop even further. When we then start to cover later in New York, conditions will be just about perfect from our point of view."

"How can you be so sure of all this, Sammy?"

"Because it's my job, Hans. Plus the fact that I made a few phone calls last night to the powers that be at the Bank of England. They have been talking to the banks that participate in the gold fixings in London. And this is what the banks told them. At this morning's fixing—which will happen in about three hours—given the number of sell orders already in hand, they will have no choice but to drop the bullion price yet another notch. Hans, I hope by now that you have figured out that I know what I'm doing."

"I certainly have."

"With all this turmoil in the financial markets, I'm going to be very busy at the bank both today and tomorrow morning," Schweizer said. "Then I'll be leaving on a short trip to Sardinia. I'll call you from the airport to see how things worked out."

Things worked out almost exactly as Schweizer had predicted.

The General Bank of Switzerland covered his entire position on the Comex before the close on Thursday. At noon on Friday, Urs Stucker called from the General Bank of Switzerland.

"I've completely closed out your gold position," he began, "but before I finalize the allocation of all your trades on the Comex—longs and shorts—to those two trading accounts, I'd prefer to review everything with you."

"I understand, Urs," Zwiebach replied.

"I know it's lunch hour, but would it be convenient if I came over to your office right now?" the banker asked. "The sooner I can close out everything, the better. Otherwise our internal auditors might get nervous."

"I'll be waiting for you."

Ten minutes later, Urs Stucker arrived. He was carrying a beat-up briefcase that was a perfect complement to his baggy pants, scuffed brown shoes, gray pallor, and stooped shoulders. He not only looked a lot older than his self-confessed sixty-two years; he looked as if he might not even last out the day.

"Let's sit over there at the conference table," Zwiebach said, "and let's both have a cigar."

The banker sat down and immediately began to methodically extract various documents from his briefcase, arranging them neatly on the conference table. Zwiebach removed two Partagas 8-9-8s from the humidor on his desk and then proceeded to carefully clip their ends. Then he handed one to Urs Stucker. The banker took a long wooden match from the box on the table, struck it, and carefully began lighting his cigar.

The ceremony completed, he leaned back, took a big puff, exhaled, and said, "Herr Doktor, I would suggest you also light yours—because as you will now see, you have a very good reason to celebrate. You have become the proud father of a lot of money. And it only took a week instead of nine months."

He cackled at his little joke.

"How big is the baby?" Zwiebach asked.

The Swiss banker shoved a single piece of paper across the table.

"That is the current combined cash position—after all the contracts have been liquidated—of the two trading accounts you have been using for these gold transactions from the original fifty-million-dollar cash deposit that came in from Italy—Q 178-5597 and J 747-2239. The first account was unfortunately wiped out. It has a balance of less than a hundred thousand dollars. But take a look at the other account."

Zwiebach put on his reading glasses, picked up the paper, and looked. There was just one number: $107,485,997.00.

It was even better than he had thought. Zwiebach put the paper back down on the table—carefully. Then he said, "You are right, Urs. This calls for both a cigar *and* a cognac."

He went to the eighteenth-century armoire that housed his bar, and pulled down one of the great treasures that was stored there on the top shelf—a nineteenth-century bottle of Gaston de Lagrange V.V.S.O.P. He poured two glasses and handed one to Urs Stucker. Holding the other glass in his left hand, he then very tenderly soaked the tip of his cigar in the ancient golden liquid. Two minutes later he finally lit it, then raised his glass. "Urs, here's to what I am sure will remain a long and mutually profitable association. *Zum Wohl!*"

Ten minutes and one hundred dollars' worth of cognac later, they returned to work, sorting out the trades. In the end, the net result was that one of Zwiebach's clients, Pietro di Cagliari, suffered a huge paper loss, while another client, Charles Black, now Chairman of the Federal Reserve, made an immense profit.

Zwiebach's final instructions to Urs Stucker dealt with the disposition—by wire transfer—of the huge profits that had accumulated in Charles Black's account. They had to be made to disappear. But they had to be made to disappear in such a way that the paper trail would lead...nowhere.

The obscure, desertlike islands of Turks and Caicos were as close to nowhere as you could get, and there was no blinder alley than account number S 1111 at the Caribbean Bank for Trade and Finance, which was domiciled there. By Monday morning the balance in that account would go from zero to a sum well into eight digits.

Urs Stucker left the lawyer's office shortly after 2:00 P.M. As soon as he was gone, Zwiebach asked his secretary to call the courier service they normally used. He had a delivery that he wanted made later that afternoon.

At four, Samuel Schweizer called.

"How did everything turn out?" he immediately asked.

"Where are you?" Zwiebach countered.

"The General Aviation terminal at Kloten Airport."

"When does your flight leave?"

"In an hour."

"I'm going to have an envelope summarizing the results hand-delivered to you. You can pass it on to Pietro di Cagliari when you get to Sardinia. I assume, of course, that it is he whom you are planning on visiting."

"It is. And I like your idea."

As soon as he hung up, Zwiebach changed his mind. Why not deliver the good news in person? A half hour later he pulled up in front of the small terminal at Kloten Airport that served noncommercial aviation. There were only a dozen or so people inside. Dr. Samuel Schweizer was one of them. An extremely attractive redhead in her mid-thirties was another. They sat side by side. They were also holding hands.

Now he knew what was making Sammy

Schweizer run. They had not yet noticed him, so he went directly to the counter.

"I'm supposed to deliver something to a Dr. Samuel Schweizer."

"I just got here," the clerk behind the counter told Zwiebach. "I'll page him."

It was a very uncomfortable Samuel Schweizer who immediately joined Zwiebach.

"I know you expected a courier," Zwiebach said, "but then I thought I'd come out myself. Here's the envelope. It's not sealed. You probably will want to open it later. I think you'll like what's inside. I came because I wanted to thank you personally, Sammy, for getting me out of a very deep hole. Believe me, I'll never forget it. You are a real friend."

Samuel Schweizer's attitude changed immediately. He actually smiled. "I don't have that many friends, Hans," he said, "so I really appreciate what you just said. Now you go home and enjoy your weekend."

The two men shook hands, and Zwiebach immediately turned and left the lounge. But just before he did, he took one more look at the redhead.

25

The Gulfstream IV was high over the Alps, at 32,000 feet, when it began to level out. The steward immediately appeared with a tray and offered his two passengers beluga caviar and a glass of Aigle poured from a well-chilled bottle. Once he had served them, he left the tray on the table that separated them.

"Wasn't this a good idea?" Simone Bouverie asked.

"Very good," Sammy Schweizer replied.

"So start enjoying it. Stop thinking about work. Why did that man have to deliver that envelope? Can't the people at your bank at least leave you alone on weekends?"

"It's not work. It's private."

"Oh. Well, if you want to read what's in it, go ahead. I'm perfectly happy." She helped herself to some more caviar, and then, with the professional touch of a former stewardess, retrieved the bottle of Swiss white wine from the ice bucket. Sammy, sitting opposite her, could not help but admire her decolletage as she leaned across the table to refill his glass. Then he opened the unsealed, unmarked envelope. Inside was a single piece of plain paper bearing no letterhead, no return address, no signature—just two lines of type:

INITIAL BALANCE: $50,000,000
CURRENT BALANCE: $107,485,997

"My God," Schweizer exclaimed.

"What's wrong?" Simone asked, instantly concerned.

"Nothing. Quite the contrary. I was

just surprised, that's all. Very pleasantly surprised."

"You're flushed."

"Really? Well, it's probably the result of drinking at this altitude."

"I think it's because you've been working too hard and don't know how to unwind."

She reached across the table to take his hand.

"We're supposed to join Pietro and Giselle for dinner at eight. I think it best if you have a little relaxation beforehand. Why don't we move to the lounge area at the back of the plane? I'll bring a blanket."

Dr. Samuel Schweizer still appeared flushed when he and Simone walked onto the terrace of the Cala di Volpe at eight that evening. Simone appeared radiant. The ever-observant Pietro di Cagliari immediately picked up on it as he rose to greet them.

"Ah, the romantic Swiss couple returns. Welcome back to the Emerald Coast."

Giselle warmly embraced Simone as the two men shook hands. As soon as they were seated, Schweizer reached inside his jacket and withdrew the now-sealed plain white envelope.

"Dr. Zwiebach asked me to deliver this to you in person."

After accepting it, Pietro said, "Should I open it? But if I do and it contains bad news, that could spoil an evening that

241

seems to be getting off to a very good start."

"Open it," Simone said. She seemed on the verge of saying more when Schweizer cut in.

"Perhaps it's confidential. So you might prefer to wait until later."

"No, no," Pietro said. "Because wondering what's in it would spoil my evening anyway."

He tore it open.

His three companions watched as he withdrew the single piece of paper, unfolded it, and read.

Pietro then put the paper back into the envelope and placed it in the inside breast pocket of his white dinner jacket.

"You were right," he said to Schweizer. "It is confidential."

Suddenly an agitated headwaiter appeared with a cellular phone. Stooping to speak to Pietro, he said, "I know you have told me never to bring a *telefonino* to the table when you have guests, but it is from the *Diana*, and they have been trying to get through to you all day. Now that they've gotten through, they are afraid they will lose the connection."

"Give it to me," Pietro said.

The phone call lasted just a few minutes. Pietro listened the entire time, only interrupting three times to say *"Bene."*

After he had given the cellular back to the waiter, who had been hovering in the background, Pietro turned to Schweizer and said, "I'd like to have some words with you in private. Would you mind joining me in the hotel for a few minutes?"

He rose from the table, and Schweizer immediately did the same.

"Excuse us, ladies," Pietro said. The two men left the terrace and disappeared into the hotel lobby.

"What's that all about?" Simone asked Giselle as soon as they were alone.

"No doubt the same thing we went to Havana for."

"And what was that?"

"This may sound strange, but I'm not really sure. It must have something to do with Castro dying. And with an American who drives around Havana in a Rolls-Royce. I saw him twice from the terrace outside our suite at the Hotel Nacional as he was leaving after meeting with Pietro. He would come to the hotel alone and call up to our room. Then Pietro would disappear for a few hours. I know he's American from his accent, because one time I answered the phone."

"So who is he?" Simone asked.

"I don't know. Pietro never introduced us. In fact, he never brought him up to our suite. They would talk somewhere else in the hotel. I do know this, though: On the day before we flew back, they went out on the *Diana*. So I thought maybe Pietro was selling the yacht to him. But apparently not."

"How was Havana otherwise?"

"Not worth talking about. How are things working out with Sammy? He seemed pretty happy when you got here."

"He should have been," Simone responded. "He had just been initiated into the Mile-High Club."

The new club member and Pietro di Cagliari had found a secluded corner in the hotel lobby.

"First, I want to thank you for introducing me to your friend Dr. Zwiebach," Pietro di Cagliari said. "That envelope you brought contained the results of his initial investments. They are fantastic."

"I'm glad to hear that," Schweizer said.

"Now I want to enlist Zwiebach's help in another matter that has just come up," Pietro said. "It's rather urgent. I wonder if he would mind if we called him at home."

"You mean now?" Schweizer asked.

"Yes. Would you by any chance know his home number?"

Samuel Schweizer had called that number three times during the past week.

"Actually, I do."

"Then if you agree, I'll get a telephone, and perhaps you can dial it for me."

The telephone arrived, and Samuel Schweizer dialed the number. When Zwiebach answered, he said, "Samuel Schweizer here. Is it convenient for you to talk?"

"Yes. Where are you?"

"Sardinia. I am with our mutual friend. He wants to talk to you."

Pietro took over. "Dr. Zwiebach, needless to say, I am most pleased with the results of your managing my money. As a small—very small—token of my appreciation, I want you to implement our fee arrangement immediately."

He listened to Zwiebach's response and then said, "I know it was to be based on annual performance. This will be an exception. Take your percentage now, and we will start over. Okay?"

Again he listened. Finally he said, "If you transferred the profits to an account at that other bank, you must have your reasons. In any case, it's fine with me. Now," he continued, "another matter has come up."

At this point, Pietro looked over at Samuel Schweizer in a way that indicated quite obviously that he preferred to continue his conversation with Zwiebach in private. The Swiss banker immediately caught on and, without a further word, headed back to the terrace to rejoin the ladies.

Pietro then resumed his conversation with Zwiebach. "I have a problem. A new client of mine wants to withdraw a substantial amount of money from the Bahamas branch of the General Bank of Switzerland. The amount involved is fifty million dollars. But he cannot go to Nassau in person. He can also not send a letter of instructions with his signature attached. He is at sea. But he wants the transfer done

245

no later than the end of next week. Can you help me?"

Five minutes later, Pietro di Cagliari rejoined the party of three at his usual table on the terrace of the Cala di Volpe.

"Let's eat," he said.

"But after we eat, let's all go to bed early, Pietro," Giselle said. "I want to take Simone and Sammy on a tour of the Costa Smeralda early tomorrow morning, before it gets too hot."

"Good idea. Take my driver," Pietro said.

The two women exchanged glances. Sammy continued to stare at the menu.

The three of them were under way at nine the next morning. Pietro had stayed behind to make some urgent phone calls.

The Emerald Coast fully lived up to its name that morning. It was a jewel in every sense of the word. Of course, it was the emerald-green waters off the northeastern coast of the island that provided the stunning background. But on the hills that rose from the sea, perched on rocky ledges, were jewels of another kind: villas that could find their match in only a few other pockets of outrageous opulence elsewhere on the Mediterranean, such as Cap d'Antibes or Marbella. As they slowly wended their way along the road that clung to the edge of those hills, Giselle explained the origins of such displays of wealth in such a remote location.

"It was the young prince Karim, the

son of Aly Khan, who originally spotted this place," Giselle explained. "He loved to sail, and it was here that he loved to sail most with his friends, especially his many girlfriends, it is said. That was in the 1950s. There was nothing here but sea and sand and rocks, a few peasants, and a few goats.

"But then, in 1957, his grandfather passed over Aly and selected the boy—some would say the playboy—prince to succeed him. Remember, it was his grandfather who used to be weighed in diamonds and gold as part of the Ismaili Moslems' commitment to tithe a portion of their income to their Imam and Khan. But I'm boring you, Sammy."

It was Simone who answered. "No, you are not. Go on, Giselle. I love it."

"Well, the new Aga Khan IV decided that he had to straighten up a bit. So he took some of the wealth that had now accrued to him, and started to put it into property development here on the Emerald Coast. First he built the Cala di Volpe hotel. Then he built a villa for himself. After that, one after the other, some of his friends did the same. The word spread among Europe's rich and famous, and this is what resulted."

Actually, there was very little to be seen from the road of "what resulted." At most, there were high steel gates with private roads beyond, leading to villas that could only be seen from the sea.

"Slow down," Giselle suddenly said to the driver. "Now pull up in front of the gate."

She took a remote control out of her bag and aimed at the gate— which slowly swung open.

"There are a half-dozen of these places for sale, and I checked them all out. This one is the best of the lot."

The car rounded a corner on the private road, and there it was. Pink stucco walls. Red tile roof. Water gushing from the mouths of the three dolphins that seemed caught in midair above the fountain that was the centerpiece of the circular drive leading to the villa's entrance.

"It is absolutely gorgeous!" Simone exclaimed.

"I have the keys. Let's go inside," Giselle said.

They followed her out of the car and up the stairs to the massive oak doors. When they entered the house, it was to step onto pink travertine marble. Beyond the entrance hall was the living room, with two fireplaces facing each other from opposite ends of the huge space. Through the windows of the living room one could see the pool area. The color of the water in the pool perfectly matched that of the emerald-green sea beyond. To the left of the pool were the tennis courts; to the right, a putting green.

"My God," Samuel Schweizer said. "What does this cost?"

"It's actually not that expensive for the Costa Smeralda," Giselle said. "It's listed at five million dollars, but I'm sure you could bargain it down to four and a half. And as you can see, it's virtually brand-new. The couple that built it never moved in. Instead they are involved in a messy divorce. They want to get rid of it as quickly as possible and divide up the cash."

"But even four and a half million dollars for what is really just a vacation home is an awful lot of money," Schweizer said. "How many people are there who could afford this?"

"More than you think," Giselle said.

"And maybe some people would use it for more than just vacations," Simone added.

The Gulfstream IV had them in Zurich at eight that evening. During the trip back, not a word was said about villas in Sardinia. In fact, very few words were exchanged. The good-bye at the door of Simone's apartment was equally cool, even abrupt. No suggestions were made about any future rendezvous in Sardinia, Crans-Montana, or anywhere else.

To make matters worse, his wife, Emma, gave him a rather odd look when he walked in the door of their apartment in Küsnacht a half hour later. Not that he really cared. What he cared about, deeply, was the woman who had opened up a whole new world for him.

But how to keep that woman and that world?

Maybe his friend Hans Zwiebach would have a suggestion. In any case, it wouldn't hurt to stay in touch. Because that new world, Simone, and Zwiebach now seemed inexorably linked through the person of Pietro di Cagliari.

26

The next morning, at the usual hour of seven, the phone rang at the home of Dr. Hans Zwiebach. It was Dr. Samuel Schweizer.

"How glad I am that you called," the lawyer said immediately. "We must talk. How about the Café Limmat again, at five?"

"Agreed. I'll see you there."

An hour later, Dr. Hans Zwiebach entered his office. The morning papers were laid out on his desk. The headlines on the front pages of all of them screamed the same message. In the *Neue Zürcher Zeitung* it read:

Fidel Castro Tot. Kuba in Chaos

The *Journal de Genève* said:

Fidel Castro Est mort. Chaos en Cuba

The *Herald Tribune*:

Castro Dead
Fighting in Streets of Havana

"That explains it," he said.

What explained it even further was a second article on the front page of the *Herald Tribune*.

Fugitive Robert Vesco
Disappears from Havana

Robert Vesco, who has been a fugitive from the law for almost three decades, has reportedly left Cuba, where he has spent the last eighteen years.

In the early 1970s, Vesco was charged by both Swiss and United States authorities with looting the IOS financial empire of Bernie Cornfeld of a reported half-billion dollars. IOS—Investors Overseas Service—was an organization based in Geneva that marketed mutual funds to investors all around the world. After fleeing Switzerland, Vesco lived in both Costa Rica and the Bahamas before being expelled by the authorities of both countries. He sought his final refuge in Cuba, where, for many years, he enjoyed the protection of Fidel Castro.

However, in a surprise move in June of 1995, Castro had Vesco arrested and held in a high-security prison in Havana on charges that he had committed "fraud and illicit activity" and "acts prejudicial to the economic plans of the state." It was hinted that Castro would extradite Vesco to the United States as a concession designed to ease tensions between the two countries in the hope that this would lead to a relaxation of the American trade embargo against Cuba. But no deal was struck.

Subsequently Vesco was tried in a Cuban court and sentenced to thirteen years in prison.

Earlier this year, in another surprise move, Vesco was suddenly released from prison and allowed to return to his home in Atabey, the choice suburb of Havana where many diplomats and VIPs reside.

Vesco's Rolls-Royce was found abandoned in Havana's port area. His yacht—which had remained anchored in Havana's harbor during Vesco's stay in prison—was reported to have left Cuban waters in the early hours of Sunday. Its current whereabouts are unknown.

Well, Zwiebach thought, *Cuba's loss will be my gain—if I can work things out along the lines I suggested to Pietro di Cagliari on Friday night.*

He picked up the phone and direct-dialed the number of the Caribbean Bank for Trade and Finance, on the island of Grand Turk in the West Indies. First he got the switchboard operator. She put him through to the president of the bank.

"Grützi," Zwiebach said in the Swiss-German dialect. *"Do isch Hans Zwiebach in Züri."*

"Dass isch e Überraschig," the exiled Swiss banker responded.

"Is your line secure?" Zwiebach continued.

"No. I'll call you back on a direct line that is."

Zwiebach gave him *his* direct number and hung up.

Ten seconds later, the banker was back on the phone. "I assume you're calling to see if the funds arrived. They did. Just a shade under $57.5 million. It was credited to account number S 1111."

"Good. Now I want you to debit that account $14,371,499 and credit half of the amount, or $7,185,749, to the other account I opened with you last week. That account number is S 2222."

"Got it. And the other half?"

"I want it transferred to my omnibus account at the General Bank of Switzerland in Zurich," Zwiebach said. Then he gave him the account number.

"I'll do it right away."

"Perfect. Now you'd better read those instructions back to me to make sure you've got all the numbers right."

Zwiebach listened, then said, "You got it. Now on to subject number two. I know that at first this will sound strange, but hear me out. Let me start with a hypothetical question."

"Go ahead."

"What if a dead man, or at least a man who was assumed to be dead, wanted to withdraw money from an account at, say, your bank?"

"He'd have to show up in person, alive.

Otherwise, if something went wrong, we would be on the hook."

"All right. Now, what if that person had his account with another bank, but showed up alive at *your* bank with all the necessary credentials, bank account numbers, and so forth? Could you persuade the *other* bank to allow their client to withdraw funds and have them transferred to *your* bank?"

"That would depend on which bank it was."

"How about the Nassau branch of the General Bank of Switzerland?"

"In principle, no problem. They know me well there. But, still, what you are suggesting—purely hypothetically, of course—is a bit unusual, to put it mildly."

"What if a front-end fee of one million dollars was made available to you, to use as you see fit—including providing incentives to one or two of your colleagues in Nassau to expedite the matter?"

"Then it would be just a matter of a few hours. How much are we talking about withdrawing?"

"Fifty million."

"Would it stay here in Grand Turk?"

"Initially. It would be credited to Account S 1111."

"Aha," the banker said, immediately adding, "I can do it. Who is it?"

"Robert Vesco."

There was a slight pause.

"No shit! But he's not supposed to be dead, is he?"

"He will be very soon."

"How will he get here? And when?"

"He'll come on a yacht—not his, but one that belongs to a friend of mine."

"When?"

"Wednesday night. They would prefer to bring him ashore when it is dark."

"They can bring him to my beach house on Grand Turk. That way he won't have to go to the bank. I can fax whatever they might need in Nassau directly from there, and personally vouch for the validity of the documentation."

"Perfect. Now, I'll need to know exactly where that beach house is."

"I'll fax a map to you within the hour."

"Great. Anything more that you need?"

"Yes. That fee. Up front."

"I will fax an authorization for you to take it out of account number S 1111. Also within the hour."

"You had better fax copies of the signature cards for both of those accounts at the same time."

"I will for S 1111. You'll get the one for S 2222 tomorrow. The originals will follow by mail."

"I like doing business with you," the Swiss banker in exile said.

"The feeling is mutual," the establishment Swiss lawyer in Zurich responded.

When Zwiebach entered the Café Limmat, Samuel Schweizer was waiting at the same table in the rear where they had met ten days earlier. Zwiebach alluded to that as soon as he sat down.

"A lot of water over the dam since we last met here."

"I agree. But it all worked out in the end," Schweizer said.

"How did Pietro react to the good news?" the lawyer asked.

"He was extremely pleased," Schweizer replied. "I think he also liked the sealed-envelope routine. That's his style."

"Good. Now here's another sealed envelope. This one's just for you."

He extracted it from his pocket and handed it across the table to Samuel Schweizer. "It's a token of my appreciation for your friendship, Sammy."

Schweizer accepted the envelope gingerly, stared at it hesitantly, then finally opened it.

There were two items inside: a signature card from the Caribbean Bank for Commerce and Finance, bearing the account number S 2222, and a blank piece of paper on which a single seven-digit figure had been typed: $7,185,749.00.

"What is this?" Schweizer asked.

"An account that I opened for you at a bank in the Turks and Caicos Islands in the West Indies, one that is owned and operated by a Swiss, under local laws that provide as much bank secrecy protection as we have here."

Schweizer carefully examined the card.

"The other piece of paper indicates the

balance in that account that will be at your disposal as soon as the signature credit is signed and returned."

"I'm afraid that—"

"Before you say anything more, Sammy, please hear me out. I was in a terrific jam. You, and you alone, got me out of it. My client has seen fit to reward 'my' performance in a very generous way—with twenty-five percent of the profits. Half of that is $7,185,749. It belongs to you."

"Hans, I know you mean well, but in my position—"

"Sammy, what's done is done."

Schweizer now remained silent.

"I repeat—what's done is done. Whether or not you accept my token of appreciation cannot change it. Don't you realize that?"

Still no response from the other side of the table.

"Besides, I have managed to find a way that will, now and for all time, completely disassociate you from any of these transactions."

"How?"

That single word did it. Zwiebach knew that he had him.

"Let's be candid. You were able to direct me to make those moves in gold futures because you found out at the BIS in Basel that, contrary to the conventional wisdom, the Federal Reserve Board was going to raise interest rates, not lower them. Who told you that?"

"We both know who. The only man who could know for sure— the Chairman of the Federal Reserve, Charles Black."

"You used those exact same words ten days ago at this very table," the lawyer said, "at which time I reminded you that, years ago, it was you who had referred Charles Black to me."

"I remember that conversation, yes."

"Well, Black subsequently became a client. And Black is—technically—still a client. He and his wife still have a fiduciary agreement with me that was never revoked. That agreement gives me control of Black's account at the General Bank of Switzerland—an account that was never closed. Follow me?"

"Perfectly."

"I booked—actually rebooked—all those gold futures trades through Black's account."

Even Schweizer was taken aback by the very audacity of it.

Zwiebach plunged ahead. "Not that there is a chance in a million— no, in a hundred million—that something would happen that could force us to revert to this fallback position. That means that where Black is concerned, he will simply never know. But it is still a necessary ultimate safeguard for all the parties involved— including Pietro di Cagliari. Nothing short of foolproof is good enough."

"Does Pietro know all of this?"

"He knows *none* of this. All he knows is

that I made a profit of fifty-seven million dollars for him. How, where, when, with whose help— he does not have a clue about any of that."

"And if he asks?"

"He won't. I know the type. And even if he did, I'd give him the usual runaround about my having to protect my relationships within the Swiss financial community, the sanctity of Swiss bank secrecy laws, and all that stuff. You know the drill. They never pursue it further. After all, they all came here in the first place to take advantage of those same Swiss secrecy laws. As long as the Cagliaris of the world make money, they don't ask questions. Even if they lose, they dare not make trouble."

"I can't really argue with anything that you have said."

"Then sign the signature card. After that, you are on your own. I will never broach the subject again; you have my word as an attorney and a friend."

Dr. Samuel Schweizer just sat there, immobile, pondering the ramifications of it all. Then he reached into this jacket, took out a pen, and attached his signature to the card. With the stroke of that pen, he now controlled a bank account that would soon have a credit balance of over seven million dollars. If he bargained hard enough, he was sure he could get that house in Sardinia for only four of those millions.

Zwiebach got home just in time to turn on the evening news on Swiss television. Cuba was the lead story. He knew almost immediately that everything was working out as planned.

After videotapes showing the turmoil in the streets of Havana, where law and order had completely broken down, a new series of pictures showed the debris of a vessel that had gone down at sea, at a location one hundred miles north of Cuba, after a spectacular explosion that could be seen twenty miles away. It had happened in the early hours of Monday. The U.S. Coast Guard was on the scene less than an hour later, and had already identified the wreckage as the remains of the yacht that belonged to the notorious American fugitive, Robert Vesco. There were apparently no survivors. In what was tantamount to Vesco's obituary, the commentator then went on to remind his audience of Vesco's looting of the Geneva-based IOS, and his subsequent flight to the Caribbean.

Zwiebach listened for a few more minutes, then turned off the set. He poured himself a drink and settled into his usual chair to reflect on what had turned out to be one of the best days in his professional career.

There was, of course, no sense in bothering Samuel Schweizer with all the details concerning the nature of Pietro di Cagliari's professional career. Schweizer's professional counsel would again be necessary when the time came to invest that $49 million of new cash that would soon be credited to Pietro's account in the West Indies.

27

That time first came five months later. There were two main reasons for the delay.

One was that Zwiebach thought it best to leave well enough alone for a while. He was sure that it would only be counter-productive if he pressed Samuel Schweizer for further investment "ideas," only to have the Swiss central banker get back on his high horse. Rather, Samuel had to be allowed first to enjoy, to *relish*, the benefits and privileges that arise when one suddenly has access to unexpected wealth. Not that Zwiebach had any doubts that, sooner or later, Sammy would come back to the well. For, now that Schweizer was running in the fast company of Pietro di Cagliari, it would only be a matter of time before he found out that $7 million did not go very far.

The other reason—over which Zwiebach, of course, had no control—was that, after the big flurry in the gold market, a period of calm had developed in the international financial markets.

In December of that year, however, that changed. As a result of a deep recession in Europe, unemployment in Germany and Switzerland had risen to levels that were untenable. At the December 3 meeting of the BIS, the heads of the German Bundesbank and the Swiss National Bank proposed a coordinated effort by the central banks of all major industrialized nations to help alleviate the situation. It was agreed that the way to do this was to realign interest rates in a way designed to readjust the value of the deutsche mark and the Swiss franc vis-à-vis both the dollar and the yen. The heads of the German and Swiss national banks agreed to drastically lower their short-term interest rates, while the Japanese and the Americans raised theirs. That would create an incentive for international investors to move out of the mark and the Swiss franc and into the dollar and the yen. In the process, the mark and the Swiss franc would move down, the dollar and the yen up. It was also decided to accelerate this process through direct intervention in the foreign exchange markets.

The next morning, Monday, December 4, Dr. Hans Zwiebach's home phone rang at 7:00 precisely. The lawyer knew who it was before he even picked up the phone.

It was two venues in London that Schweizer chose for their next foray into the exotic world of financial derivatives. The first was the interbank currency futures trading network among the hundreds of banks from all around the world that had operations in the City. The second was the

London International Financial Futures Exchange (LIFFE), where three-month Eurodollars were traded, a vehicle that allowed speculators to bet directly on the future direction of interest rates in the United States. Their price reacted inversely, and very sharply, to the direction of interest rates—that is, their price went down when interest rates went up, and up when rates declined.

The chain of command was preordained. Schweizer told Zwiebach to immediately go long the dollar against both the Swiss franc and the deutsche mark, and to begin establishing a short position in Eurodollars, since they would fall in tandem with rising American interest rates. There was more than ample cash margin available. Zwiebach had consolidated the Sardinian's cash holdings in just one account, Charles Black's account number J 747-2239. The balance was $50 million—the exact amount Pietro had transferred from Milan to Zurich in the first place.

Zwiebach called Stucker at the General Bank of Switzerland and told him that these funds should now be made available to serve as margin for two operations to be run out of London. He then precisely relayed Schweizer's instructions. Stucker relayed those same instructions to traders at his bank's London subsidiary.

Right on schedule, from the moment the markets in London opened, the Swiss franc and the German mark began to fall like rocks while the dollar rose. The prices of Eurodollar futures plummeted. At 7:00 A.M. the next day, Zwiebach received a two-word message from Dr. Samuel Schweizer.

"Liquidate immediately."

As soon as the attorney got to the office, these instructions were given to Stucker. Stucker passed them on to the traders in London. By the close on Friday afternoon, their entire position in London had been liquidated. On Monday morning, Urs Stucker called Zwiebach with the results. They had made a net profit of over $57 million. This profit was transferred immediately to the Sardinian's account in the Caribbean, where the "commissions" were deducted, and duly transferred to the accounts of Zwiebach and Schweizer.

Despite this final outcome, the week had had its scary moment—one that had nothing to do with the gyrations in the financial markets.

It had happened on Monday morning, just after Zwiebach had talked to Stucker in order to pass along Samuel Schweizer's instructions. His secretary had buzzed to tell him that a Mr. Charles Black was on the phone.

"Are you sure you got the name right?" he asked.

"Yes, sir."

"Where's he calling from?"

"I don't know."

"Put him through."

"Charles!" he said, once the connection was established. "What a wonderful surprise. Where are you?"

"I was in Basel. For the BIS meeting."

"And you're coming over to Zurich?"

"No. I'm at the Bäle/Mulhouse airport. I'm taking Air Inter to Paris in a few minutes, where I'll catch a plane back to Washington. But I wanted to call you before I left."

Zwiebach waited.

"It's about our daughter, Laura. I don't know if you remember, but you met her over lunch, maybe six or seven years ago. At the time we were still living in England and flew into Zurich before proceeding on to Zernez in the Engadin Valley, where I always went trout fishing."

"Of course I remember."

"Needless to say, she loved Switzerland. Now she's a sophomore in college back in the States and thinking about taking her junior year abroad. She is specifically interested in the University of Zurich. But she doesn't know their entrance requirements or procedures, and she's not been getting very much cooperation from the Swiss embassy people in Washington. I'll come to the point. I know you teach law at the University of Zurich. Would it be possible for you to somehow arrange for her to get that information?"

"No problem. Where should I have it sent? Go slowly because I'll be writing it down."

Black gave Zwiebach the address and

phone number of the house he and Sally had just moved into in Georgetown.

Zwiebach read it back, then said, "You'll get it within the week. And by the way, congratulations again on your appointment to the Federal Reserve. You must be a very busy man now."

"You're right," Black replied. "In fact, I've got to get moving or I'll miss that plane. Thanks for the help, Hans."

"It's a pleasure to be of service. If you or your daughter ever need anything else, just call."

"Thanks."

It was a very relieved Hans Zwiebach who hung up the phone. The last thing he needed now was for Charles Black to come over to Zurich and close his account. On the other hand, that call might be put to very good use. He rang his secretary.

"Louise, I don't know if you know that the Charles Black who just called is a client. I want to make sure that, for billing purposes, you log that call."

"Yes, sir," Louise responded. "How much time?"

"Ten minutes."

Over the next three years, Louise logged in Charles Black's name eight more times. On all but one of those occasions, she was told that the call had come in to her boss on his direct line.

In fact, the next time she got those instructions was three months later. It was, as always, on a Monday morning. It started, as always, with a 7:00 phone call from Samuel Schweizer to Hans Zwiebach's home. The sequence of events that followed precisely mirrored what had happened three months earlier. The only difference was that this time, since it was only the Fed that made a move, dropping short-term dollar interest rates by one-half percent, the market reaction was not as great, so the profit was also proportionally smaller: only $26 million.

Four months after that, it was the same thing. The same one-half-percent drop in short-term interest rates in New York. The same profit in London. It was the middle of July, and so far, for Pietro di Cagliari, Hans Zwiebach, and Samuel Schweizer, it had been a great year.

28

But it had not been a great year for everybody, as the chairman of the General Bank of Switzerland, Dr. Lothar Zopf, was finding out.

At this same time, in mid-July, it was Zopf's practice to call into his office, one by one, the senior managers of his bank. The purpose was to get a report on their performance during the first six months of the year. This was a ritual that he had established right after becoming chairman, to make sure everybody in the organization understood that there was one reason and one reason only for their having—and keeping—their jobs: making money for the General Bank of Switzerland.

The first man he called in was the senior vice president in charge of the bank's proprietary trading operations, because it was those operations that generated the largest share of the bank's overall profits. He was obviously nervous as he entered the office and approached the desk of the chairman. He handed Dr. Zopf a dossier marked HIGHLY CONFIDENTIAL. It contained a one-page summary of the trading results achieved so far that year. He remained standing in front of the desk as his boss opened the dossier and scanned the single sheet within.

The chairman finally spoke. "Not good. Not at all good. Explain."

"So far it's been a difficult year, Herr Doktor."

"Every year is difficult. What went wrong?"

"Our financial products group had a big loss. The shift in policy by the Federal Reserve at the end of last year caught them by surprise. As they gradually unwound their futures positions—they were short both the Eurodollar and U.S. government bonds—we've had to pay the price. It was a very steep price, I'm afraid."

"So how do you intend to make up for

those losses during the second half of the year?"

"I think I have an idea—if you will allow me to explain."

"It had better be a good idea," the chairman said. "Go ahead."

"It's been brought to our attention that the bank has a client who has had an amazing string of luck with derivatives. He does it on his own, with no help from our financial products group."

"How do you know about him?"

"From one of our young traders who specializes in derivatives."

"What kind of derivatives has this client been speculating in?"

"Gold futures on the Comex in New York. Three-month Eurodollars in London. Currency futures in London."

"How much has he made?"

"Just a shade over $167 million."

That produced a long pause.

"But over what time span?" the chairman asked.

"Almost exactly twelve months, starting in July of last year. The trading pattern is quite odd. It all takes place in short spurts. Four so far. But there's more. So far he's never been wrong. Every single trade he's made has resulted in a profit."

"So who is this client?"

"Our trader doesn't know. It's a numbered account. Furthermore, the trader says he was 'taken off the case.' "

"Why?"

"Because the Private Clients Group executive who takes care of this client claimed that he had screwed up on the initial trades last year."

"So who was put on the case?"

"Nobody here. The executive in the Private Clients Group directs all the trading activity himself. He channels the trades through our London office. But you know traders, sir. Whether they're here or in London, they talk to each other all day long. No gossip or rumor ever gets by them. That's how all this got back to our young trader and then to me."

"But you must know the name of the executive in the Private Clients Group who acts for this client."

"Of course. Urs Stucker."

"Have you discussed any of this with Stucker?"

"No. As you know, sir, we have instructions about maintaining a 'Chinese wall' between the Private Clients Group and our proprietary trading department. So we are not supposed—"

The chairman interrupted. "Of course not. But in this case, as you have already pointed out, that so-called Chinese wall has already been breached in London. Otherwise none of this would have gotten back to you. Right?"

"That is certainly true, sir."

"So not to maintain a careful surveillance of the situation *now* would be merely putting ourselves at a disadvantage relative to those who will."

That was a bit convoluted, but the man standing in front of Chairman Zopf was quite sure what it really meant.

"So how should I proceed?"

"If you detect another 'spurt' of activity getting under way, follow the lead and see what happens."

"Yes, sir. What kind of margin limits are we talking about?"

"What kind of cash margin does this client work with?"

"The young trader says he works with amounts up to an apparent limit of fifty million dollars."

"You can match that limit. And if things work out, double it."

"Yes, sir."

"Anything else?"

"Not really, sir."

"Then just one more thing. I want you to keep the contents of this conversation strictly to yourself. Understood?"

"Yes, sir."

The first thing the senior vice president in charge of proprietary trading did after leaving the chairman's office was to put his informant, the yuppie derivatives trader, on alert.

That paid off seven months later. The yuppie was on the phone to him minutes after the bank opened on the first Monday in February.

"He's at it again. But the tactics have changed. He just placed orders to go short Euromarks and Euro Swiss francs in London and long the DM in Frankfurt and the Swiss franc here in Zurich."

"Have the executions already started?"

"Barely."

"Good. Get in front of all of those trades for our in-house account."

"How much are you going to put up?"

"Fifty million dollars."

"For that amount I'll need signed order slips."

"You'll have them in five minutes. But get going right now."

This was known in the trade as "front-running." It was practiced all over the world. In its original form the process was triggered when an institutional client—usually a mutual fund or a pension fund—placed a very large order for a particular stock with a broker or an investment bank. That was bound to push up the price of the stock. Knowing that, the broker or investment bank handling the trade would buy the same stock for itself just *before* it began executing the order placed by its institutional client.

It was not only a sure thing for the bank or broker. It was also illegal.

On Wednesday, the central banks of both Germany and Switzerland announced that they were raising their discount rates. The next day the General Bank of

272

Switzerland covered all of its speculative positions related to the DM and the Swiss franc for the bank's own account. On Friday, after a phone call from Zwiebach, it did the same for the private client of the bank behind account number J 747-2239. Result:

The bank made $31 million.
The client made $27 million.
It always pays to be first in line.

The front-running ahead of account number J 747-2239 continued during the next ten months. Two more bursts of trading occurred during this period. Both anticipated further upward moves in German and Swiss interest rates with a timing that was nothing short of uncanny. As a result, the trading profits of the General Bank of Switzerland not only recovered, but soared to almost record levels.

At the end of the year, when the head of the bank's proprietary trading was called into the chairman's office to give his report, he was rewarded with a bonus of $11 million. The yuppie trader got one million. And there was the promise of a lot more to come. For Chairman Zopf now personally authorized a further upping of the ante.

So when, on the second Monday of the new year, Urs Stucker, acting for Charles Black's account, switched its trading activities back to the dollar, the front-running activities of the General Bank of Switzerland took on unprecedented proportions. Ten months later, on November 3 of that year, the process culminated in a massive speculation that included their accumulating a huge short position in three-month Eurodollar futures on the London International Financial Futures Exchange.

And that was when the trouble started.

29

After the collapse of the Bank for Credit and Commerce International in 1991 and the bankruptcy of Barings Bank in 1995, the central bank of central banks, the Bank for International Settlements, had felt it necessary to improve its surveillance of the banking industry. To that end, it had asked the Governor of the Bank of England, Sir Robert Neville, to set up a small team in London. He immediately did so, and assigned as its leader Derek Hambro, a recent graduate of the London School of Economics and descendent of a long line of merchant banking scions. His group was known internally as the Surveillance Group.

Using a computerized tool especially developed for it and named the Integrated Monitoring and Surveillance System, the group was to identify "sinister" trading patterns and who was behind them.

Increasingly their attention was directed at trading in financial derivatives, since this was the highest-risk type of activity engaged in by the world's financial institutions. At Barings Bank in 1995, a single twenty-eight-year-old trader operating out of Singapore built up a $22 billion speculative position in Japanese stock index and interest-rate futures for the bank's own account. He had, in essence, "bet the bank" that interest rates in Japan would go down. Instead they went up. He lost almost $1.4 billion within a matter of weeks and brought down the bank. Despite this warning of the risks involved, the volume of trading in financial derivatives had continued to skyrocket, and was now well up into the tens of trillions of dollars.

The location of the Surveillance Group inside the Bank of England was ideal, since it was just up the street from the LIFFE, and that financial futures exchange was now the center of the global financial derivatives trade. Its move up to that status had occurred after it entered into alliances with both the Chicago Board of Trade and the Tokyo International Financial Futures Exchange. Now futures trading in everything from Japanese bonds to ten-year U.S. government notes to three-month Euro Swiss francs could be traded on one floor in the middle of the City of London.

It was the massive burst of trading in interest-rate futures during the week of November 3 that first caught the attention of the Surveillance Group. Working backwards toward the beginning of the year, they identified three more such trading bursts on the LIFFE. This confirmed that something unusual was going on in a systematic fashion. And when something like this happened, their experience told them that insider trading was almost always involved. What then became apparent was that almost all the trading involved derivatives denominated in the U.S. dollar. This led them to believe that the insider was most probably an American.

So Hambro alerted Sir Robert Neville, asking his permission to concentrate their limited resources on pursuing the matter further. When he described the volume involved—volume that had risen with each successive burst of trading—Sir Robert immediately told him to go ahead, but to do so with the utmost discretion. They were obviously dealing with a very big fish out there somewhere, one who, by definition, must have connections in very high places throughout the financial world. For his part, Sir Robert would inform just one person, the Chairman of the BIS, to whom he was obligated to report on such matters. There was zero risk of any leakage there, since Dr. Samuel Schweizer also served as president of the Swiss National Bank, guaranteeing that he was the very soul of discretion.

Schweizer immediately concurred with Sir Robert's decision to assign top priority to the investigation. So the Surveillance Group again activated its Integrated Monitoring and Surveillance System, programming its computers to keep working their way backwards in time, screening every single trade on the LIFFE involving dollar-denominated derivatives.

At first it was extremely frustrating. The amount of raw data to be processed was staggering. But as the weeks turned into months, even more frustrating was the fact that no evidence of additional outbreaks of suspicious activity was brought to light.

The lull extended backwards for a full eighteen months.

But then—bingo!

A computer printout indicated that just before the beginning of this eighteen-month period, during the second week in July, a sudden surge of trading in Eurodollars had occurred. As the computers moved even further back, there it was again in the first week of March—another flurry of exceptional trading activity, again involving Eurodollars. More raw data was processed, and there it was yet again, this time at the beginning of December.

Then, as they began to put it all together, something else jumped out at them. Thus far they had identified seven bursts of suspicious trading in futures on the London International Financial Futures Exchange. The timing was nothing short of uncanny. Each surge of trading had begun just days before the Federal Reserve had announced either an upward or downward move in the federal funds rate. This confirmed their earlier suspicion that the insider was an American, most probably someone very senior at the Federal Reserve in Washington, and thus privy to the thinking and plans of the Fed's chairman.

But then one of Derek Hambro's staff noticed something even more peculiar. With just one exception, *every single burst of activity began on the Monday after the first weekend of the month.* When he was informed of this, Hambro immediately called a special meeting of the entire Surveillance Group.

"Where's the correlation?" he asked them. "What always happens on the first weekend of the month?"

Nobody came up with an answer. It was Hambro who ultimately answered his own question.

"Of course," he told the group. "How damn stupid of me. Where does the Governor of the Bank of England go on the first weekend of each month?"

"Basel," someone answered.

"Exactly."

"And who is always there also? The Chairman of the Federal Reserve. Invariably he informs his colleagues about his intentions regarding the future direction of American interest rates."

"Then it must be someone inside the BIS."

"Let's not be hasty," Hambro said. "So far, everything *still* points to someone inside the Fed. These suspicious trades have always involved dollar-denominated derivatives."

"But we don't know that," one of his staff said. "We've never checked for unusual activity on the LIFFE in Euromarks or Swiss francs or, for that matter, in Euro-yen."

"Then let's do it."

"Over the entire period?"

"No," Hambro replied. "That would take too long. Concentrate on those eighteen months when nothing happened."

"And if we find something?"

"If the same pattern emerges—involving the first week of the month—then we know for sure that it has to be someone inside the BIS."

It took just two weeks this time. Three more unusual bursts of trading had occurred during that eighteen-month hiatus. All involved Euromarks and Euro Swiss francs.

Derek Hambro immediately went to Sir Robert Neville.

"I think we've finally come up with something," he began. "Thus far we've identified seven brief periods of unusually high volume of trading in Eurodollars on the LIFFE, extending back three years. *All began shortly before the Fed adjusted interest rates in the States.*"

"So it's someone inside the Fed."

"That's what we thought. But then something else came to light. There were three similar very short periods of high-volume trading— this time in DM and Swiss franc interest-rate futures. In each case they occurred just days before the Bundesbank and the Swiss National Bank increased their discount rates."

"That defies explanation," Sir Robert said.

"That's what we thought. But now look at this." Hambro handed a chart across the desk to Sir Robert.

"It's a time line," he explained, "where all ten bursts of unusual trading are identified with specific dates. Notice anything odd?"

Sir Robert examined the chart for a full two minutes.

"No," he finally admitted.

"Look again."

Sir Robert did, reluctantly.

"Check out those dates again," Hambro said. "With *just one exception—January of last year—every single burst of activity began on the Monday after the first weekend in the month.*"

"I'll be damned," Sir Robert said.

"And what always happens on the first weekend of each month?"

Sir Robert knew the answer immediately. "The central bankers meet in Basel."

"Where the direction of *all* interest rates—not just dollar rates—is discussed," Hambro said.

"So it has to be someone inside the BIS."

"Yes, sir."

"But he can hardly operate on his own. He must be working through a financial institution."

"Exactly," Hambro replied. "And that's why I want your permission to take this investigation just two steps further. Then we'll be able to wrap this up."

"They are?"

"First, it would seem logical that whoever is behind this is not restricting himself to just the LIFFE. If you know where interest rates are going, you also most probably know where exchange rates are headed."

"Of course."

"So first I would like to have your permission to ask around the banks here in the City. Specifically to ask their chief foreign exchange dealers whether they recall any unusual surges in trading that coincided with those same ten periods of unusual volume on the LIFFE."

"You've got it."

"Then—if this checks out as I am almost certain it will—I want to ask both those foreign exchange dealers in the banks and the traders on the floor of the LIFFE if they are able and willing to identify *who* was at the center of all the action."

"You mean which brokerage firm?"

"Or which bank."

"Do it."

"Some might be very reluctant to talk to me."

"Then you will need my authorization in writing."

"Yes, sir—leaving no doubt that the full weight of the Bank of England is behind it."

"You will have it."

It was like pulling teeth, but gradually it came out. Everybody said the same thing. A lot of this had happened years ago. And there were many periods of high-volume currency trading, such as every time there was a crisis in Mexico, Italy, or Spain. But Derek Hambro, who was personally pursuing this investigation, remained patient and persistent. He was not interested in periods of currency crises; he was interested in very specific dates. Just ten in all. And it was not he but Sir Robert Neville, Governor of the Bank of England, who wanted the information.

Ultimately they agreed to cooperate. So what did the Bank of England want to know specifically? Hambro told them: the identity of the broker, investment bank, commercial bank, corporation— whatever—that was unusually active during these ten brief periods.

After he got their answers, Hambro put this same question to the traders on the floor of the LIFFE.

The same name came up time and again. It was not a British merchant bank. It was not an American brokerage house. It was not a Japanese trading company.

It was the General Bank of Switzerland.

The day after these investigations had been completed, Derek Hambro submitted a full written report to the Governor of the Bank of England. Just hours after he had delivered it, he was called into Sir Robert Neville's office.

"You did an absolutely splendid job, Derek," Sir Robert said. "I want to extend my personal thanks to you. It will now be up to me to take this matter further."

"Would it be asking too much, sir, if I be allowed to remain on this case with you?" Hambro asked. "As you must now realize, this situation goes well beyond anything we have yet dealt with. One expects hanky-panky in high places in Pakistan or Mexico. One also expects rogue traders to get their companies or financial institutions into trouble on a regular basis. But what has been going on here goes to the very heart of the system. It seriously compromises the Federal Reserve. It totally compromises the BIS. And it casts serious doubts on the integrity of Switzerland's largest commercial bank, which is a key player in the global financial network."

"That sums it up, all right," Sir Robert said.

"It is also why I would like to follow this all the way through to the end."

"Meaning?"

"I want to go to Zurich and personally confront the men running the General Bank of Switzerland with the facts—the irrefutable facts— that are in my report."

"I take it you don't particularly care for the Swiss, Derek."

"You're right. Let's say I don't particularly like Swiss bankers. They are too greedy, too smug—and, let's face it, sir, too crooked."

"They are also too clever. They invented bank secrecy laws way back in the 1930s to prevent outsiders from prying in their affairs. Outsiders like you and, truth to tell, also like me."

"So how can we proceed?"

"Only one way. Through the top banking authority in Switzerland, who, thank God, also happens to be the Chairman of the BIS. I'm talking about Dr. Samuel Schweizer, of course."

"How do you know he won't stonewall you, too?"

"Because this time, as you just pointed out, the facts are irrefutable. And Schweizer knows full well that it is my obligation to now report these facts to the central bankers at our next meeting in Basel, which takes place next weekend. I will demand that Schweizer confront the General Bank of Switzerland with these same facts before that meeting."

"And then?"

"We'll have to just wait and see what comes out."

"When are you going to talk to Schweizer?"

"Right now. Why don't you just stay put while I place the call."

30

It was a stunned Samuel Schweizer who hung up the phone in Zurich twenty minutes later.

"Verdammt, noch mal," he said, although swearing out loud at an otherwise empty office was hardly his style.

He had known that an investigation had been going on. Sir Robert Neville had informed him of this three months earlier, and had even asked his permission to proceed with it on a high-priority basis. But never in his worst nightmare had Schweizer dreamed that they would come up with anything like this. They were Englishmen, for God's sake. A bunch of lazy, supercilious, snobbish amateurs who were bound to fail in almost any serious task they took on.

This one, unfortunately, was the exception.

Now what?

He had no choice. He picked up the phone and dialed the direct number of Dr. Lothar Zopf, chairman of the General Bank of Switzerland.

"This is Samuel Schweizer," he said

after Zopf had picked up. "I've got to see you right away."

"Why?" Zopf asked.

"I'll tell you when I see you."

"But I have an executive committee meeting starting in a half hour."

"So cancel it."

There was a pause on the other end.

"I will. Expect me in your office. I'll leave here right away."

"No. I want to see you at your bank. I'll go to the private elevator off the main lobby. I'll be there in thirty minutes. Have someone meet me."

"I'll have my personal secretary meet you. She knows you."

"Good. Nobody else really needs to know about this," Schweizer said.

As soon as he had hung up on Lothar Zopf, Schweizer dialed the private line of Dr. Hans Zwiebach.

"Hans," Schweizer said immediately after the attorney had picked up, "meet me in one hour at the Café Limmat. In the meantime, don't take any calls."

Schweizer hung up without giving Zwiebach a chance to reply.

Lothar Zopf was very nervous and showed it when, a half hour later, Samuel Schweizer was escorted into his office by Zopf's personal secretary. As soon as she had left the room, and before he had even shaken hands with his visitor, Zopf asked, "What in the world prompts this?"

"Somebody's been using the facilities of the General Bank of Switzerland for some massive insider trading," Schweizer replied.

"How massive?"

"Massive enough to catch the attention of the Bank of England. They are not able to come up with exact numbers, only vague approximations. But the key fact is that they were able to identify very suspicious bursts of trading. Your bank was always a major participant in the markets in question during those brief periods and, according to the traders in London, always on the winning side."

"Doing what?"

"Trading interest-rate derivatives and foreign exchange."

"Lots of people do that."

"The difference is that *this* one never makes a mistake."

"Meaning?"

"Meaning he's got to be an insider."

"Inside of what?"

"That's what I'm going to find out." Schweizer paused. "With your help, Lothar."

"Now look, Sammy," Zopf said. "We've both been in this business a long time, and we've known each other for a long time."

"That's right."

"So you know as well as I that problems involving so-called insiders crop up all the time. And you also know full well that we take care of these things *internally*. So you tell us what's been going on, and we'll make sure it stops."

"This time that won't work."

"What makes this time different?"

"The insider."

"I don't get it."

"This time it's not some executive or board member of some corporation taking advantage of what he knows about a takeover bid his company's about to make or get. This time all signs point to someone in government. Someone very high in government."

"Our government?" Zopf asked incredulously.

"No. Of course not."

"So what did this particular insider know that allowed him always to be on the winning side?"

"Where interest rates were going."

"What interest rates?"

"Short-term interest rates."

"Where?"

"The United States, Germany, and here. Most of the trades involved the dollar, but three others involved the mark and the Swiss franc."

"You said it was the Bank of England who came onto this. Maybe it is someone inside the Bank of England who is the insider."

"Most probably not—unfortunately. But that won't be hard to find out. Again, although the Bank of England is not able to come up with any exact numbers, they are convinced that the trades originated here and were merely executed through your branch office in London. They took place over a three-year period. They always involved short bursts of high-volume trading. They always involved Eurocurrency futures traded on the LIFFE. That type of activity should be very easy for you to trace."

"Come on, Sammy. You know better than to say that. We are one of the largest players in the Eurocurrency market. You're talking about thousands and thousands of trades every month."

"I've got ten specific dates."

Lothar Zopf looked Samuel Schweizer squarely in the eye and realized he had no choice.

"All right. Give them to me."

Schweizer had written them down on a piece of paper. He handed the list to Zopf.

"How long will it take you?" Schweizer asked as Zopf looked at the dates.

"Not long. Maybe five or six hours."

"You'll call me when you know who's behind this?"

"Right away. But then what happens?"

"That depends on who it is. But I can assure you that I will do everything in my power to make sure this whole matter is handled with the utmost discretion."

"Meaning?"

"That public disclosure will not be necessary."

"I would be very thankful if you could manage that. We've had enough scandals in the Swiss banking community in recent years. We hardly need another one of these proportions."

"I agree," Schweizer said. "So I'll expect your call later today."

After that he left, exiting the General Bank of Switzerland via the private elevator and a side door.

Zwiebach was already waiting at a back table in the Café Limmat when Samuel Schweizer arrived.

"You were rather abrupt on the phone," he said as soon as Schweizer had sat down. "What's the problem?"

"You know about that investigation that Sir Robert Neville's people in London have been making?"

"Yes. You told me about it months ago. You also said it would come to nothing."

"I was wrong. They've tracked the trading activity to the General Bank of Switzerland. They've got ten exact dates."

"Jesus, Sammy."

"Hold on. *We* know everything that *they* know—so we can control the damage."

"How?"

"I just talked to Lothar Zopf. I gave him the dates. He's now in the process of tracking down the trades. So he'll come up with your B account. Then he'll call you. In fact, I'll bet he calls and then shows up at your office fifteen minutes later."

"And what do I tell him?"

"The truth. It's Charles Black's account, and all you've been doing is following his instructions. But you'll have to put up a fight first. Evoke the sanctity of the attorney-client relationship, the bank secrecy laws, the penalties you might face if you breach that relationship and those laws. Demand indemnification."

"He won't give me indemnification. You know that."

"Of course I know that. But aren't you on the board of the General Bank of Switzerland?"

"Yes."

"So, in the end, out of loyalty to the bank, you will cave in and tell them all about Charles Black. You and Lothar Zopf were both betrayed by a foreigner. So he, not you, must now face the consequences."

By midafternoon, events had played out exactly as Schweizer predicted. In the end, to the great relief of the chairman of the General Bank of Switzerland, Dr. Hans Zwiebach caved in. In doing so, the lawyer cited overriding Swiss interests that would be threatened unless swift—though discreet—action was brought to bear on the American who had so blatantly misused both of them. It was from Zwiebach's office that Lothar Zopf called Samuel Schweizer to tell him who had been behind the insider trading that, unbeknownst to him, had been done through his bank.

Samuel Schweizer then called Sir Robert Neville. The insider trading activity, he told him, had been traced to a single account at the General Bank of Switzerland. That account was a B account, controlled by a

Zurich attorney. Heavy pressure had been exerted on that attorney by both Schweizer himself and the chairman of the General Bank of Switzerland. In the end, the attorney had relented and revealed the name of the beneficial owner of that account: Charles Black.

That produced no reaction on the other end. Just silence.

So Schweizer went on to tell Sir Robert that he would expect him in his office in Zurich at 10:00 A.M. on Friday. By that time he would be in possession of all the records of the General Bank of Switzerland that were pertinent to the Charles Black affair. From what he had already been told by the chairman of that bank, the evidence against Black was totally damning.

Schweizer went on to stress that it would be in the interest of all parties to take care of this matter within the confines of "the club." He was sure that their fellow central bankers would prefer this. And as for Charles Black, when he showed up next weekend, he, Samuel Schweizer, would confront him with the facts. Schweizer prided himself on his ability to make biblical allusions, and now proceeded to draw two. Black would be told to go forth and sin no more. That would be the end of it, since the American would be the last person ever to mention any of this again. Otherwise he would be cast into outer darkness forever.

As soon as Schweizer had hung up, Sir

Robert called Derek Hambro into his office and repeated almost word for word what the head of the Swiss National Bank had just told him.

"He finished by insisting that we keep this entire matter under wraps," Sir Robert said. "Black will be thoroughly chastised and then sent off to repent in silence."

"With all due respect, sir, we simply can't let that happen," Hambro replied. "Absolutely no way. I'm coming with you to Zurich, Sir Robert. Once we have those records, I'm going to take them to the Basel police. I've worked with them before, one in particular—when we were doing the BCCI investigation. They are competent and they play straight." He paused. "That is, if I have your permission, sir."

"You do. Make reservations for both of us at the Baur au Lac."

"Yes, sir," Hambro said. Then he continued. "You know, there is still one thing that bothers me. Why in the world would a Charles Black do this? What's he going to do with all this money? We don't know exactly how much is involved, but it must be many hundreds of millions of dollars. If he *was* going to do it, then why not just once? Then take the money and run. If he'd have done that, we never would have caught on."

"These types never do that," Sir Robert replied. "Remember, Black's background is that of a Wall Street investment banker. Just like a Michael Milken. Milken did not even stop breaking the law after he'd earned his first *billion*."

"You're right. I'll make those reservations."

31

Samuel Schweizer was surprised when *two* men entered his office at the Swiss National Bank at precisely ten o'clock on Friday morning—and he showed it.

"I was under the impression that we would be alone, Sir Robert," Schweizer said, pointedly waiting behind his desk for a reply before formally greeting his guest.

"If I left that impression, I do apologize," the Englishman replied, "but my colleague from the Bank of England is much more capable of handling the details of this sad affair than I. He is in charge of the investigative unit, which, if you recall, we *jointly* set up. That is why he is here. His name is Derek Hambro."

The name did it.

"Of the Hambro banking family?" Schweizer now asked, referring to the founders of the centuries-old, London-based merchant bank.

"Yes, sir."

"Then you must have been related to Jocelyn Hambro."

"Yes, sir. He was my great-uncle."

"I knew him quite well. As you must

know, everyone in the banking world thought very highly of him." That said, Schweizer now emerged from behind his desk and shook the hands of both men.

"Where shall we begin?" he asked.

"Perhaps with the General Bank of Switzerland's in-house records of the transactions in question—assuming you now have them," Sir Robert replied.

"I do. Let's move to the conference table," Schweizer said. "It's all there, organized by date and by separate transaction. Why don't you take your seats in front of those dossiers?"

The two British bankers dutifully took their places on the side of the conference table where the dossiers, green in color and ten in number, were laid out side by side. Schweizer took his place at the head of the table, where two additional documents had been placed.

"Before we get to them, you should see these," the Swiss banker said. "One is this signature card."

He held it up and then handed it to Hambro. "As you can see, it controls account number J 747-2239 at the General Bank of Switzerland. All—I stress, *all*—the trades were made for this account. You will also note that, as I already told Sir Robert on the phone, this is a B account, meaning that it is in the name of a Swiss attorney, but for the account of one of his clients. This system evolved out of the need for another layer of confidentiality over and above the protection provided to banking customers by Switzerland's bank secrecy laws."

Hambro carefully examined the card. "The name of the attorney is Dr. Hans Zwiebach?"

"Yes."

"Do you know him?"

"Very well. He is a man of unimpeachable character."

"But was he not aware of what his client was doing?" It was Derek Hambro who posed the question.

"He merely acted as a conduit. It was only after your phone call, Sir Robert, when it was explained to Zwiebach that the *timing* of these trades was highly suspicious, that he realized the nature and immensity of the problem."

"I see," Sir Robert said.

Schweizer hurried on. "And when he did, he reluctantly offered to reveal the identity of his client. Actually, he revealed it to Dr. Lothar Zopf—the chairman of the General Bank of Switzerland—and Zopf told me. However, I have spoken directly with Dr. Zwiebach in the meantime. He is expecting your visit. When we are done here, I'll call him."

They spent the next half hour going through the contents of one of the dossiers. The documents it contained tracked all the activity related to account number J 747-2239 during the week of November 3 of the previous year—now seven months ago. Derek Hambro had various questions about some of the internal banking procedures and terminology. Schweizer always had precise answers. They finally came to the last document in that dossier.

"Now, if I understand this slip correctly, at the end of the week, when all the profits from these transactions had been credited to account number J 747-2239, they were transferred to the Bank for Commerce and Finance on the island of Grand Turk in the Caribbean."

"Yes. According to the information given to me by Dr. Zopf, there were standing orders to do that."

"So it's all gone. Out of the country," Hambro said.

"Exactly."

"And what or who is this bank in the Caribbean?"

"When I found all this out, I ran a check," the head of the Swiss central bank said. "It is owned and run by a Swiss—a Swiss who used to work for one of our major banks and got into trouble with the law. He subsequently left the country. I'm afraid there's no way that we can get at him as long as he stays where he is. And even if we could get at him and his bank, who knows where all that money has gone in the meantime?"

"This was all rather well planned and executed," Sir Robert commented.

"Exactly," Schweizer said. "Only someone at the very top of the banking profession could have managed it. It was foolproof until—"

"Until Derek Hambro and his staff smelled a rat," Sir Robert cut in. "And they never would have if Black hadn't gotten greedy."

"What does that mean?" Schweizer asked.

"Suddenly last year the volume of trading skyrocketed," Hambro answered. "It was the volume that first caught our attention."

Schweizer looked surprised. But he said nothing more.

After turning over the ten dossiers to Sir Robert, Schweizer telephoned the office of Dr. Hans Zwiebach and spoke to him very briefly in Swiss German.

"Dr. Zwiebach is prepared to meet you right away," he told the two Englishmen. "His office is just five minutes from here." Schweizer jotted down Zwiebach's address on a piece of note paper and gave it to Derek Hambro.

As he ushered them out of his office, Schweizer had one final question for Sir Robert: "How do you intend to handle this at the BIS meeting?"

"I'll let you know well before we meet again at dinner at the Schützenhaus on Saturday night."

Dr. Hans Zwiebach was waiting for them in the foyer of the suite housing his law offices just up the Bahnhofstrasse from the

General Bank of Switzerland. It soon became apparent that there was a reason for this.

After formally greeting his two visitors from the Bank of England, he asked the receptionist/secretary who had been sitting behind her desk in the lobby to join them.

"This is Fräulein Louise Stumpf," Zwiebach said. "She is not just the keeper of the gate out here. She also maintains the log of all visits and phone calls. She has been doing this for over forty years, first for my father when he was head of the firm, and then for me and my colleagues after I succeeded him."

Sir Robert and Derek Hambro moved forward and shook hands with her.

"Louise," Zwiebach now said, "I want you to get your logs going back four years."

He turned to Sir Robert. "As I understood it from Dr. Lothar Zopf, we are talking about ten very specific dates."

"Yes," Sir Robert replied.

"Could you give them to Fräulein Stumpf?"

"Now?"

"Yes. That way she can go through her logs while we talk in my office."

"Might I ask what she will be looking for?" Hambro asked.

"She knows what to look for—incoming phone calls from one of our clients. You know his name: Charles Black. It will only take a few minutes."

Derek Hambro's slight shrug indicated his reluctant agreement to go along with whatever the Swiss attorney was up to. Addressing Sir Robert, he said, "Perhaps you could proceed with Dr. Zwiebach while I go through those dossiers we just got from Dr. Schweizer. I've got my own list, but this way we can make sure that we are all talking about the same dates."

He then turned to Fräulein Stumpf, while reaching down to retrieve those dossiers from his briefcase. "Do you mind if I put them on your desk?"

"No, please," she answered. "In the meantime, I will get the logs from those previous years." She went out through a door leading off the lobby to the left.

Sir Robert and Zwiebach exited through another door into the attorney's office while Hambro, now alone in the outer office, stacked the dossiers on top of the secretary's desk and waited for Fräulein Stumpf to return. She reappeared almost immediately with four leatherbound journals under her arm.

"I assume you want to compare entries in your logs with the dates I am going to give you," Hambro said.

"Yes, sir. Those are my instructions."

"All right," Hambro said. "Let's start with the beginning of last year. The morning of Monday, January thirteenth, to be exact."

Fräulein Stumpf opened one of the black leatherbound logs and paged rapidly through it.

"There were twenty-seven incoming phone calls that morning."

"Was one of them from Charles Black?"

"Yes, sir. It came in at 11:42 A.M."

"Where did it originate?"

"That I do not know. I only record times."

"All right. Let's move up a bit. This time to the first week in March."

Again Fräulein Stumpf flipped rapidly through her log.

"Mr. Black called at 9:47 A.M."

When they were done, Hambro asked her to make photocopies of those pages in the logs that covered all the dates in question. As soon as she returned with them, he suggested that they both join the other two men in her boss's office.

Sir Robert and Dr. Zwiebach were seated across from each other at the attorney's conference table. Zwiebach motioned for Hambro to join them as he continued talking. He ignored the presence of his secretary.

"What you have there, Sir Robert, is the power of attorney that governs account number J 747-2239. As you see, it is dated fifteen years ago. Both Charles Black and his wife signed it. The fact that she signed it was not just a formality. When they lived in London, she actively traded through this account, and even took full advantage of the margin facilities at the General Bank of Switzerland. I might add that she was very successful."

Sir Robert seemed puzzled at this last remark. "Are you implying that she is implicated in all this?"

"No. Not at all. All I am saying is that the Black family has a history of knowing what they are doing when they invest. And throughout that entire history, they *always* gave me very specific instructions as to what they wanted done. I then *always* just relayed those instructions to the General Bank of Switzerland."

He now turned to address Fräulein Stumpf, who had remained dutifully standing five paces away from the conference table.

"Louise, I want you to make a copy of Mr. and Mrs. Black's fiduciary agreement. Sir Robert has the original in hand. But before you do, tell me how you and Mr. Hambro have fared together."

"Mr. Hambro asked me to look up specific dates in the phone logs. I made photocopies of those pages. Mr. Hambro has them."

"And did you find matches?" he now asked Derek Hambro.

"Yes."

"Then we will not need any further help from Fräulein Stumpf?"

"No."

Zwiebach tried hard not to appear relieved. Thus far, no mention had been made of the fact that most of these log-ins related to calls that had purportedly come in on his direct line.

"You may go back to your desk, Louise," he said. "And you will, of course, keep all of this strictly to yourself."

"Yes, sir," she said. "I will have the photocopy of the fiduciary agreement made immediately."

She retrieved the original from Sir Robert and hurriedly left the room.

Zwiebach's fears were, however, immediately revived by Derek Hambro's next question. "Before we leave the subject of those phone logs, perhaps you can tell me how the phone system works here in Switzerland—especially what is traceable and what is not."

"In essence, every call within Switzerland is a local call and not traceable. We are a very small country, you know. However, every call coming from outside the country is recorded in a way that should be traceable—within time limits, of course."

"Into what category did Black's calls fall?"

"Almost exclusively local. As you know, Sir Robert, Black was in Switzerland almost every month for the meeting of the central bankers at the BIS."

"Of course. But can you recall any of the exceptions?"

"Let me look at those dates again," Zwiebach said.

Hambro handed the photocopy of the logs across the table to the attorney, who then examined them in silence for a full two minutes.

"One immediately springs to mind.

Black called from the Savoy Hotel in London at the beginning of January of last year. According to our log, it was on January thirteenth."

He paused. "In fact, I now remember that I called him back at the Savoy. Not about the trading instructions he had given me during the first call, but about his daughter. Black had asked me to try to get her a room at the Palace Hotel in St. Moritz and I had to call him back to tell him that the hotel was fully booked."

"Any others? Preferably one that took place a few years before that."

"Yes. And I remember it because in addition to giving me his trading instructions he also asked that I help his daughter get some information from the University of Zurich. That was probably two years earlier. Let me go through the logs again."

He paged back until he found it. "Here," he said to Hambro, pointing at the entry. "The call must have originated from the French side of the airport in Bäle/Mulhouse, since I remember him telling me that he was taking the Air Inter flight to Paris. He could very well have been using one of the courtesy phones in the Air Inter VIP lounge."

He waited as he watched Derek Hambro writing in his notebook.

Then, ostentatiously looking at his wristwatch, he asked, "Is there anything else can I can help you with?"

"One more thing does bother me," Hambro said. "It is now quite obvious how Charles Black initiated his buy orders. But what about the sell side?"

Zwiebach had anticipated this question. "As I already told you, Black's instructions were always very specific. He told me what to buy and he also told me when to sell. Sometimes I was told to begin liquidating the positions in ten days. Sometimes it was three weeks. A few times he told me to buy on Monday and close out the positions by Friday."

"No matter what?"

"No matter what. Obviously—at least *now* it is obvious—he wanted to keep his communications with me at a minimum."

"And what if you got a margin call?" Hambro asked.

"We never got a margin call."

"Never?" Hambro asked.

"Never."

"And each time you not only never got a margin call, but you always made a profit?"

"Yes."

"And after you had the positions closed out, the profits were automatically transferred to an account at that bank in the Caribbean?"

"That's right. Black had me give the General Bank standing orders to that effect."

"And who opened that account?"

"Charles Black must have. I remember

not even knowing where the Turks and Caicos Islands were. I had to look them up in an atlas."

"So you never had any direct contacts with the bank there?"

"None whatsoever."

Derek Hambro again consulted his notes. "Well, for the moment that is about as far as we can take it, I think. At least until we have had a chance to examine in detail the records that the General Bank of Switzerland has given us."

"I agree," Sir Robert said as he rose from the conference table.

Derek Hambro immediately followed his lead.

Minutes later they were back on the Bahnhofstrasse.

"What now?" Derek Hambro asked.

"We have no choice but to turn all of this over to the Swiss police," Sir Robert said.

"What about Schweizer?"

"Let's walk down to the Baur au Lac. I'll phone Schweizer from the hotel, bring him up to date, and give him my recommendations on how we should now proceed. While I'm doing that, you can call your friend with the Basel police and tell him to expect you later this afternoon. As long as you're working the phone, you might as well call your people in London and have them go through the phone records of the Savoy Hotel, looking for a record of that call. When you see the Basel police, ask them to try to track that call from the airport in France. Then we'll check out of the Baur au Lac and take the next train to Basel."

Back at the hotel, it took Sir Robert a while to convince Schweizer that it would be impossible to keep this matter "within the club." But in the end he prevailed. Schweizer joined him in a conference call to Dr. Rolf Wassermann, state attorney of the canton of Basel-Stadt. They jointly filed a criminal complaint against Charles Black. The charge was suspicion of the misuse of public office for private gain, under Article 312 of the Swiss Federal Criminal Code.

As soon as the two Englishmen had arrived in Basel and checked into the Euler Hotel, Derek Hambro took a taxi to the offices of the state attorney at Heuberg 21. Lieutenant Paul Schmidt of the Fraud Squad of the Basel police department was waiting for him at the entrance.

"We meet again," the young Swiss detective said, with a broad smile on his face.

"Thank God not because of the BCCI case," Hambro replied. "This one will be a lot less complicated."

"Dr. Wassermann has told me very little about it so far," Schmidt said. "All I really know is that on the basis of an oral complaint, a warrant has just been issued for the arrest of an American by the name of Charles Black. Apparently he is expected to arrive at the Basel airport tomorrow

afternoon. We will pick him up there."
He paused. "It isn't *the* Charles Black,
by any chance? The one who was Chairman
of the Federal Reserve?"

"Unfortunately it is."

"Then we'll need a lot more than an oral
complaint if we are going to hold him for
any length of time."

"Don't worry," Hambro said, raising
his rather massive briefcase in the air.
"I've got everything you'll need in here."

"Good. Then let's go up to my office."

Derek Hambro spent the next hour
bringing the Swiss detective up to speed.
Then he began to turn over documents.
He started with a copy of the signature card
for account number J 747-2239 at the
General Bank of Switzerland in Zurich, and
the power of attorney that governed that
account. Next came the phone logs of
Black's attorney. After that, they began the
tedious task of going through the ten
dossiers containing the records of the
General Bank of Switzerland document-
ing the activities posted to Black's account
during the prior four years. By midnight
both men were exhausted.

"I think we've got Charles Black nailed
to the cross, don't you agree?" Hambro
asked.

"It looks that way," the Swiss detective
replied. "We've got all the raw material we
need, that's for sure. All we need is further
corroboration from some of the witnesses
who will eventually have to testify."

"Such as who?"

"Such as the account executive at the General Bank who was responsible for executing all of these trades—Urs Stucker. He signed off on those transactions. Why didn't he get suspicious? From what you just told me, everything always worked out. Never a margin call, always a profit—a huge profit. Did he relay his suspicions to any of his superiors? If so, why didn't they start asking Zwiebach questions? The whole thing seems too—what's the English word?—too *pat*."

"I see what you mean," Hambro said, "although I must confess that I did not jump to that conclusion."

"I'm not jumping. I just don't think we can rely exclusively on what Zwiebach and the chairman of the General Bank of Switzerland have handed us on a platter. From what you told me about the volume of trade during the latter stages of Black's activities, the numbers that we got from the General Bank of Switzerland just don't add up. My guess is that at some point, somebody else started to play the same game that Black was playing. Only the General Bank of Switzerland would know who that was. For now, they'll stick to their story that they've given us everything they've got, hoping any further investigation will become moot once Black is put away. But Urs Stucker might talk."

"When do you plan on talking to Stucker?"

"Only after we have Charles Black behind bars. And after the details of this case become public knowledge. In the meantime, the fewer people involved, the better. The state attorney has given me very strict instructions about that."

The next day, Lieutenant Paul Schmidt and two uniformed police accompanied the state attorney to the Basel airport. There, at 5:37 P.M., they arrested Charles Black and had him brought to the Lohnhof, where he was booked and locked up for the weekend. On Monday morning, Schmidt began his interrogation of Black. He continued it during most of the next day. By Tuesday evening it had become amply clear that the American intended to deny everything.

On Wednesday morning, when Schmidt arrived at his office, he was greeted by the glaring headlines of the *Basler Zeitung*, the city's morning newspaper, announcing Black's arrest and detention. So it was now in the public domain—which meant that he could begin to broaden his investigation. But to make sure, Schmidt called down to the office of his boss. The state attorney had just arrived himself and was very busy, as he immediately told Schmidt. But he confirmed that the wraps were now off. He also told Schmidt that he had gone through Schmidt's depositions of Black at home the previous evening. They were leading nowhere. What he wanted was for Schmidt to take off the gloves, confront

Black with all the evidence, and get a confession—a signed confession.

Then he hung up.

"So be it," Schmidt said after he put down his phone, "but I'm still going to get hold of that Stucker fellow." He picked up the phone again and dialed the number of the Zurich headquarters of the General Bank of Switzerland. He was told that Stucker no longer worked there. But after Schmidt identified himself, after a long wait he was given Stucker's home phone number. Schmidt then hung up and dialed again.

That phone call set in motion events that no one could have anticipated.

part
Three

32

On that Wednesday morning, all of the Swiss newspapers carried the same story. But only the *Herald Tribune* made it amply clear that the American government intended to stay out of the Charles Black affair.

After reading this, following his arrival at the Swiss National Bank, Dr. Samuel Schweizer telephoned his old school friend Dr. Hans Zwiebach, to tell him the good news.

"Hans, it's Samuel Schweizer," the central banker began.

"What a surprise," the Zurich lawyer said. "Actually, I was about to call you. I hope you have pleasant news."

"Very pleasant. Have you read this morning's *Herald Tribune*?"

"No."

"Like all the other papers, it has a front-page article on our American friend. But with more detail. I'll read the first part."

"I'm listening."

Samuel Schweizer put on his reading glasses and read.

Charles Black, the former Chairman of the Federal Reserve Board, was arrested in Basel, Switzerland, on Saturday. According to the state attorney of the canton of Basel-Stadt, where he is being held, Black faces charges of massive securities fraud. Asked to comment, the State Department, the White House, and the Federal Reserve all stated that they have no intention of intervening, since they regard the matter as a domestic Swiss affair.

"You see," Schweizer said, "the Americans have turned their back on him. That takes politics out of it. Charlie Black is going to be left twisting in the wind, all by himself. Then that prosecuting attorney in Basel is going to put him away for what will amount to the rest of his life."

"It's a pity it had to come to this," the attorney said.

"I did my best to prevent it, Hans. But once that damned Englishman began the investigation, there was no way I could stop it. And when the investigation led him to the General Bank of Switzerland and then to your fiduciary account there, what choice did we have?"

Silence on the other end of the line.

"I'll tell you the choice," Schweizer said. "Either Charles Black had to go to jail in Basel, or you and I would be on our way to jail in Zurich. Have no illusions about this, Hans. You are in this as deep as I. And although it is regrettable that we had to use our backup plan, the need for that insurance was the only reason you started using Black's account in the first place."

"I'm afraid that, unfortunately, we might have a problem there. I didn't use Black's

316

account the first time. The first trades that you and I made together four years ago were in gold futures. Remember?"

"Vaguely."

"They were *not* made through Black's account. They were initially made through the Sardinian's account. I subsequently had that 'error' corrected and rebooked the trades though Black's account. But—"

"So what? Errors like that occur every day at a big bank. Accounts are always getting mixed up."

"I know that. However, this was not the normal type of mixup. Which brings me to why I was about to call you. I got a phone call a few minutes ago from Urs Stucker."

"Who's he?"

"He was the vice president over at the General Bank who, for years, handled all my accounts there. He retired at the beginning of this year."

"Why did he call you?"

"Because, just before he called me, he got a call from the Basel police. They want to talk to him."

"So?"

"Stucker knows that what happened to those gold trades four years ago was not an error. If, for any reason, the *other* fiduciary account is brought into play, the next step will be that the Basel police will show up in my office and demand that I divulge the identity of the client who gave me signature rights for that account. *That* would bring the Sardinian to the attention of the police, and if they then started to probe deeper, they might not like what they find. Nor would we, Sammy."

"But hold on. Nobody else knows about those gold trades," Schweizer said.

"What do you mean?"

"I mean *you* know. *I* know. *Stucker* knows. And that's it."

"I still don't understand," Zwiebach said. "All those trades were in those ten dossiers that Zopf handed over to you and that you then handed over to that Hambro fellow."

"Wrong. All the trades were in those ten dossiers *except* the gold trades."

"Why?" Zwiebach asked.

"Because the General Bank did not turn over all its records related to Black's account. They just turned over what they were asked for. The Bank of England came up with ten dates, and the General Bank produced ten dossiers. Gold trades were never involved, since gold never played a role in the thinking of the Bank of England surveillance group. Even if it had, and even if they had looked for suspicious trading activity involving gold, they would have found nothing. *Because all our gold trades were made in New York.*"

"But the records of those gold trades are still here in Zurich," the Swiss lawyer said. "And as I told you at the outset of this conversation, Urs Stucker knows about them."

"What makes you think that Urs Stucker would bring this up?"

"I'm sure he won't volunteer that information now. He told me as much on the phone. But when this comes to trial and he is asked to testify before the court under oath, that might be quite another matter. Urs Stucker, as a good old-fashioned Swiss, would do his duty. I think that's why he called. To give me time."

"This is not good," Schweizer said.

"No. So we have no choice. We are going to have to tell the Sardinian."

"Tell him what?"

"Everything."

Now there was a long silence on Schweizer's end.

"When?"

"Right away."

Sally Black had just read the same story in the *Herald Tribune* over breakfast in her suite at the Euler Hotel in Basel. All it had done was add to her feeling of helpless frustration. How could what now seemed to be the entire world believe that her husband had lived a life of total deceit for the past four years?

Most worrisome of all was the attitude of the American government. Charlie had been willing to work for $135,000 a year as Chairman of the Federal Reserve when he could have been making $5 million a year as vice-chairman of Whitney Brothers.

And his reward?

Without hearing one word from Charlie, everybody in Washington—from the White House on down—had already turned their backs on him. Even her overpaid Washington lawyer had had the nerve to claim he was too busy to come over and help get Charlie out of jail. Instead she had to rely on that local Swiss attorney—with a name like Doktor Doktor Läckerlin, for God's sake—to do that. She didn't trust him any further than she could throw him. But what was the alternative?

Now what to tell Charlie? Once again she glanced down at the headline.

Former Head of Federal Reserve Arrested in Switzerland

She knew her Charles Black. He was a very proud man. Just seeing that headline—black on white—would almost kill him.

What followed below that headline would be even worse, because Charlie was still of the naive opinion that it was only a matter of time before the American ambassador got marching orders from Washington—to get Charles Black out of jail and then out of Switzerland. And to do it right now.

Fat chance that would *ever* happen. And she would have no choice but to tell Charlie the truth. She was scheduled to meet him at four o'clock in the office of that pompous state attorney. Then she had a comforting thought. Maybe they would show him the newspaper and spare her having to break the bad news to him.

33

What they were about to show Charles Black was a lot worse than that article in the *Herald Tribune*.

The admonition that the state attorney had issued to his young detective—to move the Charles Black case to a speedy resolution— produced an immediate response. After talking on the phone to Urs Stucker in order to set up an appointment, Paul Schmidt called over to the Lohnhof, where Black was being held. His instructions: Instead of bringing Black over for further interrogation at ten o'clock, as had been originally scheduled, they were to keep him locked up until further notice.

Then, using the floor of his office, Schmidt began to lay out in chronological order all the documents he had received from Derek Hambro the previous Friday. That done, he methodically developed a chronology of events on his Macintosh computer, filling in, one by one, the pieces of evidence that were laid out on his office floor. Three hours later he had it printed out.

What resulted was forty-two pages of the

most damning summation of evidence that he had ever seen in his entire career. It had not just happened once or twice, or even a half-dozen times—as if "coincidence" could have explained even that. No. It had happened *ten* times, for God's sake.

The prelude was always the weekend meeting at the BIS. Then, starting on Monday, came a huge burst of speculation—almost always in London—on how interest rates would move. Subsequently, there was always another burst of trading activity as the positions entered into on those Mondays were closed out. The results were always the same: A huge profit was made by the General Bank of Switzerland and credited to account number J 747-2239. And it was all documented.

Schmidt decided to sum it up on one page. He drew a time line that traced the path of interest rates in the United States, and covered a period of four years starting with the year that Charles Black had assumed the office of Chairman of the Board of the Federal Reserve. Then he put in arrows to indicate the key dates—which were always the first Monday of the month, with but three exceptions. Then he wrote in the specific dates under the arrows.

Finally he picked up the phone and called the Lohnhof prison. "This is Lieutenant Schmidt. Have Black brought over immediately."

Ten minutes later, after a wary Charles Black had been ushered into his office by a uniformed policeman, Schmidt said, "Please take the chair in front of the desk, and look at this." He reached across the desk and gave Black the sheet of paper on which he had drawn the time line.

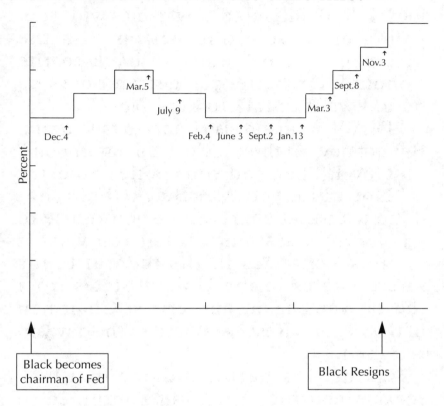

Black examined it carefully.

"What's this supposed to mean?" he finally asked.

"What do you think it depicts?" the Swiss policeman countered.

"It looks to me like a graph of the movement of interest rates over a four-year period."

"Excellent. So far you get an A, Mr. Black. Now please answer the next question. *Which* specific interest rate, and over *what* period of time?"

Black could not help noticing a new aggressiveness in the attitude of the young detective. The respectful politeness had disappeared. He decided to counter in kind.

"Why should I answer? This is ridiculous. I don't intend to play games with you, young man. So either get on with the interrogation or send me back to the Lohnhof. Or, better yet, get your boss up here. I want to talk to him. *Now*."

"Dr. Wassermann also wants to talk to you. But not now. At three o'clock this afternoon."

"Good. Then call your police escort."

"Not quite yet, Mr. Black. We're not done with that chart. Since you refuse to answer my question, I'll tell you what it depicts—changes in the federal funds interest rates in the United States from the day you began your term as Chairman of the Federal Reserve Board to the day you resigned."

Against his better judgment, Black reexamined the chart, but continued to say nothing.

The Swiss detective continued. "You will also note ten arrows. They represent the days—always a Monday—when there was an outbreak of exceptional trading activity for your account at the General Bank of Switzerland in Zurich. The records of those trades— both the purchases and the subsequent sales—are contained in those ten dossiers."

He pointed. They were lying in a row on the floor at the far end of the room.

"The results of those ten trading operations are summarized here. The dates are when trades were initiated. The first occurred three and a half years ago, and the last, six months ago—shortly before your resignation. Each time, the positions were closed out before the month was over. Each time, as indicated, a substantial profit was made. Look at it."

The detective now shoved a second sheet of paper across the desk.

Date	Place	Transaction	Profit
Dec.4	London	Short Eurodollars	
	London	Long U.S. dollars	$57,321,000
Mar.5	London	Long Eurodollars	
	London	Short U.S. dollars	$26,455.000
July 9	London	Long Eurodollars	
	London	Short U.S. dollars	$25,835,000
Feb.4	London	Short Euromarks/francs	
	Frankfurt/		
	Zurich	Long DM/	
		Swiss francs	$27,146,000
June 3	London	Short Euromarks/francs	
	Zurich/		
	Frankfurt	Long DM/	
		Swiss francs	$47,366,000
Sept.2	London	Short Euromarks/francs	
	Zurich/		
	Frankfurt	Long DM/	

		Swiss francs	$51,535,000
Jan.13	London	Short U.S. Treasuries	
	London	Short Eurodollars	$50,539,000
Mar.3	London	Short Eurodollars	
	London	Short U.S. Treasuries	
	London	Long U.S. dollars	$54,276,000
Sept.8	London	Short Eurodollars	
	London	Long U.S. Dollars	$57,321,000
Nov.3	London	Short Eurodollars	
	London	Short DM/	
		Swiss francs	$58,137,000

TOTAL $455,931,000

"To round it off, Mr. Black, here are photocopies of the telephone logs maintained by the law office of Dr. Hans Zwiebach. As you will immediately see, the dates of your phone calls to that office coincide with the dates these trades were initiated through your attorney for your account at the General Bank of Switzerland.

He stood up and handed them to the American. He remained standing as Black paged through them.

"The same dates you are seeing in those logs are entered on the graph below the ten arrows. Subsequent to those dates, and within a relatively short time, the Federal Reserve Board, under your chairmanship, adjusted American interest rates.

There were only three exceptions to this. In each case it was both Germany and Switzerland that adjusted their interest rates. You, of course, learned about this at the BIS meetings. In all cases, your prior knowledge of these events ensured that your investments were enormously profitable.

"As you must now realize, Mr. Black, these documents offer absolute proof of your guilt. There is no room for even one scintilla of reasonable doubt. The evidence is so utterly compelling that I can assure you that our Swiss courts will take no more than a week to find you guilty. Due to the immense size of the *Deliktsumme*—one, I can assure you, that is unprecedented in the annals of criminal justice in this ancient canton—the Basel court will go completely along with any sentencing asked for by the state attorney. Do you understand?"

He paused, waiting for a response. None was forthcoming. Charles Black just sat there, stone-faced.

"There is, of course, a way you could help yourself out. Confess, and show your remorse by returning the funds that you so fraudulently acquired and then transferred to your account at that bank in the Caribbean."

"Now what are you talking about? What bank in the Caribbean?"

"You know as well as I do. My recommendation, Mr. Black," the Swiss detective then said, "is that when you return to your cell, you think this over very, very carefully. I can assure you that should you choose to acknowledge these irrefutable facts concerning your guilt, and return the money, Dr. Wassermann will most certainly take this into account when formulating his sentencing recommendations to the court."

Again Schmidt paused, waiting for a response. In vain.

He picked up the phone. "This is Lieutenant Schmidt. Send over a police escort right away."

34

At four-fifteen that afternoon, Charles Black was ushered into the conference room of the state attorney of the canton of Basel-Stadt. Sally was already there, and she immediately came over to greet him. But it was obvious that this was more than just a meeting with his wife.

The state attorney was also there, in his chair at the head of the table. To his right sat Lieutenant Paul Schmidt. To his left was Black's attorney, Dr. Dr. Läckerlin. All remained seated as Black was shown to a chair at the opposite end of the table. It was indicated to Sally that she should resume her place next to his. Black noted that there were open files in front of everyone. Glancing over to the file in front of his wife, he could see that the top page was the graph Schmidt had presented to him earlier that day. She also had a copy of the *Herald Tribune* in front of her. The glaring headline showed why.

But his attention was immediately directed back to the state attorney.

"Mr. Black," Wassermann began, "I understand from Lieutenant Schmidt that this morning you were given a summary of the evidence against you. Both your wife and your attorney have been given copies of the same documentation. I now will explain to them, and to you, what the implications are. I want you to pay very careful attention, Mr. Black, because what I am about to say will be said once and only once."

He paused, but his gaze remained fixed on Charles Black.

"We have an open-and-shut case against you, Mr. Black. Seldom in my career has the evidence in a case been so complete and so overwhelming. You are guilty, Mr. Black, of massive and repeated fraud. Your fraudulent activities extended over a period of almost four years. Your personal enrichment amounted to the utterly staggering sum of $455,931,000. Not even Robert Vesco managed to steal that much. There is another difference between you. Vesco managed to flee Switzerland before we could put him in jail. In your case, we had better luck. And while we are on that subject, I think that you should not suffer under any delusions that your government is going to get you out of here. I see that your wife has brought along a copy of the American newspaper where that is made crystal clear. Perhaps it would speed things up if you would show him the paper, Mrs. Black."

Reluctantly, Sally picked up her copy of the *Herald Tribune* and handed it over to her husband.

"Take your time, Mr. Black. Read it carefully."

Charles Black's face remained completely impassive as he read. But as she watched him, Sally knew what was happening behind that mask. It was the very gradual hunching of his shoulders that gave him away. As his wife of many years, she knew that this was the telltale sign of rising tension. She also knew that it took a lot—an awful lot—to bring her otherwise imperturbable husband to this state. He finally pushed the paper aside.

"Done?" the state attorney asked.

Charles Black offered no response.

"All right. Now listen carefully," Wassermann said. He glanced over at Dr. Läckerlin and added, "All of you."

"You are now formally charged, Mr. Black, with fraud, misuse of public office for private gain, and misuse of state secrets for private gain under Articles 148, 267, and 312 of the Swiss Criminal Code. The penalties for the crimes described in these articles depend upon the size of the

Deliktsumme and whether or not the criminal activities were habitual. The place where you will serve your sentence also depends on these two factors. For lesser crimes, convicts are sent to a *Gefängnis,* where relatively liberal conditions exist. Those committing serious crimes are sent to the *Zuchthaus,* where hard labor is mandatory."

He rolled *Zuchthaus* off his Swiss-German tongue with obvious relish.

"Owing to the size of the *Deliktsumme* and to the fact that your criminal activities were habitual—extending over a three-year period—when convicted, you will receive the maximum penalty prescribed under those articles of the law that I have already cited."

He concluded, "That will amount to thirty years *Zuchthaus.*"

Despite herself, Sally Black gasped. Not caring anymore, she reached over and took hold of her husband's hand.

"This is preposterous," she blurted out.

It was in a loud, commanding voice that the state attorney responded. "Until I am done with what I have to say, you will stay silent, Mrs. Black, or I will have you removed from the room."

She continued to hold on to her husband's hand, but said nothing more.

"I have had a conversation with your attorney, Dr. Läckerlin, prior to this meeting. I informed him that it is in the interests of his client, in the interests of the canton which I represent, and which would have to bear the costs of a trial, and also in the interests of the financial institutions of which you have taken advantage, that we recognize the situation for what it is and bring it to an immediate resolution. I have made a generous offer to Dr. Läckerlin. I will now allow him to discuss it with you privately."

He nodded to the young police lieutenant who was sitting to his right. Then both left the room, closing the door behind them.

It was a furious Sally Black who was now on her feet and directing her words at the lawyer, who still remained seated at the other end of the table.

"How could you let this happen?" she asked. "How could you let us just walk into this? And how could you have a conversation with that man about my husband, *without first asking his permission?*"

Her anger was now white-hot. *"Whose side are you on?"*

"Calm yourself, Mrs. Black," the lawyer said.

"You're fired." It was Charles Black.

"Now, now, let's all settle down," Dr. Läckerlin responded.

"Get out of here," Charles Black said. "You're off this case as of right now."

"Apparently you do not understand the seriousness of the situation you are in, Mr. Black. You are now formally charged. I know Dr. Wassermann, and he meant every word he said. He will put you in prison—in the *Zuchthaus*—for thirty years, unless you listen to reason. He has made a very generous offer to me. If you submit a written confession within twenty-four hours and arrange to return the money—and I have already drafted the wording—he will be willing to arrange to cut the sentence in half. That means only fifteen years. And with good behavior, you would only have to serve two-thirds of that. That would reduce it to ten years, instead of thirty. This is a much better deal than I had hoped for. You would be a fool not to accept it."

"For God's sake, Charlie, don't listen to him," Sally said.

"Don't worry," he replied. "Please get that state attorney back in here, Sally. Then we'll set things straight."

As she stood up and went to open the door of the conference room, Dr. Läckerlin continued talking to her husband.

"I warn you, Mr. Black," he said, "you are making a huge mistake. I have seen the evidence. It is irrefutable. If this goes to trial, if you continue to deny the obvious, and if you continue to show no remorse and keep the money, the court will give you the maximum sentence. Thirty years."

The state attorney now returned to the room and stood standing with Sally at his side as he addressed Charles Black.

"I understand that you finally have something to say."

"I do. I did not authorize Dr. Läckerlin to discuss any deal with you, because I have committed no crime in Switzerland or anywhere else. I have just informed Dr. Läckerlin that he is no longer authorized to act on my behalf. I will seek to engage another attorney as soon as possible."

"You are making a huge mistake, Mr. Black."

"You and Dr. Läckerlin seem to be reading from the same page. Something is so obviously fishy here that it stinks to high heaven. I don't know who you—all of you—are protecting, but it must be a person or persons in a very high place in this country."

"Stop right there!" the state attorney demanded. "How dare you! How dare *you* accuse us—yes, *us*, because I include Dr. Läckerlin— of 'protecting' someone. In this country we have a legal system that works because of the integrity of the people who work within it. You are in Switzerland, not Los Angeles, Mr. Black. And you are now going to find out how our system works."

He now turned around to address Lieutenant Paul Schmidt, who was standing behind him.

"Arrange to have Mr. Black taken back to his cell. Immediately."

Then he turned to Sally Black. "Your visit is over."

Charles Black cut in. "Her visit may be over, but this case has just started,

334

believe me. Even in this country there must be at least one lawyer with guts. We'll find him. And then we are going to fight this all the way. *All the way.*"

A uniformed policeman entered the conference room. He went to where Charles Black was seated and touched his shoulder. Black rose and, as Sally watched, was taken from the room.

"It is also time for you to leave, Mrs. Black," the state attorney said. "I think you know the way out."

The three other Swiss—the state attorney, the police lieutenant, and the defense attorney—watched her as she left.

"It looks as if this will have to go to trial," Dr. Läckerlin said to the state attorney.

"Unfortunately, yes," Dr. Wassermann replied. "I think that all the parties who will be involved should be made aware of this right away, especially Sir Robert Neville and Dr. Samuel Schweizer, since they filed the original complaint. I'll call them immediately. Maybe you should call your colleague in Zurich. He is key to our case. Furthermore, you now have something in common. You both represented this man Black, and you both have lived to regret it."

The calls to Zurich were made within the hour. By seven that evening the recipients of those calls, Samuel Schweizer and Hans Zwiebach, were on their way from Zurich to Sardinia by way of Milan. During the flight, they decided that it would be the lawyer who would do the talking once they got there.

35

It was well into the night when they arrived at the Cala di Volpe, and well past midnight before Zwiebach had finished his monologue.

Pietro di Cagliari had sat stoically—listening, never interrupting—as the Swiss lawyer explained. Now he finally spoke.

"It is a shame that it had to come to this. But things seldom move in a straight line. The Americans are very sensible in such matters. They have a saying, 'Win some, lose some.' We had a long winning streak and made a lot of money. All of us. Now, as a result, we have a problem. All right. So we solve the problem."

"But how?" Zwiebach asked.

"As I see it, our predicament reduces itself to two men: Urs Stucker and Charles Black. Let's start with that vice president—no, you said *former* vice president—at the General Bank of Switzerland. As I understand it, only he can link us to those trades, because only he knows that those first trades—the ones involving gold—were initially made through my fiduciary account and then, subsequently, switched over to Black's account."

"Exactly."

"So one way of solving the problem would be to persuade Urs Stucker to forget about that."

"But how?"

"Pay him off."

"I'm not sure that would work," Zwiebach said.

"Why not?"

"He is a very old-fashioned Swiss."

"Are you at least willing to try?"

Zwiebach mulled that over for a long time before replying. "I think it would not be advisable to try. As I said, Stucker is a typical, old-fashioned, bourgeois Swiss. He believes that the Swiss are a cut above everybody else on earth in terms of cleanliness and honesty. Furthermore, as a lifelong employee of the General Bank, he is no doubt very well taken care of financially in his retirement. So to even bring up money with him would be running a big risk. He might well react by going back to the Basel police—remember, they have already contacted him—and blow this thing sky-high."

"Then forget that idea," Pietro said. "Perhaps there's another way."

"That is?" Zwiebach asked.

"I'll have someone take care of him."

That produced a *real* lull in the conversation.

"No," Zwiebach said. "As I told you, the Basel police know about him. His name is on all the trades, since he was the account executive handling them. No doubt that's why they contacted him. Should something happen to him, red flags would go up all over the place. Remember, records of those original gold trades still exist. The General Bank did not turn them over to the police because nobody asked for them. But if Stucker is 'taken care of,' you can be sure that they will dig out every trade that he made during the last ten years."

As he listened to this exchange of words—weighing the pros and cons of killing a man—Samuel Schweizer sat as if frozen. Then, despite himself, his mind wandered off in what was now an all-too-familiar direction. Simone. She was here, just ten minutes away, in their villa. She was not expecting him because Zwiebach had strongly advised him not to contact her. But...

"All right. So we forget about Stucker—for the moment," Pietro said. "What about Charles Black?"

"According to what his lawyer—now his ex-lawyer—told me this afternoon, he is committed to fighting this all the way. Which would mean that, sooner or later—"

"There would be no trial if there was no Charles Black to try. Right?"

"I don't think that would work, either. If something happened to Black in jail, the same red flags would go up."

"I agree," Pietro said, "if he was killed. But I'm not talking about that. What if he escapes from that jail?"

"That would certainly bring things to

an immediate halt. But whether that halt remained permanent would no doubt depend on how he escaped. If it was obvious that somebody had engineered it, the same red flags would go up. Who did it? And why?"

"Then it would have to be made obvious that *he* arranged it," Pietro said.

"Swiss jails are not like Italian jails, Pietro. They don't let visitors wander in and out. Visits are restricted to relatives— close relatives—and take place under very careful supervision. There's no way that a Charles Black could arrange to get out of that Basel jail on his own."

Then Zwiebach's face lit up.

"Hold on. Maybe we're getting closer. His wife. I've met her. She's smart, and she's feisty. And from what her lawyer—the one she just fired—told me on the phone this afternoon, she is totally convinced that the Swiss legal system is rotten to the core."

"Is she also rich?" Pietro asked.

"Very."

"Are we talking millions?"

"Tens of millions, in my opinion."

"Then that's the way to go," Pietro said.

"But even if it could be worked out, Pietro, what would happen to Charles Black?"

"The Argentines had a word for it. In the 1970s their government got rid of hundreds—no, thousands—of its political enemies. They vanished from the face of the earth. They were 'disappeared.' "

"That meant killed, did it not?" Zwiebach asked.

"No, no," Pietro said. "Their families were never sure what happened to them. They always hoped against hope that they were in hiding. Maybe in Paraguay. Or Bolivia. That someone had arranged it. And in a few cases—very few—that proved true. But what happened in Argentina many years ago is not really pertinent to what we are discussing now. The art of making people 'disappear' has been developed much further since then."

"What do you mean?"

"Should I really tell you?" Pietro said. Then: "Why not? We are in this together—irrevocably in this together. And even if we were not..."

He left the sentence unfinished as he reached across the coffee table for the humidor that contained his favorite Cuban cigar—Romeo e Juliet. He offered one to each of his Swiss visitors. Only Zwiebach accepted.

"I originally got the idea many years ago—in 1976. It started with a man by the name of David Graiver. Ring a bell?"

For the first time, Dr. Samuel Schweizer joined the conversation. "Of course. American Bank and Trust Company. At the time it was the fourth-largest bank failure in U.S. history."

"Exactly. Why do you remember?" Pietro asked.

"I was just beginning my career with the

General Bank of Switzerland at the time," Schweizer replied. "It was not just his bank in New York that went broke in 1976. So did the bank he controlled in Brussels— the Banque pour L'Amerique du Sud—as well as the Swiss-Israel Bank in Tel Aviv. He also used two small family-owned merchant banks in Argentina as his operating base, the Banco de la Plata and the Banco Hurlingham. They went out of business. We did a lot of foreign exchange business with all five banks. When they collapsed, we were left holding the bag, as far as all of our outstanding contracts with them were concerned."

"We also had dealings with Graiver," Pietro said. "He helped us finance some of our real-estate developments here in Italy. When he got into trouble, we—my father and I—felt obligated to help him."

"He was 'disappeared'?" It was Schweizer who blurted out the word. And his voice carried a sense of awe.

"Exactly. He was the first," Pietro replied. "I was barely in my twenties." His voice carried a sense of pride.

"What happened?" Zwiebach asked.

Pietro replied, "Mexico. August seventh, 1976. His plane—a Falcon jet— slammed into a mountainside near Acapulco. The plane and everybody on it was burned to a crisp." He paused. "Except David Graiver. Because he wasn't on the plane."

"Where was he?" Schweizer asked.

"By that time he was on our yacht, which anchored two days later in the harbor of Havana, Cuba."

"I'll be damned," Schweizer exclaimed.

"It is said—although I have no way of knowing whether it is true or not—that he was the banker for the Montoneros. They were the anti-government guerrilla group that was operating in Argentina in the 1970s. They amassed large sums of money through ransoms, extortions, holdups, you name it. It is known that at least forty million dollars of this eventually ended up in Cuba under a deal personally done with Fidel Castro. Whether Graiver was involved is hard to say."

"Is Graiver still living?" Zwiebach asked.

"Why not?" Pietro replied. "He was only thirty-five when all that happened."

That was obviously all he was going to say about Graiver. He took a big puff on his Cuban cigar. Zwiebach did the same. The suite atop the Cala di Volpe hotel was getting a bit smoky, but the only non-smoker in the room, Samuel Schweizer, did not even notice it. His mind was too busy trying to assimilate all that he had heard during the past five minutes.

"As I said, David Graiver was the first. But hardly the last. Remember Robert Maxwell?"

"Of course," Zwiebach replied. "He was the British press tycoon who embezzled hundreds of millions of pounds from his companies' pension funds, and when he found out that the British authorities were on to him, he killed himself by jumping off his yacht in the middle of the night. I think it happened off the coast of Africa."

"That's right. It happened during the night of November fifth, 1991. The yacht was the *Lady Ghislaine*, and was one of the world's largest—430 tons, 180 feet. It was a beauty. His body was found floating twenty miles off Grand Canary Island. The autopsy was performed at the Las Palmas Institute of Forensic Medicine. Five days later he was buried on Jerusalem's Mount of Olives."

"You mean..." Zwiebach began.

"Yes," Pietro replied, without having to hear more. "Our yacht— the new one that you have sailed on many times now, Sammy—picked him up about a half-mile away from the *Lady Ghislaine*. It was almost five in the morning, but as far as Maxwell was concerned, the circumstances were not at all unusual. He often swam alone in the middle of the night. That night was a clear one, and Maxwell, as a sailor, knew his night sky. He swam due east, and there we were."

"What about the autopsy?"

"Robert Maxwell was declared dead by natural causes. And the body was immediately flown out."

"But who is buried in Jerusalem?"

"A very obese Moroccan," Pietro answered. "As you probably know, Robert

Maxwell was a very large man. So we had to arrange not only for a very large dead man but also for an extra-large coffin. As a result, we could not get it through the door and into the plane we had originally chartered to bring it from Grand Canary to Israel. But it all worked out in the end. As Captain Bob—that's how Maxwell was known to his friends—said afterwards, his only regret was that he missed out on his funeral. It was a grand occasion. A state funeral. Both the President and Prime Minister of Israel were there. Even his wife and children thought he had died, and still think so."

"But how did you get to know men like Graiver and Maxwell in the first place?" the Swiss lawyer asked.

"Though connections. If you really want to know, it was through the Masonic lodge—the P2 branch of the Masonic lodge. For many years its very existence was unknown to anyone but its members. Membership was extremely selective— essentially restricted to Italy's leading politicians, bankers, and industrialists. Their common objective was to fight for democracy and against communism in Italy. Collectively, they knew everybody who was anybody in the world. They did business with each other. They also helped each other out when it became necessary. Sometimes I was asked to provide that help."

"I'm sure you know that, for a while, we

Swiss got very involved with all that. Both our banks and our courts," Zwiebach said.

"Of course. Because of the very unfortunate collapse of the Banco Ambrosiano in the early 1980s. Not only were the Swiss banks dragged into that affair, but also the Vatican Bank. As I said, the P2's connections were everywhere."

"Does it still exist?"

"The lodge, no. The connections, yes, although we have lost some of our most influential members. Roberto Calvi, who was the head of the Ambrosiano, was accused of making $1.4 billion in unauthorized loans to companies in Panama that were jointly controlled by the P2 lodge, the Vatican Bank, Michele Sindona, and Calvi himself. We were asked to help him. So we put him on our yacht, provided him with a Uruguayan passport, and brought him to London, where the final financial arrangements were made for his permanent 'disappearing.' He had a very large personal bank account there, with the London branch of a Swiss bank. He never told us which one. He reneged on his fee commitment, which was twenty-five million dollars cash. The next day—it was June eighteenth, 1982—they found him hanging from Blackfriars Bridge over the Thames."

Pietro took a big puff on his cigar, obviously relishing both the cigar and the memory of the untimely end of the devious ingrate Signor Calvi. Then he resumed.

"Calvi's former partner, Michele Sindona, was more sensible. Sindona, as you must recall, was one of our leading financiers, who controlled banks both here in Italy as well as a large bank in New York, the Franklin National—which went broke in the 1970s. It was the largest bank failure in U.S. history. In 1980 the U.S. court convicted him of sixty-eight counts of fraud, misappropriation of bank funds, and perjury. He got twenty-five years in a federal penitentiary. We could not help him there. But in 1984 he was extradited back to Italy, where he was accused of having made arrangements in 1979 for a hit man to kill the lawyer who had been put in charge of the liquidation of his Italian banks. Pending his trial, he was held in a jail in Milan. Here we could help him. On March twenty-first of 1986, we arranged for him to get poisoned— mildly poisoned, through cyanide in his morning tea. That got him out of prison and into the hospital—where he 'died.' In contrast to the obese Maxwell, Sindona was a man of slight build. So instead of a fat Moroccan, in his case it was a thin Milanese whose body was—and still is—buried in Sindona's grave. Unfortunately, the real Sindona was buried just six months later in Costa Rica. The whole ordeal had simply proved too much for his heart."

The two Swiss just sat there in total silence, not daring to interrupt the monologue of their Sardinian host.

"Another of our clients has fared better," Pietro continued. "Our former Prime Minister Bettino Craxi. They discovered he had accepted seven million dollars in kickbacks paid into Swiss banks to 'thank' senior Socialist Party officials for helping to secure a fifty-million-dollar loan to Banco Ambrosiano from a state-owned company. After that, the Milan magistrates issued a warrant for his arrest. He could hardly leave Italy by either air or land since they had every airport and border crossing on full alert for him. So we arranged for the *Diana* to pick him up in the harbor of Santa Margherita—you know that harbor, Sammy—and we dropped him off in Tunisia two days later. We also supplied him with a Tunisian passport and residence permit. Since the extradition treaty between Italy and Tunisia does not cover corruption—which is the principal charge against Craxi—he's still there— alive, well, and a free man."

"What does all that cost?" Zwiebach asked.

"As Calvi found out the hard way, it is hardly free," Pietro responded. "In fact, no one would take us seriously if we suggested it was anything but very expensive. Which brings us back to the real subject at hand—Charles Black, or, more precisely, *Mrs.* Charles Black. You said she has money. I think we should approach her with an offer to get her husband out of jail and Switzerland. What do you think?"

Zwiebach replied without hesitation. "Yes. And we should do it immediately. Don't you agree, Sammy?"

"Yes," Schweizer replied, "while she is still in Basel."

"All right. Where is she staying in Basel?" Pietro asked.

"Black always stayed at the Euler Hotel when he came to the BIS meetings. It's right across the street from the bank," Schweizer replied. "So I'm sure she must be there."

"All right. But before we approach her, we are going to have to make sure that we can get her husband out. Are you acquainted with the setup in Basel?" He addressed the question to Zwiebach.

"I've worked on a number of cases there," the Zurich lawyer replied.

"Any suggestions as to how we should go about it?"

"Let me think."

The room went silent.

"I'm sure they are going to continue the interrogation of Black on a daily basis," Zwiebach finally said. "That means he is going to be brought over from the jail to the building that houses the state attorney's offices—which is about five hundreds meters away. The route is along a public street."

"The name of the street?"

"I forget. I'm from Zurich. But I know that is how it is done in Basel."

"For all prisoners?" It was Samuel Schweizer who asked this question.

"No, no. Just those accused of white-collar crimes, or at least nonviolent crimes. The rest are interrogated inside the walls of the prison complex. They call it the Lohnhof. I should have made that clear, I guess."

"Why is that?" Pietro asked.

"I really don't know. I assume that as the case load increased, as it does everywhere, at some point some of the police staff had to be moved to other facilities outside of the Lohnhof. And probably, because of the low security risk where white-collar criminals are concerned, the Fraud Squad was moved into the same building where the state attorney himself has his office."

"When the prisoners are brought over from the jail, how many guards escort them?" Pietro asked.

"They are not brought over in groups. They come and go one at a time, according to the interrogation schedule. And as far as I know, there is just one guard who escorts each prisoner."

"How heavily armed is that guard?" Pietro asked.

"I really don't know. I would think he carries a sidearm at most. Certainly no automatic weapons. Remember, the guards and prisoners go back and forth along a public street. I am sure they want to attract as little attention as possible. Which reminds me of something else. There are no handcuffs or any other types of restraints put on the prisoners, until they are convicted. Then things change drastically, especially for those who are headed for the *Zuchthaus*. That's where Black will end up spending two-thirds of a thirty-year sentence. It's a terrible place. Which is another reason for going ahead with your plan, Pietro."

"I agree," Dr. Samuel Schweizer added. "I very much agree."

The Sardinian ignored this sudden outburst of Swiss compassion. "Does Mrs. Black realize what's in store for her husband?"

"I'm sure she does by now, yes," Zwiebach replied. "But I have two questions. First, assuming she goes along with this—with your plan to get him out—where will they end up? And, second, wherever that is, what is going to prevent him or, for that matter, her from continuing to stir up trouble?"

"First, we cannot assume that she will go along with this. This case is different from all of the previous ones. It was always the person who needed help who approached *us*—usually through an intermediary. In the case of Mrs. Black, it is *we* who are approaching *her*. She will have to be convinced that we are for real."

"How will you do that? And won't she wonder why?"

"We'll try to convince her by doing more or less the same as I have done tonight with you. Present our credentials. Our motive for approaching her will be made crystal clear from the outset. Money."

That motive both Swiss understood.

"If she can be sold on our plan, where they end up will basically depend on where the Blacks want to go," Pietro continued. "The options, of course, are limited—and not always attractive. Let's face it, once Black escapes, the Swiss are immediately going to issue an international arrest warrant for him. And because of the high profile of his case, Interpol is going to put him right at the top of its list of the most-wanted fugitives on earth. Under those circumstances, the safest havens are countries like Libya, Tunisia, Uruguay, Paraguay—rogue nations where you can buy immunity from extradition. But such countries are not high on anybody's list of where they want to spend the rest of their lives. Unless the alternative is that type of Swiss prison—what do you call it?"

"The *Zuchthaus*," Zwiebach said.

"*Zuchthaus*," Pietro repeated. "There are places where living standards are better. Brazil, for instance. Argentina. Costa Rica. But going there would require that the Blacks totally submerge themselves. My guess is that this is what they will go for. From what you have told me, they have more than enough money to live out their days in luxurious seclusion. And why not?"

"Which answers my second question, I guess," Zwiebach said. "The last thing they would want to do is attract any further attention from the authorities."

"Exactly. And not just the Swiss authorities. From what you have told me, Black will also be very high on the list of those most wanted by the American authorities. After all, what he did as Chairman of the Federal Reserve amounts to the use of high office for private gain on a scale never seen before, even in the United States."

"I think your analysis is correct," Sammy Schweizer added. "All the more so because of what the Federal Reserve did to a Japanese bank—the Daiwa Bank—in 1995. A rogue trader working at its New York office lost a billion dollars over a period of ten years, but none of the losses were reported. The American authorities finally caught on to him and put him in jail. But then, in what most of us thought was overkill, they publicly humiliated the entire Japanese banking community by claiming that Daiwa management had known about this and had pulled a typical Japanese-style cover-up. So the Federal Reserve closed down all of Daiwa's American operations and pressed criminal charges against Daiwa. Now it's one of their own—the Chairman of the Fed, of all people—who got caught in the act. If we Swiss put Black away for thirty years, their problem will be solved. But if he escapes, then the Americans will have no choice but to go after Black and, when they get him, throw the book at him."

"And who will know that better than Charles Black himself," Pietro said.

"Exactly."

"So we agree that once he is 'disappeared,' he will do everything he can to stay 'disappeared'?" Pietro asked.

"Yes," both Swiss answered.

"Good," Pietro said. "I have a man who has had great experience in these matters. If anybody can convince Mrs. Black, it is he. His name is Vincente Bacigalupi. He knows Switzerland well, since he was brought up just across the border. His entire family makes its living smuggling cigarettes from the Engadin Valley, in southeast Switzerland, across the mountains into Italy. Vincente was the educated one in the family. He actually went to our ancient university in Bologna, where he studied law. But we already have way too many lawyers in Italy. So, after graduation, he went back to the family business. He worked the Swiss side of the operation, which required that he spend a lot of time in the German-speaking part of the country, since that's where the cigarettes are either made or imported and sold in bulk to the smugglers. So he knows the territory. He knows their languages, including even the dialect. He also speaks perfect English and Spanish. In other words, he has both the credentials and the experience."

The two Swiss nodded their heads in acknowledgment of the man's impressive curriculum vitae. All that was lacking was Harvard Business School.

"But he will still need some help from

you, about police procedures in Basel, the exact route they take when bringing prisoners from the jail to the building where the interrogations take place, and so forth. What are your plans?"

"We are flexible," the Swiss attorney replied. "But I think that the sooner we do this, the better."

"All right. Let's meet again at eight tomorrow morning. I'll have Vincente here. I can arrange to have my plane take you back to Zurich by tomorrow afternoon. Vincente and some of his colleagues will go with you."

It was now two o'clock in the morning. Pietro had arranged that two rooms in the Cala di Volpe were available for the night for his two Swiss guests. But only one of them was used.

Samuel Schweizer had made transportation arrangements with the hotel concierge as soon as he arrived, earlier that evening. The hotel limo driver was waiting in the lobby—sleeping in the lounge area. Fifteen minutes later, his limo deposited Schweizer in front of his villa. After fumbling to find his key, the Swiss banker finally got the front door open. Once inside, he moved silently across the marble floor and up the circular staircase. The master bedroom was at the end of the corridor. Schweizer opened the door, hoping that he would not be disappointed. He was not.

She was asleep—and alone.

Five minutes later—after receiving a scolding for startling her out of her wits in the middle of the night—Samuel Schweizer and Simone Bouverie were involved in very strenuous activities. They lasted longer than either of them could remember.

At 7:45 the next morning, when Schweizer emerged from the Villa Svizzera—the name had been her idea—the limo was waiting. Zwiebach, Pietro, and one other man were already in the penthouse suite of the hotel when he arrived. Pietro made the introductions. The third man was Vincente Bacigalupi. He seemed vaguely familiar. Then Schweizer remembered. Santa Margherita. Vincente was the biggest of the men in business suits waiting for them in the dining room.

From the easy relationship he had with Pietro di Cagliari, it was apparent that if there was a Number Two in Pietro's organization, it was Vincente. He had been fully briefed, and it was he who produced a large map of the city of Basel. He knew the city well, since its port on the Rhine was where most bulk imports entered Switzerland, including cigarettes. Zwiebach, taking the map, indicated the route that Black would take each morning on the way from the Lohnhof to his interrogation. Putting the map aside, Vincente then wanted to hear from Zwiebach everything that the Swiss attorney could remember about Mrs. Black—from her physical appearance to whether or not she drank, and, if so, what her favorite drink was. He showed special interest when Zwiebach told him that she was very adept in financial matters, that she had had joint ownership of their Swiss bank account, and that, years earlier, it had been she, not her husband, who seemed to be in charge of the family's personal finances. He then asked Zwiebach to repeat, item by item, what he knew about the evidence the Basel authorities had against Charles Black. Zwiebach made it easy by producing a copy of the one-page summary of the evidence against Black which his colleague in Basel, Dr. Dr. Läckerlin, as a courtesy, had faxed to him after their telephone conversation the day before. Finally, Vincente wanted to know what the procedures were for arriving passengers at the private aircraft terminal of the airport in Zurich. When he was assured that they were minimal to nonexistent, he seemed satisfied.

At noon, the hotel limousine brought all of them to the small airport near the Cala di Volpe, where Pietro's Gulfstream was waiting. Only the two Swiss and Vincente Bacigalupi boarded. Pietro di Cagliari was staying behind. There were two other men already on the plane, seated in the rear. They remained there, unintroduced, during the flight to Switzerland.

At the airport in Zurich, they parted company. Schweizer and Zwiebach took taxis to their respective offices downtown. The three Italians got a limousine that took them to the Bahnhof, where they caught the 3:08 express train to Basel.

When they emerged from the main entrance to the train station there, Vincente immediately glanced to his left. There, as he remembered it, stood the Euler Hotel. Satisfied, Vincente then left it to one of the men who had accompanied him, Alberto, to get them a taxi. Alberto had also spent some time in Basel as a *Gastarbeiter*—"guest worker"—as had many of his compatriots. Like many of his fellow foreign workers, he had frequented Basel's red-light district, located on the other side of the Rhine, in the section known as Kleinbasel. In addition to countless bars, it also had over one hundred massage parlors. Alberto was especially fond of one of them—the Kätzchenhaus.

There were five "guest rooms" above the massage parlor. Alberto arranged that they take over three of them. No registration was required, only an advance cash payment of five thousand Swiss francs to the madam in charge. That would only apply to the rooms, however. If any of the other amenities available on the premises were used, the girls involved would have to be paid separately.

Vincente had commandeered one of the rooms for himself. He found the whole arrangement distasteful. When he was involved in such "projects," he was used to operating out of a luxurious stateroom on the yacht *Diana*. But there was an upside: This being Switzerland, even their whorehouses were spic-and-span. And the room had a shower.

He used it and then dressed carefully. He chose a white shirt, an Hermès tie, gray slacks, and a blue blazer. As he admired himself in one of the mirrors—the room was big on mirrors—he concluded that he looked more British than Italian. When he leaned down to pick up his rather worn and old-fashioned briefcase, the picture was complete.

Going down the stairs and back onto the street through the massage parlor, he hailed a cab and told the driver to take him to the Euler Hotel. When he got there, he strode into the lobby with an air of authority and, noticing the bar area off to the left, headed di-rectly for it. Once seated at the bar, using English, he ordered a Pimms.

The bartender responded in English, but from his accent, it was immediately apparent to Vincente that he was dealing with a countryman.

"You originally from here?" Vincente asked after the drink arrived.

"No, no. I'm from a little town in northern Italy. But I've worked here at the Euler for the past twenty years."

"So you've seen a lot of important people come and go."

"Some. But this is not Geneva. There they have the United Nations, which means they hold a lot of international conferences there. So a lot of important people from around the world are always staying at the hotels in Geneva. Basel's not like that."

"But you have the Bank for International Settlements."

"True. But that's the only international institution here. Fortunately, it is just across the street from the Euler. So, many of those big bankers come here at the beginning of each month. But most people have never even heard of that bank. They keep very quiet."

"Do the Americans stay here when they come to those BIS meetings?"

"Yes. And they always come to the bar."

"So you must have gotten to know Charles Black."

"Of course," the bartender answered. But then he became wary. "Why do you ask?"

"Because he was all over the papers this week."

"I know. They put him in jail. Here in Basel. It's only about ten blocks from here. I don't understand it. He always struck me as a very decent man. And so did his wife. Did you know them?"

"Only Mr. Black. I never met his wife. But I would like to. Maybe you could help me. If so, I would like to offer you a small token of my appreciation."

Vincente let that sink in. Then he switched to Italian.

"*La signora Black abita qui?*"

"*Si.*"

"Quanda sarà in bar?"

"Sì."

"A che ora?"

"Sei ora."

Having established that she was indeed staying at the hotel and usually came to the bar around six, Vincente did not mind when the bartender had to break off the conversation, since three new customers had just arrived. He looked at his watch. Another fifteen minutes to go.

It was five after six when she arrived. There could be no mistake. She was just as Zwiebach had described: a striking woman in her late forties or early fifties, tall, well built, wearing a suit that could only be a Chanel, and carrying an Hermès purse. Ignoring the bar, she immediately headed for a small table in the rear of the room. The waitress was right there to take her order, and when she returned to the bar and repeated it to the bartender—a vodka on ice, with a lot of fresh lemon squeezed over it—Vincente knew for sure that it was she. The final confirmation came from the bartender. He looked over to Vincente and, with the slightest motion of his head, indicated that the subject of their earlier discussion was here.

Vincente gave it five minutes. Then, taking his briefcase with him, he made his move.

"Excuse me, but are you not Mrs. Charles Black?"

The stare she gave him would have frozen a lesser man in his tracks.

"I don't think we know each other," she said.

"We don't. But we have a mutual friend. He told me all about your problem. And asked me to help. He gave me this."

Vincente reached into the breast pocket of his blue blazer and withdrew a copy of the fax that Zwiebach had given him. It was the one-page summary of her husband's insider trading activities. It listed the profits that had accrued to him as a result of such trading—by date, place, and type of transaction. The final line represented the grand total. It was what the Swiss police termed the *Deliktsumme*: $455,931,000.

He handed it to her.

The shock effect it had on Sally Black was immediate. She went totally pale, and when she looked back up at the man standing at her table, for a second he thought that she was going to grab her purse and hit him.

"Where did you get this?" It was meant as a whisper, but came out as a hiss.

"From a mutual friend whom I cannot identify. I gave him my word."

"What do you want from me?"

"Just to hear me out. I want to help your husband."

"Are you a lawyer?"

"Yes. But I do not come as a lawyer. I have been told what the Swiss lawyers are doing to you and your husband. I think you need a different kind of help."

Now Vincente had her attention.

"Sit down," she said.

She watched him very carefully as he took his place at her table.

"You're not Swiss, are you?" she said.

"No. Italian."

"What is your name?"

"That is not important at the moment."

"Fair enough. What kind of business are you in?"

"Helping people who get into trouble."

"What kind of help?"

"In your case, helping you get your husband out of Switzerland."

"How?"

"By arranging for his escape from Swiss custody, and then by providing transportation to the destination of your choice."

That stopped her. But not for long.

"Assuming you can really do that, why would you?"

"For money."

"Well, at least you're up front about it."

Again she examined the man who was sitting opposite her.

"I can't believe this conversation is taking place," she said.

"You probably also find it hard to believe that your husband is in jail, and facing a thirty-year sentence."

"You are very well informed about my husband's situation."

"Yes. We always try to do our homework."

"So you've done this sort of thing before."

"Yes. Quite often."

She thought about that for a moment.

"Can you document that? Like who? When? And how?" Sally asked.

"Yes. But first I must know whether you are interested in pursuing this. In principle."

Sally answered without hesitation. "In principle? Why not?"

"All right," Vincente said. He reached down, opened his briefcase, and extracted two folders. "Let's start with a recent case. Are you familiar with the name Robert Vesco?"

"Of course. My husband's spent his whole life in the financial business."

"Then you know that for many years he was a fugitive, wanted by both the Swiss and American authorities."

"But they never got him. He ended up in Cuba," Sally said.

"Exactly. Then Castro put him in jail."

"I remember."

"Then you must also remember that when Castro died, Vesco escaped from Cuba. In his yacht."

"But he died at sea when his yacht blew up, didn't he?"

"Not exactly. The yacht blew up. But he didn't die."

Vincente opened one of the folders and drew out three photographic prints. He placed one of them in the middle of the table, facing her.

"Recognize him?"

"Yes."

It was a picture of a man who, though old and drawn, was unmistakably Robert Vesco. He was lying on a deck chair and reading a newspaper. From the background, it seemed apparent that he was at sea, on board what appeared to be a large and very well-appointed yacht.

"All right. Now look at this one."

He placed the second photo in front of her. It was a close-up.

"Can you make out the details of the newspaper?"

Sally picked up the photo and drew it nearer to her eyes. The bar was not well lit, but she was able to make out the masthead of the newspaper, the headline, and the picture. The paper was the *Miami Herald*. The picture in the *Herald* was that of a younger Robert Vesco. The headline said:

Vesco Dies at Sea

Now Vincente put the third photograph in front of her. It was the same scene, the same deck chair, the same newspaper, the same old and haggard Robert Vesco. Except that now a second man was standing beside Vesco.

That man was now sitting across from Sally Black in the bar of the Euler Hotel.

"Amazing," was all that Sally could manage

as she kept staring at the third photograph. "But how dare you show me this?"

"Why not? It's just a picture."

"But hold on. I distinctly remember that they found parts of the wreckage of Vesco's yacht at sea."

"They did."

"Then whose yacht was he on when these pictures were taken?"

"Ours," Vincente answered.

"You have a yacht like *this*?" she asked.

"Yes."

"Where do you keep it?"

"In the Mediterranean."

She mulled that over.

"Could you arrange for me to see it?"

"Certainly. Pick your port."

"All right. Let's say Nice."

"When?"

"It's Thursday evening. How about this Sunday?"

"That can be arranged."

Sally Black leaned back in her chair, and for the first time since the Italian man had joined her, she reached for her drink and drained what was left in the glass.

"Let's go back a bit, to where you started. You said that you are here because a friend of Charlie's sent you."

"I wouldn't say 'sent.' He just asked if we could help."

"But how would any of Charlie's friends know about *you*?"

"You just told me that your husband has

been in the financial business all his life. As I understand it, before he worked for the government he held a very high position with an American investment bank. So he knew powerful and wealthy people from all around the world. And he no doubt provided help to some of them when they needed it. One of them now wants to help your husband."

"But why does he insist on remaining anonymous?" Her discomfort with the idea was obvious.

"I can see why this bothers you, Mrs. Black," Vincente said, "but that's the way he wants it. At least for now. He will contact your husband directly once this operation has been completed."

"How would you expect to be paid?" she now asked.

"Cash. Or a wire transfer to a bank that we would specify."

"How much?"

"Three million dollars. Half up front. Does that sound reasonable?" It was a price that was far below what they normally charged, but for reasons that Pietro di Cagliari had kept to himself, this was the cut-rate fee he had been told to ask for. The number did not seem to shock her. But she also offered no response.

So Vincente continued. "Perhaps you would like to hear about more examples of our work. Some of the men involved you might know about. Others, probably not."

There was still no response from Sally, so he went ahead and described to her how

Robert Maxwell was "disappeared" and Bettino Craxi was smuggled to Tunisia.

Then he asked, "Would you like me to tell you about a few more?"

"No," Sally said. "I've heard enough. And it really wouldn't make any difference. If you are not what you purport to be, you could make up any story you wanted to, and probably fake pictures to prove it. Conjuring up a yacht like that on short notice—that's another thing."

She went silent now as she watched Vincente gather in the three photographs from the table and put them back into his briefcase. The one-page summary of the evidence against her husband he left lying in front of her.

She picked it up and again asked, "I still don't understand how you could get hold of this."

"It has apparently been circulated among those who are involved in your husband's case."

"So it is one of those who are involved, as you say, who is behind this?"

"I didn't say that. But quite obviously banks are involved. What I can say is that your benefactor knows a lot of bankers in this country— just as your husband must have. When you are a big player in international finance, that is inevitable, I am told."

"Fair enough," Sally said. Then: "Assuming we went forward with this, what time frame are we talking about?"

"The sooner the better. The way things are now, we know how to go about it. If circumstances change…"

"But you can hardly do it alone," she said.

"I have arranged for help," Vincente replied.

"That help is already here in Basel?"

"Yes. But I will also need your help."

"You mean the up-front money?"

"Not just that."

"Then what?"

"You will have to be there when we get your husband. To ensure that it is him, and not somebody else. Pictures won't help. We want to be absolutely sure."

"I understand. So you already have a very specific plan?"

"Yes. At least for the first part of the operation—getting him out of custody. I will get to that in a moment. But the second part depends on where you want to go—to end up. And I think I'd better also discuss that with you now, very openly and very frankly. Because this is going to mean a drastic change in the way you spend the rest of your life."

"All right. Let's start with the first part."

During the next fifteen minutes he spoke without interruption. When he was done, she put a single question to him.

"By when must I make up my mind?"

"As I already said, the sooner the better."

"How will I be able to contact you?"

He thought it over for a moment, then said, "As you know, the train station is a half-block away. It has a huge restaurant—the Bahnhofbuffet—where people are constantly coming and going, day and night. Why don't we meet there for breakfast? At, say, seven-thirty?"

"I'll be there," Sally replied.

He rose from her table and reached over to take her hand. To Sally's surprise, he did not shake it but bent to bestow an air-kiss as only an Italian can do.

Then he left.

36

Five minutes later, Sally was back in her room. Her first impulse was to pick up the phone and call somebody to ask for advice. But who? Dan Lash, their Washington lawyer? She knew what his advice would be without calling.

Her daughter?

Yes. But how could she know whether or not the Basel police were monitoring her phone calls? Her experience thus far with the way things were done in Switzerland told her that they probably were. And would it be fair to ask Laura in any case? It would only worry her to death if she became aware of the hopeless position her father was in.

Hopeless—that was the right word. Sure,

she could try to find a new Swiss lawyer. She could bring over Dan Lash to back him up. But she already knew that, in the end, that would not change things one iota. Because—and it was time to face up to it realistically—there was the "evidence."

By any measure, it was thoroughly damning to Charlie.

They had everything nailed down from the day, even the hour, when Charlie had purportedly made those trades, to the exact amounts he had earned each time. Sure, their lawyer in Zurich had cooked the books. And no doubt he had cooked them in collusion with the General Bank of Switzerland.

But prove it.

It was Charlie's word against that of everybody else in Switzerland— which meant that Charlie's fate was already decided. It had become crystal clear that in this country, if there was a prima facie case, if a foreigner was involved, and if the Swiss establishment wanted it, conviction was a certainty.

But it was not just the Swiss who wanted Charlie put away. It was also the Americans and even the British. Where were Charlie's former colleagues at the Fed? Or Sir Robert Neville of the Bank of England, of whom Charlie had always spoken so highly? Sir Robert was now one of Charlie's *accusers*, for God's sake, and the people at the Fed wouldn't even take Dan Lash's phone call.

So what was left? *Who* was left? So far,

just one person: that Italian in the bar.

But was he for real?

If he was a con man, he had certainly put together a very elaborate story on very short notice. Take the yacht. What if she had insisted on seeing it? Or take that summary of the evidence against Charlie. How had he gotten his hands on that? Then there was the story about Robert Vesco, *cum* photographs. You could call it a woman's instinct, but the more she thought about it, the more she was convinced that the Italian really *had* made Robert Vesco disappear.

So, what to do about his offer? In the final analysis, what did they have to lose? If something went wrong, Charlie would probably end up in even greater trouble with the Swiss than he was now. So they'd keep him in jail for forty years instead of thirty. By that time he'd be dead anyway.

She would no doubt end up in trouble, too. She knew that women got no special treatment in Switzerland when their banks and big money were on the line. She vaguely remembered reading about the sister-in-law of Mexican President Salinas. She had walked into a Swiss bank a few years ago and tried to remove some documents from her husband's safe-deposit box. The bank had called the Swiss cops, who had arrested her on the spot. They claimed she was laundering drug money, but she was released shortly afterward, and no charges were brought against her.

That's what would no doubt happen to her if she went along with the Italian—except that *she* wouldn't be released. But so what?

Her mind was already made up. Sure, the ultimate decision should be left to Charlie. But could she communicate this to him without their finding out? They had had their first real visit between four and five that afternoon. It had been in the office of that young police lieutenant. He had worked at his desk while she and Charlie talked together at his conference table. They had kept their voices down, but it was impossible to know whether or not the policeman was really listening in.

As she had left, the lieutenant had suggested that she return tomorrow at noon, and that she might want to bring a picnic lunch along so that she and her husband could share a meal together. Maybe that was part of a good-cop, bad-cop routine. But it could also be that he was simply a decent young man who was trying to be considerate. In any case, the opportunity would be there.

She had come away from that visit worried about Charlie. During the hour she had spent with him, it had become increasingly apparent that beneath the calm surface, Charlie was building up a boiling rage. He had been under interrogation the entire day, a three-hour session in the morning and another two hours in the afternoon, before she arrived. He had immediately told her that the questioning was now taking a new direction: Where had he hidden the money? Now he was being reduced to the status of a common thief. At the end of the morning session, the state attorney himself had put in a brief appearance. He had said nothing, just sat there and listened—like the ever-present stenographer. But as he heard Charlie's consistent denials, the smirk on his face betrayed his utter scorn.

What would happen when that contempt for her husband was put on display in an open court, where Charlie would have to just sit there and take it while all the world was listening in?

It would utterly destroy him.

To try to end the session on an upbeat note, at the end of her hour with him, she had brought up the subject of finding a really good new Swiss lawyer who would take on the bastards and dig out who was behind all this.

His sarcastic response had told all: "Lotsa luck, Sally."

So she already knew what Charlie's decision would be. She looked at her watch. It was eight o'clock. She knew she ought to eat something because she sensed that tomorrow would be a very long day. She'd seen a McDonald's next to the train station. She'd only eaten at a McDonald's once in her life—years ago, at Laura's insistence. Afterwards, she had sworn that it was the first and last time. But after all that she had gone through in this vastly overrated little police state they called Switzerland, the last thing she wanted to eat was their Wienerschnitzel and Rösti. She yearned for something American. Really American.

So she put her shoes back on, took the elevator back down to the lobby, and walked up the street to McDonald's. She was not disappointed. The Big Mac, the french fries, the ketchup, and the Coke that she ordered were as junky as food could get. But it was *American* junk. She relished every morsel. On the walk back to the hotel she recalled what the Italian had said about where they might end up if this worked out. Maybe their first stop would be Paraguay, but she knew that, somehow, their ultimate destination would have to be home. And for her and Charlie, that meant only one place: the United States of America.

Back in her room, she felt better. The little excursion had put things back into perspective. There was still a normal world out there. She was asleep by nine-thirty.

37

Ten hours later, when she walked into the Bahnhofbuffet at exactly seven-thirty, she was surprised at how large it was. There were probably two hundred people having breakfast there. All, it seemed, were having the same thing: milk coffee, rolls, butter, and jam.

It took a few minutes, but then she spotted him. He was sitting at the corner table at the far end of the room, his back to the wall. As she approached, he rose and, after shaking her hand, assisted her in taking her seat at the table. He was dressed like an Englishman on his way to his country estate in Surrey.

"You look very radiant this morning," he began. "You must have slept well."

"I did. I also made up my mind. I want to proceed." She had decided to leave Charlie's name out of the decision making. In case things went badly wrong, it would be her responsibility, and hers alone.

"You are absolutely sure?" the Italian asked.

"One hundred percent."

"Good. Now let me order some breakfast. What would you like?"

"What everybody else seems to be having."

"They call it *café complet*," he said.

He caught the waitress's eye, and the breakfast was served almost instantaneously.

"Do you have any thoughts on timing?" the Italian asked.

"The sooner the better," she said. "But you will need the money first."

"Where will it come from?"

"A bank in New York."

He looked at his watch.

"It's one-thirty in the morning in New York. When do the banks open there?"

"Nine o'clock, I think."

Vincente frowned. "That would make it three o'clock here."

"Yes."

"You can't call from the hotel. You'd have to come back here. Do you have an AT&T calling card?"

"Yes."

"There are phones in the main hall of the train station that accept them," he said, adding, "I checked."

"The down payment is one and a half million dollars?" she asked.

"Yes. Have it sent by way of an urgent wire transfer. Insist that it be there within the hour."

"Where is 'there'?"

"A bank in the Caribbean. I have written down the details."

He reached into the pocket of his tweed jacket for a piece of paper. "Here. I will want it back."

She took it and began to get up.

"Hold on just a minute," he said. "I want to know about your husband's schedule today."

She sat back down. "I assume that they will continue interviewing him."

"During what hours?"

"So far it has been between nine and twelve in the morning, and two and four in the afternoon."

"And in between they take him back to the Lohnhof for lunch?" he asked.

"Yes. But not today. They have arranged that I meet him at noon in the building where he is interrogated. They suggested that I bring along a picnic lunch so that we can eat together. That's when I will tell him about all this."

"Then, after lunch, you will leave, and he will go back into interrogation?"

"I assume so."

"And after his interrogation is done—at four—he will be brought back to the Lohnhof?"

"I would think so. Although yesterday they brought him back to the jail at five, since we had our visit between four and five. But today, since we will meet over the lunch hour, they will probably bring him back to the Lohnhof at four. But I can't be sure."

"I don't like uncertainty," he said as he again looked at his watch. "Would you mind trying to get hold of your banker now?"

"In the middle of the night?"

"Yes."

"I could try. I know where he lives. But I don't know if his phone number is listed."

"Would it upset him?"

"Maybe. But I'm sure it won't be the first time he's had to take calls in the middle of the night. I know that it happened to my husband all the time when he was with Whitney Brothers. Somebody would call from Hong Kong or Istanbul without realizing what time it was in New York. It never seemed to bother Charlie."

"You Americans work too hard," he said.

"Have you ever been there?" she asked.

"Twice. Once in Miami and once in New York."

"Did you like it?"

"Sure. But I like it better in Italy."

"Will we be going to Italy?" she asked.

"Yes. Going *through* Italy."

"To?"

"Probably Sardinia."

"And then?"

"Africa. Tunisia."

"Isn't that a rather circuitous route?"

"Not really. Most people don't realize that Sardinia is only one hundred twenty-five miles from Bizerte."

"By yacht?"

He laughed. "You are way ahead of me."

"What about passports?"

"We are set up to handle that. All we will need are photographs of you and your husband. We are also equipped to take care of that."

"Right away?"

"Right away."

"Where?"

He told her about the place in Kleinbasel, and then again looked at his watch.

"The more I think about it, the more I feel

that you should make that phone call to New York now. I have to make a call, too, in order to alert my people. I'll get the check."

After he had paid, he led the way out of the restaurant into the great hall of the train station. The bank of pay phones was to the left of the main entrance.

She immediately got to an international operator, who put her through to information for the 203 area code in the United States. She knew that he lived in Greenwich. There were two John Wrights. She went for the second one. It rang five times before someone answered. She immediately recognized his voice as that of the man who had succeeded her husband as vice-chairman of Whitney Brothers.

"John," she began, "this is Sally Black. I'm terribly sorry to have to disturb you at this hour. But it is because of something that is urgent and of extreme importance to both Charlie and me. We need some help."

"Sally," he responded, "where are you?"

"In Switzerland."

"Look, we've all heard about what you are going through. So if there's anything I can do to help, just name it."

"Thank you, John. As soon as you get to the bank this morning, I want you to wire one and a half million dollars from our account to another bank."

There was a pause on the other end.

"No problem. Although I will need written instructions—addressed to me at

Whitney Brothers. You know the address?"

"One World Financial Center. Right?"

"Right. The zip code is 10281."

"This is Friday. I'll write you the letter and make sure you have it Monday morning. But it is absolutely essential that the funds be transferred as soon as you get to the office. I'll need confirmation of their arrival today. This is extremely important to me."

Another pause.

"All right, Sally." The reluctance was all too obvious. "Which bank?"

She referred to the piece of paper the Italian had just given her. "I want it to go to the Caribbean Bank for Trade and Finance, account number S 1111. It's located in the Turks and Caicos Islands."

"Are you sure you know what you're doing? I've never heard of such a bank."

"I know exactly what I'm doing." There was steel in her voice.

"All right. I'm sticking my neck way out for you, Sally, but I'll take care of it. Would you mind repeating those instructions so I can write them down?"

She did. Then she thanked him again, mumbled a quick good-bye, and hung up. Her hand was trembling as she did it.

When she emerged from the phone booth, he was waiting outside.

"You wanted this back," she said, handing him his piece of paper.

"Thank you. Did everything work out?"

"The money will be there today."

"Excellent. Now that we're in business

together, Mrs. Black, here's what I propose we do next. I have arranged that—"

Sally interrupted him. "But won't you have to wait for confirmation from your bank that the funds are really there?"

"No, I trust you. Just as you now trust me—which I greatly appreciate."

Sally looked at him in surprise. "The feeling's mutual."

"Thank you. I think it's time you used my name, Mrs. Black. You would say Vincent, although here it's Vincente."

"I like Vincente better."

"Good. I have arranged that we be picked up in fifteen minutes in front of the train station."

"By whom?"

"My two colleagues. They have a car."

"And then?"

"We will drive six blocks to the Barfüsserplatz and park there."

"Then?"

"We will walk diagonally across that square to an ancient stairway known as the Leonardsgässli. It leads up the hill to the Heuberg."

"That's the street where the offices of the state attorney are located. By now I know its address by heart: Heuberg 21."

"Exactly. It is also the street that they use when they walk your husband over from the jail. In fact, the winding stairway comes up to that street almost exactly halfway between the jail and the building where your husband is interrogated."

"Is that where you are going to get my husband?"

"Yes."

"This afternoon, on his way back to the jail?"

"No. Now. At nine o'clock."

"But first I have to explain to him—try to explain to him—what is happening. I already told you that."

"No. I've thought it over. That's too risky. They are probably listening in to every word you say. And also recording it."

"But what about my things at the hotel?"

"I assume you have your wallet and your passport in your purse."

"Yes, I do."

"So the rest you leave behind."

"But..." Then she stopped. "You're right. It just comes as a shock that we are actually going to do it."

"But you're okay, aren't you?" he asked, looking carefully at her.

"I'm shaky, but I'm all right."

"And you are still sure you want to go through with it?"

"Yes."

"Good. Because we are going to need your help."

"To make sure that it's Charlie?"

"Yes. And maybe a bit more." He looked at her feet. "Can you run downstairs in those shoes?"

"I'm not sure. Walking shoes with a rubber sole would certainly be a lot better."

"Did you notice if there is a shoe store around here?"

"Yes. There's one right next to the McDonald's, which is next door to the train station."

"Could you manage to buy a pair in less than ten minutes?"

"Yes. If the store is open."

"In Switzerland, stores open early. But let's go and find out. I'll wait outside."

The store had just opened, and she was the only customer. She went right to the rear, where the women's shoes were on display. There were at least half a dozen Bally shoes that fit the bill. She grabbed one that looked like it was her size and looked around for a place to try it on. By this time one of the salesgirls had caught up with her.

"Please?" she said.

"I'm in a hurry," Sally replied.

She got a blank stare.

Sensing that it was hopeless to try to get through in English, Sally went into a little routine indicating that she wanted to try on the shoe. It worked. The girl took the shoe, led her to a bank of chairs, and, once Sally was seated, knelt to put the shoe on her right foot. It was not perfect, but it was sure a lot better than the Ferragamo she still had on her left foot.

"I'll take it," she said, repeating, while pointing at her watch, "I'm in a hurry."

The girl nodded and reached to unlace the new shoe.

"No, no," Sally said. "I'll keep the Bally on. Bring the other one." She leaned down and took the Ferragamo off her left foot.

The girl understood. She disappeared and returned almost immediately with the box containing the matching shoe. When the second shoe was on, Sally grabbed the empty box, stuffed her old shoes into it, got up, and headed to the counter at the front of the store. There she pulled her wallet out of her purse.

"Pay," she said. "Cash."

It came to 185 Swiss francs. Sally gave the clerk two one-hundred-franc notes, stuffed the change and her wallet back in her purse, grabbed the box containing her pair of Ferragamos, and was out of there.

Vincente was waiting outside. The moment he saw her, his face became wreathed in a broad Italian smile. Now it was he who pointed at his watch.

"Nine minutes," he said. "Only an American woman could do that. Now let's walk back to the station."

They were no sooner there than a black Fiat sedan appeared on the left and cautiously began to approach the curb. Two men were in the front seat—two large men.

As soon as it came to a halt in front of them, Vincente opened the back door and within seconds both Sally and he were in the car and it was moving off. A uniformed policeman, stationed there to keep traffic moving, took absolutely no notice of them.

Vincente now spoke in rapid Italian to the driver. Then he turned to Sally. "Still all right?" he asked.

"Yes. But concerned. Are you absolutely sure this is really going to work?"

"Don't worry. This morning, at dawn, while nobody was around, I went through the drill with my two colleagues. We know what we are doing, Mrs. Black. We're professionals. So from now on, just do what I tell you. Okay?"

"Okay."

Vincente now leaned forward and, in a steady flow of Italian, gave directions to the driver. Five minutes later they entered an ancient square near the center of the city. It was dominated by a large medieval structure, originally a church, the Barfüsserkirche, which was now Basel's Historic Museum. The quadrangle in front of the church was no longer a place of meditation for the barefoot monks after whom the church had been named, but was now a parking lot. It was still early in the morning, and there were still many parking places available, including one immediately adjacent to the exit.

"*Perfetto,*" Vincente said as the driver pulled into it and stopped. Then more words in Italian, directed at the man sitting adjacent to the driver. His response was to reach into the duffel bag that was in front of him between his legs. He extracted a gun. It was a nine-millimeter Beretta. After checking the parking lot for any possible onlookers, he turned around and handed it to Vincente. Then he reached back into his bag, withdrew a second Berretta, and handed it to the driver. The third one he kept.

Sally watched as Vincente checked his weapon. Apparently satisfied, he carefully stuffed it into the side pocket of his English tweed jacket. The two men in the front seat of the Fiat could not have been attired more differently from him. They wore what appeared to be surplus army combat dress, loose-fitting olive-colored jackets and trousers. They both wore sunglasses that wrapped around their eyes. Their hair was short-cropped. They resembled young Italian men trying to look like American paratroopers. To the casual Swiss observer, that made them typically macho Italian and thus amusingly harmless. They would have changed their minds had they been able to watch as both slid guns into jacket pockets that were there for exactly that purpose. Sally could not help recalling Vincente's reassuring words: *We're professionals.*

Vincente again consulted his watch.

"*Cinque minuti,*" he said. As if on signal, both men in the front seat lit up cigarettes. Then all four of them sat in silence as the minutes ticked by. Exactly five minutes later, Vincente leaned forward and tapped the shoulders of both of his men. Then he turned to Sally.

"Now," he said.

There was increasing activity on the Barfüsserplatz, a major hub in Basel's municipal transportation system. One green-colored tram after the other came silently gliding to a halt. Most of the passengers who emerged headed out of the square and into the narrow Gerbergasse, which was lined with elegant stores. Sally had always come down here during her earlier trips to Basel to do her shopping, or at least her window shopping. She had once enticed Charlie to come with her by describing it as the Rodeo Drive of Basel, with the slight difference that the stores were often housed in buildings that dated back to the fifteenth century, the shoppers wore real clothes instead of gold chains and leather pants, and the girls were prettier.

This time it was not Charlie who was at her side. As soon as they emerged from the Fiat, Vincente had taken a firm hold on her arm, and now steered her out of the parking lot, across the tram tracks, and onto the sidewalk on the other side. There they joined the stream of shop clerks and early shoppers streaming down the Gerbergasse. They walked fifty meters, and then Vincente pressed her arm. They came to a halt in front of a very elegant jewelry store. Sally knew it. She had once bought a gold bracelet for her daughter there. They now stood in front of the store window, apparently checking out the Vacherin and

Constantine watches and the stunning collection of black pearl necklaces displayed behind the thick glass. The store was at the intersection of the Gerbergasse and a narrow medieval passageway called the Leonardsgässli, and its showcase windows extended around the corner. Still holding on to her arm, Vincente steered Sally around that corner. On display there was the unique Swiss-made Jetzler silverware. The Leonardsgässli, though in the heart of Basel, was totally off the beaten path, so now they stood alone. But not for long. The two would-be paratroopers had also arrived.

Again Vincente consulted his watch. He then spoke to Sally for the first time since they had left the car.

"In two minutes we are all going to start climbing these stairs. You and I will lead the way. When we get to the top, where the stairway meets the Heuberg, I want you to stand behind me. If they stick to their normal schedule, in less than five minutes you will see your husband coming in our direction, accompanied by a guard or guards. Once you are absolutely sure it is he, I want you to tell me, and then go back down the stairs far enough that you are no longer visible from the street above. That is very important, because if your husband should see you, he will inevitably react. Then the guards will react. And this whole thing could go up in smoke. Understand?"

"And if my husband does not appear on schedule?"

"We wait another five minutes. Then we break it off."

Vincente fell silent. He seemed to be counting off the seconds to himself.

"Let's go," he finally said.

The stairway was narrow and dank. It had been there for almost a full millennium. On both sides rose the windowless walls of three-story medieval buildings. All were private residences owned and inhabited and immaculately kept by Basel families who had been ruling that city for almost as long as the Leonardsgässli had existed. When they were halfway up, Vincente gave a signal and they all paused. To their left was an open gate that gave onto a small courtyard. In the center of the courtyard was a fountain. Behind the fountain stood an ancient lamppost. Overlooking the courtyard, and the city below, was a house, all of whose shutters were closed.

Vincente carefully took all this in. Satisfied by what he saw, he tugged on Sally's arm and they resumed their ascent. Two steps from the top, Vincente stopped. Remembering what he had told her, Sally took her place just behind him. He was right. If she pressed up against him, she had a full view of the Heuberg as it curved off to the left. She could even see the open gate that led into the prison courtyard. From her vantage point, nervously looking first up, then down the stairway, there was nobody else in sight. Then Vincente abruptly turned his head and hissed a command she did not understand. The young Italians must have caught it, though, since they now moved up to a position immediately behind Sally. She pressed her body up against Vincente's back and forced herself to look up the Heuberg. Two men were just emerging from the prison courtyard. One of them was Charlie.

"It's him," she said. As she spoke into Vincente's ear, she had involuntarily pressed even closer to him. He suddenly turned and, whether on purpose or not, put one hand on her shoulder and one on her breast and pushed her flat up against the wall.

"Don't look and don't move until we return," he ordered.

He hissed another order to the two young Italians, and then all three of them moved up the stairway and onto the street above. The Heuberg was a narrow cobblestone lane that had been closed to through traffic for many years. Vehicles were only allowed if they were making deliveries or picking up and dropping off residents and visitors. This morning there was no such activity. There was no pedestrian traffic, either, except for a hand-holding pair who were approaching from the right. After pausing, they decided to take the stairway down. They glanced a bit curiously at Sally as they passed by, but kept on going.

Sally was still in shock at the sudden rough treatment she had just experienced.

"Who does that son of a bitch think he is?" she muttered. Ignoring his orders, she moved up to the top stair of the Leonardsgässli and peered around the corner.

What she saw was Vincente and his men moving up the Heuberg at a leisurely pace, heading straight toward the two men approaching them from the opposite direction. Even at a distance, it was obvious who was who. Charlie was tall and well dressed, and his stride was that of an athlete. The person at his side was a good six inches shorter, ill-clad in a greenish-colored suit that did not quite fit. His haircut reflected his working-class origins; his almost sickly pallor was what one expected of a prison guard. There was no sign that he was carrying a weapon. And, much to Sally's relief, Charlie appeared to be in no way handcuffed, shackled, or otherwise restrained.

It happened very swiftly.

Still behaving in a very relaxed fashion, Vincente and his men passed to the left of Charlie and his guard, who seemed to be taking no notice of their surroundings. Then the three Italians wheeled. The two young strongmen grabbed the guard from behind, one from the left, the other from the right. They immediately had him in a vise and literally lifted him off the ground. In a simultaneous action, Vincente grabbed Charlie from behind and spun him around, talking rapidly as he did so. She could not see Charlie's face, but she did see him nod his head. Vincente released him. Then both men began to walk in her direction. At first the guard appeared to be resisting, but after receiving a swift fist to his ribs, he allowed himself to be hustled forward in the wake of Vincente and Charlie.

Sally stepped out of the Leonardsgässli onto the Heuberg. Charlie saw her immediately. He broke into a sprint as she stumbled forward to meet him. As soon as she was in his grasp she said, "It's okay, Charlie. It's okay. I arranged it. We're getting out of here."

"Then let's go," he said.

Following the lead of Vincente, all six of them moved into the shadows of the Leonardsgässli and began their descent. Halfway down, Vincente stopped beside the open gate that led into the courtyard with the fountain. The two thugs then followed the prearranged drill. They dragged the guard through the gate and across the courtyard until they stood in front of the fountain. One of the Italians drew out his Beretta. But instead of shooting the guard, he used the gun to strike a powerful blow to his captive's skull. The man immediately slumped to the ground. They now dragged him to the other side of the fountain, where the lamppost stood. From his paratrooper garb, one of the Italians produced two strands of wire to bind the guard's hands and feet, and a thin rope to tie him to the lamppost. The other had a roll of tape. Both knelt down next to the man lying on the ground below, though he was now shielded by the fountain and thus out of sight from the Leonardsgässli.

Within less than a half minute they were done. They crossed back over the courtyard and into the Leonardsgässli, leaving the gate open. Everything was as it had been. Vincente delivered a firm congratulatory slap to the shoulder of each man and then turned to Sally.

"We are going to proceed very briskly down the rest of the stairs. Below, we are going to slow to a fast walk, cross the Barfüsserplatz, and go directly to the car. No talking until we are in the car, okay?"

It was Charlie who answered. "Get going. We're right behind you."

Then he took hold of Sally's hand, a grasp that was so firm it hurt. Looking directly into her eyes, he said, "You're crazy, Sally. But it's the only way. And I think it might even work."

Five minutes later they were in the backseat of the Fiat. So far there was no sign that anything had been noticed. There were no sirens, no police cars, no policemen running. Nothing. Vincent was the last one into the car.

"*Lentamente,*" he said to the young Italian at the wheel as he began to slide the Fiat out of the parking lot and onto the Freiestrasse.

"Where now?" Charlie asked.

"A whorehouse," Sally answered. When she saw the look on Charlie's face, she actually giggled. Despite himself, Charlie could not help but laugh too.

"First jail and now a whorehouse. What's next, Sally?"

"The end of the nightmare. We'll be out of Switzerland within three days." She turned to the other man in the backseat of the Fiat. "Right, Vincente?"

"Right," came the terse answer. "But first we have to get to that whorehouse."

Charlie now took a good long look at the man sitting on the other side of his wife. Then he looked at Sally. She knew what was on his mind, knew the questions he was dying to ask, but she just stared straight ahead. He knew what *that* meant. Not now.

The Freiestrasse ran into the Marktplatz, which had always been the central gathering place of the citizens of Basel. They passed the red sandstone Rathaus with its Holbein murals and statue of Munatius Plancus, the Roman general who was the founder of the city. Immediately beyond was the Mittlerebrücke, which spanned the Rhine and led to Kleinbasel, on the other side. Still no sirens, no police cars.

"We're almost there," Vincente said.

On the other side of the bridge, not only did the street name change to Klarastrasse, but the city itself changed radically. The ancient elegance was now replaced by seedy hotels, smelly fast-food joints, and one massage parlor after another. It was not as openly decadent as the red-light district of Amsterdam, or as grossly crude as the Reperbahn in Hamburg. But it was obviously a place where women were for sale, where drugs were peddled, where a tourist in search of a night to remember entered at his own risk. But since it was barely nine in the morning, there were no tourists, no neon lights, and no hookers on the prowl. There were just dingy streets and a few bums sleeping in doorways.

The Fiat suddenly turned right off of the Klarastrasse onto an even dingier street.

"Non vada cosi presto," Vincente told the driver. Halfway down the block, a car was just pulling away from the curb. The Fiat slowed and then stopped. The driver proceeded to ease it gradually into the now open parking spot.

Once the car's engine had been turned off, Vincente again spoke to his two companions in the backseat. "See that place on the other side of the street with the sign that says 'Kätzchenhaus'? That's where we're going. The door should be open. When we get inside, we will be in a small, dark entrance hall. Beyond is a curtained entrance that leads to the main part of the establishment. At the far end of that room is a staircase. We will go directly to it, and up the stairs. Our rooms are on the second floor. But first I want to have a look around. Stay here until I signal you."

"Quanto dovrò?" the driver asked him.

"Due minuti," Vincente answered.

Then he got out of the car. Sally and Charlie watched as he carefully walked up the sidewalk on the right. A delivery van appeared, but it kept on going. Vincente walked another twenty meters. He then paused and, looking carefully in both directions, crossed the street. On the other side he now stood directly in front of the Kätzchenhaus. He tried the door. It opened. But instead of going inside, he stepped back and again checked the street and sidewalks on both sides. Then he turned in their direction and gave them the signal.

"Here we go," Charlie said. He opened the back door on the driver's side and stepped out into the street. Sally slid over to follow him. Suddenly a taxi came racing up from behind. Charlie flattened himself against the Fiat as the taxi roared by with its horn blaring and its driver shouting.

Unfazed, Charlie reached inside the car and helped Sally clamber out. "Those fucking Swiss keep trying to get me, don't they?" he said.

"They'll never get us now, Charlie," she replied.

Vincente almost pushed them through the door when they arrived in front of the massage parlor. It was dark inside, just as he had warned. There was also a woman inside.

"Oh, it's you," she said to Vincente.

Then she turned to look at Charlie and Sally. "These are also friends of yours?"

"Yes. I believe our arrangement covered three rooms. They will occupy the third."

She again eyed Sally and Charlie.

"Where's Alberto?"

"He's parking the car."

"I made the arrangements with him," she said.

"I know, but—"

"I'll have to talk to him."

"Fine."

"In the meantime, bring your friends inside."

She turned and drew aside the curtains from the doorway leading into the inner sanctum. Although the room was almost as dark as the foyer, it soon became apparent that its main features were a bar and five booths, all also curtained. The madam steered them toward one of the booths, and drew aside the drapes. Inside was a table, and behind it a red plush sofa with pillows on both ends.

"Please make yourself comfortable," the madam said.

Vincente appeared to be uncertain what to do.

"Why don't you stay here?" he said to the two Americans. "I'll wait for Alberto in the foyer."

"Is there going to be a problem?" Sally asked.

"No. It will just be a matter of money."

"How much?"

"Don't worry. I've got more than enough to take care of it."

"How long are we going to stay here?"

"Until tomorrow morning."

Suddenly there were voices from the far end of the room. Two women had just come down the stairs. Seeing the madam, they came forward to greet her.

"*Salü*, Betty," they said, both eyeing Vincente as they did so.

"No, girls," the madam said. "He's here on business. Why don't you go and make your coffee?"

One of the women was of Middle Eastern origin and was clad in a dressing gown that might very well have been bought in a bazaar in Istanbul or Cairo. The other was Asian, wearing a tight silk robe that was slit up to her thighs on both sides. Despite the early hour and the fact that neither seemed to be wearing makeup, both were women of exceptional good looks. Before heading toward the bar and the coffee machine behind it, they managed a quick look inside the booth where Sally and Charlie were now seated.

"Would you care for some coffee too?" the madam asked them.

"Yes, please," Sally answered.

"They'll bring you two cups, won't you, girls?"

The madam watched as they left to follow her orders. Then, turning to Vincente, she said, "Let's go back to the foyer.

Maybe we can work this out by ourselves."

Now, for the first time, Sally and Charlie were finally alone.

"Who is he?" Charlie immediately asked.

"I don't know exactly. He's Italian. He claims he was sent by someone who knows you, someone you helped out when you were with Whitney Brothers. So far I've paid him one and a half million dollars. And so far, so good."

"So far, so very damn good," Charlie responded.

"Then you don't think I've made some terrible mistake?"

"No, no."

"But what if they catch us?"

"I'd just be back where I was. And no worse. They intended to ask that I get thirty years. And I have no doubt whatsoever that the courts here would have given them what they asked for. This was the only way out. I just can't believe that it is happening. Because I actually thought about it."

"I wanted to discuss it with you first. But he said they were no doubt listening in to every word we said."

"I'm sure he was right. But I've got to know a lot more. You said he was sent by a friend of mine from the Whitney Brothers days."

"Yes. But he absolutely refused to say who."

"Should I press him to tell me?"

"You could try. But I don't think it would make much difference now."

"You mean we're now in his hands whether we like it or not."

"Exactly."

"What persuaded you to go along with him, other than his telling you that a friend sent him?"

"He convinced me that he is a professional. That he's done this sort of thing many times before."

"What does that mean?"

"That he's in the business of making people disappear, people like us who find themselves in desperate situations with no way out. He does it for money, pure and simple. He gave me some examples."

"Such as?"

"A former Prime Minister of Italy, Bettino Craxi. He was sentenced *in absentia* to eight and a half years on corruption charges. They got him out the day before he was going to be arrested. He's now in Tunisia, where the authorities refuse to extradite him. And Robert Vesco. They got him out of Cuba when Castro died. They helped him sail his yacht out of Havana's harbor. Then they blew up *his* yacht and got him away in *their* yacht. Vincente showed me photographs, including a picture of Vesco talking to him and holding up a copy of a Miami newspaper with the headline proclaim-ing Vesco's death at sea. They did the same with Robert Maxwell. He didn't drown. He was 'disappeared.' By them. I know this all sounds absolutely farfetched. But less than an hour ago you were in jail and I had run out of ways to help you. Now we're here, Charlie."

"I would have done exactly the same thing, Sally. Let's move on. Did they tell you where we're going from here?"

"First to Italy. Then Sardinia. Then Tunisia. After that it will depend on us."

She abruptly stopped talking. The reason: The women were back. One was carrying two huge cups of coffee, the other a tray with croissants, butter, and jam. They both smiled at Sally and Charlie as they served them.

"Be careful," the Asian girl said. "The coffee is very hot."

"We will. This is very kind of you," Sally said. "Thank you."

They did not leave, so Sally continued. "You both look very lovely. Where are you from?"

"Cambodia. And my friend is from Iran. Have you ever been there?"

"To Cambodia, yes. My husband was on business in Phnom Penh, and I went with him. We visited the temples at Angkor Wat. They are wonderful."

"They must be. I was never able to see them. You are Americans?"

"Yes."

Then Vincente was back.

"It's all been arranged," he said. "When you're done, we can go up to our rooms."

He turned to the two young women and said in a commanding voice, "I'm sure you must have other things to do. So if you don't mind…"

This produced a scowl on the face of the Iranian woman and she seemed about to say something, but when the other woman touched her arm, she just turned and strode off. When Sally again thanked her, she smiled back before following the Iranian. Vincente's eyes tracked them until they had disappeared through the curtains into the foyer.

"You talked to them?" he asked.

"We had no choice. They were nice to us," Sally responded.

"I don't like the looks of that dark one," Vincente said. "Let's get out of here before somebody else shows up. Follow me."

He led them to the back of the room and up the stairs. The narrow corridor at the top of the first flight of stairs was as badly lit as every other room on the premises. Their room was dominated by a large bed. Beside it was a table and a lamp. There was one chair, a chest of drawers, and a small closet. The door to the tiny bathroom was open. The bidet was its main attraction.

"Welcome to the Ritz," Charlie said.

"At least it's clean," Sally answered. "It also appears to be well used. I think I'd better check the sheets."

"Don't worry," Vincente said. "We're not staying long. Too many people have seen us. I did not anticipate that."

"So when do you plan to leave?" Charlie asked.

Vincente looked at his watch. "It's still only half past nine. Do you think they know by now that you are missing?"

Charlie thought that one over. "Maybe. Maybe not. The procedures that they follow are pretty relaxed. In my case, they seemed to have established a routine where my hours of interrogation were nine to twelve and two to five. But no one really checks you out when you leave the jail and—except for the first time, at least in my case—no one checks you in when you arrive for interrogation."

Vincente liked that. "So, theoretically, the guard who takes you over could show up late for work, which would mean that you would arrive late for interrogation. And nobody would think much of it. At least for a while."

"That's my impression," Charlie responded.

"But at some point—probably right about now—somebody's going to figure out that something is not quite as it should be," Vincente said. "Even then, it could still take them a while before they realize you're really gone. But they will have no way of knowing *how* you got away. They won't find that guard for hours, maybe even days. In any case, they will be expecting you to head straight for the border—of either France or Germany. As you know, both borders are less than five kilometers away. Does that make sense to you?"

"Yes," Charlie said.

"That should give us at least another half hour to get as far away from here as possible—in the opposite direction."

At that moment the two young Italians appeared at the door. Vincente immediately involved them in a rapid-fire exchange of words. Then they disappeared.

"Okay. We're leaving right now," Vincente said. "They parked the car two blocks away. They are on their way to get it. I don't want the madam or any of the girls here to see what kind of car we're driving. So they are going to wait at the intersection just up the street. We'll meet them there. Then we'll drive to the Swiss Autobahn and head toward Zurich."

"Okay."

Within seconds they were down the stairs, through the room below, into the foyer, and out the door. On the way, they encountered no one. Once outside, Vincente paused to check the street. The madam was nowhere to be seen, nor were the two girls. So they began walking rapidly up the street and away from the Kätzchenhaus. They were almost at the intersection when they could see the Fiat coming down the street in their direction.

"When it stops, we're getting in," Vincente said. "Fast."

Thirty seconds later they were in the backseat of the car. Vincente was seated behind the driver. This time he gave no warning to take it easy. Rather, he issued a series of staccato orders as they zigzagged through the narrow back streets of Kleinbasel. Five minutes later they were on the Swiss Autobahn—the Nationalstrasse 3—and headed east at 120 kilometers an hour. During the first ten kilometers, the Autobahn ran parallel to the Rhine.

Vincente was again checking his watch. "It's now a quarter to ten. In a few minutes we will be coming to the exit that leads into the town of Rheinfelden, where there's a bridge across the Rhine. Germany's on the other side. It's heavily traveled, and the border checks are minimal. When they start looking, here is one of the places where they will be looking first. My guess is that by now they know you've escaped."

As the minutes ticked by and the Fiat sped down the highway, nobody in the car said a word. They did not see even a single police car on the road, moving in either direction. The Rheinfelden exit came—and went.

"Okay," Vincente said, "we're by that one. But there's still one more border crossing ahead, where the highway and the Rhine converge in the town of Stein-am-Rhein. It's about twenty minutes down the road. After that we'll be moving out of the danger zone."

Stein-am-Rhein also came and went. No police. No roadblocks. No nothing.

This was the signal for the three Italians to light up cigarettes.

"You can relax, even take a nap," Vincente said to his two companions in the backseat of the Fiat. "It's going to be a long trip. My guess is that it will take between seven and eight hours to get there."

"Where is 'there'?" Charlie asked.

"Pontresina. Do you know where that is?"

"Not really," Charlie answered.

Sally gave her husband an odd look when she heard his answer. Of course he knew where Pontresina was. During the time Charlie had worked in London, they had spent many a ski vacation in St. Moritz, which was just two kilometers from Pontresina, and even more summers in Zernez, which was no more than thirty kilometers away. That was the village where they had stayed—always in the same small hotel—when Charlie and his Swiss buddy, who owned that hotel, went fishing for trout in the streams of the high mountains above Zernez. She and her daughter had spent their days hiking in the adjacent Swiss National Park, or taking the bus to St. Moritz to shop and have tea or hot chocolate at Hanselmann's. Even after they moved back to New York, they had returned on occasion.

But if he now chose to play dumb, he must have a reason.

"It's in the Engadin Valley. The most famous town there is St. Moritz," Vincente continued. "I know that valley very well. My family has been doing business there for many years."

"I thought you were Italian," Sally said.

"I am."

"But aren't the Swiss very strict about foreigners working here?"

"My dear, when you have the right connections, everything is possible. Even in Switzerland."

Charlie gave her a slight nudge in the ribs.

"Oh," she said. "Of course." Then: "Do you mind if I open the window?"

"Go ahead."

She did, and sweet, warm, early-summer air now poured in, driving out the stale cigarette smoke that had filled the car. It was June in Switzerland, and despite all that had happened, there was no denying that it was a green and lovely country that they were passing through. Charlie leaned toward her, now also drinking it all in.

"You know," he said, "if it wasn't for the Swiss, Switzerland would be a great country."

They were just going by a road sign indicating that Zurich was only twenty kilometers away when two police cars, lights flashing, came into view. They were traveling at a very high speed, and they were going in the opposite direction.

"I don't like that," Vincente said.

"Maybe we should get off the Autobahn," Charlie suggested.

"No. In ten minutes we'll be past Zurich. That's where they're coming from. The sooner we get by that city and put even more distance between us and Basel, the better.

I think we're still one step ahead of them. Though barely."

Suddenly a low-flying police helicopter passed overhead, headed in the same direction as the police cars. In response, Vincent spoke two words to the driver: *"Pi;agu presto."*

The reaction was immediately apparent on the speedometer. It moved up to 140. "Everybody keep an eye out,"Vincente said.

During the next fifteen minutes, his eyes were mostly peering out the rear window of the Fiat. They flashed by the Zurich turnoff, staying on the N-3, which now took them down the west side of the Zurichsee in the direction of Chur.

"Okay," he said, "now we can slow down again."

"Jesus," Charlie said to him, "you sure seem to know what you're doing."

Vincente flashed his Italian smile back at him. "That's what you're paying me for, Charlie." It was the first time he had used his name. "Which reminds me of something. I don't know whether your wife has had time to explain the details of our business arrangement, but when we get to our destination, another payment will be due."

"You mean when we get to Tunisia?"

"No. I mean when we get to our last stop in Switzerland."

"No problem. Whatever you and Sally agreed to."

Sally was going to say something about

that, but changed her mind. Instead, she said, "This reminds me of something. I promised our banker in New York that he would get a written and signed confirmation of the instructions I gave him this morning. And I assured him that he would have it in hand by Monday morning."

"You didn't tell me that," Vincente said.

"I didn't get a chance to tell you," Sally replied. "But I know our banker, and he's going to need it before he can arrange for another payment to be made. Right, Charlie?"

"I'm afraid so."

"If he is to get it Monday," Vincente said, "then it will have to be sent off today. This is Friday, and on weekends the post offices in Switzerland close down. In small places like St. Moritz, so does Federal Express. Let me think about that."

"Why not stop in Chur?" Charlie said.

"What do you know about Chur?" Vincente demanded in a sharp voice.

"Nothing whatsoever," Charlie answered. "It's just that the road signs say that's where we're headed next."

Vincente thought it over for a while. "You know," he then said, "I think you've come up with a good idea. We are going to get off the N-3 in Chur in any case. So this would cost us only an extra twenty minutes or so. And I think we can risk it. My guess is that Chur is about the last place that will get the word that they're looking for you, Charlie. Anyway, there is no reason why you should even get out of the car there. Your wife and I can handle it."

Chur, a city of thirty thousand, was chiefly a transportation hub, where one changed trains before moving on to Davos, Klosters, or Arosa. So it was a busy place, both winters and summers. The post office was on the main drag, right next to the train station, and there was a stationery store right next to it. But on this warm June Friday, there was not a parking space in sight.

As they passed the train station, Vincente told the driver to pull to the curb at a loading zone and stop. "Mrs. Black," he said, "you and I are getting out. Charlie stays here. While we're gone, they will drive around town a few times. That's even safer than parking."

With Sally in tow, Vincente headed directly for the Papeterie Gaumont. There he bought writing paper, plain white envelopes, and a pen. Five minutes later they entered the post office. One wall was lined with tables at which the local burghers stood, addressing their envelopes or making out payment slips of the postal banking system, which most Swiss use instead of checks to pay their monthly bills. One table at the far end was vacant, so Vincente proceeded to commandeer it.

"Here," he said to Sally, handing her the bag full of supplies from the stationery store. "Let's get it over with fast."

She unwrapped the package of writing paper, took the pen, and was about to start writing. But before she did so, she asked, "What was the name of that bank in the Caribbean again?"

"I'll write it down for you."

She gave him the pen, and he reached over for a sheet of stationery.

"I'll also write down where I want the second payment to go," he said. It was an account he had opened at a bank in St. Moritz using a false name and passport.

When he was done, he gave her back the pen and the sheet containing his notes. She began to write.

Mr. John Wright
Whitney Brothers & Pierpont
1 World Financial Center
New York, NY 10281

Dear John:

This is to confirm our conversation of today in which I instructed you to withdraw $1.5 million from our account at Whitney Brothers and wire it to the Caribbean Bank for Trade and Finance in the Turks and Caicos Islands.

Please withdraw an additional $1.5 million from our account and wire the funds to: Account #783522, The Swiss Bank Corporation, St. Moritz, Switzerland. I will call you Monday to confirm this.

Sincerely,
Sally Black

She handed the letter to Vincente. He read it.

"Okay?" she asked.

"Is it necessary that you call him again?"

"If I don't, he won't do it."

"All right." The reluctance in his voice was obvious. He reread the letter.

"You forgot to date it. Please do so."

She did as she was told.

"Now address an envelope. Use your home address in America as the return address."

Again she did as she was told.

He took the letter, folded it, stuck it in the envelope, and sealed it.

"Wait here," he said.

He got in line at the Express Mail counter. It moved fast, and in less than ten minutes he was back.

"That was expensive," he said. "But don't worry, I won't charge extra. Now we'll go outside and wait for the car."

Although it was only midday, the traffic in downtown Chur was heavy. The reason was the weather. This promised to be the first really warm weekend of the early summer, and many of the German Swiss had gotten into their cars early in order to get a head start on the weekend rush to the mountain resorts that surrounded Chur, all within easy reach of the big cities in the north of the country. So it was ten minutes before the black Fiat finally pulled up in front of the post office.

Once inside the car, Vincente again gave the driver instructions. On the outskirts of Chur, instead of heading back to the main highway, which led south to Belinzona in Ticino, the Italian-speaking canton of Switzerland, they turned south on a road that, although well paved, was narrow and became increasingly winding as they began their ascent into the foothills of the Alps. Now the traffic had thinned out to a trickle. After forty-five minutes they were on a high plateau and in Lenzerheide, where the pristine forest grew to the edge of a series of small Alpine lakes. In the now dazzling sunlight, the reflections of trees on the lakes' surfaces, with the panorama of snow-covered peaks in the distance, was a stunning sight. Even Vincente was impressed.

"*La bella Svizzera,*" he said.

They passed an inn with a canopied terrace overlooking one of the lakes. It was crowded with tourists having lunch.

"I know you must be getting hungry," Vincente said, "but now that we have gotten this far without any trouble, it would be stupid to stop."

On the other side of Lenzerheide, the road began to zigzag downhill, as they plunged ever deeper into a ravine. At the bottom of the ravine was the village of Tiefencastel. As they passed through it, a road sign told them that they were almost at their destination: ST. MORITZ 42 KM. But it was an illusion. Because now the road began to climb steeply up the other side of the ravine. Soon their forward progress was down to twenty kilometers an hour as they navigated one switchback after another. Suddenly there were high walls of snow on both sides, pushed there by the plows that had opened the road for traffic just weeks earlier. Finally, at shortly after three, 2,284 meters above sea level, they came to the Julier Pass, which, two millennia earlier, the Roman military had used as their main north-south crossing through the Alps. Beyond and below lay the Engadin Valley.

"We'll be there in less than an hour," Vincente announced.

By a quarter to four they were approaching the outskirts of St. Moritz. In the forest to their left, they could see the Suvretta House, where the Shah of Iran used to park his girls while he lived in even greater splendor next door in the private villa he had always maintained there. There was surprisingly little traffic as they approached the intersection in the middle of the small resort town. Parked there was a police car, and the two uniformed policeman in it watched as the Fiat came to a stop.

"Don't look at them," Vincente warned.

Nobody did. The driver took the Fiat around the corner—and nobody followed. As they rolled down the hill to St. Moritz Bad, where the spa and the railroad station were located, to their left was a lake, famous for its winter horse races and *skikjoring* on the ice. Overlooking the lake was Badrutt's Palace Hotel, where Europe's royalty and millionaire playboys gathered both summer and winter. Few others could afford it. But now it was between seasons for the super-rich, which accounted for the fact that, in contrast to Chur with its crowd of weekend-trippers, St. Moritz seemed almost deserted.

After another two kilometers across the flat valley floor, they were in Pontresina. To their right they could see the cable car station, the jumping-off point for a huge red gondola that took skiers almost two thousand meters up the Diavolezza. Starting from the top of that mountain, skiers could cross the glacier in one of the most spectacular downhill runs in Europe. On the edge of town the Fiat suddenly turned left off the main road and went fifty meters up a lane. At the end of the lane was a three-story chalet, its wooden balconies lined with boxes of red geraniums. A large garage was adjacent to the chalet, and behind it stood an even larger barn. The Fiat stopped in front of the house.

"We're here," Vincente announced, "safe and sound."

For the first time in seven hours, Charlie Black got out of the car. As he took in the grandeur of the surrounding mountains with the icy blue sky above, and drank in the crisp Alpine air of late afternoon, for the first time in a week Charlie Black knew that he was again a free man. Sally let him be for the moment. She knew what must be going through his mind. It was Vincente who broke the silence.

"What do you think?" he asked. "Very nice, isn't it? You'll like the inside even better."

As he spoke, an older woman dressed in black emerged from the chalet.

Vincente immediately went forward to greet her.

"This is a cousin of my mother. She is the housekeeper and cook *extraordinaire*. She speaks only Italian. But if you need something, just show her, and she'll somehow figure it out."

He then gave instructions to the woman in Italian.

"She will take you to your room," he said. "It has a private bathroom. I suggest you just take it easy for an hour. Then, at six, we'll have dinner. Somebody will knock on your door to remind you. In the meantime, I have a few things to do."

The room was on the third floor, and it was huge and airy, furnished as a bedroom in a Swiss chalet should be, with white lace curtains, a huge bed covered by a billowing *Federbett*, two wooden chairs, and two ornately carved wooden chests. On top of one of the chests were a bottle of white wine, a corkscrew, and two glasses.

"Who gets to use the bathroom first?" Sally asked.

"You. But make it quick. It's been a while," Charlie answered. "After that, we are going to take a shower. Then we will drink the wine. Then we are going to take a nap. And we are going to postpone any serious discussion until after dinner. Okay?"

They were still in bed when the knock on the door came.

Fifteen minutes later, when they were in the hallway at the bottom of the stairs, they could hear voices. They came from the large room that took up the rest of the ground floor. It was a living room, dining room, and kitchen, all in one. A fire was burning in the fireplace at the far end of the room, and Vincente and his two men were standing in front of it. They had changed clothes and were now wearing the typical attire of Swiss mountain people: open-necked wool shirts, baggy trousers that appeared rough and warm, and boots. All three had glasses in their hands.

"Buona sera, signora et signor," Vincente said in a booming voice. "Now we can really begin to celebrate."

The woman in black came from behind the counter that separated the kitchen from the rest of the room with a tray bearing two glasses filled with champagne.

After Sally had her glass in hand, Charlie took his and said, "I would like to thank you—to thank all three of you—for what you have done. It was perfectly planned and perfectly executed. My wife and I will be eternally grateful." Then he raised his glass to the three Italians and said, *"Grazie. Grazie tante."*

The Italians beamed when they heard those final words. Then all three drank what was left in their glasses and called to the woman in black to refill them immediately.

"Now we eat," Vincente said.

The table was set in the rustic fashion of the Grisons, or Graubünden, as it was known in German. The hand-painted plates depicted Alpine pastoral scenes. The ceramic wine mugs and pitchers bore sayings in the ancient language of this region, Romansch, an obscure dialect that was a direct descendent of Latin and was now spoken by less than forty thousand people. But when the food began to arrive, it was all Italian. It was being prepared by the woman in black and served by a pretty young woman dressed in a peasant blouse and skirt. The antipasto could have come from one of the finest kitchens of Rome. The salad could have been served in Ravenna. The pasta was Milanese at its best. But it was the steak, done Florentine style, that was the *pièce de résistance*.

The wine flowed freely. Pitchers were filled and emptied and filled again. The white wine was a Valtelina Bianca. But when the steak arrived, it was a hearty red Valpolicella that they drank. Neither wine had had to travel far since both were the products of grapes that grew in northern Italian vineyards located less than a hundred kilometers distant.

"This is unreal, isn't it, Charlie?" Sally

said to her husband, trying to be heard over the loud Italian voices that constantly filled the room that evening. "The food's great, but the wine's even better. I'll bet they smuggle it in."

"What makes you say that?" Charlie asked.

"Because that's the other business they're in—smuggling. They smuggle cigarettes from here over the nearest border into Italy."

"You sure know how to pick your friends, Sally," he said. "Which reminds me, how and when are *we* supposed to be smuggled across that border?"

"Let's ask. They all seem to be rather loose by now."

"You or me?"

"I'll ask, since I made the deal with them."

Vincente was sitting on her left at the head of the table, jabbering away in Italian. She tapped his arm and he stopped talking and looked at her.

"We have a couple of questions," she said. "How are we going to get out of here and into Italy? And when?"

His voice was a bit slurred as he answered. "We will stay here until Monday, maybe Tuesday, to let things cool down. How we do it depends on the weather. If it stays good, maybe we will hike over the border. We know routes. If the weather's bad, we drive. Maybe in a car. Maybe in a truck."

"But if we drive, and they check us at the border?"

"They won't check on this side unless something seems obviously wrong. And we'll make sure it doesn't. Maybe on the Italian side, in Madonna di Tirano."

"Let's assume they check us there. Won't we need passports?"

"You'll have passports."

"When? You will first have to have passport photographs. You said that you were fully equipped to take care of that right away."

"That's right. We are. Don't you believe me?"

She remained silent.

Vincente turned back to the men sitting to his left and barked an order. The man named Alberto immediately sprang to his feet and left the room. Then Vincente turned back and looked at Charlie.

"You can't dress like that for the passport picture. Come with me. I'll give you something else to wear." He looked at Sally. "You're dressed wrong, too. You should be wearing a blouse like the serving girl. She rooms upstairs. I'll tell her to get one of hers for you. And maybe you could do something with your hair. Make it look different. Less fancy. And no makeup. Look plain. Like a Swiss."

He got up and went behind the counter and talked to the girl. Then he waved at Charlie and Sally. They followed him and the girl into the hallway and up the stairs to the second floor.

"Wait here," Vincente said.

He returned almost immediately with an open-necked shirt and a thick knit sweater. "Try them on upstairs," he said to Charlie. "I think they'll fit. We're about the same size. When you're done, come back down. You will see that we are equipped to take care of this—just as I told your wife."

The girl appeared next and shyly handed Sally a beautifully embroidered peasant blouse that was no doubt reserved for very special occasions. Then both she and Vincente disappeared down the stairs.

When they were inside their bedroom, Charlie said, "You sure got him going on this passport thing."

"The sooner we get them, the better," Sally answered. "Wasn't it Ronald Reagan who used to say, 'Trust but verify'?"

"Something like that. In any case, Vincente sure seems eager to prove that he can come through."

"And I know why. The money. If I don't call New York on Monday, Vincente doesn't get his next million and a half dollars. He wants it sent to his account at the Swiss Bank Corporation in St. Moritz."

"I don't quite understand," Charlie said.

"I put it in the letter that I just sent to John Wright at Whitney Brothers. But I'll explain that later. Let's get ready for the photo op— before they are too drunk to point the camera in the right direction."

When they returned to the big room

on the ground floor, the camera was all set up, tripod and all. A straight-backed chair stood three meters in front of it.

"In case you are wondering," Vincente said, "we have all the facilities to process film in the basement. We are in the import-export business. It is a business that requires documents. If necessary, we make our own. Roberto is the expert for that."

Roberto wasted no time. Within five minutes the pictures were taken, and he disappeared once again. But not for long. Twenty minutes later, just as the rest of them were finishing dessert—Linzertorte—he reappeared. He handed two small blue passports to Vincente. Engraved on their covers was a white cross against a red background. Vincente opened the first one, looked up at Sally, then down to the passport, then back up at Sally, finally nodding his approval. He went through the same routine with Charlie.

"Bene, multo bene," he said to Roberto.

Vincente rose from his place at the head of the table and, with mock ceremoniousness, handed one passport to Sally, the other to Charlie.

"Good, huh?" he said as they opened them. "They are real Swiss passports. They were just stolen, I am told, not made. We bought them from very reliable people whom we have often dealt with on other occasions. I called them last night to give them the specifications. They delivered them this afternoon. They did not come cheap, believe me. All we had to do was change the photographs. What do you think, Mrs. Black? Don't you look like a real Swiss *hausfrau*? And Charlie—in that shirt and sweater, nobody would ever suspect that you used to be a very famous American banker, would they? You look like a Swiss mountain guide."

Sally leaned over to look at her husband's passport picture.

"You actually do, you know," she said. Then, addressing Vincente: "But why Swiss passports? Why not Paraguayan or something like that? I thought that was what was usual. At least it is in all the novels that I read."

"Anybody can get a Paraguayan passport. The government there will sell one to anyone who has the money to pay for it, no questions asked. And the border police all over the world know that. Anybody can buy a Polish passport, too, and cheap. But they're all bad fakes. A Swiss passport is like a Rolls-Royce. The only people who qualify for them are six million Swiss, a people who are known everywhere as law-abiding citizens. So they command respect everywhere. And where better to steal real Swiss passports than right here in Switzerland?

"Take another look at them," Vincente continued. "You'll see visas. Australia, Brazil, even the United States. A passport is no good in those countries without a visa. And we usually don't know in advance where our clients might want to end up. The people we buy these passports from are real experts in forging visas. You see, Mrs. Black, we know our business. When I promise to do something, I do it right, and I do it right away. Although we could have done better on the names."

Both Blacks reexamined their new passports—first the visas, then the names. He was now Hans Zurbriggen and she was his dear wife, Annemarie. Their home canton—it is the canton that confers citizenship in Switzerland—was Valais, the mountainous canton in southwest Switzerland. Their hometown was the Alpine village of Saas Fee. He was fifty-six. She was fifty-two.

"So I think we must again celebrate. And I have just the thing to do it with."

He went back to the kitchen and retrieved a bottle from a cabinet in the rear. Out of another cupboard he got five small glasses, which he proceeded to fill. He motioned to the serving girl, who brought one to each person seated at the table. Vincente came back to the dining room and stood at the head of the table. He raised his glass. "To *Herr und Frau* Zurbriggen. May they live a long and happy life." He tossed the entire drink down his throat.

Everybody, including the new Mrs. Zurbriggen, followed his example. "What on earth is it?" she asked when she could finally speak.

"Grappa," Vincente said. "Only for strong men and strong women. Do you want

424

another? If you do, I'll get another bottle. I have one that's even older. Much older and much stronger."

"Absolutely," Sally answered, while her husband looked at her in awe.

That was her last, but it was hardly the last for the three Italians. By ten o'clock the new bottle was empty. And the three Italian men, who had left the table and were now standing—or swaying—in front of the fireplace, were nursing what was left in their glasses. Charlie and Sally had remained at the table and were nursing the rest of their third cup of coffee.

"I think it's time," Charlie said.

"I agree. But just wait a minute longer."

The passports were lying on the table in front of them. Watching the men in front of the fireplace to make sure that they were not watching her, she slid the passports onto her lap, and from there into her purse. Then she got up from the table.

"Hold on." It was Vincente who gave the order.

Sally froze.

"I think it's time for a little TV. The ten o'clock news is just about to come on. Maybe we'll be the stars of the show."

There was a television set on a table to the right of the fireplace. Vincente turned it on just as the talking head of a newscaster came on the screen. He was speaking in German. First there were pictures of what was happening in Jordan. Then came something to do with China. Next—a full-screen picture of Charles Black. As the newscaster continue to speak, Charlie's picture was replaced by one showing the Federal Reserve building in Washington. Then back to Charlie.

"What's he saying?" Sally asked.

"Hold on a minute while I listen."

When the talking head came back on, the picture in the background changed once again, this time showing Steffi Graf chasing tennis balls. They had moved on to sports.

"All right," Vincente said as he turned off the television set. "They said that earlier today your husband escaped. They explained that he was the former head of America's central bank, and that he was being held in Basel on charges of massive fraud. The details of what happened today remain a mystery. The prison guard who was in charge of your husband is also missing. Collusion between the guard and your husband has not been ruled out. An international search is under way for both of them. That was it."

Sober reality had returned. Sally could not help looking at Charlie, now standing at her side. His jaw was clenched in anger.

"Let's go upstairs," she said to him. Then, to Vincente: "Thank you for the dinner and everything. It's been a long day. Please excuse us."

Two minutes later they were back upstairs in their bedroom.

38

"Are you too tired to talk?" Charlie asked.

"No. We've got to talk. Maybe it was just that stuff on television, but I'm worried," Sally answered. "Call it a woman's intuition, but I've got this nagging feeling that something's wrong here. Who *are* these guys, anyway? There's something else. His calling you Charlie. Who the hell does he think he is?"

She decided to leave out his groping her at the top of the stairway in Basel.

"We are thinking along the exact same lines," he said, "so let's go right back to the beginning. There must be some clues somewhere."

"Okay. Where do I start?"

"Why don't you lie down on the bed. I'll sit in one of those chairs."

She took off her shoes and, after arranging the pillows, stretched out.

"You met him in the bar of the Euler Hotel last night. Right?"

"Yes."

"How did he know you were there?"

"I don't know. Maybe that mysterious friend of yours told him that we always stayed there."

"Okay—although that's stretching it. How did he know that you were Sally Black?"

"I thought about that. After seeing you

that afternoon, I came back to the hotel and decided to have a drink. I went directly to a table. He must have been sitting at the bar, waiting. He could have asked the bartender. The bartender knows who I am. I know that because after I checked into the Euler Hotel at the beginning of the week, I went down for a quick drink. He recognized me immediately. He even remembered what I always drank—vodka and lemon juice. I think that's part of his standard routine, remembering the drinking habits of out-of-town visitors. It flatters them and probably results in bigger tips. So it may well be that Vincente asked him, and he pointed me out."

"That answer makes sense. So then he came to your table and introduced himself as a 'friend of a friend' of mine from my investment banking days, who had sent him on a mission of mercy—as an act of gratitude for past favors."

"That was what he said, yes."

"That's stretching it even further, isn't it?"

Suddenly Sally's hands went to her face. "Oh, I forgot to tell you the most important thing."

"What?"

"I wasn't even going to ask him to sit down at my table until he pulled a document out of his briefcase. It was a copy of that one-page summary of the trades you made. The same one that the state attorney showed all of us on Wednesday afternoon in his conference room when he said it constituted enough evidence to send you away for thirty years. When Vincente put it in front of me, at first—"

"How in the world could he have gotten hold of it?" Charlie interrupted.

"I asked myself the same question. At first it crossed my mind that the police were somehow trying to set me up. But for what? That didn't make sense. What did make sense was that the 'friend' who had sent Vincente was for real, that he was a person who must have a very close relationship to someone at the top of the banking hierarchy in this country who was in on your case. Who? Most probably someone at the General Bank of Switzerland. At least that's what immediately came to mind. I mean, that's where all those numbers had to come from. Or am I missing something?"

"No, no. You're right. That's where they had to come from."

"So they were real trades?"

Charles Black remained silent for a minute. "That's what really got to me, Sally. They had to be real trades. The General Bank of Switzerland could hardly have just fabricated the whole thing. There were too many records, including trading slips for each and every transaction. No, that stuff was real. In reconstructing what happened, there had to have been a constant back-and-forth between the General Bank in Zurich and the police in Basel. When they both were pretty sure that they had covered all of the trades, the young lieutenant came up with that one-page summary. I'm sure he provided a copy to the General Bank so that they could double-check. And from there—"

"From there to your 'friend,' who, when he saw it, came to the same conclusion you did, Charlie. That your goose was cooked."

"Jesus, Sally. It does make sense." Her husband mulled that over. "Okay, keep going. So far, Vincente's story is holding up pretty well."

"At that point I asked him to sit down. Then he moved on to presenting me with his credentials. Vesco, Maxwell, the Italian Prime Minister. I've already told you that part of it. No. One detail I didn't. They always seem to use a yacht in their operations. When I brought that up, he offered to bring the yacht to Nice this weekend and show it to me there. By that time I was convinced that he was real, so I told him to forget it. Then we moved on to the money. Three million dollars. Half up front. I didn't argue."

"Then?"

"He told me how he planned on getting you out. He said the sooner the better— and that his people were already in Basel and ready to go. I told him I had to think it over, and he proposed that we meet in the restaurant at the train station the next morning. That was *this* morning, Charlie, although as I tell all this to you it seems like it all happened a long time ago, and that it happened to somebody else, not me. It's weird."

"So you met him this morning and then came to get me."

"Not quite. First I had to make arrangements for the money to be sent. He wanted a wire transfer of the first million and a half. So I went to a pay phone in the train station and called up John Wright. I woke him up in the middle of the night. He was very hesitant at first, but then he finally agreed to do it."

"I can understand why he was hesitant. This thing must have been all over the New York papers."

"It was not just that. It was also that bank in the Caribbean."

Her husband went dead silent, then said, "Say that again."

"I said that when I told John Wright where I wanted the money wired—to that bank in the Caribbean—it made him even more hesitant. He said he had never even heard of it."

"Hold on. Hold on." Charlie was now on his feet.

"What's wrong?"

"Maybe I'm getting really paranoid, but that's where they said I had stashed all my ill-gotten profits. In a bank in the Caribbean."

"What was the name of the bank?" Sally asked.

"We never got to that. It was such an

absurd suggestion I just lumped it together with all the other stuff that was untrue and didn't even bother to press them for the name of the bank. And let's face it, there are hundreds of banks in the Caribbean, and probably half of them cater to crooks."

"Wait a minute," Sally said. "When I wrote that confirmation letter to Whitney Brothers this afternoon, I had to ask Vincente to give me the name of the bank again."

She got off the bed and retrieved her purse from on top of one of the wooden chests. Then she pulled out a piece of paper.

"Listen to this. It's called the Caribbean Bank for Trade and Finance, and it is located in the Turks and Caicos Islands."

"Show me that," Charlie said. He looked at it for a long time. "No wonder the Swiss authorities are unable to get the money back."

"What do you mean?"

"I mean this. I'll bet that's where the money really did end up. Except that it is their account, not mine." Now he was practically shouting.

"Easy, Charlie," Sally warned. "But if it is their account, why would they use it again now?"

"Because by doing so they could get our money and further incriminate me— all at the same time. This would be the last nail in my coffin. Now the Swiss authorities have hard evidence that I—or now we—

are beginning to empty out our accounts in the States before they are frozen by the American authorities, and transferring them to the same old account in the Caribbean that I had been using all along, knowing that it was out of reach of anybody who came after me. I'll bet the banking authorities in the Turks and Caicos Islands don't even have an office. They probably operate out of a P.O. box, and when a letter of inquiry comes in from the authorities in Switzerland, the United States, or anywhere else, it ends up going through the shredder. Remember, Sally, I used to run the Fed. This happens all the time."

"But if you're right, that would mean—"

He took up where she left off. "That the guys that got me out are the same guys that set me up and got me in."

"But why get you out?"

"To stop the investigation and to prevent a public trial where something might turn up that would blow their case against me sky-high. That would lead to a new search for who was really behind all this."

"But what if we are caught and you end up back in Basel?"

"That they will not allow to happen."

"My God, Charlie," Sally said, "now I'm really scared."

He went over and put his arms around her. She was shaking.

"Easy, easy," he said. "We'll find a way out of this."

She was crying.

"Don't worry, Sally. I know how. It just came to me. We start by getting out of here."

"But don't they know that we might find them out? I mean, they must know that at some point we are going to start comparing notes and come to the conclusion we've just come to."

"Maybe. But I don't really think so. At least not tonight. They've done this before and it seems to have worked every time. They are going to bleed us as long as they can."

Sally had stopped crying.

"You're right. I didn't tell you where the next million and a half is going. In that letter, I gave instructions to Whitney Brothers to wire it to the Swiss Bank Corporation here in St. Moritz. Vincente wants it here by Monday."

"I'll bet he's free-lancing. That million and a half is going to end up in his personal pocket. I'll bet further that we won't leave town until he withdraws it from the bank in St. Moritz. *That's* why he's celebrating. And that will hardly be the end of it. At our next stop, which will be Sardinia, from what you told me, he'll demand another one and a half million, and next time it will go where it is all supposed to go—to that same bank account in the Caribbean which is controlled by his masters, whoever they are. Then another hit when they get us to Tunisia. They've got us, and they know it. And in the end, when we run out of money, they'll *really* make us disappear. Permanently. Just as they undoubtedly have done with all, or almost all, of the others."

"What do you mean?"

"First they engineered their escapes, like they did ours. Then they milked them dry financially, just like they are starting to do to us. Then—"

"Then they just killed them?"

"Do you really think that Vesco and Maxwell are alive and well in Paraguay?"

Sally started to tremble again.

"That's why we've got to get out of here right away," he said.

"How?"

"They're all thoroughly drunk by now. So drunk that until they wake up tomorrow morning, they will not even notice that you managed to swipe those passports. And drunk enough not even to suspect for one moment that we might try to get out of here tonight. After all, we're still in Switzerland. Where are we going to go?"

"Where *are* we going to go?"

"I know where."

"When?"

"First we have to be sure that they have all finally stumbled into bed."

"How will we know that?"

"We literally play it by ear."

He went to the bedroom door and opened it. At first there was nothing to hear. But then a loud shriek—a female shriek—followed by a giggle. Then a man's voice.

Vincente's. The voices came from the hallway on the second floor. A door slammed. Then silence once again.

Five minutes later, still total silence.

Charlie closed the door and again bolted it. "I think Vincente's banging that serving girl in one of the bedrooms on the floor below. Which means that the party must be over. But we have to be sure that the rest of them have also gone to bed."

"How?"

"We wait. And listen. Until it is near dawn. Then we go down the stairs and out the door. And trust our luck. So far it's been pretty good."

"And what do we do in the meantime?"

"Go to bed."

They went to bed, but neither went to sleep. At around midnight, both heard it at the same time. Somebody was outside their door. A half-minute later, there came the unmistakable sound of someone very carefully working the latch on the door—until it must have become obvious that the door was bolted on the inside. Then the noise stopped. And the presence outside the door disappeared.

Sally's hand had gone to Charlie's the moment all this began, and it now stayed there as she finally dozed off. But then it was his hand squeezing hers as he began whispering very softly in her ear.

"We're leaving, Sally. No shoes. Carry them."

No light was turned on and none was

really necessary, since the night outside was clear and, despite the lace curtains, the moon bright enough to bathe the bedroom in enough soft light so that they could move around with ease. They were both fully dressed within minutes. Then Charlie went to the bedroom door. Slowly, carefully, he drew the bolt. Then even more slowly and more carefully, he opened the door. Both had their shoes in their left hands as they moved down the hallway, trying to avoid bumping into the walls in what was now almost total darkness. Finally they were at the head of the stairs. Holding the railing with their right hands, they descended, step by careful step, the first flight of stairs. Someone was snoring behind the door of one of the bedrooms on the second floor. But that was the only noise to be heard.

Halfway down the second flight of stairs, as Charlie put his foot down, it produced a loud creak. He froze. She froze. They listened. Nothing. They continued down, now moving faster. From the hallway of the ground floor they could see the main room off to the left. There were still embers smoldering in the fireplace. But the room, dimly bathed in moonlight, was empty.

There was enough faint light in the hall for Charlie to see that the front door was bolted. But was it also locked? He wasted no time worrying about it. He drew the bolt and turned the latch and pulled gently.

The door swung open.

He grabbed Sally's arm and drew her through the door. Then he closed it softly. Again taking Sally's arm, Charlie tugged her in the direction of the driveway. Just as they reached the driveway and were about to turn down it toward the street, Charlie stopped.

"Time to put our shoes on," he whispered.

For some reason, as she struggled to do so with her purse hanging from her left shoulder, Sally looked back to the garage. There they were, leaning against the garage wall.

Two bicycles.

Now it was she who tugged on Charlie's arm. She pointed at the garage with her other arm. He immediately saw them too. Twenty steps later, they stood in front of the bikes. No lock on either. Probably one belonged to the woman in black, the other to the serving girl. They pulled them away from the garage wall and began walking them down the driveway. As bikes are prone to do, they emitted clicks as they rolled, clicks that sounded to Sally and Charlie more like gunshots. But finally they were out the driveway and onto the lane that led to the main road.

"It's now or never," Sally whispered.

She mounted her bike and, wobbling crazily at first, began rolling down the street. Charlie followed her lead. He was more sure on the bike, but was hardly destined for the Tour de Suisse. They both rolled to a stop at the main road leading back to the center of Pontresina.

"Where now?" she asked, still in a whisper, even though they were now a good fifty meters from the chalet.

"As long as it's still dark, we can't stay on this road. If somebody sees us, they'll call the cops for sure. Follow me. I think I know where we can wait until dawn."

She followed him down the cyclist path adjacent to the road. After going three hundred meters, Charlie's bike suddenly swerved across the road and into the lane leading to the Diavolezza gondola lift and the large parking lot behind it. She could see why he had come here. It was a cul de sac, and since it was off-season, the lift was shut down, meaning there was no reason why anybody would be there or come there. She followed Charlie into the parking lot, where he stopped behind the building that housed the base station for the gondola. There was a rear stairway leading up to it.

"Let's sit on the stairs and catch our breath. Then we'll make our next move," Charlie said.

The signal for that next move came a half hour later, when dawn began to break. A rooster crowed in the distance, and the first sound of a passing car reached them from the main road.

"We give it another ten minutes," Charlie said, "and then we're off to St. Moritz

Bad. It's only two kilometers from Pontresina, and as you saw when we drove here, it's as flat as a pancake all the way. So you should have no trouble. When we get there, we'll leave the road and park our bikes in front of the little train station. Okay?"

If it hadn't been for the circumstances, it would have been a trip to remember. Surrounded by snow-capped Alps gradually turning pink in the reflected light of the rising sun, Charlie and Sally Black pedaled their way as fast as they could down the road between Pontresina and St. Moritz, all alone except for the passing of three cars and a milk truck. When they got to the train station and parked their bikes in the stands that were still empty but had room for another fifty bikes, there were actually two people already there. Soon a dozen more arrived. The reason was given on the timetable posted outside the station. The first train out—destination Belinzona—would leave in twenty minutes. But it was the schedule for the *Postauto*—the yellow Swiss bus that bore the painted emblem of a bugle as its trademark and that carried the mail and passengers to and from even the remotest villages in the Swiss Alps—that Charlie was interested in. The next one was due to leave in twelve minutes. It would head east and stop at every hamlet between St. Moritz and the Austrian border at the extreme eastern limits of Switzerland, then turn around and do the same thing on the way back.

Charlie pointed his finger at the column on the schedule so Sally could see what he had in mind.

"So we're going to Austria and not Italy," she said. "That's already a relief."

"Maybe. But not yet. First we're getting off at Zernez."

"And visit your fishing buddy there?"

"Exactly."

"You think he'll help us?"

"We'll soon find out. Here comes the bus. Wait here."

Charlie disappeared inside the station, where he went to the ticket counter and bought two tickets to the last stop before the Austrian border. As soon as he was back outside, he took Sally's arm and they boarded the yellow *Postauto*. They were the only passengers on the bus when it pulled away from the train station exactly eight minutes later. They had taken a seat halfway back. Charlie's eyes were peeled to the window.

Just as they were about to pull onto the main road and head toward the main town of St. Moritz, a Fiat sedan came into sight, approaching fast from the opposite direction.

"Damn it," Charlie said.

"What's wrong?" she asked in alarm.

The Fiat roared by. It was green, not black.

"False alarm," Charlie said. "I thought it was their Fiat."

"I don't think I can take a whole lot more of this," Sally said in a very strained voice.

"Don't worry. We'll be out of here and in Zernez very soon," he said.

"Not so soon. Remember, I used to take this bus on little shopping trips to the big city while you were fishing. It stops about ten times between here and Zernez."

It did exactly that, picking up passengers each time. Charlie kept checking the traffic every time they stopped. Still no black Fiat sedan. After they had left the village of Zuoz, Sally reached over to touch the arm of her husband, who was still glued to the window.

"Now *you* can relax, Charlie. Zuoz is the last stop before Zernez. Anyway, that Fiat was probably a rental car. I'm sure they've got other cars and trucks they keep in that big garage of theirs—even in the barn."

"*Now* you tell me," Charlie said.

For the first time that day, she laughed.

39

They were the only ones to get off the bus in Zernez. It was a small village of only five hundred inhabitants, and was squeezed right up against the side of a mountain, which seemed to soar straight up behind it. The main road was its one and only thoroughfare. The downtown district consisted of unimpressive stucco buildings: a small grocery store, the co-op, a bakery, a butcher shop, and a *Milchladen* where the villagers went every morning with their gleaming metal canisters to fetch milk and buy the butter and cheese that were made in the *Molkerei* situated right behind the store. St. Moritz was only twenty-nine kilometers away, but it could have been on another planet. Zernez was what the Swiss Alps were before the English tourists discovered them in the nineteenth century, before their trees were cut down to make room for yet another ski lift, before their forests started dying from the pollution emitted by the millions of cars that now converge on them every summer.

The bus had stopped right in front of the only hotel in town, the Alpenrose. And that was where the two Americans went as soon as the bus had pulled away and was out of sight.

The Alpenrose was simple, immaculately clean, and cheery. All the rooms, including the small dining room and bar, were furnished in an almost crude Alpine style: wooden chairs and tables and, on the walls of the dining room and on the wooden chests in each guest room, pewter vases full of Alpine roses that had been just picked in meadows above Zernez. It was June, and they were in their full glory.

There was no one behind the reception desk in the small lobby, but there was a bell. So Charlie sounded it.

A big man appeared almost immediately. As soon as he saw them, his face lit up in a broad smile.

"Mr. and Mrs. Black," he said. "What a wonderful surprise!"

He came around the counter and took Sally's hand and shook it vigorously. After doing the same to Charlie, he put his arms around him and almost smothered him in a bear hug. Then he went back behind the reception counter and looked at the open pages of the hotel register.

"I remember the room you always had," he said, "number seventeen. And I see that it's free. But we are still not very full since the season has not really started, so if you would like a different room this time..."

"No, seventeen," Sally said.

"Good. You can have it for as long as you want. Now let me help you with your luggage."

Charlie and Sally looked at each other.

"We've got no luggage," Charlie said. "It's a long story, Primus, but it got left behind."

"That happens all the time," the innkeeper said. "Those airlines are getting worse and worse. Don't worry. Until it gets here, we can provide you with what you need." He looked at both of them once again. "Mrs. Black, I think the first thing you'll need are some different clothes. You can't hike in the mountains in what you have on now. So let me fetch Ingrid."

Ingrid, dressed as always in her black and white maid's uniform, was all smiles when she appeared.

"You remember Mr. and Mrs. Black, don't you, Ingrid?" Primus asked. "They will be staying in the same room where they always stay, seventeen. Their luggage got lost, so they'll need some things right away." He switched to the local dialect for the rest.

The room was not very different from the one they had occupied in the chalet in Pontresina, except for the vases full of *Alpenrosen* and the view from the balcony. As they stepped out onto it, their eyes were immediately drawn to a simple white church that glistened in the morning sun. Immediately behind it was a meadow and, behind the meadow, a mountain.

The forest that grew up its steep side had been scarred by a massive avalanche that had cut a wide swath through it. The only sound that could be heard was that of the bells worn by the cows that were grazing in the pasture behind the church.

"Oh, Charlie," Sally said, "if we could just stay here for a month— right in this room, without leaving it even once. And then wake up one morning to find out that all that happened this past week was just a bad dream."

There was a knock on the door. When Sally opened it, it was Ingrid and another maid, a younger one, both with armfuls of clothes.

"Take what you like," Ingrid said. "They are all freshly cleaned. And if you need hiking shoes, we have a whole selection downstairs that were left behind over the years. They are not very nice to look at, but they are practical. And when you go fishing, Mr. Black, you will have to borrow some of our rubber boots. Just let me know."

After the maids had closed the door behind them, Sally said, "I don't think any of them has a clue about what happened to us, do they?"

"Obviously not. Which does not surprise me. Remember, Sally, this part of Switzerland has always been totally remote from the rest of the country. And their dialect made them a people apart. People like Primus Spöl couldn't care less about what happens in Zurich or Basel or Geneva. I'm sure they don't read their newspapers. Nor watch their television. If I remember correctly, around here they mostly watch Italian TV. So, at least as far the locals are concerned, we should be safe. It's the hotel guests that we are going to have to worry about. In any case, I know we can depend on Primus. That's why we came here."

"I know. He really likes you, Charlie. Because of the way you've always treated him. Like a buddy. Not like he's treated by some of the other guests. I've watched over the years. Maybe it's because you're American. By the way, I've always wondered. How did he get a name like Primus?"

"Didn't I ever tell you?" Charlie replied. "Well, I asked him the same question years ago when we were having a beer in the bar downstairs after coming back from a day's fishing. He said it's fairly common around here. It goes back to Latin, which their dialect descended from. If you remember, Sally, *primus* is Latin for 'first.' So since he was the firstborn son, he got the name Primus. Second son: Secundus. Third: Tertius. And so forth."

"What about daughters?"

"I didn't ask him about that."

"Maybe Prima."

"Maybe not, too. I don't think daughters used to count for much around here."

"You're probably right."

Abruptly she asked, "How are we going to get out of here, Charlie?"

"I don't know."

"What about Vincente and his pals? Can they find us?"

"They are sure going to try."

"How?"

"By asking around. Like talking to the clerk at the train station who sold me the bus tickets. Except that might not help much, since we got off here instead of where we were supposed to get off, at the last stop before the Austrian border. If they find that out by talking to the bus driver, and if he remembers us—two big ifs— they'll come here. This is the only hotel in Zernez."

She said nothing more. Instead she

started to lay out some of the second-hand clothes on the bed. Charlie took off his sweater—actually Vincente's sweater—and went back out onto the terrace, where he stretched out on one of the two lounge chairs that had been arranged to face the morning sun. Five minutes later, Sally joined him. She took her place on the other chair.

"I found this map on top of the chest," she said as she unfolded it and laid it out in front of her. "Unless I can't read maps right, it seems to me that our options are not too many. It's a case of either/or. Either we can go south and into Italy, or east and follow the Engadin Valley to the Austrian border—like the bus is doing—and take our chances at that border crossing. But as you just said, if Vincente asks around, that's where he will think we are headed. So, despite what I said earlier, maybe Italy is still the better bet."

She reexamined the map.

"From here to Italy is exactly forty kilometers. Just twenty-five miles. We could bike that."

"Not you or me. Remember, we're in the Alps. To get to Italy from here, you first have to go over the Ofenpass. Between here and the pass—which means the first few kilometers—you have to climb two thousand meters. So forget bikes. And you can forget cars—we can hardly rent one in Zernez. There are also no trains. So we are back to the bus."

"Or back to Primus," Sally said. "He's got a car. And he's also a professional mountain guide. That opens up some pretty good possibilities."

"That's right."

"So how are you going to approach him?"

"That's what I've been thinking about."

"And?"

"I'm still thinking. By the way, how much money have you got with you?"

"Let me check."

She got up, hurried back inside, and then returned with her purse. She dumped its entire contents on the lounge chair and then knelt beside it.

"First, cash." She counted. "I'm down to three hundred twenty dollars and five hundred ten Swiss francs. I used the rest of the Swiss francs to buy shoes in Basel."

"I wondered where they came from."

"It was Vincente's idea."

"That's it?"

"No. I've got American Express traveler's cheques. I was taught—probably by you— never to leave home without them. That was before they started to take credit cards all over the world."

"How much?"

"A lot. Because I never used them." She had three checkbooks. She went through them one by one.

"How much?" Charlie asked again.

"Six thousand three hundred eighty dollars," she answered.

"Wow. Good for you."

"But some of them are pretty old. Are they still good?"

"They stay good forever. As long as you don't cash them in, American Express gets to keep your money. For nothing. It's a pretty good racket."

"But if we use them, won't they be able to trace them back—to us?"

"That would take forever," Charlie said. Then he sat straight up in his deck chair. "But something else won't take forever."

"What do you mean?"

"That letter you sent to John Wright at Whitney Brothers."

"What about it?"

"You told him to send the next million and a half to the Swiss Bank Corporation in St. Moritz. Right?"

"Yes."

"He'll have that letter on Monday. If he doesn't hear from you again—and you said you'd call—he might very well feel obligated to report it to the American authorities. Then..."

"They would tell the Swiss?"

"Yeah."

"So should I call?"

"I don't think so. We can't do that to him."

"So what *do* we do?"

He looked at his watch. "We wait until lunch. I'm sure Primus will come by our table to see if everything's all right. He'll also want to establish a schedule. Maybe he's already put together a fishing party for other guests, as he usually does. After we've got past that, then, depending, I'll talk to him."

When they entered the dining room shortly after noon, there were only two other couples there. This being Switzerland, no one paid any attention to them as the waitress took them to a table.

As soon as the waitress had given them the menus and left, Sally leaned forward across the table. "Charlie," she whispered, "what about that guard? What if he's still lying there, tied up behind that fountain?"

"I thought about that. Look, it's not as if it's the dead of winter. If it's this warm here, it must be even warmer in Basel. He'll survive."

They both ordered the same thing—a platter of the local cold cuts, complemented by pickles and freshly baked bauernbrot. He had a beer, she ordered tea. They had just finished when Primus arrived.

"Do you mind if I join you for coffee?" he asked.

"Please do," Charlie said.

Primus looked Sally over. "I see you found some clothes that fit. Now nobody would guess that you were an American."

He turned back to Charlie. "I'm afraid I've got some bad news for you."

He saw how they both reacted to what he had just said, so he hurried on.

451

"No, it's nothing serious. Nothing to do with you. It's me. I'm not going to be here for the next two weeks. It's something I've been doing every June for the past three years now. Since the last time you were here was at least five, maybe six years ago, there is no way you could have known that, Mr. Black. But I will try to line up another guide for you before I leave. I'm sure you will end up catching many trout. And when you bring them back, our kitchen will prepare them especially for you, as they always did."

"When are you leaving?" Charlie asked.

"Very early tomorrow morning, while it is still dark. You'll never guess where I'm going."

His face was all smiles.

"Alaska," he said.

"You're kidding," Sally said. "Why?"

"To fish. The Alaskan peninsula has the best fishing in the whole world. And there you are in the middle of nature, real nature, as far as you can see in any direction. It is fantastic," Primus said. "It is like it must have been around here thousands of years ago, when only a few people lived in Europe."

"That sounds wonderful," Sally said, trying not to show her disappointment while keeping up the conversation, "but isn't it very expensive?"

"In dollars, yes. In Swiss francs, no. Maybe you forget, Mrs. Black. When you started to come here years ago, we had to pay four Swiss francs for one dollar. Now they are almost even. And we go by a charter airline, so the airfare is not that bad, either."

"What kind of a charter?" It was Charlie who asked the question, and in a sharp tone of voice that Sally knew well. He was on to something. So she leaned back and just listened.

"Balair. It's a subsidiary of Swissair. From the middle of June to the middle of August, it flies from Zurich to Anchorage once a week. It leaves every Sunday at noon. The people who go are just like me, sportsmen. Some take their wives."

"And how are the arrangements made?"

"In groups. I organize one group of Swiss with the help of a travel agency in Zuoz. There are now twelve of us, mostly hoteliers and mountain guides from around here. Then there are groups that come from Austria, Bavaria, even from the South Tyrol, right across the border in Italy. What we have in common are two things. We all love to fish. And we all speak German—in many different dialects, of course."

"Amazing," Charlie said. "There are enough people to fill up a charter flight each week?"

"Almost. Tomorrow is the first flight of the year, and it is usually not full because it is not yet vacation time in Europe for most people. But it is the best time to go. You see, the sockeye salmon start their run next week. They come from the ocean and go up the rivers by the millions—no, the *tens* of millions. You have to see it to believe it."

"I've never seen it," Charlie said. "In fact, I've never been to Alaska."

"Then you've really missed something, Mr. Black," Primus said.

Charlie remained silent for a moment. "You know," he then said, "this might sound crazy, but maybe we could join your group, Primus. Then you can show me how to fish in Alaska, just as you did in Switzerland. That is, if you would like to. And if you've still got room for us."

Now Sally jumped in. "Say yes, Primus. This is an absolutely fantastic idea. I'll even try fishing in Alaska if you show me how."

Primus looked startled, and at first seemed to not know how to respond.

"Are you really serious about this?" he finally asked.

"Absolutely," Charlie answered.

"But you'd have to pay the full airfare—to and from Anchorage— even if you don't come back."

"That wouldn't matter," Charlie said.

"And I would have to make sure that the lodge where I go every year still has room. You see, after we get to Anchorage, the groups go their separate ways—some to the Kenai region, some way up to Prudhoe Bay, on the Arctic Ocean. There are fishing lodges scattered all around Alaska, a lot in very remote areas. From Anchorage you get to most of them by chartering a small plane, often a seaplane."

"Couldn't you call and find out?"

"I could. What time is it in Alaska?"

All three had to think that one over. Sally was the first to answer. "I think it's either nine or ten hours' difference. So it's still three or four in the morning."

"You are absolutely sure you want to do this?" Primus asked again.

"Yes," Sally answered.

"All right. First I'll check with the travel agent in Zuoz to see if she can still arrange to get both of you on that charter flight tomorrow. If it works out, I'll call the Arrowhead Lodge to see if they still have room." He paused. "You know, only Americans would do a thing like this. That's why I like you."

He got up to leave, and Charlie did also. "Sally," he said, "you probably want to go back up to the room and get some rest. I'll be up soon."

She looked at him, and then did as she was told.

Fifteen minutes later her husband returned. Sally was out on the terrace.

"What was that all about?" she asked immediately.

"I told him that we were having a problem. And that if anybody came around and asked about us, he should tell them he never even heard of us."

"Did he agree?"

"Yes. He gave me a kind of funny look, but he agreed."

"What about Alaska? You *were* dead serious about that, weren't you?"

"Absolutely. And it's simple. Even if we do manage to get across the border into Austria or Italy, then what?"

"I don't know. I just want to get out of Switzerland," she answered.

"So do I. But that's no solution."

"Why Alaska? Is *that* a solution?"

"No. But at least we're back home, where we know how things work. That might lead to a solution. I don't trust the Italians or Austrians any more than I do the Swiss. If they catch up with us there, they'll just toss me right back over the Swiss border. If they catch up with us in Alaska, we've got the legal system on *our* side. You know? Innocent until proven guilty—for a change."

"All right." She knew better than to push it further. "But how can you be sure the Swiss won't catch us before we can get on that plane to Alaska?"

"I'm not sure. But we won't even try it unless the odds are pretty good."

"At this point, I'd be willing to settle for fifty-fifty," Sally said.

"Me too," he answered.

"Did Primus find out if there is room on that plane?"

"No. The travel agent was out to lunch. Primus will let us know as soon as he gets hold of her."

An hour later there was a knock on the door. Charlie went to open it, while Sally remained on the terrace. It was Primus.

"I've got to talk to you, Mr. Black," he said.

"Sure. Come in."

Primus came in and closed the door behind him.

"You were right. Somebody came to ask about you," he said.

"And?"

"I did what you told me and he went away." Primus stopped, and then asked, "Do you know who it was?"

"I think so, yes. I don't know his last name, but his first name is Vincente."

"Exactly. He is a dangerous man, Mr. Black. A *very* dangerous man."

"I know. I found that out. That's why we came here."

"You were at his place in Pontresina?"

"Yes."

"He's a smuggler. The entire family is a band of smugglers. And worse. Much worse. They're Italian," he added, as though that explained it. "I won't ask how you got involved with him, Mr. Black. But I know you and your wife very well. I will help you get out of here."

"Thank you, Primus. I will tell you the whole story if you want."

"No. I don't want to know. Maybe on the airplane. The travel agent called back. There is room on that charter flight. I still have not called the Arrowhead Lodge to find out if there is room there. But I don't think that really matters to you."

"You're right. Then we'll just go and get the tickets from the travel agency," Charlie said. "In that connection, there's one other thing. We do not have our regular passports with us. So we will be booking those seats on that charter in different names. If that's a problem, then just forget the whole thing. I don't want to involve you in our problem."

"You're not. But you have to have passports. Without them, you will not be able to get on the plane to America."

"We do have passports. Just not in our names."

"But they must also be stamped with a valid visitor's visa."

"They are."

"Then give them to me. I'll go to Zuoz right now and make all the arrangements. You stay here in the room. And don't leave it until I get back. I don't trust that Vincente one bit."

"My wife has the passports. She also has the traveler's cheques."

"I don't need traveler's cheques. I'll take care of it. We can settle up when we get to Alaska. And I don't think it is a good idea for your wife to be outside on the terrace. You both stay in the room. I'll have dinner sent up."

40

When the Blacks came down to the hotel lobby at five the next morning, it was still dark. A maid, who doubled as a waitress, helped them with their luggage, which Ingrid had brought to their room the prior evening. A minibus was waiting outside. Primus was waiting inside.

"It's all set," he said. "I've got your airplane tickets. And your passports." He handed them to Charlie, who then gave them to Sally, who put them in her purse. "I'll put your luggage in the minibus for you. You'll need more clothes, but we can fix that up in Alaska. I finally got through to the Arrowhead Lodge. I've also got good news there. They have room, though just for two weeks. After that, they are fully booked until the end of August."

"Perfect," Charlie said.

"Everybody else has already boarded the minibus. I explained to them that you are Swiss-Americans, born here but raised in America, which explains why you don't speak our languages. That's not so unusual. So I think we're set, unless you have any questions."

"No," Charlie said. "How can we thank you, Primus?"

"No thanks are necessary. We fishermen have to stick together."

There were two open seats immediately behind the driver, and Primus indicated that he had reserved them for the Blacks. They were no sooner seated than the minibus pulled away. An hour later they were at the top of the Flüela Pass, where they began their descent to Davos and, beyond that, Chur, where they would get back on the *autoroute*. They had left the Engadin Valley, and Vincente, behind.

Sally spoke for the first time. "Charlie, I think—"

"So do I. But we've still got the airport."

"I'm confused. Do we get checked on the way out?"

"No. Not in Zurich. You just go to the check-in counter after you get inside the terminal, get your boarding pass, then go into the transit lounge and wait until they call your flight."

"Are you sure?"

"Yes."

"But have you ever been on a charter flight before?"

"No. But it can't be much different. Maybe whoever's in charge of the group just collects all the tickets and passports, gets all the boarding passes, gives one to everybody, and that's it. That would be even better."

That was exactly what happened. By eleven o'clock they were safely inside the transit lounge at Kloten Airport. It was the time of day when there was always a lull in traffic there, and this was especially true on Sundays. So the transit lounge was sparsely populated.

Everybody had been told that they would be leaving from Gate 17, and should be ready to board no later than eleven-thirty. The Blacks had gone directly to that gate area and sat down in a row of seats facing the window that looked out onto the tarmac. The Balair Airbus was already parked there.

As soon as they were seated, Sally's hand found her husband's. Hers was ice cold.

"I didn't see one policeman so far," she said. "Did you?"

"No."

"What about the Sunday newspapers?"

"What do you mean?"

"Won't they have pictures of us or something?"

"In Switzerland they don't have Sunday papers like they do in the United States and England," Charlie answered.

"How do you know that?"

"I don't know how, but they don't."

"What about the *Herald Tribune*?"

"They don't either. Saturday, yes. Sunday, no."

"Then maybe I should go to the kiosk and see if they've still got a Saturday paper."

"Sally," her husband said, "you're getting edgy. Look, the last thing we want to do is call attention to ourselves. It's almost exclusively Americans who buy the *Herald Tribune*. It's a dead giveaway. So forget newspapers. Period."

"You're right. I'll shut up."

"No, I didn't mean that. Just take it easy. They've got to start boarding soon."

Ten minutes later the flight was called. When they handed their boarding passes to the Balair representative at the gate, she didn't even bother to look up.

As they entered the airplane, Charlie said, "It's open seating, so we go all the way to the back."

All the seats in the back of the Airbus were still free. Charlie took the window seat in the second-to-last row. Sally sat down in the aisle seat. It seemed to take forever for the plane to fill up. Neither said a word. Charlie kept checking his watch. At five to twelve, they saw Primus coming up the aisle, checking on both sides as he did so. Then he spotted them.

"I was getting worried," he said to Sally. "The rest of us are up near the front of the plane, and we saved two seats for you. But I see you're settled in back here. If you want to change later on, let me know. That won't be any problem, since they tell me the plane will be only two-thirds full."

At that point the voice of a stewardess could be heard on the public address system, asking everybody to be seated. Five minutes later, at exactly twelve noon, they could feel the plane move as it was slowly pushed away from the gate. Soon they were near the end of the runway, third in line, according to the pilot. According to Charlie's Rolex, it was exactly ten minutes after twelve noon when, with engines now at full thrust, the Airbus began hurtling down the runway. Eleven seconds later they were airborne.

"Oh, Charlie," Sally said as she grasped his arm so hard it almost hurt, "we've made it. I never really believed we could do it, but we've made it. I think I'm going to cry."

"Go ahead and cry. I'm just going to sit here and—"

She patted his arm. "You just sit there and relax. The worst is now over." She paused, then said, "The Swiss won't ever be able to get you back, will they?"

"No. But they'll try. In fact, I'll bet they're trying real hard right now."

"I only hope they've found that prison guard by now."

41

At two o'clock that Sunday morning, the prison guard had been found. A stray dog had wandered into the courtyard where he had been lying behind the fountain, and its incessant barking had roused the neighbors. Dogs are not allowed to bark at night in Switzerland, so the cops were called immediately.

The guard was taken directly to the Bürgerspital, where it was determined that he was suffering from a mild concussion as well as a minor case of hypothermia. So the police let him recover for the rest of the night. But at eight that morning, four detectives, including Lieutenant Paul Schmidt from the state attorney's office, began their interrogation of him. Their questioning was rough. He was told that he was under suspicion of having colluded with the American in his escape, that the slight injury to his head, his being tied up behind that fountain, was an obvious charade. How much had the rich American banker offered him? How was he going to be paid? Where was the American now hiding? Or where was he headed?

The guard stuck to his story. He had gotten the American from his cell at shortly before nine, as he always did, and they were at about the halfway point between the Lohnhof and the office of the state attorney when it happened. It had come as a complete surprise. There had been three men. All of them looked like Italians. They had simply grabbed him from behind in the middle of the street and dragged him to the top of the Leonardsgässli, where a woman was waiting. They had pulled him halfway down that stairway and then into the courtyard, where one of them had hit him on the head with a gun. Was he sure it was a gun? He was absolutely sure. Then they must have tied him up and gagged him. That was it. By the time he regained his senses, they were gone. And nobody else came—until the dog started barking.

Nobody else saw any of this? they asked. How could he tell? the guard answered. It had all happened so fast. From beginning to end, the whole thing had taken maybe three minutes. Had they talked among themselves? Yes. Just a few words—in Italian. No English? Not that he had heard. How was the woman dressed? Very well. Like a rich woman. How old? Maybe fifty. Good looking? Yes.

At eleven-thirty, Lieutenant Schmidt called a halt to the interrogation. The state attorney wanted them all in his conference room at noon. He was there, waiting, when they arrived. He was not in a good mood.

"All right, what's the story?" he asked as soon as the four police officers were seated.

It was Lieutenant Schmidt who replied. "We were wrong. I'm quite sure the guard was not involved. It was an outside job, so it had to be organized from the outside. In my opinion, the person who did that was Black's wife. Let me explain."

When he was done, the state attorney said, "So you think this was a professional job?"

"Absolutely," Schmidt replied.

"And that the road to the professionals and the current whereabouts of the Blacks is through Mrs. Black?"

"That's right. And we start with what we found in her room at the Euler Hotel. Everything—all her clothes, her make-up, even her address book, which was lying beside the telephone—was left behind. Everything except her purse and her passport, which was probably in her purse."

"So either she left in a big hurry or she expected to come back to the hotel."

"Yes. My guess is that she must have been meeting someone—the Italians—and events overtook her."

"But she must have met them before."

"Certainly. Probably more than once."

"Where?"

"Even before we found out what we just learned this morning, we've been asking every taxi driver in town if any of them remembered her. So far, no luck. I don't think she knew her way around town well enough to take a tram. And she didn't have a rental car. So she met those people either in the hotel or somewhere within walking distance of the hotel. Which means we have to go back to the staff of the hotel and ask them the right questions this time. Who was seen with Mrs. Black, and when? The same for the restaurants and cafés in that neighborhood."

Now the state attorney was getting very impatient.

"What good is all that going to do us if they're already out of the country?"

"It's going to broaden the search. We've already filed an international arrest warrant for Charles Black with Interpol. Now we'll file one for his wife. And if we can now find somebody who can give us a description of one or all of those three Italians, we'll have every policeman and border guard in Europe looking for them too."

"So you think they're already gone?"

"Maybe. But maybe not. If this is a professional job, which I am now sure it is, before attempting to get out of the country they might decide to lie low until things cool off. They probably have a place in Switzerland where they can do that. They seem to know their way around this country very well. Otherwise they could not have done what they did and then disappeared into thin air. But we now know something about who they are and where they are most probably headed. So we have to increase—greatly increase—our surveillance at every border crossing into Italy."

"I'll arrange it immediately," the state attorney said. "But one thing bothers me. How in the world was a Mrs. Charles Black able to organize this?"

Lieutenant Schmidt paused before answering that question. "Frankly, that also bothers me, sir. There's something missing."

In Pontresina, Vincente was wrestling with the same problem: the missing. His problem was compounded by the fact that it was only he who knew that they were missing. The others thought they were still upstairs, locked inside their third-story bedroom, because that was what he had told them. And he had also told them that until further notice, he and only he, Vincente, would have any contact with the Blacks, including taking them their meals. Nobody had asked why; they knew Vincente too well to do that. After all, he was the only educated man in the entire family. He always knew what he was doing.

Their faith would not have been so secure had they known what was racing through Vincente's mind. He looked at his watch, as he was so prone to do. It was now twelve-thirty on Sunday afternoon, and the Blacks had been missing for well over twenty-four hours. That was bad enough. What was worse was that he had still not told the Sardinian.

He desperately hoped that he would never have to tell the Sardinian. If he could get those two Americans back, then he could just continue with the original plan as if nothing had happened. Except for his million and a half dollars. He could forget about that. Even if he caught them, she'd never make that phone call to New York. Somehow they'd figured it out and were on to him. Which made it all the more important that they be taken care of.

He was pretty sure they were still in the Engadin Valley, because yesterday he had talked with one of the Italian guards who was posted at the border crossing just beyond the last stop of the Swiss *Postauto* before it turned around. He had told the guard, who had been on the take from him for many years, to ask around among his colleagues and then report back. His call had come through just an hour ago: Nobody recalled anybody resembling either of the two Americans coming through during the past forty-eight hours. They were now on full alert for them. If they were spotted trying to cross, the border guard would call again.

So he would have to start all over again and check every hotel, every inn, even every hostel on that bus route. And he'd have to start right away. But could he leave Alberto and Roberto, the housekeeper, and the maid alone in the house with the two nonexistent occupants of the bedroom on the third floor? One of them might get nosy.

Vincente solved that problem during the next fifteen minutes. He told the two young men to drive the rental car to Zurich and turn it in there. If the Basel police eventually caught on to what had happened, they were bound to check out the car rental agencies. And if the black Fiat was traced to Zurich, that would only confuse them even more. That would keep the men away for two days. Then he gave the housekeeper and the maid the rest of the day off. Their stolen bicycles had been found in front of the train station in St. Moritz Bad and returned by the local police. Who had stolen them? Probably local teenagers. It happened all the time. Vincente now suggested that the two women celebrate the return of their bikes by taking a Sunday afternoon trip on them. He waited until they were gone. Then he took one of his cars out of the garage and resumed the search.

At one o'clock this same afternoon, Dr. Samuel Schweizer, Dr. Hans Zwiebach, and their wives sat down to lunch on the terrace of the Grand Dolder Hotel, high on the hills overlooking the Lake of Zurich. It was a celebratory lunch, but only the two men knew that. What they were celebrating was the closure of an episode that, if it had been allowed to continue unchecked, could have had disastrous consequences for both of them. Both had heard of the escape Friday afternoon. They had discreetly talked to each other on the phone and decided to have lunch together on Sunday—to the delight of their wives, when they were told.

All four were in their Sunday best, since all four had gone to church that morning. The Zwiebachs had gone to the Frauenmünster in Zurich, the cathedral where their family had had the same pew for centuries. The Schweizers went to a small church in Küsnacht. They had not been there for months, since, of late, he was almost always out of town on weekends. His wife, Emma, thought that whatever had been

470

going on might now have ended, and that this might represent a new beginning. At least that was her fervent prayer in church that morning. Samuel was also in a prayerful mood, giving thanks for his release from the possible consequences of a financial arrangement that had been on the verge of going badly wrong—through no fault of his own. But now, with the disappearance of Charles Black, that problem had been solved. Now he could look forward to once again enjoying life to the fullest—with his newfound wealth and Simone.

It was such a lovely June day that the Zwiebachs and the Schweizers lingered at the Grand Dolder until four o'clock, finishing up their Sunday lunch with the traditional meringue glacé, coffee, and cognac. Even Emma had a cognac. Then they went their separate ways.

That evening both couples watched the seven o'clock news. The escape of Charles Black was the main subject. The prison guard who had been in charge of him had been found, badly injured, according to the police, and suffering from severe hypothermia. The Europe-wide search for the perpetrator, the American banker Charles Black, and his wife, who had acted as his accomplice, was being intensified. The Swiss authorities had also announced their intention to seek the assistance of the American Justice Department in finding Charles Black and bringing him to justice.

42

The two American fugitives were already four time zones to the west, high above Greenland, and fast asleep. They stayed asleep until Sally felt her shoulder being shaken gently. It was a stewardess. She spoke to her in German, but it was obvious what she was saying. They were about to land in Anchorage.

Sally reached over and woke her husband. He seemed confused when he opened his eyes.

"It's okay," she said to him gently. "We're almost home."

When he was fully awake, she spoke again. "Charlie, do you think the American authorities would arrest you if they recognized us?"

"I'm afraid so. I'm sure the Swiss have been in contact with our Justice Department all the way. Based on the 'facts' they've been fed from Basel, I'm sure they're convinced that my so-called crime of insider trading is even a more serious matter in the United States than in Switzerland, if you can believe that. As Chairman of the Board of the Federal Reserve, I betrayed the public trust for personal enrichment on a scale never seen before in this country. No, the way things stand now, if they spot us they'll lock me up in the nearest brig and then throw the book at me. My chances of getting out on bail would be zero."

The passenger terminal at Anchorage was small, even though there were a lot of very large aircraft there. The reason was that Anchorage was the major terminal for air freight moving to and from Asia. As a result, and because Anchorage was an entry point for foreigners coming in on flights using the polar great circle route, the customs and immigration facilities were proportionately large and intimidating.

Primus and his group were standing at the end of the ramp waiting for them when they finally emerged from the plane.

"We take the line for foreigners," he said.

"So do we," Charlie said.

The line moved slowly. When they got there, Charlie handed their two Swiss passports to the uniformed woman in the booth. She checked her computer. It took thirty seconds.

"Welcome to the United States," she said. "Next, please."

The customs procedure was just as cursory. Inside the main terminal, Primus was again waiting. "The plane we will be taking to Lake Iliamna is supposed to leave in forty-five minutes. Those of us from Zernez who are going there have been booked on it for a long time already. The Arrowhead Lodge people told me that they would try to get you on, too. But it's a pretty small plane, so we'd better check in right away."

An hour later they were again airborne. This time it was in a Sea Otter, a high-winged plane that could take off and land on both land and water. It headed southwest. As soon as it was over the Cook Inlet, the channel leading into the port of Anchorage, it began climbing steadily. The reason could soon be seen outside the windows. High mountains lay straight ahead. An hour later they skirted the most spectacular one—a ten-thousand-foot volcano. The captain came on the loudspeaker to explain that it was the Iliamna volcano, part of the Aleutian Range, which stretches hundreds of miles into the Bering Sea and has fifty active volcanoes along its length.

Beyond the mountain range lay a flat wilderness, in the true meaning of the word. No roads, no railroads, no airports—except for a half-dozen gravel landing strips, one of which was located on the northern shore of Lake Iliamna. That is where the Sea Otter landed at seven o'clock that Sunday evening. It turned around at the end of the runway and then taxied halfway back and pulled into a small parking area, where it stopped in front of a wooden shack.

Primus was the first to emerge from the Sea Otter, and he was barely on the ground when a man stepped out of a waiting Land Rover and came rushing up to him.

"Godammit, Primus," the man said, "you made it. And I've got good news. You're in luck. The salmon run began yesterday. So if you want to go out later tonight, that's fine with me. Now, who else is here?"

There were six other Swiss in the party, and the man knew them all. One by one he shook hands with them. When he was done, Primus intervened.

"Dan, I've brought those two new-comers that I telephoned you about. Here they are. Charlie and Sally."

"Welcome to God's country," Dan said as he stepped forward to pump their hands. "I hope Primus told you that our place is not fancy. But we've got the best damned food in Alaska, and the sooner we get out of here, the sooner we can all have dinner. So let's load up."

Two men had now come out of the wooden shack to help unload the luggage from the Sea Otter. Everybody who was headed for the Arrowhead Lodge picked out his own suitcase, and then Dan and another man who was with him loaded them on the back of a pickup. It was a tight fit, but all of them managed to find a place in the Land Rover or in and on the pickup. As they bounced down the gravel road, there was a view that seemed to stretch a hundred miles in every direction. The Blacks were seated directly behind the owner of the Arrowhead Lodge, who obviously relished having some first-time visitors.

"You're on the only road within two hundred miles in any direction. And it's only seven miles long. Total. Gravel, like the landing strip. See that little lake on the right? It's called Schoolhouse Lake. See that red frame building beside it? That's the schoolhouse. Only schoolhouse in the entire region. It's for the Indians and Eskimos. Yupik Eskimos. Nice people. Now we're coming to their village. Them shacks over there. That's where they live. See those huts and wooden racks right near the water? They dry-cure salmon on the racks or smoke them in the huts. Fish is a big part of their diet all year round."

The road now followed the north shore of Lake Iliamna in a westerly direction.

"We're almost there," Dan said. "See that inlet ahead, where the seaplanes are parked? That's Eagle Bay. Now, see those buildings up on that hill overlooking the bay? That's our place. The Arrowhead Lodge. The big building's the lodge proper. The others are cottages. You'll be staying in one of the cottages. Now, I want to tell you something before we get there. The Alaskan peninsula is full of bears. Brown bears. *Hungry* brown bears. They're big, they're fast, and they're mean. So nobody goes very far from the lodge without a gun. Nobody. If you don't know how to use a gun, and you want to wander around, let us know and we'll arrange for a guide to go with you. They're always armed. And they've all shot their share of bears."

When they pulled up in front of the lodge, a tall, handsome, busty blond woman was waiting outside. Primus, who had been riding in the back of the pickup truck with the luggage, jumped out and was the first to greet her.

"Primus!" she shrieked. *"Du bist wieder da. Und alle deine Freunde auch. Wie schön."*

Then she grabbed him and bestowed a big kiss right on his lips.

"That's my wife, Hilda," the lodge owner explained as he helped Sally Black get out of the Land Rover. "She's originally from Vienna. I sometimes think all these Krauts come here as much for her as for the fish. She is the best cook in all of Alaska."

She was the one who took the Blacks to their cottage.

"It's simple," she said as she showed them around, "but here in Alaska, you don't expect anything fancy. When I first came here, after marrying Dan, I thought I would go crazy out here in the middle of nowhere. I missed Austria so much. But now the Austrians and the Germans and the Swiss all come here. So I no longer have *Heimweh.*" She paused. "I forgot. *Heimweh* means being homesick. Primus said you no longer speak German. You've been in America too long. Don't worry. They all speak English too. Now you freshen up and then come to the main lodge for something to eat."

When they got to the lodge twenty minutes later, all the men from Zernez were already there. A fireplace dominated the huge room. The wood-paneled walls were lined with trophies, from moose heads to salmon of all varieties. And in the corner, beside the fireplace, loomed the prize trophy, a huge bear standing erect, eight feet tall, and dominating the room. Beside the bear was a bar. On top of the bar was a large platter of smoked salmon canapes. Behind the bar stood Hilda.

"First, a drink," she said to the Blacks as they come up to her, "and then we go to the dining room."

Charles Black asked, apologetically, if they could possibly have two very dry martinis.

"Natürlich," Hilda said. "With or without olives?"

Twenty minutes later, Hilda announced that dinner was ready. The dining room could not have been more simple: three long wooden tables with four wooden chairs on either side, and one at either end. Only one of the tables was set. The eight men and one woman who had come from Zernez all had room, leaving one chair at the head of the table open for their host, who immediately came to take it. Four carafes of wine stood waiting in the middle of the table. They did not remain full for long. As soon as the wine had been poured, Dan stood up, holding his glass.

"You all know I don't speak German. But

this much I can manage," he said. *"Willkommen zu der Arrowhead Lodge. Prosit!"*

Poached rainbow trout was the first item on the menu. Then venison served with red cabbage and new potatoes. A choice of Linzertorte or Sachertorte was offered as dessert. At ten o'clock came coffee and schnapps.

The owner of the Arrowhead Lodge came to his feet once again. "Now, how many of you want to go on a night fishing expedition?"

Seven hands went up.

"All right. Everybody get your gear. We meet outside in fifteen minutes."

As everybody rose and began leaving the dining room, Dan came over to the Blacks.

"I'll make arrangements for you to go fishing tomorrow morning. That way you will be able to get a good night's sleep. If you come over from your cabin at ten, you can still get breakfast."

"I don't know if Primus told you," Charlie said, "but we don't have any fishing gear with us. Not even boots."

"He told me. Don't worry. We can provide you with everything. One more thing. Remember what I said about the bears. Don't wander around outside alone."

As the Blacks hurried along the path between the main lodge and their cabin, the Arctic sun still lit the sky as if it were late afternoon. But after going through all those time zones since Zurich, they did not even think about it. They were both out of their clothes and into bed in less than five minutes.

"This is almost surreal," Sally said as she snuggled up to Charlie for warmth. "Here we are in the middle of the Alaskan wilderness, and everybody but us speaks German, eats red cabbage, and guzzles schnapps."

"And couldn't care less who we are or where we come from," Charlie added. "So we can finally sleep in peace."

When they entered the dining room at ten o'clock on Monday morning, they were the only ones there. Breakfast had been laid out buffet style, so they helped themselves. They had just begun eating when Dan appeared, accompanied by a young man in his late twenties or early thirties.

"The others came back around eight o'clock this morning. They're all in bed now. You said you wanted to give it a try, and I thought you wouldn't mind going out by yourselves. You'll need a guide. This young man's name is Bill. He's our schoolteacher. During summer vacations he works with us. He was born and raised here, so he knows Lake Iliamna better than almost anybody."

The young man stepped forward to shake hands—very respectfully. He was an Indian, black-haired, brown-skinned, and slim. He had the lithe movements of a natural athlete.

"Have you ever fished here before?" he asked.

"No," Charles answered, "but I have fished for trout all my life."

"That will help, but not much. To catch sockeye salmon requires a very special technique. I'll show you. It's easy to learn."

"But first we'll have to outfit them," Dan said. "They'll need windbreakers, waders, and fishing rods. I've already got it together in the shed, ready to go. You can take the pickup to the dock."

The dock was a half-mile back up the road they had taken in from the airport. It jutted out into the waters of the same small cove where the seaplanes were parked. Two motor launches were tied up there.

"We'll take the small one," the guide said. "I'll help you get in."

After he had them seated on the side benches facing each other, he went back to the pickup truck to get the poles, the tackle box, a net, a blanket, the basket containing their picnic lunch, and his rifle. Then he untied the boat and started the engine. He pulled away from the dock very carefully and, once the boat was clear, said, "Hang on. We're off."

The boat accelerated from zero to twenty knots in what seemed to be about ten seconds. They headed straight north along the eastern shore of Eagle Bay. It was a perfect day—blue sky, a dazzling sun—but they were glad they had the windbreakers. The air that streamed by them was cold, and the occasional spray of lake water that hit their faces was frigid. It was also extremely noisy. Their guide had to yell when he spoke to them.

"We're headed for the northern tip of the bay, where it narrows into the Eagle River. We go as far up the river as we can—until we hit the rapids. That's where we get out. It usually takes an hour, but there's no wind today, so my guess is that we'll be there in about fifty minutes."

"Fifty minutes," Sally muttered. She pulled the parka of the wind-breaker over her head. Beneath it, her face indicated that she was definitely not having fun yet.

Halfway there, the young man pointed at the very large birds circling high above the trees that lined the lake on the other side. "Bald eagles," he yelled. "Hundreds of them nest in those trees. That's why they called it Eagle Bay."

It was almost noon when the Indian guide slowed the boat to a stop and then cut the engine. The rapids of the Eagle River lay dead ahead. He poled the boat very carefully to the rocky shore and then leaped out to tie it up, using the scrawny trunks of two scrubby trees that had grown up through the rocks. Then he helped them get out of the boat.

"Be very careful," he warned. "The rocks are slippery and the water coming down these rapids is extremely cold. I'll lead the way."

It took them twenty minutes to go the next 250 yards. There was no real path. With

Sally hanging on to Charlie most of the time, they went from rock to rock, tree to tree, sometimes pausing to lean up against the side of the hill that rose almost like a cliff from the shore of the rapids. Twice they had to wade into the rapids to get around a rock that blocked their way upstream.

Finally they arrived at their destination. The river had cut a swath into the hill in times past, leaving a small, flat, rock-strewn space along its shore. Bill stood there waiting.

"Sorry about that," he said, "but it's the only way up here. This is a very special place for salmon fishing. You'll soon see why I say that. All the shoreland around Iliamna Lake belongs to the Native Americans, but this we respect as a spot reserved for the Arrowhead Lodge. So do all the guides who work for the other lodges in the region. Now, you might want to sit on one of the rocks here and catch your breath. I'm going back to the boat to get our stuff."

"You okay, Sally?" Charlie asked as soon as Bill had disappeared.

"I guess so. But now I see how smart I was to never go fishing with you before. I already hate the thought of having to go back."

"You're a good sport to at least give it a try, Sally. And you've got to admit one thing. If you want to get away from trouble, this is about as far away as you can get. Or 'git,' as our host would probably say."

"They are all such nice people. It makes

you kind of wonder about the people we've been hanging around with lately. Like all your old colleagues at the Federal Reserve. And those at the BIS. Or our wonderful lawyer in Washington. The only person who came through—reluctantly— was John Wright at Whitney Brothers. Everybody else took a hike."

"I know. I've been thinking about the same thing, trying to come up with some-body who might still trust me enough to help me get out of this mess—if I can raise sufficient doubts in his mind. It has to be somebody who has sufficient author-ity to gain access to facts. But he can't be Swiss. They will protect each other to the death. So I'm talking about somebody who is an insider and an outsider at the same time."

"But who would fit that bill?"

"I think I know."

"Who?"

"I don't want to get your hopes up now. I'll tell you if it works."

"But how in the world could you get hold of whoever it is and try to raise those doubts in his mind? You can't just pick up the phone in the lodge. If he doesn't believe you, he will report it to the author-ities, they will trace the call, and we'll be finished. By the way, how does that phone work, anyway? There can't be a telephone line stretching from here to Anchorage."

"No. But I did see telephone poles along the road from the airport to the lodge. They must be a connection. I'll ask our young schoolteacher about it when he gets back. I also want to ask him something else."

"What?"

"Whether he's got a computer."

"Why?"

"I want to borrow it."

"How would that help?"

"You'll soon see. I hope."

The Indian guide managed to bring all the stuff from the boat in one trip.

He spread the blanket out on the one sandy spot between the rocks, then asked, "Ready?"

"You try it first, Charlie," Sally said. "I'm just going to sit on the blanket and watch for a while."

"All right," Bill said. "Let's start with the rod. You see it's not one like you're used to for trout fishing. It's much longer, and much more flexible." He demonstrated by waving it back and forth. "For the lure, we use a wet fly. I tie them myself. The key to success is color."

He reached down into the tackle box and retrieved one, a dazzling combination of yellow, red, and chartreuse yarn that disguised a medium-sized hook.

"The idea is to catch the salmon's eye in the split second the lure passes in front of its mouth. Then, and only then, will a sockeye go for it."

He attached the fly to the leader at the end of the line and then reached down into his tackle box again. This time he took out some split-shot sinkers and attached two of them to the line, about eighteen inches above the fly, explaining, "We only want the lure to settle about two feet below the surface of the water and ideally about a foot or two above the bottom. Now come with me."

He stepped out into the relatively calm waters in front of them and waded about ten feet into the river, stopping where the shallows ended and the swiftly flowing waters of the rapids began. Charlie Black followed his every move and then stood at his side.

"Look," the guide said.

The water was crystal clear and about four feet deep. Suddenly he saw them. Fish, large fish, dozens and dozens, jammed up close to each other, struggling up the rapids. Row after row of salmon swam right past them, like soldiers in formation, marching unwaveringly in a straight line toward their certain death upstream, after they had reached their spawning grounds and laid their eggs.

"Truly awesome," Charlie said. "I never would have believed it."

"Now let's get to work," Bill said. "The idea is very simple. You cast out about fifteen feet upstream—upstream—and then, keeping the line as tight as you can, just let the lure float downstream. Ideally, if we have the right sinkers relative to the speed of the water today, the lure will float down the rapids at eye level—the eye level of the salmon—or about two feet below the surface. If one of the salmon sees it coming and is irritated by the lure, it will take it. But the take is very subtle, barely perceptible. When you sense it, or if you see the line swerving, it means that something is on the other end, causing it to deviate ever so slightly in its downstream drift. Then you instantly snap the rod up with one hand and pull down on the line with your other hand. If you're lucky, you've set the hook. Watch."

He raised the rod above his head and then, with an easy motion, brought it forward like a wand, releasing line as he did so and laying it in a short arc fifteen feet upriver. As the lure sank below the surface, he let it float down past where they were standing and beyond. Nothing happened. He reeled the line in and did it again. Still nothing. A third time. The lure had just floated past them when it swerved. He instantly brought the rod up. The line started to quiver. He tugged on it, and in the next instant the fish broke the surface and went airborne like a silver skyrocket on a tether. When it landed back in the water, the salmon immediately started swimming toward midstream. Then it was airborne again. The guide kept the rod up and only gave the fish enough line to prevent it from breaking. Finally the fish appeared to be tiring in its struggle to escape. Only then did he begin to reel it in.

He kept the line taut, and the fish in the water, as he drew it out of the rapids and into the shallows. Finally he yelled to Sally, "Bring me the net!"

She came to her feet, looked frantically for the net, and when she saw it beside the blanket, she picked it up, scrambled to the edge of the water, and handed it to the Indian. He took it, scooped up the fish, and stepped back onto dry land. There he drew the hook out of the salmon's mouth and replaced it with a short fishing line, which he drew through its mouth and gills.

"We're going to keep it alive in the waters of one of those shallow pools down there between the rocks. When we've got our limit, and before we head back, I'll fillet all of them."

When he returned, he said, "Okay, Charlie, now it's your turn."

The two of them went back out to the same spot in the shallows right beside the rapids. Now Charlie had the rod. Bill stood behind him and, with his arm under Charlie's, helped guide the motion of the rod, first taking it back, then gracefully casting the line upstream. Again. And again. And again.

"Okay," he finally said. "You've got it. Now you're on your own."

Charlie arced the line into the water and watched it float downstream. Then he reeled the line in and did it again. Eleven times. On the twelfth try, the line swerved. He drew the rod up as Bill had done.

"Pull on the line!" Bill yelled.

Charlie did. The fish leaped straight up into the air. Five minutes later he had maneuvered the salmon into the shallows, and almost instantly the guide had it in the net.

Within less than two hours, Charlie had caught his limit of ten. So had Bill. Sally had decided to remain a spectator. Laid out on top of two rocks was a board that had been there when they arrived. Using it, Bill now filleted the twenty sockeye salmon with his hunting knife. Then he washed them in the icy waters of the rapids and tossed them into a plastic bag.

By four o'clock, after again struggling over the rocks, they were back in the boat, and by five, back at the dock. After Bill had helped them out of the boat, he said, "Wait in the pickup. I'll get all the stuff out of the boat. Then we'll head back to the lodge. It will only take a few minutes."

They did not argue.

"Are you as cold and as pooped as I am?" Sally asked when they were both inside the truck.

"I hate to admit it, but yes," Charlie replied. "I'm ready for one of those martinis. Maybe two."

"You read my mind, Charlie."

A few minutes later the guide joined them in the front seat of the pickup, and soon they were back on the gravel road.

"I wanted to ask you something," Charlie said to him.

"Sure."

"I know you're a schoolteacher. Do you by any chance have a computer?"

"Of course. A Macintosh PowerBook."

"With a modem?"

"Built in."

"So you can connect up with the Internet?"

"Sure. I do it all the time, via a server in Anchorage. But I usually do it at school, because from there it's a local call to Anchorage. The state government has provided all the rural schools with computers and Internet access. We've got three of them in our school here. All Macs. The kids love it. It makes them feel part of the world, instead of totally isolated."

"That's really wonderful," Sally said.

"I agree. But school's out, and the kids are more interested in other things right now. So if you want to use one of those computers, just ask. Nobody will mind. Just the opposite."

"I would like to pay for it," Charlie said.

"No," the Indian guide said firmly. "My people know what tourism does for us. So if, in any way, they can help you, they will, and hope you come back. Why don't I show you the school? It's just up the road."

"Actually, we saw it coming in from the airport. Dan pointed it out."

"Do you want to see what it looks like inside?"

"Sure," Charlie said.

It was a school in the middle of the Alaskan wilderness, but—except that it was just one room—it could just as well have been in a suburb of any city in California or New York. From the desks to the projection equipment to the small "lab" set up on a table at the back of the room, everything looked state-of-the-art and brand new.

"I see that the state of Alaska takes care of its children," Sally said.

"They really do. That's why, when I finished college in Seattle, I came back here to teach," Bill replied. Then he pointed across the room. "Over there against the wall are the computers. Macintosh 8500s, all with 28.8-thousand-baud modems built in. All three are connected to each other and to an Apple laser printer. All the software you need is in them, from word processing to spread sheets. And Netscape. Are you familiar with the Mac?"

"Yes," Charlie said.

"Then you know that all you have to do is go to Netscape Navigator in the Apple menu, and you'll be up and running."

"I know exactly," Charlie said.

"When do you want to start using it?"

"If it would be at all possible, tonight. Among other things, I'm going to be communicating with Europe. Which means that because of the time difference, I would like to begin around midnight."

"No problem. Around here at this time of year it never gets dark, so everybody does stuff at strange hours. Look, I'll just give you a key and you can come and go whenever it suits you. Just lock up after you're done. By the way, our E-mail address is *iliamna@alaska.com*. We use Eudora Light for our E-mail. To get access to it, the code word is *sockeye*. Not too original, I guess, but hard to forget."

Bill went to the large desk on a podium at the front of the room, unlocked a drawer, and withdrew a key. "Take this. It's a spare. One other thing. Because of the bears, you'll have to drive over here. I'll ask Dan if you can use the pickup. I'm sure he'll agree."

When they were back in the truck, Sally said, "Bill, I also want to ask you something. How does the phone work? I mean, how do phone calls get in and out of here?"

"Via the airport. Since they use the landing strip for search-and-rescue missions and for emergency medical evacuations, they installed a microwave link to Anchorage years ago. The tower is behind that shack that serves as the terminal. Later they strung lines to the village and the lodge."

"Just as you thought, Charlie," Sally said.

During cocktails and dinner, Charles Black was unusually quiet. Sally knew this was a sign that he was thinking. When dinner was over, Dan came up and told him that the guide had mentioned that he wanted to use the computers over at the schoolhouse and needed the pickup for transportation. The ignition key was always in the truck, he told him, since it would be kind of dumb for anybody to try to steal it. Where would he go? When they got back to their cottage, Charlie was fidgety.

"Why don't you go over there now?" Sally asked. "Then you can take your time in figuring out the computer setup."

"Okay. Do you want to come along?"

"No. I'm tired. All those damn rocks. Anyway, you'll be better off without me. I'm going to bed. And, Charlie—good luck."

43

It was eleven o'clock at night when Charles Black reentered the one-room schoolhouse. He didn't have to search for the light switch, since there was ample light from the midnight sun coming in through the windows. He went directly to the bank of three computers, sat down in front of one of them, and turned it on.

The Macintosh came instantly to life. After it had gone through its warm-up routine, Black checked the Apple Menu to see what type of software was built in. All he really needed was an E-mail link, and an Internet access program. Netscape Navigator was there, just as the schoolteacher had said. So was Eudora Light.

"All right," he said to himself, as he was prone to do when trying to think something through, "let's see if I can figure out how to get their addresses."

He activated Netscape Navigator, and within seconds the screen lit up with Yahoo!, the search engine located at Stanford University. He moved the cursor to the "Search" box and typed in, "Anonymous Remailer." A list appeared, and he began to scroll down.

He recalled that the most famous, or most infamous, remailer of all had been located in Helsinki, Finland: Johan Helsingius. There had been articles written about him in many places, ranging from *The Wall Street Journal* to *Time* magazine. The stories all had a common theme. People from all over the world were pressuring the Finnish police to close Helsingius and his computer down, complaining that his service was a primary conduit for child pornography transmitted on the Internet. The police dismissed these allegations as groundless, but Helsingius finally closed shop anyway. He said he did this because, in a copyright infringement suit against him, the court had ordered him to identify one of his users. He claimed that this order would open the floodgates to myriad suits of this kind and that he would rather close down the system than spend all of his time in court.

Black, however, remembered that another remailer had filled the breach. That operation was based in Iran, had the support of the government there, and was thus beyond the reach of the courts. He continued scrolling and its E-mail address suddenly appeared on the computer screen: *an@anon.teheran.ir.*

He wrote it down on a notepad that was on the desk beside the keyboard. Then he moved the cursor to the "Back" box, hit "Return," and Yahoo! came back on the screen. He again went to the "Search" box, and this time typed in, "Bank of England." The search engine came up with a dozen different E-mail addresses, depending upon whether you wanted to read their bulletin or get in contact with their currency trading desk. Black wrote down what appeared to be the main one: *bankeng@ukfinancial.com.*

Now that we know 'where,'" Black said, "we come to the hard part. What am I going to say?"

During the past couple of days—on the plane and while fishing—he had finally had time to think about that, to think through the whole bizarre episode, from beginning to end. And he now knew the answer. They had fully documented all those trades he had supposedly made. That list. But at no time had there been any mention of where the cash margin for the first trade had come from!

He went to the Apple menu and opened Eudora Light. The computer asked him to fill in the password for *iliamna@alas-*

ka.com. He typed "sockeye," and after the modem had connected him, he clicked on "New Message" and started to fill in the text.

To: an@anon.teheran.ir
From: iliamna@alaska.com
Subject: Please remail to Sir Robert Neville at *bankeng@ukfinancial.com*
CC: None
BCC: None
Attachments: None

Dear Sir Robert:
   This is Charles Black, and I am using this peculiar method to communicate with you for obvious reasons. I will keep it as brief as possible.
   I would like to begin by assuring you that all the accusations made against me in Switzerland are false. When the opportunity to escape from Swiss custody presented itself, I felt I had no choice but to take advantage of it. I have good reasons to believe that the men who engineered my escape are directly connected with people who were engaged in the insider trading at the General Bank of Switzerland, and who subsequently set me up in order to conceal their identity. I managed to also escape their custody and am now in a secure place.
   There can be only one person who has served as the common link to the

General Bank of Switzerland—common to both me and those who were behind all this. That is Dr. Hans Zwiebach, the Zurich attorney, who must have set up fiduciary accounts at that bank for both of us. He and his client must have decided at some point to use my account, instead of their own, for their trading. Now I will come to the point.

I was given a list of the date, place, type of transaction, and profits for each of the transactions in question. I understand that it was your team at the Bank of England who tracked them down, using your computer. I now realize, after giving this a great deal of thought, that one crucial item has been overlooked—namely, where did the original cash margin necessary to finance the first trade come from?

That first trade occurred four years ago, on December 4, and generated a profit of over $50 million. My guess is that that would have required a cash margin of at least $25 million. My account at the General Bank of Switzerland had been dormant for years, with a token balance of one thousand francs. So I repeat: Where did the cash that was added to my account in order to finance this transaction come from? I strongly suspect that came from that other account, administered by Dr. Zwiebach.

As bankers, we both know

paper trail that will answer this question must exist inside the General Bank of Switzerland. My only request of you is that you ask your team at the Bank of England to attempt to uncover that trail. If they are successful, I can assure you that it will totally exonerate me.

If you wish to communicate with me, I believe that the address of a specific E-mail box, to which I will have exclusive access, will be substituted for the real one at the top of this message.
Sincerely,
Charles Black

He ordered the computer to print it out, so that he could go over it carefully before sending it. It told him to turn on the printer, so he did. He read it three times, went back to the computer, and pressed "Send." Then he waited.

Fifteen minutes later the computer beeped, indicating that an E-mail message had just come in. He went to the "In" box. It came from Iran, and was very brief:

Your message has been remailed. Your anonymous address here is *an57q4anon.teheran.ir.* Your password is x3533.

He printed that out. Then he erased both messages from the computer's memory.

Black locked the schoolhouse door on the way out and left the ignition key in the pickup after he had parked it in front of the Arrowhead Lodge. When he entered their cottage, the first thing he saw was Sally, sitting straight up in bed.

"I thought you were going to sleep," Charlie said.

"Are you kidding? With you out there communicating with the mystery man? Did it work?"

"I think so. I mean, I think my message is on its way to him."

"Who?"

This time he answered the question. "Sir Robert Neville."

Sally thought it over. "I can see why you picked him. He is a totally decent man."

"Exactly."

"But how could you get to him without somebody being able to trace it back here?"

"I used something called an anonymous remailer, in Iran." He explained how it worked.

When he was done, she asked, "So what did you tell Sir Robert?"

"This. Read it." He withdrew the computer printout from his jacket pocket and handed it to her.

She read it.

"Get it?" he asked.

"I get it. But how do you know that the

499

original cash margin didn't come from that bank in the Turks and Caicos Islands?"

"I don't. But something tells me that it didn't."

"But what if it did?"

"Then we are really screwed. Because after you had Whitney Brothers transfer that money there—and at some point the authorities are bound to find out about it—it will represent further 'proof' that I am guilty. But, believe me, Sally, it's not your fault. It's the only thing you could have done."

"Then what do we do if they do find out about it?"

"I don't know."

He suddenly looked worn out and haggard.

"Come to bed, Charlie," Sally said. "There's nothing more you can do. Now it's up to Sir Robert."

44

It was ten o'clock on Tuesday morning when a copy of Charles Black's E-mail message arrived on the desk of Sir Robert Neville's secretary. She read it and reread it, trying to make up her mind whether or not to pass it on to her boss. Even the Bank of England was not immune to receiving messages from kooks. But she had been following the case of Charles Black. It had been all over the Sunday papers, and on Monday she had handled a series of phone calls between Sir Robert and the Swiss, in which they must have been discussing it. The E-mail had the ring of authenticity, she concluded. So she got up from behind her desk, knocked on Sir Robert's door, entered his office, and laid the message on his desk. He didn't bother to look up. He was reading the *Financial Times.*

But five minutes later he buzzed for her.

"I want to talk to Derek Hambro. Right away. In fact, when you find him, tell him to come straight up to my office."

The young Englishman arrived ten minutes later. Without even bothering to say hello, Sir Robert held out the E-mail message and said, "Read this."

Hambro did.

"What do you think?" Sir Robert asked.

"I'm sure it came from Charles Black. Via what they call an anonymous remailer in Iran. By using such a facility, Black could conceal where he sent it from."

"Frankly, I don't understand one single word of what you just said."

"I'll explain," Hambro said.

It took a while, but finally the Governor of the Bank of England got it.

"So Black could literally be anywhere."

"Exactly. But even if we don't have the faintest idea about where he is, we can still communicate with him at any time."

"Amazing. How do you know all this?" Sir Robert asked.

"Because people who launder money have also figured out how to use anonymous remailers to cover their tracks. That's in my department, sir."

"If you feel sure that this message is authentic, what do you think we should do about it? First, does what Black says make sense?"

"About the cash margin?"

"Yes. How much cash margin was in Black's account before that first transaction that he mentions took place? Do you remember?"

"Yes, sir. I distinctly remember. Around twenty-five million dollars."

"Where did it come from?"

"I don't think it came from anywhere. It was just there. We assumed, I guess, that it had been building up over the years as a result of Black's legitimate investment activities. Remember, before he became Chairman of the Federal Reserve, he was chairman of one of the world's most prestigious investment banks, Whitney Brothers & Pierpont. So, by definition, he knew how to make lots of money legally. Just not a half-billion dollars within three years, as he did after he became Chairman of the Federal Reserve."

"But he says that the account had gone dormant, and that he only had a token balance of a thousand Swiss francs there."

"That's what he says, yes."

"Why would he say that if it wasn't true?" Sir Robert asked.

"Good question."

"If what he says is true, and it came from another source, there would be a paper trail, wouldn't there?"

"Yes, sir. But the way this case stands now, I'm very doubtful about whether anybody in Switzerland is going to help us find it. The General Bank of Switzerland sure won't."

"Unless they're ordered to do so."

"You've met that state attorney in Basel who's in charge of this case. Do you really think he would give such an order? All he is interested in now is finding Black, bringing him back to Switzerland, and getting the courts to put him away for the rest of his life."

"I'm afraid you're right. He was on the phone three times yesterday, assuring me that they were doing everything possible to find him. So even if Black is telling us the truth, there's nothing we can do about it. Is that what you are saying?"

Derek Hambro did not reply immediately. Then: "There's one man who might help us. And if he's willing, he will also be able."

"Who?"

"The detective lieutenant in Basel who is in charge of the investigation. I've worked with him from the very beginning, and I like him a lot."

"Well, call him," Sir Robert said.

"Right now?"

"Why not? My secretary's got the number of the office where he's located."

"Should I tell him about Black's message?"

"No. Tell him that I was thinking things over and was puzzled about where the original cash margin came from. That's all. Use my phone."

Hambro got through to Lieutenant Paul Schmidt right away. He explained that the reason for his call was Sir Robert Neville's alleged puzzlement concerning the origins of the cash margin in Charles Black's account that was there before all his insider trading began.

He finished by asking, "Is Sir Robert right to be concerned?"

That question produced a pause on the other end.

"Well, it is certainly something I should have looked into," the Swiss police officer said. "In fact, on general principles, I was going to interview the man who handled Black's fiduciary account at the General Bank of Switzerland. I never got around to it, for obvious reasons."

"Can you tell me his name?"

"Yes. Urs Stucker. He retired at the beginning of this year. He lives in Zurich."

"Maybe we could interview him together," Hambro said, adding, "in Zurich. I'd be happy to come over."

"Actually, I'll be leaving for Zurich in about an hour. Some men who fit the description of those who helped Black escape returned a rental car to the Hertz office at Kloten Airport on Sunday evening. We just found out about it. I'm going over there with some of our men to check the car for fingerprints or whatever else we might find, and to talk to the man at Hertz who remembered them."

"Maybe I could come to Zurich too, meet you at the airport, and when you are done, we could both go and see Urs Stucker."

That produced a longer pause on the other end.

"All right. But if I can arrange it, I'd prefer to do it in an unofficial way and to treat it as confidential—for the moment."

"I agree. And so will Sir Robert."

"I'll see if I can get hold of Stucker," Schmidt said. "Then I'll call you back."

"In the meantime, I'll check what flights are available," Hambro replied.

45

At this same time, many time zones to the west, Vincente had just finished checking into the Hilton hotel in downtown Anchorage, Alaska, after an odyssey that had taken him from Zurich to New York to Seattle, where, at nine that evening, he had caught the last Alaska Airlines flight to Anchorage. Once inside his room, he opened the bottle of Scotch that he had bought at the duty-free shop in Kloten

505

Airport many hours ago. He poured himself a stiff one, added a little water, eased himself into a lounge chair, and stretched out his legs. Then he emptied half the glass in one go. He was very pleased with himself, even though, in the final analysis, it had proven to be so easy.

The breakthrough had come on Sunday evening. Earlier that day he had resumed his search for the Blacks, which had proven just as fruitless as the one he had made on Saturday after he discovered that they were missing. Nevertheless, he had also decided to give the Hotel Alpenrosen in Zernez one more try. From his hostile behavior the day before, he knew that the owner of the hotel thoroughly disliked him. So he had decided to try a different tack—to avoid Primus by going into the hotel through the restaurant entrance, and trying his luck at the bar. The Alpenrose had the only restaurant and bar in town, so if the locals gathered somewhere on Sunday evenings to gossip, that had to be the place.

His instincts had proven correct. There were three other men already at the bar, all mountain guides from the lower Engadin Valley. They were speaking together in Romansch, sure that nobody but they could understand a word. But, Italian though he was, Vincente had spent more than enough time in that valley to pick up a lot of the dialect, even though he never dared speak it. This being the time of year that it was, the three men were discussing fishing. And at some point the name of Primus came up. That was when Vincente intervened.

"Excuse me," he said in the Swiss-German dialect, "I could not help hearing you mention Primus. I came here to ask him something."

"You're out of luck," one of the men replied, switching to Schwyzerdütsch. "He'll be gone for two weeks. Fishing in Alaska."

"Really? Then maybe I could talk to his assistant."

Then it was the girl behind the bar who intervened. "That's Ingrid. She's not here, either. Except during high season, she always takes Sunday evening off. So I take care of both the bar and the front desk. Why do you want to talk to her?"

"I wanted to ask her about those two Americans who were staying here. They left something behind in a coffee shop where I work in St. Moritz, and the owner asked me to bring it back to them."

"What was it?"

"A new clock. An Atmos. It's still in a box. They must have just bought it. It's in my car."

"You're too late," she said. "They went with Primus to Alaska. I helped them with their luggage. They left together, early this morning."

"Maybe I could forward it to them there. Where would they have gone in Alaska?"

"I don't know. But Ingrid might," she replied. "Come back tomorrow."

Then one of the men spoke up. "I know who else might know. That travel office in Zuoz. Primus wanted me to come along a couple of years ago, and that was where he sent me to get the details and make the arrangements. It costs a fortune. So I didn't go."

Vincente finished his beer within minutes. The next morning he was there when the travel agency in Zuoz opened its doors. Fifteen minutes later he knew all about the Arrowhead Lodge on the shores of Lake Iliamna, in the middle of the Alaskan peninsula. Five and a half hours later he was at the airport in Zurich, about to board a plane to New York.

But before he did so, he went to a phone booth in the terminal and called the Sardinian. He had had no choice. One way or another he was bound to find out that the Americans had gotten away. Now he could at least tell him how he was going to rectify that. The Sardinian's response was immediate and clear. Take care of them immediately.

But before he hung up, the Sardinian added to his instructions. "From now on, until this is done, no matter where you are, you will check back with me every twelve hours. Without fail. Understand?"

46

Derek Hambro and Detective Paul Schmidt arrived at the house of Urs Stucker at four that Tuesday afternoon, central European time. It was a modest home, full of overstuffed furniture, and musty. Stucker was visibly nervous when he opened the door and asked them in. He took them into the living room, where they all sat down, facing each other over the coffee table.

"As I mentioned on the phone, Mr. Hambro is from the Bank of England and is working with me on this case," Schmidt began. "So do you mind speaking English, Herr Stucker?"

"No, of course not," Stucker answered.

The next words that he blurted caught both of his visitors by surprise. "I think I know why you are here, Lieutenant Schmidt. After you called me last week requesting an interview, I've been expecting to hear back from you. But I guess after that American escaped, you've been too busy."

"That's right," Schmidt answered, "but now we're here."

"It's those gold trades, isn't it? The ones we shifted from one account to the other account. That was four years ago, but I still remember every detail. See that cigar humidor on the coffee table? It must have cost a thousand francs. Too expensive for the likes of me. It arrived the day after I altered the books. It was filled with Partagas cigars. The card that came with it—it's still inside the humidor—said it was with the compliments of Dr. Zwiebach."

Hambro and Schmidt exchanged glances, but said nothing.

"I never did such a thing either before or after, believe me. That's why it's been bothering me ever since you arrested that American."

"Go on, please," Schmidt said.

"It started with a wire transfer from Italy of fifty million dollars. It came from a bank in Milan and went into Zwiebach's omnibus account."

"Then what?" Hambro asked.

"Just a week later, Dr. Zwiebach called me and said he wanted to transfer twenty million of that new money to a brand-new fiduciary account he had just established with us, and invest it in gold. That's not very unusual; a lot of our clients buy gold bullion. But this was different. He wanted to buy gold *futures*. If you're from the Bank of England, sir, you must know how risky that is. I told him that futures were way over my head. But he insisted. So I got a young trader to buy them. A nice young man, very capable. But he just got fired from the bank. He called me. He's very bitter."

"So you bought gold futures for this new account. You're sure it was new?"

"Absolutely. And that was one reason I

remember it so well. Here was a newly opened account, and Zwiebach was using it to speculate in derivatives. We put down twenty million dollars' cash margin with a broker in New York and bought thousands of contracts, betting the price would go way up."

"Then what happened?" Hambro asked.

"The price went up for a while, but then it sank to a level well below where it was when we had bought those futures. We got a margin call from New York and had to wire another five million cash. Zwiebach went into a panic and said we were to reverse course. Cover our long contracts, take the loss, take what was left of that fifty million in the omnibus account and use it as cash margin to go short. It was crazy."

"Then what happened?"

"The gold price collapsed."

"Why?" Hambro asked.

"Because a day or so later the Federal Reserve raised interest rates in New York instead of cutting them like the smart guys expected."

Again Hambro and Schmidt exchanged glances.

"Then?"

"I got another call from Dr. Zwiebach. He said there had been a mixup between two of his fiduciary accounts. The second round of gold future trades should not have gone through the new account, but through an old account that he had kept there for many years. I knew full well that something funny was going on, but I went along with him."

"Then?"

"Zwiebach told us to cover. We did. You know how much we ended up with in that account? One hundred seven million dollars. It was incredible."

"What then?"

"Dr. Zwiebach asked me to transfer the profits from the gold futures speculation to an account at a bank in the Caribbean, one that, frankly, I had never even heard of before. I had to look it up."

"In the Turks and Caicos Islands," Schmidt said.

"Exactly. Of course you know about that. We transferred the profits there, but always kept fifty million in cash in Zurich."

"You kept it in the 'old' account now?" Hambro said.

"Exactly. Everything was now consolidated there. Those were Dr. Zwiebach's instructions. After those gold trades, as you must know, we used that account for many other investments. They almost always involved speculation in either currency futures or derivatives related to interest rates. We always made money. We always transferred the profits to that bank in the Caribbean. And we always maintained that fifty million cash balance—until the end of last year. Then the fifty million was also transferred to the Turks and Caicos Islands. What happened after that, I don't know. I retired."

"That 'old' account was the American's?" Hambro asked.

"All I ever knew was that it was a fiduciary account in Dr. Zwiebach's name. But you must have found out who the client behind it was. It was Charles Black, wasn't it?"

"That's right," Schmidt said. "But we never heard any of what you have just told us."

"I've been thinking about this day and night since you called me, Lieutenant Schmidt. Now I'm sure of one thing. The American did not do it. Dr. Zwiebach just used his account as a cover."

The unspeakable had now been said.

"It was all done for a new client. One who sent that fifty million from Milan. One for whom they did that gold speculation. One for whom they opened that account in the Caribbean to keep the money out of reach of the Swiss authorities if something went wrong—as it did, in the end. This had to be planned in a cold, calculating, cruel fashion. And I was party to it. I'm sorry. I'm very sorry."

Stucker slumped in his chair, a visibly broken man.

Paul Schmidt got up and went over to comfort him. "Take it easy," he said. "Whatever you did four years ago, you've more than made up for it right now. Are you willing to repeat what you have just told us in court? Under oath?"

"Yes," came the whispered answer.

Their good-byes were hurried. As soon as he was back in Schmidt's car, which the police officer had driven over from Basel earlier that day, Hambro could no longer contain himself.

"What a fucking mess," he said. "How could we have missed this?"

"Neither of us went back far enough," Schmidt said. "We didn't have to. We had more than enough evidence against Black as it was."

"There's something else," Hambro said. "Maybe it is more an excuse than a reason, but our paper trail in England first started six months after those gold trades took place. We did go back further. But we found nothing. Now we know why. All the gold trades were done through a broker in New York, not London."

They both fell silent as Paul Schmidt maneuvered his Opel through the Zurich rush-hour traffic.

"What now?" Hambro finally asked.

"I know my boss," Schmidt said. "He won't even listen to me unless I have a paper trail to back up what Stucker just told us. So after I've dropped you off at the airport, I'm going to check into a hotel here in Zurich and call the head of the General Bank of Switzerland first thing tomorrow morning. Then I'm going to go over there and get it."

"So you're now as convinced as I am that Charles Black has been set up?" Hambro asked.

"Absolutely."

"If not Black, then who?"

"Dr. Zwiebach for sure."

"I agree. Who else?"

Schmidt hesitated before answering. "You're now treading on very dangerous ground."

"What do you mean?"

"Your basic premise is still valid. These trades were engineered by somebody who was privy to the information that only became available at the beginning of every month at the BIS meeting in Basel. I'll bet you anything that if the note in Zwiebach's humidor is dated, it will further confirm this. You heard Stucker. Right after they reversed course on those gold futures, the Fed raised interest rates."

"What you're really saying is that if it was not the head of the Federal Reserve who did this, it has to be another central banker."

"Exactly."

"How many central bankers did Zwiebach know?"

"I think I can answer that," Schmidt said. "Two."

"Just two?"

"Just two. One was his client Charles Black. The other was a person who went to school with him—primary school, *Gymnasium*, even the University of Zurich. They are best buddies to this day. I ran a quick check on Zwiebach right after this case broke. I wouldn't have had to. Their close friendship is common knowledge in Zurich. In fact, I think that Zwiebach is probably the only close friend Schweizer has."

"So it's Schweizer."

"It's got to be Dr. Samuel Schweizer, the pious head of the Swiss National Bank."

"But he surely could not have come up with that original fifty million?"

"No. That's the missing link. I think it is somehow connected with Italy. That's where the original fifty million came from. The three men who freed Charles Black were definitely Italian. This was confirmed earlier today. Two Italians returned a black Fiat rental to the airport Hertz office on Sunday. We checked it out. Black's fingerprints were all over it."

"So Zwiebach had an Italian client—a new Italian client."

"That's my guess."

"And Herr Doktor Schweizer helped his buddy Zwiebach make money for that client."

"Lots and lots of money. More than enough to go around."

"Jesus," Hambro said. "How are you going to prove that?"

"I don't know. First we nail Zwiebach. Then maybe he'll tell us."

"What will you tell the press?"

"Nothing. That's up to the state attorney in Basel. I know him all too well. He's going to keep a total lid on this until he's got overwhelming physical evidence against

Zwiebach and his cronies in hand. It's going to kill him when he hears all this, because it is going to blow the Swiss establishment sky-high." Schmidt did not seem unhappy at the prospect.

"But what about Charles Black? Shouldn't he be told?"

"No. As I said, I have to clear this with the state attorney first. Anyway, it won't kill Black if he has to wait a few more days."

47

It was eight o'clock on Tuesday morning in Anchorage, and Vincente had just entered the sporting goods store right across the street from his hotel. Half an hour later he walked out with rubber boots, fishing tackle, a hunting knife, a high-powered Enfield 383 rifle, and a box of ammunition. The salesman assured him that it would stop a bear at a hundred yards. He had also bought a large map of the Lake Iliamna region of the Alaskan peninsula. He took a taxi directly to the airport.

The first thing he did after arriving there was go to the same phone booth he had used the night before to call the Sardinian. From the background noise, it sounded like Cagliari was out on the terrace of the Cala di Volpe, having dinner. Vincente told him what his plan was, and that if it worked out—and even if it did-n't—he would call again in exactly twelve hours. The Sardinian just grunted and hung up.

It proved almost as easy to charter a sea-plane in Anchorage as it was to buy a gun. He wanted it for just a day trip to Lake Iliamna, he told the man behind the counter at the airport. No problem, he was told. You want one of our floatplanes, and it will cost you a thousand dollars. The man put a sign reading BACK IN 15 MINUTES on the counter and told Vincente that he would take him to the plane himself.

The pilot was waiting in a small shack right beside the basin on Cook Inlet, where at least another twenty seaplanes were anchored.

"He wants to take a day trip to Lake Iliamna," the man from the airport said. "He's already settled up with me." Then he left.

"You know it's two hours each way," the pilot said. "Although since it never gets dark this time of year, that doesn't mean you can't get a good day's fishing in."

"It's the only day I've got," Vincente said. "I've got to return to Argentina tomorrow morning."

"It's okay by me. I just thought you should know. We'll take an inflatable rub-ber dinghy to and from the plane. Give me your stuff. Then just follow me. I'll take care of everything. By the way, have you got someplace in particular on Lake Iliamna that you want to head for?"

"Yes. The Arrowhead Lodge. Know it?"

"Hell, yes. Sometimes during the summer I operate out there. Take guests from the lodge to small lakes they can't get to otherwise."

"A friend of mine is staying there. I want to surprise him. And also get in a day's fishing."

"Whatever you say."

After the pilot had warmed up the single-engine floatplane for five minutes, he taxied it farther out into Cook Inlet, turned into the wind, and then gunned the engine. They were airborne almost immediately. The two men talked very little during the trip. The pilot asked about fishing in Argentina. Vincente made up an answer. Vincente asked where the guests at the Arrowhead Lodge usually went to fish. The pilot told him that after they got there, he would go to the lodge and find out. They landed in the inlet in Eagle Bay just down the road from the Arrowhead Lodge. Three other floatplanes were anchored there.

"Now you want me to find out where the Arrowhead Lodge people went to fish today, right?" the pilot asked. "Maybe I won't even have to go to the lodge. It's a pretty good hike. If I can find the pilots who belong to those other planes, maybe they'll know. Or one of those Indian kids fishing off the dock. You wait in the plane. I'll take the dinghy."

Vincente watched him as he paddled to the dock. Without even getting out of it, he started talking to the Native American kids. Then he came back.

"Lucked out," he said after he had stowed the dinghy and climbed back into his seat beside Vincente. "The kids were here when they left. Ten of them, in a big launch that belongs to the Arrowhead Lodge. They headed up Eagle Bay. For the rapids of the Eagle River, they thought."

"Let's look at the map," Vincente said. "I've got one here somewhere."

"Don't bother. I'm sure mine is better," the pilot said.

He reached into his leather pouch, pulled out a map, and unfolded it. "Here we are," he said, pointing his finger, "and there are the rapids just up from where the Eagle River flows into Eagle Bay."

Vincente pored over the map without saying anything.

"Like I said, I want to surprise my friend. See that lake? Pike Lake? My guess is that it's about a half-mile from the mouth of the Eagle River."

"Let's see." The pilot looked. "That's about right."

"Is that a trail?" Vincente pointed at the tiniest of lines leading from the lake to the river.

"It is. Now I'm getting the drift of what

you're thinking. You want me to land in Pike Lake, and then you're going to hike over to the river and take your friend by stealth. He thinks you're in Argentina?"

"You got it."

"When he sees you walking out of the wilderness in the middle of Alaska, he'll have a goddamn heart attack." The pilot was obviously beginning to like the idea. "Just one problem," he then said. "This entire area is full of bears."

"I've got a gun, and believe me, I know how to use it."

"Okay. It's your funeral. Let's go."

They were back in the air within minutes.

"Let's first take a look at the rapids of Eagle River and see if there is anybody there fishing. Otherwise we're wasting our time," the pilot said.

Ten minutes later they approached the upper limits of the bay at about a thousand feet.

"There they are," the pilot suddenly said. "On the western bank of the river. See them? If you want to get to them from this side, you're going to have to wade the rapids. So don't forget your hip boots. I'll try to count them." He peered through the windshield with great intensity. "If I got it right, there are ten of them, just like the kids said—nine men and one woman. And you can see the motor launch anchored in the lake right below the rapids. I'd say we've lucked out again. Now hang on. That's Pike Lake right in front of us. I'm going to take it straight in."

After they splashed down, the pilot said, "I think I spotted that path right over there." He pointed through the side window, then slowly began to taxi in that direction. He finally anchored the plane very near the southwestern shore of the lake.

"You're not going to take all your stuff with you, are you?" he asked Vincente. "My guess is that it is at least a forty-five-minute hike from here."

"No. Just the gun. And, like you said, I'll wear the hip boots."

"I'll put them in the dinghy for you. How soon do you think you'll be back?"

"In two hours. Maybe a little more. Then we'll either go fishing here in this lake or go back to the Arrowhead Lodge, where I could spend some more time with my friend. We'll see."

"Okay. I'll get the dinghy ready, then you take it. I'm going to have a little nap in the plane. And take your time. We've got all day. If your friend wants to come back with you, as long as he's not too big, we can probably manage to fit him in, at least for that short hop back to the Arrowhead Lodge."

"I'll see what he wants to do. Thanks."

The trail began just yards from where he landed with the dinghy. It had been in very recent use, probably by fishermen with the same idea he had. Well, maybe not exactly the same idea.

Vincente set out at a good pace. The terrain was flat, and though it was rocky in places, he was making good time. But would they both be there? That was not unlikely. After all they had just gone through, they were probably sticking together like glue. And the pilot had seen a woman down there.

On the other hand, if neither of the Blacks were there, then he'd have to try a different approach—such as going back to the Arrowhead Lodge and finding out which room they were in. He didn't have to use the gun. He also had that hunting knife.

Suddenly the brush on both sides of the trail got thick. Then the path broke into the clear. He found himself on top of a cliff. He immediately dropped to the ground. Then he began a careful survey. Fifty meters below lay the rapids of the Eagle River. A rugged path led down to the rocks on the edge of the rapids. The rapids themselves were about twenty meters wide, and the water that rushed down them seemed not very deep. There was no one to be seen on his side of the rapids.

But on the other side, there they were. Ten of them, just as the pilot had said. They were strung out along the rapids, some at least a hundred meters farther upstream. But Vincente's eyes were immediately drawn to the group of people downstream from where he was lying. There were four of them. One was Charles Black. One was his wife. The third was Primus. The fourth, a stranger. From his looks, he was certainly not a Swiss. The stranger and Primus were closest to where he was lying, working at a board that had been stretched across two large rocks near the side of the hill on the other side. They were filleting fish. Ten meters downstream from them, Mrs. Black was sitting on a blanket, reading a book. Charles Black was farthest away, standing in the shallows right on the edge of the rapids, leaning out over the water, in the process of reeling in a salmon.

Vincente slammed a clip into his rifle. He had made up his mind. He would take out all three of them. First Charles Black, then that disrespectful son of a bitch Primus. Then Mrs. Black. Then out of there.

He did not hurry. He brought the rifle scope to his eye, adjusted it, adjusted it again. Finally he was satisfied that he had the head of Charles Black lined up just right.

Then he squeezed the trigger.

48

Maybe it was jet lag. Maybe it was Vincente's lack of familiarity with the new rifle. Maybe it was the fact that in the instant before the shot was fired, Charles Black's feet had begun to go out from under him, the result of his trying to reel in a salmon while also trying to maintain his precarious balance on the slippery rocks. Probably it was a combination of all three. In any case, Vincente's bullet did not even graze Charles Black.

But nobody else knew that yet. The shot, the sight of Black falling, produced a piercing scream from Sally.

It produced another reaction in the two men upstream from her. Both Bill and Primus went instantly for their guns, which they had left behind the cutting board, propped up against the side of the steep hill.

"Get behind a rock!" Bill yelled as both he and Primus scrambled to do just that.

Charles Black was crawling on all fours through the shallows. When Sally saw him move, she moved also. A second shot was heard. Nobody seemed to be hit. Before the third shot, all four of them had found cover behind rocks—with Primus and Bill each behind one of the rocks that held up the cutting board.

"Who is it?" Primus asked.

"Must be some crazy. Some drunk crazy, maybe," the Indian answered.

"Do you think he has any connection with the plane that came over a while ago?"

"Maybe."

"Did you spot where he is?"

"He must be lying on the ground just over the ridge at the top of the path that leads up from the river. I saw the top of his head there when he fired that third shot."

"Do you think he's going to keep this up?"

"Yes."

"So what are we going to do about it?"

"Get him before he gets us. Are you any good at this?"

"Yes. I'm a sharpshooter in the Swiss Army reserves," Primus replied.

"I'm not that good," Bill said, "but neither is he. He's already missed three times."

"The elevation is probably giving him trouble," Primus said. "He'll soon learn to compensate for it."

"Then let's try to get it over with right away. You get ready to line up the spot right at the top of that path. I'm going to stand up and get off as many rounds as I can. When he tries to get me, you get him. All right?"

"All right. Just say when."

Thirty seconds passed. There was now complete silence on the banks of the Eagle River.

"Now!" the Indian yelled.

He stood and began firing. From his crouch, Primus moved over to brace his gun against the rock and take aim. The rifle and the head of the shooter on the other side suddenly became visible above the ridge.

Primus fired a single shot.

There was a scream. The shooter disappeared from view. Both the Indian and Primus went back behind their rocks.

"You hit him," the Indian said.

"But we don't know how badly," Primus replied. "What do you suggest we do now?"

"Go get him," the Indian replied. "Wounded animals running around loose are dangerous."

"I'll get help," Primus said. Then he yelled at the top of his voice, "Rolf! Jacob! Sepp!"

"*Jo!*" came the replies, as in a chorus, from the three men farthest upstream.

"*Hän dir euri Gwehr?*"

"*Jo,*" they replied again.

"*Wenn I sag 'jetzt,' denn gömer!*"

"*Jo.*"

"What's going on?" the Indian asked.

"Those are my three buddies from the Swiss Army. They've also got their guns with them because of the bears. I told them that when I yell *jetzt*—which means 'now'—we're going to go get him. All right?"

"I'm ready."

Primus waited five seconds, crossed himself, and yelled, "*Jetzt!*"

All five men now rose from behind their rocks and, with rifles held above their heads, charged into the swift waters of the rapids. It was only twenty meters wide, but it was chest-deep in the middle. No one went down. All reached the other bank at almost the same time. And so far, no more shots had been fired at them.

Now Primus shouted out new orders, but this time it was in English. "Let's climb it! When you're on top, yell out!"

It was a test even for the Swiss mountain troops, but after five minutes, one by one, each of his comrades reported in. Bill, now crouching at Primus's side atop the cliff, was not even out of breath.

"The spot where he fired from is just thirty yards from here," Bill said. "You stay put. I'll take a look."

Primus stayed where he was and remained in a crouch. But after three minutes he got impatient and stood up to look in the direction where Bill had gone. Suddenly there he was, standing and waving, indicating that he wanted Primus to join him. When Primus got there, the Indian was carefully looking at the path that led off into the wilderness.

Drops of fresh blood were clearly visible on the trail. "He's gone, but he's bleeding," Bill said.

"What now?" Primus asked.

"Get your men. Then we'll spread out on both sides of the trail and go after him."

Suddenly, in the distance, there was the sound of an aircraft taking off.

"That's him!" Primus said.

"No. Impossible," the Indian replied. "That noise is coming from the direction of Pike Lake. It would take even a healthy man at least forty-five minutes to get there from here. He must have come in on that floatplane we saw earlier. Whoever flew him in must have heard those shots and decided to get out while the getting was still good. Bush pilots don't like trouble."

"Then he's out there somewhere."

"Yes. But now we've got to be even more careful. He heard that plane, too. He knows there's no easy way out now. If there's one thing even more dangerous than a wounded animal, it's a wounded animal that suddenly finds itself cornered by its enemies."

"What about the people we left behind on the rapids?" Primus asked.

"You and your buddies wait here while I go back down and suggest they return to the Arrowhead Lodge immediately. There they can alert the state troopers in Anchorage. I'll also tell them to make sure someone from the lodge comes back here with the launch and waits for us."

Fifteen minutes later the Indian returned and the search began. The vegetation in the wilderness of the Alaskan peninsula is sparse—no trees of any size, mostly brush, and that spread out over the flat landscape. It was not the ideal place for either man or beast to hide.

It was Primus who spotted him, just fifty meters away. He seemed vaguely familiar. He was sitting on the ground and leaning against a rock. Even at a distance, the blood dropping from his scalp onto his soaked jacket was a nasty sight. So was the gun that he held across his lap.

At almost the same time that Primus saw

him, the man saw Primus. He immediately staggered to his feet, brought the gun up, pointed it in his direction, and fired. And fired. And fired.

Primus had dropped flat to the ground. Not one of the shots came even close. The return fire, however, came from three sides and was delivered with Swiss precision. Vincente was dead before he hit the ground.

The first thing they did after making sure the shooter was dead was go through his pockets. They came up with ammunition, a hunting knife, a wallet, and a passport. It was an Argentine passport that identified the dead man as Raoul Tescari of Buenos Aires, an engineer. His driver's license verified all this.

But Primus knew better. He had been right when he thought that the shooter looked familiar. The dead man was not an engineer from Argentina. He was Vincente Bacigalupi.

Should he tell the others? If he did, how to explain it? Especially when even *he* could not explain it. Then it dawned on him—the explanation, the connection. It had to be Charles Black. Vincente had been looking for him in Zernez and had found him in Alaska. Because he wanted to kill him. But why? Only Charles Black could answer that question. So until he talked to Black, he would say nothing. But why talk to Black at all? There was no sense in getting involved. Something very odd was going on with the Blacks. Back in Zernez, Charles Black had told him he had a problem, and that was why he wanted to get out of Switzerland. So he had brought them here, no questions asked. But there were problems and there were *problems*. It was now obvious that the Blacks' problem was so serious that it had led to attempted murder, and to the death of the would-be killer. As the Blacks' helper, he was implicated. That could turn out very badly. He was a Swiss national on American soil. The American police did not have a very good reputation for their treatment of foreigners. Maybe the best thing would be for him to cut the fishing trip short, get on a plane, and get back onto Swiss soil as soon as possible. Meanwhile, the best policy would be to just act dumb and play along.

Following Bill's suggestion, instead of going back to the rapids, they carried Vincente's body to the shore of Pike Lake. From there he could be flown out on a state trooper floatplane or helicopter. The Indian guide said he would stay there until the police arrived. There was no need for the others to stay. In fact, the sooner they got back, the sooner they could tell the state police where to find him. So the four Swiss mountaineers headed back to the mouth of the Eagle River to wait for the launch that would take them to the Arrowhead Lodge.

It was well past six that evening when they arrived at the lodge. After they told the owner what had happened, he telephoned the state troopers in Anchorage. They asked if anybody needed immediate help. When assured that this was no longer the case, they said it would be a while before they could dispatch a plane to pick up the body.

49

Three hours later, when everybody at the Arrowhead Lodge was at dinner and consuming a lot of wine while discussing what had happened that day, ten time zones to the east in Sardinia it was seventhirty in the morning the next day. Pietro di Cagliari was in the study of his villa in the hills above the Cala di Volpe, waiting beside his phone. Two hours later he was still waiting. He had the sinking feeling that something had gone wrong.

Five hundred miles to the north, in Zurich, just as Dr. Hans Zwiebach arrived in his office, the direct line on his phone began to ring. He was about to experience a similar sinking feeling. It was Dr. Lothar Zopf, chairman of the board and CEO of the General Bank of Switzerland.

"I just got a call from a Lieutenant Paul

Schmidt of the Basel police. He is in charge of the Charles Black investigation. I say *is*, not *was*, because the investigation is on again. I don't know why. I thought it was dead after Black disappeared. What's happening?"

"Maybe they found Black," Zwiebach replied.

"No. I asked. That's not the reason."

"Then what is?" the lawyer asked.

"Something about trades in gold futures. Schmidt says they were originally made for one of your fiduciary accounts with us, a new one that you just opened, and then transferred later to another of your accounts, the now-famous account you opened up years ago for Charles Black. I really didn't quite understand what he was driving at. Do you?"

"Who told him that?" Zwiebach asked, barely managing to get the words out.

"One of our managers in the Private Clients Group who retired this year. The one you always worked with, Schmidt said. His name is Stucker, Urs Stucker."

Now the sinking feeling in Zwiebach's stomach turned into a gut-wrenching spasm.

"Are you still there?" the banker asked.

"Yes."

"Schmidt's already in Zurich and on his way over here. I'll have to give him what he wants. What's he going to find?"

"Look, that was years ago," Zwiebach

said. "I'll have to go back through my records."

"Do it right now. I don't want this case reopened. Hear?" the banker said.

There was that as-yet-undiscovered history of his bank's front-running. Black might have made a half-billion dollars from his insider trading. The General Bank of Switzerland had made even more by taking advantage of its knowledge of what he intended to do, and getting in ahead of him.

"I'll get on it right away," Zwiebach said.

"You do that. I'll expect to hear back from you today," the banker said. "Understand?"

"Yes, sir," Zwiebach said. He had not called anybody "sir" in decades.

The banker hung up.

Zwiebach was so stunned that he just sat there behind his desk with the dead phone still in his hand.

Then he reached over, clicked the receiver, and began to dial the number that would connect him directly with the head of the Swiss National Bank.

"Samuel," Zwiebach said when Schweizer answered, "this is Hans."

"I'm in a meeting, so keep it brief."

"There's trouble. Remember that discussion we had with Pietro in Sardinia last week? Specifically about making sure that Black's case was closed so that nothing ever came out about those gold futures? Well, I just got a call from Lothar Zopf. The Basel police are coming to his bank this morning to take another look at all the account files related to the Charles Black case. The name of Urs Stucker came up. So did the subject of gold. I'm going to have to tell Pietro."

"After you've talked to him, call me back," Schweizer said.

"I will," Zwiebach said.

He dialed the number of Pietro di Cagliari's villa in Sardinia. The phone was picked up after just one ring. It was Pietro.

"Vincente?" he said. "Everything all right?"

"You must be expecting another call, Pietro. This is Hans Zwiebach. In Zurich."

"Oh. What do you want?"

"We've got a problem."

He then repeated what he had just told Samuel Schweizer.

"Why now?" Pietro asked. "Did they find Black?"

"I was told no."

"Strange. Look, the three of us have to talk this over right away. I'll send the plane up to Zurich immediately. It will be there by three o'clock. We'll talk here. Then you can get back on the plane and be home by midnight, so nobody will even have to know that you left town. All right?"

"All right as far as I'm concerned. But I'll have to see about Samuel."

"Tell him that I consider this extremely important," Pietro said.

"I will."

"And, Hans, bring my entire dossier with you. I want to go through it. In detail."

"No problem."

"Then I'll be seeing you and Samuel in about five hours," Pietro said.

Zwiebach and Schweizer took separate cabs to the general aviation terminal at Kloten Airport and arrived within minutes of each other. Shortly after their arrival, a uniformed pilot entered the terminal, looked around, and then approached them.

"Would one of you by any chance be Dr. Hans Zwiebach?" he asked in a very quiet voice.

"Yes," Zwiebach replied, "and this is Dr. Schweizer."

"Great. We're ready to go if you are. Any luggage?"

"No. Just this briefcase," Zwiebach said. "I prefer to keep it with me."

"Okay. Then just follow me."

Fifteen minutes later they were cleared for takeoff. The flight plan that had been filed indicated that the Gulfstream IV was headed for Paris. There was a two-man cabin crew on the flight. Once the jet had leveled out at twenty thousand feet, they came to serve a light snack and to offer wine or beer. Both men chose beer.

Forty-five minutes later they were over the Mediterranean. After their beer glasses were taken away, both passengers pushed back their seats and closed their eyes. The two cabin attendants stayed in the lounge area in the rear of the plane, watching.

Now they came forward.

Both had pistols.

Dr. Samuel Schweizer and Dr. Hans Zwiebach were shot in the head simultaneously. Both died instantly.

After making sure both were dead, one of the flight attendants went to the front of the cabin and knocked on the cockpit door. The plane immediately began to descend.

The flight attendants began to open the baggage compartments. They pulled out two body bags, two canvas tarpaulins, and many coils of rope, and dumped them in the aisle in the middle of the plane. They stuffed the two bodies into the body bags and zipped them up. Then they went to the galley, opened the metal doors leading to the food compartments, and pulled out cinder blocks that had been cut into halves. They spread out the tarps, placed the body bags on them, and then put a row of cinder-block halves on top of each body, lashing them firmly together with rope. Finally they wrapped the tarp around each "package" and wound rope, lots of rope, around the tarp.

All this time the small jet was descending, and the pilot was steadily easing back on the throttle. He leveled the plane at five hundred feet. It is not easy to open the door of a Gulfstream while in flight, but with the help of the copilot the two cabin attendants managed. All three men had tethered themselves with rope to prevent being sucked out. It was a struggle, but they finally managed to push one, then the second body through the door, from where they plunged into the waters of the Mediterranean and sank. Then they slammed the door shut.

Forty-five minutes later they landed in Sardinia. Pietro di Cagliari was waiting on the tarmac. One of the flight attendants walked up to him and handed over the only piece of luggage that had been on the flight: a leather briefcase.

"Everything worked out all right?" Pietro asked.

"Yes, sir."

"You know, I got the idea from the Argentines. Years ago, the government there used to 'disappear' people this way. But instead of doing it the humane way, they dropped them into the Atlantic Ocean from twenty thousand feet while they were still alive."

The Sardinian was a content man as he sat in the backseat of his Rolls-Royce as it headed back toward the Cala di Volpe. The only remaining paper trail that could have led from account number Q 178-5997 to him was now safely in his hands. The other one that could have led to him—the original transfer of that $50 million to

Zurich—had been taken care of. Already years ago, the lodge brethren in Milano had made sure that those records had been destroyed. In the absence of any paper trail, the only men who could have linked him to all those profits that had been made for him at the General Bank of Switzerland were at the bottom of the Mediterranean. There was, of course, Vincente. The Blacks must somehow have caught on to who he was and gotten away. But Vincente appeared to have disappeared in the Alaskan wilderness. And even if he did show up eventually, he would simply have to be killed.

So he was safe. And so was the money.

There was, however, one other matter that had to be taken care of. Schweizer's woman. Simone. She was in her villa, just down the road from his. He was going to pay her a visit later that evening. He would plan on spending the night, the first of many nights.

It was only fair. The victor *should* get the spoils.

50

It was not until the morning of the next day that the first alarms began to sound in Zurich. The wives of both men called their husbands' secretaries to find out whether the men had come to work. They told the same story. Their husbands had not shown up for dinner the night before. They had also not come home to sleep. Had they gone away on a trip unexpectedly? No? Then where were they?

The second call that the lawyer's secretary got that morning came from Lieutenant Paul Schmidt of the Basel police, asking her to put him through to Zwiebach immediately. It was in regard to a matter that was extremely important and extremely urgent. When she told him that her boss was apparently missing, he told her that he would be right over.

Schmidt called the state attorney in Basel from Zwiebach's office. He told him where he was calling from, and why. Newly found records in the General Bank of Switzerland had proven beyond any doubt that Zwiebach had framed Charles Black, that all the speculation they had accused Black of masterminding had been done for the benefit of another of Zwiebach's clients. Schmidt had that client's account number: Q 178-5997. All he had needed to wrap it up was the dossier in Zwiebach's office that would match that account number with the name of Zwiebach's other client.

But Zwiebach had disappeared. So had the client file for account number Q 178-5997.

He now switched to the subject of Dr. Samuel Schweizer, Dr. Zwiebach's best friend. This was when the state attorney cut him off.

"Are you crazy?" he yelled over the phone. "I want you to stop everything, right this instant. You will talk to nobody else until you talk to me. You will leave that lawyer's office immediately and head straight for my office. Do you hear? You've got two hours to get here."

An hour and fifty minutes later, when Schmidt walked into the state attorney's office at Heuberg 21, he was waved to a chair. The great man was involved in an intense conversation with his counterpart in Zurich. Ten minutes later he finally hung up.

"You must have overheard what we were talking about. Now Samuel Schweizer has disappeared. The state attorney in Zurich is getting a court order. Then the Zurich police are going into the offices and homes of both missing men to go through all their records, looking for clues that might lead to their whereabouts. By the way, I'm sorry I yelled at you that way. I'm afraid you were right about Schweizer. I only hope now that something concrete turns up that will *prove* you're right."

What turned up that afternoon, in Samuel Schweizer's private safe in his home, was a dossier containing statements from the Caribbean Bank for Commerce and Finance in the Turks and Caicos Islands, for account number S 2222. The latest statement indicated that Schweizer had a balance there of just over $45 million. When this information was relayed to the state attorney in Basel, he immediately picked up the phone and called Sir Robert Neville at the Bank of England.

51

That Wednesday morning in Alaska, two state troopers showed up at the Arrowhead Lodge. They had flown in from Anchorage, bringing Bill back with them. The Indian guide had gone to Anchorage with them and the body the night before and had already thoroughly briefed them on what had happened. It was breakfast time, and all of the guests were gathered in the dining room. The police introduced themselves, explained that Bill had told them the story, and that they would be contacting the Argentine consulate general in Los Angeles, which was responsible for taking care of its country's citizens in the western part of the United States. The consulate general probably could help them find out more about the dead man. So far, his fingerprints had led nowhere. Then came a question: Could any of those who had been on the Eagle River rapids the day before, when it had all happened, be of any help? No one could. So the police excused their intrusion and left.

After breakfast, Sally and Charles Black decided to give fishing a rest that day.

The events that had taken place on the Eagle River had upset them both. Logically, it had nothing to do with them. After all, it was some crazy from Argentina. But still, the man had shot at Charlie first. They picked up some books from the small library of the Arrowhead Lodge and then went back to their room to read.

When breakfast was over, everybody else got together their fishing gear and left for the launch, which was going to take them to a new fishing site that day. No one had said so, but nobody wanted to go back to the Eagle River rapids for a while. Only Primus stayed behind. He explained that he had to make some phone calls to Switzerland to ensure that, in his absence, everything was going smoothly at his hotel.

An hour later he informed the owner of the Arrowhead Lodge that something had come up that urgently required that he return to Switzerland. He had already booked the first flight out. He offered to pay whatever penalty would be appropriate for this sudden cancellation, but the owner declined. After all, he said, Primus and his friends would be coming back next year. A half hour later the hotel van deposited him at the small Lake Iliamna airport. By eleven o'clock he was in Anchorage, where he took a noon Air Canada flight to Vancouver. Later that afternoon he boarded a nonstop flight to Europe.

At seven o'clock that evening, Charles said he had had enough of reading and was going to check for E-mail. Sally decided she would go along. The pickup was in its usual place. Ten minutes later they were inside the schoolhouse.

Once he was seated at the computer, it only took a few minutes for Charles to get through to his mailbox in Iran. He typed in the password, and the computer responded: *You have new mail!!!*

"Come here," he yelled at Sally, who was wandering around the schoolhouse, checking out the artwork on the walls. She came over and stood behind him.

"Look," he said once she stood behind him. "I'll hit this key, and..."

And there it was on the screen. E-mail from *bankeng@ukfinancial.com*. It read:

The Swiss authorities have just informed me that they have withdrawn all charges against you, with apologies. New evidence has revealed that Dr. Hans Zwiebach used your account to cover the insider trading activities he conducted in conjunction with Dr. Samuel Schweizer. Both have disappeared. International arrest warrants have been issued.

Please call on me at any time should you need further information, or assistance in any other matter. I would like to extend my heartfelt best wishes to you and your wife.

Sir Robert Neville

Sally threw her arms around her husband and squeezed.

"You did it. My smart husband did it, just like he always does."

He got up from behind the computer, turned around, and lifted her in the air.

"With a little help from his wife," he said. "Thank you, Sally."

"Hold on," she then said. "How do you know this isn't just a trick to get you out of hiding?"

He put her back down.

"It's eleven-thirty in New York, right?"

"Yes. Why?"

"That's when *The New York Times* puts its next-morning edition on the Internet. If what Sir Robert says is true, I'm sure they will carry it."

"Do you know how to get it?"

"Sure. I do it all the time. Watch."

He sat back down in front of the computer, went back to the home page of Netscape, and, in the blank space after "Go to," he typed, *http://www.nytimes.com*.

Seconds later, a pictorial replica of the front page of the next day's early edition of the *Times* appeared on the screen. And there was the headline:

Former Head of the Federal Reserve Exonerated in Swiss Banking Scandal

From there he went to the full text of the story. Everything that Sir Robert had told him was true.

"You know something," Sally said when they had finished reading. "I had a funny feeling that Schweizer was somehow involved. I never did like that man.

"What now?" she then asked.

"First we call Laura. Then we go back to San Francisco. Then I am going to raise holy hell in Washington. By taking advantage of me—and, by extension, of the government of the United States of America—somebody has gotten away with a half-billion dollars, stashed it in a crooked bank in the Turks and Caicos Islands, and is going to be able to keep it unless I do something."

"Don't forget the million and a half bucks I sent there," Sally said.

"I won't."

"So let's go get it."

As soon as they were back at the lodge, they telephoned their daughter to tell her the good news and suggest that they meet the next day. The first local flight out was at ten o'clock the next morning, so they booked a United Airlines noon flight from Anchorage to San Francisco. By now it was eight o'clock, so they went to the dining room to look for Primus. Now they could tell him the whole story and thank him for his help. They were both surprised when the owner of the lodge told them that Primus had left that morning and was on his way back to Switzerland to attend to urgent business. After hearing that, they broke the news that they too would be leaving early the next morning. They did not explain why. The owner looked disappointed, but said that he would have the bill ready for payment that evening. When they paid it, it included a one-thousand-dollar surcharge for early departure.

After dinner, Charles and Sally Black went right to bed. But before they went to sleep, Sally said, "You know, after all this, what we need is a really good vacation. Not one climbing over slippery rocks."

"I agree. Where?"

"Well, I've been reading this travel book that I found in the lodge, and it gave me an idea."

"All right. Tell me."

"We didn't go to Italy after all, did we?"

"I thought that was the last place you wanted to go."

"I've changed my mind. The book says that there is a wonderful, romantic resort hotel on the island of Sardinia. It's called the Cala di Volpe. That means 'Den of the Wolves.' Let's go there after San Francisco. Now we can even check into hotels again using our real names."

"All right. But first I've got a few things to attend to."

52

Charlie had never seen their new apartment in San Francisco. When they decided to sell their Georgetown home and move out there, he had left it up to her. After all, she was a California native and knew her way around that beautiful city.

But he fell in love with it from the moment he stepped out of the elevator door onto the marble floor of its elegant foyer. After they had taken what little luggage they had to the master bedroom, Sally gave him the grand tour. She ended it by insisting he take a chair in the living room, from which there was a magnificent view from Nob Hill of Huntington Park, Grace Cathedral, the Fairmont Hotel, and, beyond that, the sweep of San Francisco Bay.

Then she left the room, and when she returned she was carrying a tray, on which was an ice bucket containing a bottle of Dom Perignon. There were also two crystal champagne glasses. "Now let's celebrate," she said.

He poured, and when the glasses were full, he raised his and said, "To my beautiful wife, our new home, and a new life."

Their daughter, Laura, arrived a half hour later, and after a tearful reunion, they all decided to go out for an early dinner. Laura had heard all about Stars, but had never been there, so that was where they went. The restaurant, a French brasserie with a unique flavor of San Francisco in both its food and atmosphere, was a complete hit. So the early dinner turned into a late dinner. When they got back to the apartment, Charlie said that he was going to bed. Sally and Laura could stay up as long as they wanted and sleep in the next morning, but he was going to get up before dawn. There were a few phone calls that he had to make.

He made the first call just before 5:00 A.M. That would make it almost 2:00 P.M. in Switzerland. He knew that Lieutenant Paul Schmidt of the Basel police always brought lunch to his office, and that he ate alone between noon and two. He picked up on the first ring.

"Lieutenant Schmidt *hier*," he said.

"And this is Charles Black."

After a stunned silence, Schmidt said, "What can I say, Mr. Black? We made a mistake. We're sorry."

"You did what you had to do. Now I need a little help. Very little."

"If I can help, I will."

"Well, try hard. First, there is the matter of who was behind all this. Do you now know who that was?"

"No. His dossier disappeared, along with Dr. Zwiebach. And the records of the bank in Milan from which his funds originally came have also disappeared."

"Maybe I can help," Black said. "I know a man who is linked to that person. He is the one who got me out of your jail. His name is Vincente. He lives in a large house on the outskirts of Pontresina with some of his family. They are all Italian. I only know his first name, but a man by the name of Primus Spöl, who owns the Hotel Alpenrose in Zernez, knows all about him."

At first he had not planned on bringing up Primus's name, but now it could no longer hurt him.

"Thank you, Mr. Black. I will have the police in the canton of Graubünden get on this as soon as our conversation is over."

"Good. And I'd appreciate hearing from you when you find something out. My number here in San Francisco is 415-950-4141."

"I've noted it."

"Second and last favor. I want to know the numbers of those accounts at that bank in the Turks and Caicos Islands. And I also want to know exactly how much was transferred from Zurich to those accounts over the years."

"I'm not sure I can do that."

"I'm sure you can. I want the information to come directly from you, and I want it on paper, within the hour. Otherwise I will have to go to the Governor of the Bank of England and ask him." Black paused to let that sink in. "My fax number is 415-950-4142. Understood?"

"Yes, sir."

"Good. Thank you."

"Thank you, sir."

When Black hung up, he noticed that his hands were shaking. Just hearing that voice again had done it.

The fax came just twenty minutes later. As soon as it had arrived, he picked up the phone to make the next call. It was to Sir Robert Neville at the Bank of England.

"How wonderful that you called, Charles," the Englishman said as soon as he came on the phone. "I've been wanting to call you, but nobody knew where to find you. Where are you?"

"San Francisco. It's going to be our new home."

"And you're all right?"

"I'm in fine shape, and so is Sally."

"I'm so glad to hear that."

"Sir Robert," Black said, "I've called for two reasons. The first is to thank you for responding so quickly and so effectively to that message I sent you."

"You were right about that cash margin," the Englishman replied. "How we missed pursuing where it came from in the first place is beyond me. We slipped up. I'm sorry."

"I understand. But this brings me to the second subject. Whoever was behind all this—and that mystery has apparently not been solved—still has not only his original cash, but all the profits that he was able to generate illegally by using it in his hugely successful speculations."

"I know. It bothers us, too. But we both know the problem. It's in that bank on those damn islands in the Caribbean, and we can't get at it."

" 'We' being who?"

"The Bank of England."

"But as I understand it, the Turks and Caicos Islands are a British dependency."

"That's correct. It is under British *political* jurisdiction. Their governor general is appointed by the Queen."

"But it is the British government, not the Queen, who tells the governor general what to do."

"Precisely. We—the Bank of England—*cannot* tell him what to do."

"Does the power that the British government holds over the Turks and Caicos Islands through its Governor General extend to financial matters?"

"Yes. In fact, it was our government that originally put them on the road toward becoming a tropical version of Switzerland. It was thought that if it became a thriving offshore banking center, the resulting income would create a level of prosperity there that would allow us to discontinue the rather substantial financial aid that we have been providing them with, year after year. It worked. The banking industry now accounts for fifteen percent of the national income of the Turks and Caicos Islands. But it also backfired in the sense that some of the island's banking activities are crooked."

"But are you telling me that if the British government could be convinced that, in our case, those illicit banking activities had gone beyond what was acceptable, they would have the power to intervene?"

"Yes. But who is going to convince

them? I tried and got nowhere."

"Maybe the American government can," Black said. "After all, our national interests have suffered in that it was chiefly our Federal Reserve that was taken advantage of."

"If you can get something going from your side, you can be sure that you will have my complete support."

"What about the Swiss?"

"They are so damned embarrassed about this entire mess that they will go along with any solution you Americans might come up with."

"Including their commercial banks? Some of them might claim that they were also injured parties, since they lost money on some of those trades and will want a share of whatever we might get back."

"They will do what the Swiss government tells them to do," Sir Robert replied. "Nevertheless, if you can persuade our government to retrieve those funds and to appoint the Bank of England as custodian, we will make every effort to determine who the losers were—including those Swiss commercial banks—and arrange for compensation."

"That's an excellent suggestion," Black said. "I intend to pursue this immediately and vigorously."

"Good luck. As I said, you have my complete support. If you need anything more, feel free to call on me at any time."

"I will. Thanks again, Sir Robert."

It was a highly satisfied Charles Black who hung up the phone. He looked at his watch. It was now almost 6:00 A.M. in San Francisco, meaning that it was almost 9:00 A.M. in Washington. He was sure that his successor as Chairman of the Fed never got to the office before nine. So he went into the kitchen and made a pot of fresh coffee. It took him a while, since the kitchen was new to him and he had to first find both the coffeemaker and the coffee.

It took a lot longer to get hold of Arthur Lake than it had either Paul Schmidt or Sir Robert Neville. For a while he thought maybe Lake had refused to take the call after his secretary told him who it was. But then he finally came on the line.

"Charles," he began in his booming voice, "how good to hear from you. None of us believed one word of what the Swiss were telling us. But we couldn't do anything about it. It became a political matter. So our hands were tied."

"Well, Arthur, I'm calling to get you to untie them. This matter cannot be allowed to stand where it is now. Somebody misused information illegally gotten from the central bank of the United States, and used it for criminal purposes. He made almost a half-billion dollars that way. I know where that half-billion dollars is. I know the bank. I know the account numbers."

"Hold on, Charlie. I also know where that bank is. The Turks and Caicos Islands. You know as well as I that the Fed has no power or authority that would enable us to get that money released."

"I'm completely aware of that. But as you just said, this became a political matter. In my judgment, it still is. Therefore it is up to the only person who has sufficient political clout to do something about this to correct the situation. I am talking about the man who appointed you as my successor, Arthur."

"What do you expect me to do?"

"Set up an appointment for me with the President. I'll take it from there."

"He's a busy man, Charles."

"Look, I think that after all I've been through, that's the very least that both you and he can do for me now."

It had worked with Schmidt, and now it also worked with Arthur Lake.

"All right. What time frame do you have in mind?"

"Right away. You set it up for Monday, and I'll fly out on the weekend."

"That's asking a lot, Charles, but I'll try to have him see you as soon as possible." He then changed the subject. "How's Sally? Was she able to stand up to this ordeal all right?"

"She stood up like a soldier. She was at my side and *on* my side the entire time. She was the only one."

That produced silence on the other end, so Black continued. "If you switch me back to your secretary, Arthur, I'll give her my new phone and fax numbers and my new address here in San Francisco. I expect to hear from you very soon."

"You will."

Arthur Lake called back exactly one hour later. The President had agreed to receive both of them at ten o'clock on Monday morning. Lake's limousine would pick him up at his hotel—Black told him it would be the Four Seasons in Georgetown—at exactly a quarter to ten.

The President was all smiles and geniality when he greeted Charles Black.

"I very much appreciate your receiving me on such short notice," Black began.

"We owe you one, Charlie. Sit down and tell me how I can help. I should say at the outset that I have been fully briefed on this appalling situation, and that I am as outraged as you are."

Black spent the next ten minutes explaining exactly what he proposed be done.

When he was finished, the President responded, "Everything you say makes complete sense. I will have my people find out what the British Prime Minister's schedule is, and try to arrange a call to him later this morning. If he agrees to act, I will ask him to do it in cooperation with your friend at the Bank of England."

The meeting was over.

The Governor General of the Turks and Caicos Islands was a bit eccentric. From his opulent residence in Cockburn Town, the islands' capital, he would ride the short distance to his offices in a black and white limousine—a converted London taxi bearing the island chain's coat of arms, which featured a lobster and a pelican flanked by pink flamingos.

On the morning after that phone conversation between the American President and the British Prime Minister, the limousine kept rolling past the government offices and stopped one block farther down the town's main street. It stopped directly in front of the Caribbean Bank for Trade and Finance. When the governor general emerged from his car, he was joined by two uniformed members of the local constabulary who had been instructed to meet him outside the bank. Accompanied by them, he now strode into the lobby and demanded to see the man in charge, Werner Weber.

It was a highly flustered ex–Swiss banker who came out of his office to greet his unannounced visitor. He became even more flustered when the governor general refused to accept his outstretched hand and, instead, thrust a highly official-looking document into it.

Then the governor general spoke: "In my capacity as Governor General of the Turks and Caicos Islands and representative of Her Majesty the Queen, and in my further capacity as chief justice of these islands, I hereby demand that you immediately follow the directive that I have just handed you.

Otherwise I will have no alternative but to close down your bank and arrest you."

One hour later, instructions were given to the correspondent banks of the CBTF in London to transfer from its accounts with them a grand total of $597,426,435 to a special account at the Bank of England. Of this amount, well over a half-billion had been held in account number S 1111, and just a shade under $45 million in account number S 2222. Zwiebach had no account there. His share had always been transferred back to his omnibus account at the General Bank of Switzerland in Zurich, from where it had disappeared.

Weber demanded a receipt, and he got it.

Under a confidential agreement reached the next day between the governments of the United States, Great Britain, and Switzerland, the Bank of England agreed to transfer $1.5 million from this special account to the account of Sally Black at Whitney Brothers in New York. The Bank of England immediately initiated a search to determine who had been injured as a result of the insider trading, in order to arrange for compensation. Because of the myriad transactions involved, their complexity, and the lack of transparency in the futures markets, they were not optimistic about the results. Whatever was left over after an exhaustive search had been completed would go to UNICEF, to help the starving children of the world.

When Charles and Sally Black were informed of this, they went to take one last look at their old house in Georgetown, since the new owners were already in the process of moving in. Then they checked out of the Four Seasons Hotel and caught the late-afternoon flight back to San Francisco.

They were still so excited about what had happened that it was well after midnight when they decided to go to bed. Just then the phone rang. They looked at each other in alarm. Then Charlie picked it up.

"This is Lieutenant Paul Schmidt in Basel, Mr. Black. Excuse me for calling you this late. I've been trying to get you, but nobody answers the phone."

"We were out of town. What's wrong?" Charlie asked. Apparently Sally had not gotten around to installing an answering machine.

"We followed your lead regarding Vincente Bacigalupi and determined that he and his entire family have disappeared. That house you mentioned has been totally abandoned. The occupants were apparently all Italians, so it will be very difficult for us to track any of them down. But we did find out more about Vincente. He's dead. He had apparently followed you to Alaska and was going to kill both you and Mrs. Black, but instead it was he who was killed. Primus told us the entire story. I suspect that the Alaskan police will be contacting you to verify this."

So it had been Vincente. It made sense. But now what?

"So you still don't know who was behind all this?" Black asked.

"No. As I told you last week, the paper trail has disappeared. Both Schweizer and Zwiebach have vanished. Vincente was killed. The only possible link left was the secretary of Dr. Zwiebach. But after all that has happened, she has undergone a total mental breakdown. She vaguely remembers that he was an Italian. But he was only there once, and that was four years ago. She has difficulty recalling what happened four *days* ago. So we are at a dead end. But I have heard that at least you arranged to get the money back."

"I did, yes."

Now, suddenly, Charles had had enough of all this. It was time to move on.

"Thanks, Lieutenant Schmidt. I appreciate the call, and I wish you all the best in your career."

He hung up.

The next morning Charlie slept in. He was awakened at ten o'clock by Sally, who had brought him a cup of freshly brewed coffee.

"Honey," she said, "remember my talking about taking a vacation?"

"Of course. You wanted to go to Italy."

"Actually, Sardinia. Well, I've got good news. I got the reservations. We can leave tomorrow."

53

Two days later the Blacks were sitting on the terrace of the Cala di Volpe, having dinner. Pietro di Cagliari, dressed in a stunning white suit and accompanied by two very beautiful women, came to the table next to theirs. He had just surreptitiously checked the hotel register for new arrivals, as he often did, and had taken particular note of the name of a couple who had asked for an eight o'clock dinner reservation. He paused for a moment, looked the Blacks over very carefully, then turned his back on them and sat down.

"Do you know that couple?" Simone asked.

"No," Pietro answered, "and they obviously don't know me. I think I will keep it that way."

If you have enjoyed reading this large print book and you would like more information on how to order a Wheeler Large Print Book, please write to:

Wheeler Publishing, Inc.
P.O. Box 531
Accord, MA 02018-0531